Liver

Liver

A Fictional Organ with a
Surface Anatomy of Four Lobes

WILL SELF

NEW YORK BERLIN LONDON

Published by Bloomsbury USA, New York

All papers used by Bloomsbury USA are natural, recyclable products made from
wood grown in well-managed forests. The manufacturing processes conform to the
environmental regulations of the country of origin.

LIBRARY OF CONGRESS CATALOGING-IN-PUBLICATION DATA HAS BEEN APPLIED FOR.

ISBN-10: 1-59691-664-8 (hardcover)
ISBN-13: 978-1-59691-664-7 (hardcover)

First published in Great Britain in 2008 by Penguin Books Ltd (UK)
First published in the United States by Bloomsbury USA in 2009

1 3 5 7 9 10 8 6 4 2

Printed in the United States of America by Quebecor World Fairfield

For Marc, Georgia and family

Who sees with equal eye, as God of all,
A hero perish, or a sparrow fall,
Atoms or systems into ruin hurled,
And now a bubble burst, and now a world.

Alexander Pope, *Essay on Man*, I, 87–90

Contents

Foie Humain

Val Carmichael credited Pete Stenning – who was always called 'the Martian' – with getting him off the gin and on to the vodka.

'Clever cunt, the Martian,' Val said to the assembled members, who were grouped at the bar of the Plantation Club in their allotted positions. Left to right: Val on a stool by the till, Scotty Henderson ('the Dog') on the one next to him, Dan Gillespie ('the Poof') on the one after that – a tricky position, since, if the Poof tipped back, which he often did, he would be struck by the door if someone happened to come in.

In the second row were Bernie Jobs ('the Cunt') and Neil Bolton ('the Extra'). While the other nicknames were mostly referential, as in, 'Poof bin in?', Bolton was called 'the Extra' to his rubbery-handsome face. He was a leading British character actor, and Val, who had known Bolton the longest, had issued one of his draconian decrees, to the effect that, having prostituted himself on the West End stage – and in a number of hugely successful Hollywood filmed musicals – the Extra was no longer entitled to any more familiar form of address. Bolton took this in good part.

At the back, completing this scrum of drinkers, was Phillip McCluskey ('His Nibs'). McCluskey was the diarist on a mid-market tabloid, and celebrated on Fleet Street for the McCluskey Manoeuvre, which consisted of his putting a drunken hand up a young woman's skirt, then falling unconscious with it clamped, vice-like, around her knickers, the waistband a yanked communication cord in his sweaty hand.

The success of the Manoeuvre rested, in part, on McCluskey's saintly demeanour: until he made his move he looked – and behaved – like a choirboy who had stayed on in the stalls for five decades, ageing but never growing up. Besides, at the beginning of McCluskey's long career such behaviour was pretty standard, while latterly he was protected by his proprietor, who, as well as appreciating the reliably incendiary gossip the diarist poked through the letter-boxes of Middle England, was also an enthusiastic molester himself.

His Nibs wasn't in the Plantation that often; long lunches at Langan's or Bertorelli were essential to his métier, and this was an afternoon club. His frequent absences meant that the three other solidly dependable members were usually able to join in free intercourse with the barflies, even though their stations were some way off.

The Martian himself, and Margery De Freitas ('Her Ladyship'), sat at a small, round, melamine-topped table, set against the bit of wall that separated a niche where an upright piano lurked from the sloping embrasure that terminated in the bleary eye of a sash window. Meanwhile, on a stool midway between the piano niche and the main door, perched the Honourable Sarah Mainwaring, who, having more rightful claim to a title than Her Ladyship, was instead known as 'the Typist', a nod to the fact – not obvious from her county-set manner, her twin set and her solidly set hair – that she was the senior commissioning editor for an august – and famously high-brow – publishing house.

'See,' Val went on, 'the Martian says that all the juniper berries in the gin make it an impure spirit. Toxins build up. Cunts. Too many vitamins. Gotta stop it. But vodka's completely fucking pure: just grain – nothing else. It's a well-known fact' – Val cupped his elbow in his hand and pointed out indecipherable smoke slogans with the tip of his cigarette – 'that vodka drinkers – and I'm talking absolutely fucking pure stuff – can live for bloody ever. Ain't that so, Marshy?' He turned on his stool to acknowledge his life coach, and the Martian raised his glass of vodka and orange in salute.

The other members were sceptical and expressed it in their several ways: the Dog (Scotch) snuffled; the Poof (Campari and soda) tittered; the Cunt (Scotch also) sniggered; the Extra (lager) openly guffawed. Neither the Typist (gin and bitter lemon) nor Her Ladyship (gin and tonic) gave voice, although both evinced dissent, the former puckering her long top lip so that her thick foundation cracked, the latter pulling at one of her hideous novelty earrings, which were in the shape of bunches of red grapes.

'It is so,' the Martian pronounced. His voice was at once low and nasal, so that each carefully enunciated syllable vibrated. 'That's why I drink vodka myself, although with orange juice as a mixer, rather than tonic, on account of certain . . . health issues.' Then he took a swig of his drink, replaced it on the table and ran his stubby fingers through his greenish hair.

It was this greenish hair that had given the Martian his moniker – the hair, and a slightly other-worldly manner that, although difficult to pin down, was none the less there. The Martian lived by himself in a large and mouldering house on Melrose Avenue in Kilburn. The house was damper in than out; sodden rendering flopped from the façade, and on one occasion a lump narrowly missed the postwoman.

The Martian was a printer by trade. The others never asked him about his work – shop talk was derided at the Plantation – but it was generally assumed, from the closeness he enjoyed with the Cunt – who managed Sadus, the sadomasochistic porn shop on Old Compton Street – that the Martian spent his mornings and evenings checking the registration of tormented flesh.

'Course, tonic water', the Martian continued, 'has quinine in it – even that Schweppes piss Val flogs – and quinine's what they used to take out to the colonies for malaria. Used to be more valuable than fucking gold by far. Lowers the body temperature, see, stops the malarial parasites getting into yer red blood cells, then fetching up in yer bloody liver.'

5

This was a long speech for the Martian, whose remarks were usually one-liners, and the other members remained silent, stunned by his verbosity.

It was left to the final occupant of the Plantation to essay a reply. Hilary Edmonds ('the Boy') stood behind the tiny semicircular bar – no more than an apostrophe of wood and cloth, denoting the absence of some far more solid thing – facing the front row of the scrum and rubbing dirt into a dirty glass with a dirty cloth. 'B-But, P-Pete,' he charmingly stuttered, 'you ain't gonna get malaria in Soho, are you?'

Perhaps not, although the Soho the miasmal Plantation Club floated above was certainly a swamp: pools of urine and spilt drink reflected the low grey skies, while for its slithering denizens the solid four-storey terraces had all the insubstantiality of reed beds.

Not that any of this was immediately apprehensible from the confines of the Plantation, which was a world entire, accessed via two flights of stairs from Blore Court, a grimy alley that linked the filmic commerce of Wardour Street to the sweetly rotten fruit and veg market in Berwick Street.

Blore Court was a time portal, a fossilized trace of a thoroughfare around which the living city had continued to grow. If a passer-by noticed this four-foot-wide crevice in the brick bluffs and ventured inside, he would be transported back to the era when a huge rookery of slums roosted here, its smoke-blackened hovels, festooned with smutty laundry, over-toppling a maze of alleyways that, as thin and dark as ruptured veins, wormed their way crazily through the face of the drunken city.

The right-hand side of Blore Court was a single sweep of brick-work sixty feet high, and unrelieved by window or door. Behind this were the offices of a film distributor, where men in shirtsleeves shouted down phones at space salesmen, and runners panted as they waited for their tin discuses.

If our hypothetical flâneur had the temerity to venture deeper into Blore Court, he might – not being one of the prostitutes' clients, who scurried, heads down, their turgid cocks dowsing for moisture – look up and notice that the left-hand side of the alley had a queerer aspect: these were the snub façades and sawn-off porticoes of a row of late-nineteenth-century retail premises, erected presumably during an odd hiatus, when the right wall of the court was temporarily lower-rise, or absent altogether.

In subsequent years these once prosperous drapers and mercers had been worked over, again and again, by the troubled genius of enterprise. Their windows had been smashed, boarded up, reglazed, then smashed again; their sign boards painted over and over, as business after business infested the light-starved showrooms, while artisan after artisan lost his – or her – eyesight in the dingy flats and garrets up above.

During the period that our story takes place – the second great epoch of the Plantation Club – Blore Court was on the skids. Chipboard covered most of the former shop windows, except for a single 'boutique' – as anachronistic as this designation – that struggled on at the Berwick Street end, trying to flog 'gear' that hadn't been 'fab' since the publication of the Wolfenden Report.

Elsewhere along the alley multiple door bells studded the flaky pilasters, tangled wiring connecting those that pushed them to a multiplicity of sole traders, the bulk of whom had put their pudenda on the market. Yet there were also dental mechanics and hat blockers, Polish translators of French and French polishers, furriers whose customers were as elusive as sable and knife grinders who were none too sharp.

At 5–7 Blore Court there was one bell push labelled, quaintly, 'French Lessons', and a second offering the services of a 'Model', presumably for an artist who required neither natural light nor a subject that appeared particularly lifelike. If our wanderer had stood outside Nos. 5–7 and looked up, he would have seen the whores' red lights cheerily illuminating the two topmost windows, and casting their russet glow on the opposite wall.

However, had he stepped in through the heavy door – an original feature, much assaulted and always ajar – he would have been assailed by the nutty odour of roasted coffee – a domestic aroma, at odds with the grimy vestibule, that was the sole legacy, besides their defunct sign, of Vinci Brothers Neapolitan Coffee Importers, who had decamped some years previously. The Brothers' ground-floor tenancy had been taken over by a Mr Vogel, whose name plate advised that he, too, was an importer, although of what none of the other tenants had the slightest idea, never having clapped eyes on him.

Climbing the stone steps, our wanderer might well gain a sense of purpose from the ring of his steel Blakeys alone. Passing by Oswald Spengler, Rare Books, and Veerswami the locksmith on the first floor, he might detect a certain 'come on' in the cartoonish sign that beckoned him up the next flight: a bulbous gloved hand with *The Plantation Club, Private Members* painted on its index finger. To succumb would be a grave mistake, for, were he to ascend these stairs – the treads worn wood, the runners long since fled – and push open another heavy door – this one with shreds of green baize drooling off it – he would only have been confronted by the faces of the Poof, the Dog, the Extra, etc., their fleshy convolutions trapped in the gelatinous atmosphere like whelks in aspic. Then his ears would be smitten by the discord of Val's voice – at once a whine and a grate – speaking English with an intense affectation, suggesting it was only his second language, while his mother tongue had been the now defunct theatrical – and latterly gay – argot, Polari, and enunciating the salutation that was at once a damnation: 'Who's this cunt, then?'

Although, to be fair, Val's greetings even for the most staunch of his members – and they were *his* members, since the club was a business, and Val its only owner – were hardly more welcoming:

'Look what the cunt's dragged in'; 'Managed to hoik her cunt up the stairs, has she'; and even the paradoxical 'Hello, cunt.'

As the stage upon which these cunts strutted and fretted was now fully revealed to our imaginary wanderer, it would be – as De Quincey, another habitual Soho *boulevardier* once remarked – as if the 'decent drapery' had been twitched away, and an elderly maiden aunt were caught struggling into her Playtex 24-Hour Girdle.

A single room, twenty-four feet by seventeen; to the immediate right of the door, which was set obliquely, was the bar; behind it the expected shelves of bottles and glasses, together with a small set of optics holding the gin, whisky, vodka and rum. The dusty glasses and faded labels – Bass Ale, Merrydown, Harp – had been interposed with novelty postcards sent by roving members. At the far end of the bar sat Val, beside a large and ornate, old-fashioned cash register; sometimes he sported a collared shirt and a silk cravat, but mostly a Breton fisherman's jersey plotted blue and white contour lines on to his hillock of a torso. However, Val's costume was of absolutely no significance when set beside the horror mask of his face – but more of that later.

On a tall table beside Val there was a money plant, its leaves coppery in the homely light of a standard lamp with a flock shade that was always on; behind his head an orange plastic modular shelving unit had, circa 1973, been pinioned to the ancient wallpaper – wallpaper that, with its oppressively vertical bamboo motif, was the cause, not, as most neophytes assumed, the result of the club's name. The rounded slots of the unit were crammed with girlish tat: sequinned purses; dyed peacock feathers nicked from Biba; gonks, dolls and trolls all looking faintly surprised by the pencils rammed up their jacksies. Propped on top of this excrescence there was a single artefact that summed up the desperately puerile and frantic ironizing of the establishment: a framed gold 45 rpm disc, the label of which read 'Chirpy-Chirpy-Cunt-Cunt by Middle of the Cunt'.

On the bar-room floor was a carpet the colour of middle-aged shit, while in the opposite corner to the door an ancient partition concealed, behind its plaster and laths, a lavatory the size of a draining board: an antediluvian crapper with cracked eggshell enamel and a bird-bath sink, both reeking of ammonia.

Since nobody ever said anything in the Plantation that wasn't facetious, there was a punning fittingness to the way the toilet intruded into the main body of the club; what little daylight leaked from the sash window to splash against its prow provided the only indication of the passage of time in this static universe. Which brings us back to the table habitually occupied by the Martian and Her Ladyship, beside the niche like a rock-cut tomb, in which stood the melody-devouring casket of the piano.

The Poof dabbled his fingers on its keys from time to time, so that it spurted out old show tunes that the others would join in massacring. On top of its lid there stood a china bust of Albert, the Prince Consort. It still had the bright glaze applied by the Royal Doulton pottery in the 1850s, but had been customized during the Punk era with a safety pin nose ring and a length of toilet chain.

This entire compromised space – at once private and public, intimate and horribly exposed – was illuminated solely by sash window, standard lamp, a few candles stuck in old Chianti bottles and a permanently fizzing rod of neon screwed to the nicotine ceiling, lending a mortuary ambience to the already deathly scene.

For the above is by no means exhaustive; we have omitted to mention the snapshots of former patrons, the un-taken-up invitations, the press clippings and 'outsider' canvases – their thick surfaces compressed by awful demons – that were stuck to the walls. Nor have we fully inventoried all the World Cup Willies, stolen pub ashtrays, vintage biscuit tins, voodoo dolls, brass bells, snow globes, and several more skip-loads of useless tat that had been deposited over the decades by decorating skills that were glacial in their slow indifference.

Indeed, given that our chance wanderer, had he happened upon the Plantation Club in 1999, would have found its appearance unaltered from 1989, 1979 or even 1969, it's questionable whether we can speak of this interior as being 'decorated' in any meaningful sense of the word at all; rather, the contents of the club were more akin to the symbol set gathered together by a shaman, then arranged and rearranged in the pursuit of magical effects.

With this one proviso: the shaman of the Plantation Club, Val Carmichael, had never been known to rearrange anything, and, although Maria, a Filipina hunchback, came in punctually every morning to clean, she dealt only with the wipeable surfaces, leaving all the rest of this brooding stuff to become, over the years, set not in concrete but in a far more transfixing substance, to whit: dust. 'Dust', said Trouget, who was only an occasional visitor to the club, yet perhaps its most revered member, 'is peace.'

Trouget, who was a world-famous painter – and therefore known to his fellow members merely as 'the Tosher' – was given to such gnomic utterances, and, while he himself may have discovered a certain repose in the furry interior, he none the less never ventured that far inside, preferring to position himself midway between the stools of the Typist and the Poof, erect in his habitual, tightly zipped, Bell Star motorcycle jacket (he lacked a machine himself but was keen on motorcyclists and liked them to ride him hard), while listening to the arch badinage of the others and buying them all round after round.

When Trouget swung open the green baize door and Val saw the painter's oddly vestigial features – which were partly innate, although also a function of liberal rouging with shoe polish – he would exclaim, 'Cunting cunty, cunt!' The point being that in the Plantation 'cunt' in its nounal, verbal, adjectival, adverbial and even conjunctive forms was the root word of an entire dialect, the main purpose of which was to communicate either extreme disapprobation or, more rarely, the opposite.

If you were in with Val, and therefore in receipt of the right kind of 'cunt', then you were a made man – or, more rarely, woman: you were allowed to come, or go; to remain in the Plantation for an hour, or a month. You could run up a hefty tab; you could even borrow money from the huge till, leaving a scrawled-upon coaster as an IOU. But if you had bestowed upon you the wrong kind of 'cunt' – and, mark well, this was an instantaneous and irrevocable decision on Val's part – then, like the black spot, it stuck to you unto the grave. It didn't matter if you were vouched for by the oldest of the regulars, or if you tried to ingratiate yourself with Val in the most egregious fashion: buying his *Racing News* from the newsagent on Old Compton Street; running his bets to the bookie on D'Arblay Street; fetching him cigarettes and meat pies; lighting those cigarettes; and, of course, standing many, many rounds – it would all be to no avail. You might be tolerated for a week, or three years, but it would only be under sufferance, and sooner or later Val's Embassy filter would be raised at a threatening angle – like the crozier of a battling bishop in the medieval church – and anathema would be pronounced. 'You're barred,' Val would whine-grate, and if you failed to obey as quickly as could be expected of the average sot, by the average sot, then he would follow this up with: 'Get that cunt out of here.' Which was an appeal to the cuntishness of the Cunt himself, who had boxed at Toynbee Hall in the 1950s, then served a further apprenticeship in the early 1960s, wiring car batteries to genitals on behalf of the Richardsons.

Yes, Bernie Jobs knew a thing or two about chucking people out – you don't acquire the nickname 'the Cunt' somewhere as cuntish as the Plantation without special qualifications; and Bernie, with his Wermacht helmet head – shiny-bald, save a black moustache that ran from ear to ear across the back of his bulldog neck – and his squat build – a brick shithouse built to withstand a direct hit by an ICBM – was fully accredited.

Alternatively, were you in receipt of the right kind of 'cunt', you might, on any given afternoon between, say, 1976 and 1983 – for the procedure took this long to fully complete – have witnessed the ritualized humiliation and – this is by no means too strong a term – dehumanizing of the Plantation's resident barman, Hilary Edmonds; who, until this procedure was completed, was denied even the consolation of a nickname, being referred to by Val and his cronies – or ordered about by them – purely by means of a specially inflected 'she'.

On this particular afternoon – a Tuesday one, not that it matters one jot, it was *always* a Tuesday afternoon in midwinter in the Plantation, even if outside it was a steamy midsummer evening or a lemon-bright spring morning – 'she' was being teased remorselessly.

'She's something stuffed in her crack,' the Dog observed as Hilary bent down to fetch a packet of crisps from one of the cardboard boxes under the bar. 'I hope it doesn't work its way up inside her.'

The Dog licked his chops – literally: a carpet tongue unrolled from chapped lips, touching first one of the pendulous jowls that had secured him his moniker, then the other. He had once been a tall cavalryman, the Dog, and he still dressed in regulation tweed hacking jacket and twill slacks, with a paisley cravat tucked behind the collar of his Viyella shirt. It may seem a solecism that so much whisky could have engendered a burgundy hue to his bloodhound's muzzle – but it had.

Hilary, still at a comparatively early stage of his conditioning, felt enough shame with the Dog's, the Cunt's and of course Val's eyes on him to, still bending, reach back to yank down the hem of the Breton fisherman's jersey he wore in emulation of his controller. Losing his balance, he tipped forward and banged his head.

'Ooh!' cried the Cunt. 'She's hurt herself; clumsy girl – silly fucking girl. Won't be giving *her* a china dolly.'

Val chuckled indulgently; it sounded like the first stages of emphysema. 'Heugh-heugh, *she* should give that little cunt of hers a bit more of a sluice, filthy little trollop.'

Hilary straightened up and handed the crisps to the Poof, who negligently thanked him. Gillespie was the only regular male member of the Plantation who was nominally heterosexual; and, while he cast a benign eye over the taunting, he seldom joined in. As for the Martian, his sexual orientation was ambiguous, if it even existed at all.

Gillespie was a well-known photographer, the extempore chronicler of the beautiful and the damned of London's West End. Gillespie, who always wore a lush brown leather coat and a white silk shirt. Gillespie, thrice married but pulling behind him a string of blondes that stretched, taut with yearning, from Billericay to Barnes. Gillespie, whose gypsy-raffish good looks still as yet uncorrupted by the trays of Campari and soda he was undeveloping them in – the features becoming more blurred with every year. Gillespie, whose barrel trunk and columnar thighs every red-blooded queer in Soho wanted to feel battering against him, and who, for that very reason, warranted the ironic title 'the Poof'.

Descending from her bar stool as if it were a glittering rostrum on the stage of the Windmill, and she was still the statuesque brunette she had been during the last war, the Typist sashayed up to the bar and placed her empty glass on a mat. Leaning forward, she gazed down the back of Hilary's orange loons and remarked in clipped, headmistressy tones, 'Isn't that the string of her Tampax poking out? I think she must have the curse, poor thing.'

General sniggering.

Val said, 'In that case *she* probably needs a drink, eh? Pity I've nanti dinary, or I'd stand her one.'

This rare lapse into his native Polari was a sign that Val was in an uncommonly good mood. There was nothing quite like humiliating Hilary to cheer him up. His rubbery face mask stretched with amusement, pushing his beaky nose into still greater prominence.

Ah! Val Carmichael's nose – a treatise could have been written on it; indeed, it looked as if an unseen hand had begun to do exactly that – poking with steely nib at its sub-surface blood vessels and pricking them into the raised, purplish calligraphy of spider angiomas, a definitive statement that the Plantation's owner was already in the early stages of cirrhosis.

Now, quietly, unobtrusively, the Martian joined the torturers at the bar, murmuring so casually, 'I'll stand everyone a round' that the others barely registered his largesse, even when, with a loud 'ting', Val fed his twenty-pound note into the till.

Then. A hiatus. Drinks were poured by Hilary and guzzled – as something for nothing so often is.

This interlude gives me the opportunity to admonish you, gentle reader, not to sit in stern judgement of the Plantation's members and their decadent airs. Weren't, aren't, won't Soho's denizens always be thus? More truly subject to an almost mathematical recursion than any other cultural grouping in the world?

This 5 × 6 grid of streets has been a *quartier* specializing in the division of the human spirit for decades – centuries, even. Since Marx burst his boils and buried his kids on Dean Street; since Hazlitt expired from his 'happy life'; since Johnson's club strutted; since young Wolfgang tinkled the ivories and Casanova got his oats on Frith Street. Back and back, the same divisors have been applied to each term of the series: alcohol and insouciance.

Back and back, until Huguenots destroyed their eyes with needle-point, while Billy Blake bunked off from his dad's drapery to trip, off his head, down to the satanic mills of Farringdon. Soho! Your very name a cry thrown over the shoulders of hunting noblemen. Is it any wonder that generation after generation of your inhabitants have been brought to bay, then stood – or slumped, or lain legs akimbo – frozen, waiting to be dispatched by the hounds of time? If the Plantation Club (est. 1948) was still lost in the foggy forties,

15

with its members aping the mores of Maclaren-Ross and Dylan Thomas, and lapsing into the secret language of formerly outlawed inverts, then this was only as it should be. And yet . . . And yet . . . there was a deeper timelessness to the bar-room above Blore Court, a holier stasis. For, while the black plastic bags piled up in the streets during the Winter of Discontent, and then, come spring, were hauled away, the trash in the Plantation remained. As the upper echelons of West End Vice ran amok and the streetwalkers became entire formations, the Plantation stayed just as whorish. While the social revolution of the 1980s raged, and merchant bankers sprayed every surface matt black, in the lavatory of the Plantation Club the toilet paper was still the consistency of Formica.

No change at all was wrought in this sequestered cell. To say of any of its members that they were 'gay' would be a nonsense, for, while outside in Old Compton Street everyone became openly gayer and gayer, inside the club they only grew sadder and sadder. No popper was ever popped, no T-shirt was tightened, there was no house music in da house.

To apply the epithet 'gay' to Val Carmichael would have been worse than ridiculous; while to say of him – or of any of the rubbery plants in the Plantation – that they were 'queer' would have constituted a gross understatement. The term 'homosexual', if it was taken to imply that Val sought intimacy with – or simply ingress to – to a member of his own sex, was also no longer applicable, and hadn't been for two or three years now; not since Val had discovered Hilary Edmonds in the Wimpy Bar at King's Cross.

The young man was too old and too unmissed to be described as a runaway; he was rather a stroll-off, who had sauntered away from the repression of his home town – some Market This or Thatminster – much as a dazed passenger staggers, fortuitously unharmed, from the smoking wreckage of a car crash.

Hilary had no money and knew no one in London. For three

nights he had been scratched under a holly bush in Bloomsbury Square. When Val spyed him, sitting in the window of the burger bar, Hilary was consuming his last few pence in the form of a sweet bun seamed with beef. His collar-length brown hair lay in dangleberries on his spotty neck – an imperfection that the older man found particularly arousing.

Beyond this Hilary was no great catch. He was tall, scrawny and had features that, cruelly, already bore a mean-spirited impress exactly the same as his father's, although Edmonds Senior had taken thirty-odd years of rankling behind the grille of a bank branch to acquire them.

Val took Hilary home, which was a third-storey walk-up on the old LCC estate off Harrison Street. At that time these redbrick warrens had been overrun by punks, who lolloped furtively along their balconies, halting in the stairwells to nibble amphetamines, their soap-stiffened mohicans twitching like rabbit ears. Val noticed none of this; it belonged to a parallel universe.

If anything, the flat was even more time-locked than the club. Unhemmed yards of blackout cloth kept out the day; a plush-covered sofa slumped on the herringbone wood block floor, twenty-six inches in front of a black and white television. In the tiny kitchen, the tea cups were kept in a broken Baby Belling. In the bathroom the porn was kept in the bath.

Strictly speaking it wasn't *all* porn. There were early German magazines of the burgeoning homosexual community, such as *Die Insel*; there were the homoerotic leaflets of proto-Nazi hiking clubs; there were even bound volumes of the works of Magnus Hirschfeld. This was heavy water at the bottom of the bath; above it was half a fathom of health and fitness magazines, together with outright penis-in-anus stuff brought from Copenhagen. However, the froth on top of this was touchingly innocent: underwear advertisements cut out of *Titbits* and *Reynold's News* that showed men in navy Y-fronts with white piping. There were a few knitting patterns featuring chaps posing in cardigans, and even bobble hats, which Val now found oddly affecting; for, as his ability to construct a viable erection declined, so the objects of his desire became more and more remote: a typology of the masculine, rather than the man himself.

On this exceptional evening Val did try to have sex with Hilary. Being obliging, and a complete ingenue, Hilary was more than happy to lower his dirty polyester houndstooth check trousers – with the stylish flat front – and allow Val's doughy face to knead his crotch. But once the foreplay had been completed – a matter of seconds – and Val was about to munch on the poisoned apple of Hilary's behind, his worm turned and bored back inside him.

Behind the bar at the Plantation, in a votive niche hollowed out between the liquor bottles, so that she was surrounded in death by the alcohol she had worshipped in life, there stood a framed photograph of Ivy Oldroyd, the self-styled 'Queen of Soho'. (An absurd pretension: Soho was, is, and always will be a republic of queens governed by a parliament of whores.) Ivy, even in the sepia tones of the old photo, had a face that recalled Titian's *The Flaying of Marsyas*; she had been a whale of a woman, whose blubber was still constrained by whalebone when she died – of liver failure – in 1966.

Despite her legendary acerbity – wit as quick and bitter as a salted lemon hurled in your eye – Ivy had suffered the same humiliation at the hands of Val Carmichael, as was now, just as unwittingly, being perpetrated upon him by Hilary Edmonds. She, too, had taken a shine to a young man from the provinces whom she had discovered drifting in the London streets. In the photograph Ivy was standing, jade cigarette holder held upright, with Val beside her, looking ineffably young and handsome and manly. His hair was thick and blond, his tie (yes, tie!) was straight – but can she really ever have convinced herself that he was, too?

We will never know; the only certain thing is that when, eventually, he rejected her advances, far from rejecting him, Ivy Oldroyd clamped Val to her Ben Nevis of a bosom, suckled him with wormwood and resolved that he would never be weaned.

As it had been with Val, so it was to be with Hilary. They were both brainwashed into becoming the tireless workers for their respective Queen Bees, and fed with increasing doses of alcoholic royal jelly until they were no longer willing – or even able – to buzz off.

Although 'brainwashed' hardly caught it at all, for, once a new barman had been installed at the Plantation, the process by which he was turned into an alcoholic was more akin to the force-feeding – or *gavage* – whereby a poultry farmer in the Dordogne transforms the liver of a duck or a goose into foie gras. Hilary had no great predilection for drinking; it was only that even to stand in the Plantation for a matter of hours was a health risk.

A tipsy hepatologist, who was once stranded in there for an afternoon, later claimed that he could actually feel his liver cells mashing into steatosis, as drink after drink was augered into him, the spirit scarring his oesophagus, the fluid swelling his abdomen. While mixed with the liquor there was also – he said – an undiluted and poisonous anger.

Anger is what Val Carmichael supplied by the sixth of a gill from the optic of his psyche; shot after shot of spiritous rancour, distilled from his copper full of humiliation. And, as the years engorged with resentment prolapsed into decades, so this rage grew as well, until it obscured the bamboo-patterned wallpaper of the Plantation quite as much as the miasma of cigarette and cigar smoke.

Bernie Jobs – lest we forget, the Cunt – said, 'My gaff, Sadus, is reopening today after its refurb. The boss-man is gonna make an appearance.'

19

(I make no apology for plunging you straight back into the highly provisional, yet simple, past tense of our narrative; this is congruent with what it was like to be in the club. Blubbing to the surface of the boozy pool, he – or rather, she – would become aware of her rescuers, speaking with the cold intimacy of paramedics and firemen: *Are you all right, dearie?* Or laughing with the falsified yelps of whores faking orgasm: *Ha, ha, ha!*)

'Oh, yes,' Val said, 'and who's she when she's at home?'

'Oh, y'know, Denny Wilson.'

'Brrrr,' Val shivered. 'The big brute, she is.'

Two things: 1. To describe Denny Wilson as a 'big brute' displayed a casual attitude in the face of human depravity that was almost laudable, because at this time Wilson still had West End Vice tucked in his crombie pocket, and, had he so much as suspected that pond life like Val was denoting him with a feminine pronoun, would have unhesitatingly instructed some other cunt to do to Val what the Cunt used to do at the behest of the Richardsons. 2. That female pronoun itself requires a little further elucidation. Hilary wasn't the only one so called; it was the sole pronoun in common usage at the Plantation. There were no male members in this club, only shes and cunts.

'Well, Val,' Bernie said, waxing philosophic, 'what you say about Denny may well be true, but she'll be mightily offended if we don't troll round to Old Compton Street and wet the baby's head.'

'With *what*?' Val sneered, darting feverish looks around the bar-room as if the most obvious thing was that it was empty of liquor. 'I've told you cunts already that I've nanti-fucking-dinary!'

The Dog, for many years the London stringer for some Scottish rags, moved to calm him: 'Now, Val, don't take on so.' But his ministrations were unnecessary, because at that moment the baize door wheeled open and Trouget inched in, followed by His Nibs.

'Cunty, darling!' Val cried. 'It's been a bloody age. Cunty, my sweet,' he hurried on, 'that fucking bruiser Wilson is pitching up at the Cunt's smut shop on Old Compton, and we've all got to go down and hob-fucking-nob. You'll stand the 'poo, now won't you, cunty?'

Trouget, whose canvases were already selling for substantial five-figure sums, was notoriously profligate. He orbited the economic sphere of mere solvency, casting bills upon the darkness of its waters. Long before, he had done a deal with his Cork Street gallery – at that time a considerable punt for them – whereby he supplied x number of daubs per year, they took the entire sale price and paid him an annuity of £100,000.

It was a bet that Trouget, a dreadful gambler, lost in the longer term. As his prices rose and rose, and his art became the bamboo-patterned wallpaper of the Met, MoMA and the Tate, his annuity, proportionately, was reduced to a derisory payout. However, it was an arrangement that meant the Maître was free to work all day, then gamble, get soused and flogged all night, which is what he enjoyed more than any splendoured thing.

'Cuuuunty?' Val appealed again, and the Tosher puckered up his polished brown boot of a muzzle in acquiescence – he hardly ever spoke.

'Thank goodness!' Val screeched – although goodness had nothing to do with it. 'Get down half a dozen of 'poo, you,' he ordered Hilary, 'and put it on the Tosher's tab. C'mon, you lot,' he called to the other members, 'hands off cocks and on socks' – this an epithet from his National Service. 'We'll *all* go round and toast her gaff.'

And so they all did. McCluskey, who was a genius at such things, even managed to insinuate a small item concerning the reopening into his column, which disguised the nature of the enterprise that a party was being thrown for – with drink supplied by the famous painter – from those of his readers who wouldn't have been able to stomach it, while artfully exposing it to those who were potential customers. This was a favour that Denny Wilson didn't forget.

He *was* a big brute, and Sadus, while not a small shop, was dominated, after its refurb, by the two new long racks holding its merchandise; goods that were brown-paper camouflaged so that our hypothetical wanderer – remember *her*? – on slapping through the multicoloured plastic strips that dangled in the doorway, might think she'd chanced upon a stationer's with a single product line.

In point of fact, Sadus (est. 1978) was a new kind of porn vendor. Wilson had seen the future – and it wanked. No longer need onanists be separated by mere orientation; the important thing was *what* got you off, not who you got off with. If beating, whipping, bending, masking, gagging or twisting was your thing, then Sadus was your one-slap-shop. Cause, indeed, for celebration.

And if, to begin with, the party was divided – the Plantation members, looking raggle-taggle and out of place, squatted in one aisle, while Wilson and his heavies prowled up and down the other – then after the first five bottles of Trouget's champagne had been drunk, a definite common purpose emerged; humiliating Hilary.

Not that Trouget himself participated. He stood in the corner by the riding crops, an enigmatic crease in his boot-browned features, his Bell Star jacket zipped to his chin, while Hilary was passed from one suedehead in a Harrington to the next, his feet stamped upon at every step, his ribs poked as he poured the 'poo. Yes, the heavies cruelly goosed him, and Val, who had been furnished with a stool by the till, cackled fiendishly.

If what Hilary was being subjected to in the Plantation was indeed a protracted *gavage* – taking place over months and years, not days and weeks, with the force-feeding of alcohol, not grain – then these excursions were those periods in the life of Val's captive goose when the creature was kept outside, voluntarily grazing on the tougher grasses of humiliation, so that his throat became sufficiently toughened to withstand the *finition d'engraissement*.

Val cackled, the heavies assaulted Hilary, the Plantation members were so many plaster casts propped against the Artex walls.

Trouget slipped away into the rainy night. The Typist and Her Ladyship, who might, by reason of their sex alone, have been expected to object to the long-drawn-out assault that was being perpetrated right under their noses, did nothing of the sort. Although their antagonism to one another was legendary, there came a point in a long session (especially one where fresh air acted as a catalyst to their intoxication) when they rediscovered their sisterhood, and so they hung round each other's neck, blabbing emotional confidences that the following morning's hangovers would ruthlessly send to the dustbin of *her*story.

It was left to the Martian to resolve things: he called off Wilson's attack dogs and unobtrusively shepherded the members off down Old Compton Street to the Admiral Duncan, where he equally unobtrusively bought them all a drink – two for Val – before herding them on to the Swiss for the same again – two of the same for Val – and so, by easy stages, home to the Plantation, where everything terminated in a welter of drunkenness.

They were all, of course, alcoholics – every last one of them. But it would be a mistake to equate that alcoholism with unruly behaviour, incontinent emotion or wholly unmanageable lives. The welter of drunkenness that ended the Festival of Sadus would have been barely discernible to an outsider; even an habitué of the club could only tell when consumption was peaking due to an added dankness in the atmosphere, an extra film of dirt on the sash window and a multiplication of 'cunts', until they were not only the most frequently employed words but also their punctuation.

No, the members of the Plantation led lives of remorseless continence: deeply trammelled, painfully organized. They had chosen this mode of existence and bowed down to its limiting constraint: that for the greater portion of their waking lives their forebrains would be completely sedated. If they had work, then their performance was characterized by its stereotypy; if they had a family, then home life was typified by their absence, for on the rare occasions that they were in the vicinity, it was as a Tupperware Moloch in a suburban Gehenna.

Getting the money to spend on drink, getting to the Plantation, leaving the Plantation, and – in the case of the majority – getting on to other pubs and clubs, until they beat the night to death in some chthonic shebeen deep beneath the West End, required a steadiness and fixity of purpose that militated against any reckless behaviour whatsoever.

If the club had had a motto, it would have been – to paraphrase Suetonius: 'Make waste slowly.' The huge volume of alcohol poured into the wonky vessel of the Plantation was as formaldehyde decanted into a specimen jar, with this distinction: these spirits preserved everything but the flesh.

Hilary Edmonds had for years now rented a cupboard in Kensal Rise from Margery De Freitas, aka Her Ladyship. De Freitas, who once shared Mandy Rice-Davies with Peter Rachman, had followed the slum landlord's trajectory rather than the whore's, moving straight on to a brief stint as a madam, before finding the management of the girls too onerous. So, she dispensed with the chickens but kept their coops; verminous Victorian houses, subdivided and subdivided and partitioned again, in which she incubated as many blacks and Irish as she could lay her fat bejewelled hands on.

She had skipped the prime of life, cutting straight from slim, angular, Mediterranean good looks to a dropsical version of them: mountainous hair, vulturine beak, tits avalanching into her lap. Her legs plagued her, and, as if the treatment he received in the club wasn't enough for the poor boy, when they got back of an evening Hilary was ordered to remove Her Ladyship's support hose, unwind fathoms of crêpe bandages, then bathe the porphyritic columns in salt water.

Promptly at noon each day, the two left Kensal Rise and took the Bakerloo Line to Piccadilly Circus. Her Ladyship stumped up

Shaftesbury Avenue to the French, where Gaston helped to correct the balance of alcohol in her blood. Meanwhile, Hilary opened up at the Plantation: checked the Filipina had done her wiping, supervised deliveries, re-stocked the shelves; all in all enjoying his hour or so alone, dabbling in the dusty peace, before Val Carmichael dragged himself in from King's Cross, and the long dark sousing of the afternoon began.

On this particular afternoon – one in May, not that you'd feel merry buried in Blore Court – the regulars trickled in, in their usual order: first the Cunt, crowing over this scam or that rip-off; then His Nibs, immaculate in suit, tie and puce face mask, with dry talk of lubricious scandal. Next came the Dog, the only member who took the stairs to the second floor at a bound, a gesture to his Highland boyhood that cost him long minutes heaving on his stool, slobbering on a cigarette as he battled with his necrotic lungs.

Then up came the Poof, frowsty from a young girl's perfumed bed and snapping at Hilary to make haste with his Campari, as he hid his shakes by patting his curly locks. The Typist and Her Ladyship arrived within seconds of each other, separated by leagues of hatred; then, *finalement*, the Extra made his entrance. Bolton, narrow of skull, sandy of hair, his malleable features writhing with the effort required to corral six personae into the role of a single actor. The Extra, whose big day this was, for, together with a jejeune TV comedian in the role of Clov, while he himself – perhaps inadvisedly – attempted Hamm, they were opening in a production of *Endgame* at the Peacock Theatre on Portugal Street.

Oh, yes – and then there was the Martian, although to say of Pete Stenning that he had 'come in' to the Plantation at any given time was difficult. He seemed always to have been there, sitting at his little table between the piano nook and the window embrasure, his greenish hair shining faintly in the pallid light, his glasses tilted forward and the lenses holding two orange saucers, the reflections of the drink he held in his ink-stained fingers.

Even in an establishment where stasis was the prevailing mode, the Martian stood out for his refusal to be moved by the times. He was still wearing the same serviceable suede jacket in 1983 that he had been sporting in 1980, and 1973. The same yellow shirt, too. He spoke seldom, and when he did his interventions had a surgical character, as, sidling up to the bar, he got right to the point: 'What're you having, Val?' As if he didn't know.

So Hilary built the bubbly edifice of another vodka and tonic, and another Campari and soda, and another whisky, and another lager. Round and round it went, the drinking in the Plantation, a perpetual motion of alcoholic fluid like a water feature with a concealed pump.

At some point during the afternoon Bolton handed out the tickets – even Hilary got one – and at 5.30 he left the club, admonishing them to 'Be on time, you cunts. There's only one act and no admission after curtain up.'

'We know that,' Val snarled, although heretofore he had never evinced any familiarity with the joyful pessimism of the Irish Nobel Laureate's œuvre. 'Don't get yer lavender scanties ridden up yer crack.'

In the weeks running up to this big day, Val had been finding the Extra's increasingly thespian airs altogether intolerable. As Bolton pulled open the green baize door, his fellow members croaked 'Break a leg' (perhaps a superfluous remark, given that had any ordinary man drunk as much as the Extra had that afternoon, he might well have broken a leg descending the kerb of Wardour Street), but Val only sneered, 'He oughta stick to choccie bars.' A put-down occasioned by the fact that in the last year the Extra would have gone under, were it not for the residuals from a TV advert for Crunchie that settled his bar tab.

An hour later Val said to Hilary, 'C'mon, Boy, let's shut up shop.' A remark that while commonplace to almost anyone, was to Hilary a warm gush of the sweetest, most nurturing intimacy.

No one knew who had first started calling Hilary 'Boy', or, if he were absent, referring to him as 'the Boy', but gradually the nickname had begun to stick. Initially, Val was having none of it. If the Dog barked, 'Where's the Boy?', his bloodhound eyes too myopic to see that Hilary was emptying one of the heavy cut-glass ashtrays into the bin under the bar, then Val would snarl, 'Boy? Boy? There's no fucking *boys* in here, girlie, only you bunch of cunts.' Yet, as time stalled, and Hilary became as much a fixture of the Plantation as the bust of Prince Albert on the piano, so even Val was driven to moderate his sneeringly impersonal shes and hers.

Hilary locked the till; Val pocketed the key. Hilary checked the toilet to see that no one had collapsed in it (a common occurrence with members' guests, who, invited in for a singular 'drink', found themselves indoctrinated by a cult of libations); Val finished his V & T. The members slopped down the stairs into Blore Court, sniffing the astringent bouquet of the early-evening piss left there by the dossers. Hilary switched off the lights and locked the door of the Plantation; Val pocketed the key.

Crossing Wardour Street, then rounding the corner by the Vintage House and proceeding up Old Compton Street, the Plantation members – who appeared in public, en bloc, perhaps only once or twice a decade – presented a curious spectacle: overgrown children, their clothes a lustrum or two out of date, holding hands to form a crocodile that swam upstream against the current of fluvial time.

Out in front was the Dog, sniffing the route ahead, then darting back – if an overweight Scots drunk can ever be said to 'dart' anywhere, unless, that is, he's actually playing darts – to round up the others.

Val and Hilary had linked arms – but out of desperation, not defiance. Val had a spotted silk scarf knotted around his scraggy throat; dark glasses pinched his ruby nose with its bloody filigree. In his free hand a walking stick wavered over the paving; he looked like a sick old man – he was forty-six. Alcohol had done ageing's business – psychically as well as physically. Val was so long accustomed to the furred tranquillity of the Plantation that rush-hour London had a furious, insect intensity for him; as he proceeded among them, the pedestrians buzzed and flitted, settling in the food-spattered roadway, then taking flight when a lumbering lorry tried to crush them.

Up to Cambridge Circus, then dazedly across and on to the Seven Dials. Hilary staggered over the cobbles of Neal Street; he needed Val's support almost as much as vice versa. The slim hips that Val had once impotently coveted were now pulpy. Beneath his Breton fisherman's jersey Hilary's liver was swelling, as fatty globules accumulated in its cells. Already the macrovesicular steatosis was under way, and, to confirm further still that Hilary warranted the feminine personal pronoun, a spongy mass was building up in concentric rings around his nipples; a foretaste – for the paps that ne'er gave suck – of alcohol-induced gynaecomastia. Val's clawed hand, its nails striped with the paired bands of hypoalbuminemia, dug into the soft underside of Hilary's wing. He guided his fattened goose past the ugly pile of the Freemasons' Hall on Great Queen Street – possibly the pre-eminent club among the many who would never have accepted these members as members.

Her Ladyship was flagging on the long march, while the Typist collapsed hopelessly on the lip of a concrete cup spiky with greenery. A passer-by, confused by her two pieces of tweed and general air of respectability, leant down to inquire if she was 'all right', then recoiled from her gin breath and hurried on.

The stony canyon of Kingsway terrified the members; they hugged the ankles of the buildings, keening for mercy. They almost scampered into Lincolns Inn Fields, and made their escape, via the Old Curiosity shop, into Portugal Street.

They didn't properly regain their breath until, cigarettes lit, they were ensconced in the theatre bar, and the Martian had bought them all a drink – a triple for Val, who was most in need. 'Why – why the fuck,' Val panted, 'did we fucking walk here?'

But, of course, none of them knew.

The crowd in the bar were not the usual sort of first-nighters. These sports-jacketed men, with British Home Stores bolsters of wives, had driven in from the outer suburbs, or even further afield; some with teenage children, others with elvers still more jellied. No more familiar with Beckett than Val Carmichael (less so, in point of fact, because he had met the playwright, once, with Trouget. 'What's he like?' the Extra had asked. 'Her?' Val replied. 'Total cunt.'), these punters had come to see Terry Pierce, the fresh-faced and rubber-legged star of the hugely popular peak-time sitcom *Baloo's Den*, in which he played an accident-prone young Scout master.

Backstage, Pierce had been appalled by the state that Bolton had arrived in. The Extra caromed off the distempered walls and nutted the safety lights' wire basketry. However, after applying to an attentive stagehand for medicinal cocaine, the actor, who was to be the very embodiment of Beckett's joyful pessimism, did indeed achieve a kind of . . . joyful pessimism.

'Terry, darling,' he slurred, propped in the doorway of his co-star's dressing room. 'Don' worry 'bout nuffin, sweetie. All I gotta fuckin' do is sit there, babes – iss you gotta do the work!'

This, while technically accurate, was still not particularly re-assuring for Pierce, who, in common with so many *farceurs*, had a deep – almost pathological – yearning to be taken seriously. The Extra, as Hamm, might well be able to sit in 'an armchair on castors' for ninety-some minutes, but whether he could bring the right kind of sonorous asperity to lines widely regarded as the very acme of bleak Absurdism seemed altogether doubtful. He couldn't even remember the *names* of the actors playing Nell and Nagg – who fluttered about solicitously in their grey weeds, faces doubly whitened – merely waving them away with an idle, 'Will you fuck off, you little cunts.'

Bare interior. Grey light. Left and right back, high up, two small windows, curtains drawn . . . The spartan set and insufficient lighting mandated by Beckett's anal-retentive stage directions may have temporarily dampened the audience's spirits – they were, after all, anticipating an evening rich with belly laughs – but the entrance of their hero, and his funambulist compliance to those self-same directions, soon ignited outbreaks of giggling, especially among the teenagers.

. . . goes and stands under window left. Stiff, staggering walk . . . He turns and looks at window right. He goes and stands under window right. He looks up at window right. He turns and looks at window left. He goes out, comes back immediately with a small step-ladder . . .

With each wobbly revolution and spring-heeled gyration, Terry Pierce called forth gales of laughter. Then, when he eventually closed in on the shapeless form centre stage and whipped away the sheet shrouding it to reveal Bolton in a dressing gown, stiff toque on his head, bloodstained handkerchief covering his features, the merriment faltered.

In the wings, the director of the piece was on his knees, a prayer on his lips, albeit a secular one – an adaptation, to suit these harrowing circumstances, of the playwright's own *aperçu* concerning Hamm: that he was 'The kind of man who likes things coming to an end but doesn't want them to end just yet.'

Midway back in the stalls, strung out along the best seats in the house, sat the membership of the Plantation. They had already attracted whispery opprobrium in the bar, as they sucked up booze, spurted out smoke and cratered the haze with their 'cunts'. Now, in the blacked-out auditorium, their purse-lipped critics discovered that the Plantation members not only looked off, they smelt it, too.

Very red face. Black glasses. Handkerchief removed, a reversal began the very instant the Extra spoke Hamm's first line: 'Me –' (*he yawns*) '– to play.' The Extra hadn't needed much make-up at all to conform with Beckett's instruction that Hamm have a 'very red face', and, while he may have been drunk, he was still an old trouper: he remembered his lines, and gave them a slushy, sibilant delivery that sent out small puffs of spume, clearly visible in the footlights.

Bolton's fellow members – who, while possessing little culture themselves (with the obvious exceptions of Trouget and the Typist), none the less knew perfectly well how to be snobbish about it – were appalled by the levity with which their country cousins were responding to the crepuscular vision of the great dramatist. They tut-tutted, and the Poof even poked the eleven-year-old boy sitting next to him and hissed, 'Shut up, you little prick.'

But then the hicks became transfixed by the Extra's Hamm. He may have remained seated, but his performance was definitely a high-wire act. The unutterable pathos of the human condition, as revealed by the desperate, halting exchanges between Bolton/ Hamm and Pierce/Clov, fell heavily on them: a mighty weight crushing their bourgeois complacency. The mums and dads ceased chuckling; the teenagers stopped tittering; the smaller kids struggled on with their giggles for a few more minutes, but soon, flummoxed by the weirdness of it all, they, too, shut up and lapsed into that state of shocked boredom that Theodor Adorno characterized, *vide Endgame*, as the 'gerontocracy of late capitalism'.

However, *Very red face. Black glasses.* Hamm, calling upon the dogged, hapless, slavish Clov to poison himself. Hamm, static unless wheeled; self-obsessed unless rebarbative. Nell and Nagg in their bins, the whitened after-images of human affection, condemned for ever to an atemporal realm in which they acted out, and acted out, and acted out the pathetic dependency they called love.

Very red face. Black glasses. It didn't need Ken Tynan – the only individual who had known both mise en scènes intimately – to recognize that this set-up was uncannily like the daily psychodrama in the Plantation Club; nor to grasp that Hamm, as portrayed by the Extra, bore close comparison with Val Carmichael himself. By the time Bolton reached the line 'Do you not think this has gone on long enough?', and, worse, delivered it with an accurate imitation of Val's whining croak, the overseer of the Plantation could bear it no longer and whined back, 'It certainly has, you cunt.'

The Extra was too much of a pro to react to this, but Terry Pierce fumbled, then dropped the three-legged toy dog. Having got this off his sunken chest, Val had no intention of leaving; besides, he had wittingly planted an evil seed, and in the last half-hour of the play was delighted by its burgeoning, as, unable to control himself, Bolton began to gash Hamm's gnomic utterances with more and more 'cunts'.

Now it was the members' turn to be convulsed, while the small town burghers sat – possibly as Beckett had intended – desperate for it all to end *right away*.

By the time the Extra glossed Hamm's final weary remark thus: '. . . speak no more . . . Old cunt! You remain,' they were shuddering with embarrassment, whereas Val was clucking with delight. Backstage, the director lay unconscious in a pool of his own tears.

The critic from *Time Out* declared Bolton's Hamm to be a 'masterful improvisatory tour de force', restoring 'a much needed contemporary bite' to a piece that was beginning to petrify in the gorgon stare of academic eyes. Others were not so sure, and, although *Endgame* smouldered on at the Peacock Theatre for another sixteen performances – with most of Bolton's expletives deleted – it was soon enough stubbed out by lawyers acting on behalf of its author, who, whether or not he may've been a total cunt, totally objected to any bowdlerization of his work.

However, that night at the Plantation – which Val, in an almost unprecedented move, had reopened – the Extra received a hero's welcome. No Larry Olivier or Ralphie Richardson could have been more lauded. Val ordered Hilary to suck Bolton off in the toilet. Trouget loitered, standing everyone champagne for an hour or so, then slipped away. The Martian made good the deficiency, buying round after round – always triples for Val – and Val, pressing on with Hilary's *gavage*, took care to pour a little of each V & T into his understudy's glass.

The Poof mounted the piano stool and pounded out, over and over and over again, '(Don't Put Your Daughter on the Stage) Mrs Worthington', a ditty that, although risqué in its own day, took on a filthy contemporary tinge as the members bawled their heads off, adding 'cunts' in all the irrelevant places.

The Prince Consort, safety-pin nose-ring jangling, pogoed on top of the piano; Her Ladyship's dewlaps jiggled; Bolton cut a wonky caper. By the till, Val Carmichael lit Embassy after Embassy, each from the tip of the last, while surveying the giddy pavane with a dangerous leer. The Cunt roared, His Nibs smiled sardonically, the Dog howled with drunkenness.

Some time after midnight, the Typist, who had long since concertinaed into blackout atop her stool, wet herself; but no one paid this the least attention, as they were all caught up in the whirling circularity of dervishes, who, as they spun faster and faster, became more and more abandoned in the devastation of their short-term memories, until they metamorphosed into figures with no more ability to think of the next move than a chess piece.

Each on its appropriate square, left to right at the bar: Val, the Dog and the Poof. In the second row the Cunt and the Extra; dumped on a stool her own colour, the queenly Typist; trapped at the end of the board, the Martian and Her Ladyship; taken by it all, slumped against the wall, His Nibs. And observing the whole scene, that silly goose, the Boy. Hilary, who on this dark night was granted a painful moment of not to be repeated clarity, and grasped that this was a zugzwang from which he could never escape.

*

33

A couple of years later they were all still on the same squares. Entire civilizations of dust mites had arisen, then fallen, while in the human realm nothing had changed, except that it was June, earlier in the day, and the Tosher was in. He stood by the door, diffident as ever; that was how Trouget made his way in the world: light as a fly sensing its way across a soufflé. Give him a tin of brown shoe polish and a bottle of vintage Taittinger, zip him into his Bell Star jacket and hand him a first-class plane ticket, and away he'd go with no thought to the morrow, intent on dropping ten, twenty, fifty grand on the tables at Biarritz or Monte Carlo.

When the Tosher was in town he toshed all day at his studio, which was above a sanitary-ware manufacturer in Peckham Rye, fuelled only by successive glasses of champagne. Then, in the late afternoon, he applied his polish, lacquered his hair into a hard helmet and went up to the Plantation, where he stood by the door and drank champagne. Cunty, darling.

Without the Tosher, the other members would have been mere mudlarks grubbing on the foreshore for trinkets discarded by the Truly Significant as they swept past on their gilded barges, heading downstream to the silvery sea of posterity. Without Trouget their ossified mores would have been a stylization that had forgotten style. Trouget – by virtue of his great success alone, for he was as daft as one of his own brushes – belonged to the world without; a world that was steadily growing faster and brighter, while in the club it only grew slower and dustier.

'Are you well hung, cunty darling?' Val asked him on this particular day. The Tosher murmured an affirmative. 'It's all in the *hang*, isn't it, Tosher?' Val continued. 'I mean, if your daubs ain't hung just so, no cunt'll buy 'em.'

Again, Trouget's weird young-old face contorted consent. The world-famous artist suddenly spasmed forward, pecked a few peanuts from the bar and popped them into his mouth. He brushed his fingertips on the flanks of his jacket; the grains of salt fell to the carpet, poisoning the peaceful fields of dust.

Val took another line: 'Have you got our cunt-boards? And are our names on the silly list? You know I can't be doing with a wait.'

Trouget dropped his weak chin to his strongman's chest.

The Boy, who had been tidying up the bottles of Britvic orange beloved of the Martian, couldn't prevent himself from breaking in at this point: 'Um, T-Tosher, c-can I come, too?'

Over the years Hilary had lost any awe he may have once had in the presence of the others, who, while they were hopeless sots, were none the less what his mother quaintly referred to as 'your betters'. But with Trouget, Hilary was still tongue-tied; and this despite the fact that the painter had once, very civilly, asked Hilary to beat him with a small hammer, the kind railway engineers formerly used to check tappets. More of that, never.

Val, outraged, froze: his Embassy aloft, his claw gripping the till, as if it might give him the strength of money.

Had you, for the past two years, been spending all afternoon, every day, in the Plantation, you probably wouldn't have noticed the changes in Val – the changes, specifically, in his nose. The spider angioma was far more advanced: ruptured blood vessels now entirely enmeshed his fleshy beak in a net of angry bluey-red lines.

The sight was so arresting that newcomers to the club – of whom, admittedly, there were few at this time – would be altogether transfixed by the nose as it shone, a warning buoy bobbing in the whirlpool of booze. If, at some later date, these neophytes were asked about their visit to Soho's oldest and most celebrated private members' club, they would only ask in return: 'That man who says "cunt" all the time, what's wrong with his nose?' As if *you* would know.

It was comforting to think of Val Carmichael's nose as evidence of bad character – each bloody filament a wrong choice or an evil deed – but the truth was far sadder, and more desperate. True, Val had not been exactly *nice* to begin with, but for a long time now it had been the nose that was lighting his way into the most Stygian recesses of human nature.

The nose burnt with unholy indignation.

Trouget said nothing, then unzipped his jacket and, withdrawing a thick deck of engraved invitations, dealt one on to the bar in front of the Boy. It read *Trouget 1955–1985, A Retrospective at the Hayward Gallery*, then the usual guff. The Tosher didn't stop there: he went on from place to place, silently dropping invitations into the hands and the laps of the members. It was a fait accompli; however much the ugly old sister hated it, the Fairy Godmother had decided: Cinders would go to the ball.

In the Methuselan lifespan that it was taking for Val's indignation to subside into resignation, the Martian rose and slowly scuttled the five steps to the bar. 'Have a drink, Val,' he cautioned him. 'On me – Boy, get Val a V & T, a triple, I think.'

'She, she, sheeeeoooo.' Val's attempt to become the screaming pope and excommunicate Hilary ended with a sound the members had never heard before: his sighing. Hilary, who had been holding his own bad breath, at last managed to swallow.

This time they didn't make the mistake of walking. Even so, when the two cabs pulled up on Belvedere Road, and the ten members of the Plantation party struggled out into the summer evening, they found the light and the noise and the air and the people almost overwhelming.

His Nibs, who had more cause to venture outside the square mile of the West End than the rest, took the lead. Yet even he, once they had entered the labyrinth of stairwells and walkways that corrugated the cardboard Brutalism of the South Bank, was altogether bamboozled.

McCluskey halted and looked back. Coming up behind him, arm in arm, were Val and the Boy; while to their rear limped the rest of the members: defeated Tommies retreating across a concrete no man's land. At the very back was the Martian, one hand on each of Her Ladyship's buttocks so that he could propel her forward.

His Nibs was oft times precluded from deep insight – by reason of alcohol, of course, and also for professional reasons: so much of his intellect was adapted to the secretion of shmaltz – the heating up of it, and then its smearing across the tabloids – that he had lost his nose for what might, or might not, be kosher.

The Boy, almost a decade on now, had reached a peculiarly affecting stage: plump and dazed, subject at least once or twice a week to blackouts, his suffering lending his thin nose and flabby cheeks a kind of nobility.

McCluskey was no gastronome; he knew neither of the *iecur ficatum* – the livers of geese force-fed with figs – originated by Apicius, nor of the manner in which the medieval European Jews had, as a by-product of their own dietary laws, preserved the practice of *gavage*. Nevertheless, observing the Boy and his tormentor, His Nibs grasped that what existed between them was no Beckettian stalemate; and that no matter the extent to which the Plantation and its members were outside time, there was still a linear process at work here, one that, no matter how haltingly, was limping towards some strange fruition.

According to Pliny the Elder, when the Romans' geese were fat enough, they were drenched with wine and immediately slaughtered. In Hilary Edmonds's case the drenching was taking years, and His Nibs now realized that the only thing that might prevent his eventual demise was the saturation and slaying of the poultry keeper himself.

McCluskey was not the only one to be granted insight on the night of Trouget's triumphant retrospective. (The prices paid for the

Tosher's canvases quadrupled in the first few days of the show, while he was levered from a position of undoubted avant garde pre-eminence to a pedestal of Portland stone. The OM was spoken of – and we're not talking Buddhist chants here.) In the topsy-turvy galleries of the Hayward – spaces at once airily vast and oppressively claustrophobic – some hundred and fifty of the Maître's mighty oils loomed and brooded, deepening the mystery.

Trouget's brushwork may have changed over three decades, from the smooth viscosity of Léger to the scraggy abrasion of Kokoschka or Jasper Johns, but his fidelity to his palette and his subject matter was absolute. In picture after picture, using his favoured bile-greens and bathroom-tile blues, Trouget portrayed well-built nudes, willowy youths and neotenous golems, their heads part skull, part the melted plastic of dolls. There were also a lot of dogs – cartoonish and naturalistic.

In many of the paintings, pricks ('penises' would be to dignify them) stuck out of the pictorial space as scaffolding poles do off the back of a flat-bed truck. Trouget employed them to support the drapery of his backgrounds, which were divided, laterally, into three, or stretched into astigmatism, or simply dumped in the corner, a heap of old Euclid.

Art critics – who *never* know better – ascribed both the persistences and the discontinuities in the Tosher's works to ideological conflicts, and to modes of being and seeing that were at once lofty, yet, for him, gnawingly ordinary. The reality – as any of his fellow club members could have told them – was that he was always pissed.

But the most salient thing about Trouget's paintings – a fact long since ignored, now that you can see a Trouget replicated in an advert for arch supports, or a poster of one stuck up in the toilet of a small town library – is that, without exception, whether seated, standing, recumbent – or, in the case especially of the dogs, on their haunches – all of the figures were upended: dangling men and women, their painterly hair draggling the heavy gilded frames Trouget's gallerist favoured.

Whether this made of his subjects brachiating apes or lynch victims, it was difficult to say – and the critics expended a great deal of energy not saying either; but on that balmy evening in mid June, in the mid 1980s, there were few among the attendees of the private opening who did not experience these serried ranks of gibbeted figures as anything except premonitory of Death.

Their shoulders hunched in their outsized shoulder pads; their scalps contracted beneath their big hair. Whether they were drawn into the horror show of an individual painting, or hurried past them all in a blur, even the most corpulent bankers visibly shrank into the boxy confines of their double-breasted suits, while their Adam's apples shrivelled behind the huge knots of their Valentino ties.

The artist himself blew and spun through the Hayward, a maso-chistic spindrift of a man, who was wafted along by the artistic director, the curator and even – for a good part of the evening – the Minister for the Arts himself. (A ludicrous goofy fatty, who later that year was to lose his portfolio, after getting his prick stuck – like a scaffolding pole – in a prostitute.)

When Trouget finally found Val and the others, they had gone to ground in one of the smallest spaces – no greater than a well-lit coal hole – where he had placed three of his 'sculptures'. Which were nothing more – and possibly even less – than the rags Trouget used to clean his brushes. Glaucous, pyramidical piles of these – the arse-wipes of his art – now lay under perspex. This, an astute memorializing of his thrilling praxis, anticipated the wholesale iconography that was to be constructed after his death, when the 'dilly boy Trouget had named as his heir flogged off the Maître's studio. It was systematically broken up, the 597,644 bits individu-ally numbered, then crated and shipped to Indonesia, where they were reassembled in a Jakarta shopping mall, much to everyone's satisfaction.

The supplies of 'poo were perfectly acceptable for anyone who called it champagne – but not for the Plantation workers. Seeing that they were getting restive, and perhaps fearing a scene, the Martian had discreetly palmed a waiter a twenty pound note; subsequently, tray after tray came winging down into the coal hole.

Val sat on a padded bench bracketed by the Typist and Her Ladyship, while His Nibs, the Poof, the Extra, the Dog, the Cunt, the Martian and the Boy leant against the outside-inside walls. Seeing them all clearly – which, after all, was what he was good at – abstracted from their usual habitat, even the other-worldly painter was taken by how anachronistic they all seemed. In this brave new world of matt black and mirrored glass the Dog's terrycloth shirt and flared trousers, the Extra's leather waistcoat and floor-licking knitted scarf, the Cunt's Harrington jacket and polyester trousers, even His Nibs' suit – brown, Burton, gleaming at shoulder and elbow with wear – let alone Val and the Boy's matching Breton fishermen's jerseys – all set them as firmly apart as the Appalachians do remote hillbilly communities. Their arch cuntishness and man-nered Cockney was as bizarre to the ears of the passing crowd as Elizabethan dialect in the mouths of modern Americans.

Trouget saw this – and grasped it entire. Life, properly conceived of, was not his subject, which was why he preferred to work not with life models but with pages torn from magazines, old anatomical drawings, postcards and osteopathy instruction manuals. So, now that the members of the Plantation Club had been torn out of their own era and pasted on to another, he could apprehend them for what they truly were.

'Blimey,' Trouget softly exclaimed. 'You lot should get out more.'

Ten years passed.

In the thick green atmosphere of the Plantation – an aquarium filled with absinthe – time was experienced as a limpid thing, with no current, only the muted bubbling of artificial oxygenation. If a time-lapse camera had been mounted in the corner of the bar-room and left running for a decade, the film would show only the strobe of night and day, and the fishy flip of its patrons swimming in the door, to the bar, and then back to their crannies.

It was 1995, and time again for Trouget to have a major London retrospective. In the intervening years more canvases had been dealt into his collectors' hands, just as the painter himself had been dealt more cards at the baccarat tables. More 'poo had been poured down his polished throat, more belts had been thwacked on his backside, and now he stood zipped into his Bell Star jacket, once more dealing out pasteboard invitations to the Poof, the Cunt and the Dog.

To say that nothing had changed in the Plantation would not have been strictly accurate. His Nibs and the Typist had died. Their funerals had been at Mortlake Crematorium and Kensal Rise Cemetery respectively. Although all their fellow members – looking, in full daylight, like living dead themselves – had attended, it was part of the Plantation's voodoo that these passings away went largely unremarked. Life events – and indeed, much of the very stuff of life – were never spoken of at the club. Under the blank eyes of the Prince Consort, and the furious ones of Ivy Oldroyd, there was never any mention of the following: children, pets, kisses, food, travel (including foreign parts of any description), politics, religion, music, romance, architecture . . . and so, wearily, on.

Picture a Red Admiral butterfly poised on a purple spear of buddleia – a sight that can often be witnessed, even in the very stony heart of a city. See its painfully delicate wings part with a quiver, marry with another; observe their tawny tips, their backs, which become denser, more rubescent, as they curve into the plush runnel of the thorax. Then scrutinize the outsides of the wings, taking time, trying to identify the precise point at which the tawniness distorts, then explodes into vivid orange bars. All this while the Red Admiral continues to feed on the flower, perfectly poised on its legs, which are banded black and white like the finest electric flex.

This is not an experience that would *ever* – not even if human lives were geologic in span – be spoken of at the Plantation.

There were the deaths of His Nibs and the Typist – and there was the imminent death of Val Carmichael himself. (Or should we say 'herself' of an individual who had not, to anyone's certain knowledge, employed a masculine pronoun since the late 1960s.) Of course, Val had been moribund for years, but at some point in the early 1990s his massively engorged liver passed beyond mere macrovesicular steatosis into the irredeemably gothic realms of steatonecrosis.

We may set to one side the fact that Val was also suffering from hepatic encephalopathy – with all the brain-warping confusion that this entailed – because, after all, since he had been continuously drunk since the Macmillan premiership, it was impossible for him, or anyone else, to tell where one kind of mental discombobulation blundered into the other.

Even so, given the radical internal restructuring of Val Carmichael that those hectolitres of vodka and tonic – interspersed with the very occasional bottle of 'poo – had undertaken, it is strange to note that his view of his body remained curiously un-differentiated: a child's conception of a plasticine blob that might be rolled into a ball, then a sausage, then a snake, yet remaining throughout the same stuff of Life.

Perhaps this is the real saving grace of chronic alcoholism? That, as the completion date is neared, and the architecture of the liver has been fatally altered – portal hypertension opening the umbilical vein to the portal venous system, so the entire property is sprayed with blood – its sitting tenant stays put, blissfully unaware.

Poised on his stool by the till, Val's quivering wings parted, then married, as he lifted the V & T to his creased lips. His thorax had impacted, throwing into upsetting prominence his gynaecomastic tits. His alcohol-induced hypogonadism meant that he had to sit with his stick thighs parted: his soiled flies were an open incitement to . . . nothing. He smelt of piss and death and booze and cigarette smoke.

In common with the Red Admiral's wing tips, all the extremities of Val's body were tawny; a good match, if it could have been contrived, to the dappled beige-brown, russet-yellow of his liver. *Kirrhos*, the Greek for 'tawny', is the root of 'cirrhosis', and as the absinthe light from the sash window spilt on to the dusty carpet and spattered the bamboo-patterned wallpaper, it turned the whole interior of the Plantation tawny. Thus Val was superbly camouflaged: all of him but the dreadful beak, as bright and hollow and heavy as a hornbill's.

Hilary stood behind the bar smearing glasses and swapping cunts with the Dog, the Poof, the Cunt and the Extra. The years had not been kind to the Boy either, extinguishing every last glint in him of party-time attractiveness, while helping him into the whole-body fat-coat of alcoholic middle age, then showing him, firmly, to the door.

Perversely, it was only now that it was too late, that Hilary dared to assert some independence, abandoning his striped jersey for a woeful bovver boy costume of cropped Levis, white T-shirt and red braces. However, it wasn't much of a breakaway, because the Boy remained in sync with the older members, whose butterfly collars, flowery ties and Fair Isle tank tops were once again in fashion. In sync with them, and also with the replacements for His Nibs and the Typist; newborn members, who, well lubricated, had slid into the cauls of their predecessors.

They were so hip that it hurt: a posse of young conceptual artists, whose bloody flux of creation – preserved animal carcasses, shit-daubed canvases, inflatable wank dollies – was at that very moment coagulating into a big scab of success on the cultural body that would be picked away at by the critics for decades to come.

It had been Hilary himself who had reached out to these Soho apprentices and invited them to join the Plantation's death cult. Voodoo Val thrust his Embassy filter in their downy faces, and, pronouncing proscription, whined, 'Look what the cunt's dragged in', once, twice, three times an afternoon, but they paid no attention. There was a new wind blowing through the *trompe l'œil* bamboo, an awareness that soon enough the old overseer would be gone.

In the meanwhile, the Martian sidled up to the bar and got a round in: a Campari and soda for the Poof, whose nights in white satin were now over. Instead of scaling legs-up-to-her-arse, he was reduced to summitting a mountainous mixed-race girl called Berenice, who lived in a council flat on Brick Lane. His leather coat hung on his shoulders, the flayed skin of a vanquished sex-warrior.

The Martian got a Scotch for the Dog, who, the preceding month, had been offered voluntary redundancy by his one remaining rag, in the way a real dog is 'offered' being put down. The Dog snarled at the injustice, and yapped of a cottage outside Dundee, but he was never going to go walkies further than the Coach and Horses, and he died the following year.

'Bernie?' the Martian needlessly inquired, and the Cunt growled an equally redundant assent. Hilary poured a second Scotch for the hard man, whose days of intimidation weren't over, although now it was he who was on the receiving end. Tottering back to his flat at World's End, he was mercilessly ragged: 'Look atcha, yer pissed old cunt!' Everyone on the estate knew him, true enough, but nobody feared him any more.

The Extra was in rehab, emoting in the round of plastic chairs. He had written a letter of amends to Val, apologizing for the nine hundred-some quid he'd racked up on his tab, and asking for the Bard's Complete Works to be sent into him, the text adapted to contain a half-bottle of vodka. Val used the missive to light a fag, then told the other members it would be better if 'the cunt were dead'.

Hilary shook hands with the optic and set the highball glass half full of vodka down in front of Val. While the Boy turned to get the tonic – and still, after nearly twenty years, Her Ladyship spluttered, '*She* should mind her back!' – Val added half the contents to the Boy's lager.

No doubt Hilary Edmonds no longer knew what lager should taste like; after all, this mixture of grains had been pumped into him for so long now that uncontaminated pints were as the brown remembered ponds he had splashed in as an ugly gosling. And if we calculate a day of a goose's *gavage* to be a year of a human's, then the job was almost done. *Entier*, *cuit* or *mi-cuit* – which cut of Hilary would Val consume? Or, instead of Hilary *frais*, would he send the inferior Boy off to be turned into *mousse*, *parfait* or even *pâté en bloc*?

The Martian headed back to his stool, his vodka and orange in one hand, Her Ladyship's gin and tonic in the other; there he resumed his position. Even in an environment characterized by stasis, he was the stillest of things. The black rims of his spectacles were more mobile than his watery blue eyes; his greenish hair was no more likely to fly away than a barnacle.

Unlike the other shivering denizens of King Alcohol's mad realm, the Martian seemed always to keep his head. Some three years before, in an unguarded moment, he'd confessed to Her Ladyship that he'd had to let go of the print shop. 'Health and Safety cunts,' he'd muttered; but she was as incurious as a dead cat, and since he kept on getting them in, everyone else assumed he was still working.

Hilary poured the Tosher a flute of 'poo from a freshly opened bottle. 'Thank you, cunty,' the painter said and handed him the stack of invitations. 'Pass them on, will you, Boy?' Then he was gone. Hilary lifted the flap and stepped between the Dog and the

Poof. He headed for the toilet, passing out the invitations as he went.

Trouget seldom stuck it out in the Plantation for long nowadays: the sycophancy of the younger piss-artists sickened him, and, like Val, he professed to be appalled by their cocaine-sniffing. Val grew depressed by the painter's departures; he knew that whatever élan his era at the Plantation possessed was derived from Trouget's massive profile alone. In too short a time all cunty witticisms would be forgotten; all that would remain of three decades of barring and bitching, belching and kvetching, would be a blue and white English Heritage plaque at the Wardour Street end of Blore Court that read: *Louis Trouget, 1922–1998, was Pissed Here.*

The toilet properly stank.

When the Typist died in St Tom's it had been a deeply disinfected expiration: she was surrounded only by the ample flesh of the Filipina cleaner from the Plantation. After the funeral Maria had drunk her own bleach. No one had known they were that close, let alone 'Minge monkeys!', as Val had spat. He neglected to hire another.

As for Hilary, he didn't bother with the wiping of wipeable surfaces – except with his index finger. Bending to tap the creamy granules on to the dirty tiling, he admired the way the young piss-artists' fingers had mixed a gouache from the residue of previous snorts and left smeary contrails on this tiny inverted sky.

They only just made it to Trouget's retrospective that night. The same cortège pulled up on Belvedere Road, and, scattering pork scratchings from the folds of their clothes, the members crept up under the concrete skirts of the Hayward Gallery. It was the last time that Val Carmichael was seen out in public. No matter the hogsheads of vodka and the butts of tonic; no matter the muffling of the sound and the fading of the light; no matter the high dive his psyche was taking into the pool of total oblivion – he could still hear it perfectly when a young woman (young enough, in a parallel world, to have been his granddaughter), wearing a miniskirt that wouldn't have been out of place in the Plantation the year Val took the club over, cried out: 'Eurgh! Look at that old woman's disgusting nose.'

She was drunk, of course.

Those last few months the Martian came in from Kilburn by minicab to pick up Val from his flat in King's Cross. It was summer, and the Martian chose to ignore the flies dogfighting over the dirty dishes in the sink, and the soiled underwear that, each night, was torn from Val's rotting body by the impact of sleep. Once a week the Martian brought fresh underwear for Val: seven pairs of Y-fronts.

Twice a week they called in at the Parkside Medical Centre on Dean Street, where Val's bandolier of pill pots was refilled by an idealistic young doctor, who felt himself – with his clientele of street sleepers, junkies and drunks – to be performing noble triage on the urban battlefield. This general practitioner – who himself liked to smoke dope in front of foreign cinema – would have regarded it as the most reactionary paternalism to have in any way implied, let alone said, that he thought Val should stop, or even moderate, his drinking.

Instead, favouring an 'interpersonal' approach, Val's doctor embraced the fetor and the cunty chatter, as if these were, respectively, the odour of good food and the table talk of a sagacious wit. Inscrutable, the Martian propped himself by the door and fiddled with the Velcro on a blood-pressure cuff. Then, to fill in time until the Boy opened up the club, Val stopped at the Coach and Horses, while the Martian went to fill his prescriptions at Bliss on Shaftesbury Avenue.

Soon enough, the doctor began coming into the club. On one occasion he even took Val's blood while he was sitting on his stool.

The doctor thought he could handle his drink. Needless to say, he couldn't: alcohol is a fluid, it can never be held. He fucked the miniskirted girl from Trouget's retrospective in the toilet, and she left bite marks on his shoulder that he explained away to his wife as those of an epileptic patient. The doctor was going down, and eventually he ended up in the same stacking-chair circle of hell as the Extra: strolling Sunday shrubbery with angry wifey; making miserable toast in a toaster that takes half a loaf; loitering on the forecourts of provincial garages, waiting for the country bus to the self-help group.

However, this lay in the future. In the meantime he was in the Plantation, although not on the afternoon when Val quipped – apropos of a famous singer, discovered dead from an overdose that very morning by her manager-cum-fuck buddy – 'Ah, well, I s'pose those who live by their cunt, die by one.' Then slowly pitched forward and executed a near-perfect forward roll on to the incontinence pad of the carpet.

For long moments nothing happened. Only the regulars were in – it was too early for the arty party – and, even though Val was lying directly at the Cunt's feet, Bernie Jobs's days of bending over were long gone. Val wheezed like a cat with a hair ball, chalky bubbles gathering at the corners of his mouth.

Eventually, Hilary, who had been observing his tormentor with interest from behind the bar, while trying to assess whether this was the end game, came out and got Val back up on his stool. But even if Hilary propped Val's Punch profile against the till, he couldn't get him to stay upright, let alone hold a glass. The regulars pretended nothing untoward was happening. It was left to the Martian to go to the payphone and call for an ambulance.

They came, heartily efficient young people – a man and a woman. The woman went back to fetch a stretcher chair from 'the van', on account of the tight manoeuvring needed to get anyone out of Blore Court, dead or alive. It wasn't until a full quarter of an hour had elapsed since they had borne Val off – with sure tread and snappy cooperation – that anything was said.

The members sat there: the Dog and the Poof on their stools, Her Ladyship seated, the Cunt standing. They were all resentfully nursing their glasses – the only things they had ever nursed in their lives – and waiting for the Martian to get a round in. At last, Hilary whined, 'You silly cunts, Pete went with Val in the fucking ambulance. If you want a drink, you'll have to stump up for it yourselves.'

And with that, he lifted the counter, waddled through, and, assuming Val's position at the end of the bar, pulled across his own pint of vodka-laced lager, tapped it like a gavel and reiterated, 'Yes, if you cunts want a drink you'll have to stump up for it yourselves. There are', he whined on, 'gonna be a few changes round 'ere.'

Then he toasted the icon of Ivy Oldroyd, who looked down on the proceedings with imperial detachment, the corners of her mouth as downturned as the thumbs of a plebeian multitude.

The next day, when the Dog came snuffling up the stairs, and swung open the ratty green baize door, he discovered that a full-blown coup d'état had taken place: not only was Hilary on Val's throne, but there was a new 'Boy' installed behind the bar, dressed in a sad emulation of his master's own sad emulation of a style.

'Scotty,' Hilary whined croakily, 'this here is Stevie. *She'll* be serving while Val's in hospital.' Then he went back to reading his *Daily Mirror*, a newspaper that told him very little about things he didn't particularly want to know.

Hilary had, of course, been waiting for this; and, in anticipation, had had Stevie on hold for several weeks, stashed in a cubbyhole at Her Ladyship's Kensal Rise stately doss-house. Stevie, who Hilary had found crying underneath the arches outside Heaven, was indeed heaven-sent. Once the amyl nitrate had been wrung out of his system, he was perfectly presentable, if a bit emaciated. Hilary certainly fancied Billy, but the time-honoured ritual whereby a new goose was penned at the Plantation had yet to take place. Hilary had to wait until the Old Queen was dead, and have it confirmed that he was the sole heir.

In the meantime, Hilary accepted tributes from the subjects of the mad realm in the form of vodka, undiluted by beer. It was too early to say whether Val Carmichael's *gavage* had been a complete success; Hilary was definitely well on the way to full-blown cirrhosis, and, like his farmer, he had an impressive bosom, but, more importantly, he was swollen with pride and stuffed with arrogance.

Val had cleverly utilized the masochistic tendency he had first intuited in the young Hilary when he saw him through the window of the Wimpy Bar. Thereafter, Val had forced Hilary to swallow so much humiliation that it had stuck in his craw, in much the same way the poultry farmers of the Dordogne made use of their geese's natural tendency to store grains in their oesophaguses.

At the St Charles, the gloomy Victorian hospital in back of Ladbroke Grove where Val ended up, a junior registrar had to give him a shot of Ativan to stop him fitting. She was no expert on this spectacular form of self-abuse, which involved relentless terrorist attacks on the temple of the body; but then few are. However, even a cursory examination of Val's dropsical body was enough to tell her that: 'This, uh, man – Mr Carmichael, is so close to suffering a portal haemorrhage . . . Well, I don't suppose . . .' She looked up from the bed, where Val's head, a crushed grape, lay on the pillow. 'Mr?' she queried.

'Stenning,' the Martian replied matter-of-factly. 'Peter Stenning. Val – Mr Carmichael – is my cousin. And, yes, I do know what a portal haemorrhage is.'

Although while in the dusty confines of his adoptive habitat the Martian was notable for his tranquillized manner, strange to relate that here in the St Charles he appeared studiously efficient. And while in the tawny interior of the club his garb and even skin had a tinge that matched his greenish hair, in the cold-old light of the general ward he didn't look like anything much: just another late-middle-aged, middle-class man wearing slightly anachronistic spectacles and a suede jacket.

There was little to be done with Val, so the medical staff did nothing: there was no heroism in giving this spavined old nag a painless trip to the knackers. The Martian, however, did plenty. He had told the junior registrar that he was Val's cousin, and, since he was so willing to undertake the palliative care that they couldn't be bothered with, they saw no need to inquire any further when he signed the relevant paperwork as next of kin.

The Martian had Val moved to a private room. He gently petitioned the doctors for all the medication necessary to make the dying man comfortable. All agreed that in the case of this most determined waster of it, it was only a matter of time. A matter of time before pancreatitis, hepatorenal syndrome, hepatitis, cancer and, of course, cirrhosis jostled together in Val's engorged liver, kidneys and gall bladder, and, finding a common pathway out, ruptured the walls of his weakened arteries, so that blood gushed into his throat and drowned him.

It was only a matter of time, but, despite waiting for decades now, the Martian was succumbing to a mounting impatience. He went down to the convenience store on the corner of Cambridge Gardens and bought quarter-bottles of vodka; a tacky brand called something mock-Slavic like 'Gogol', but that hardly mattered at this stage. It was also a hot summer, but that didn't matter a damn either.

The Martian fed Val tiny sips of the burning spirit through a straw, and the patient croaked his gratitude. No one else came to see him – not that he would have been able to recognize them if they had. The Plantation Club members had a well-justified fear of hospitals, given that any self-respecting mental health practitioner would've sectioned them more or less on sight.

Her Ladyship, escorted by Hilary, did make it as far as the main lobby of the St Charles; there, upon seeing an immunization flyer that depicted a doting mother and her winsome baby, she was utterly overcome by her own pathological self-pity and had to adjourn to the nearest pub for much needed medicinal gin.

Hilary himself couldn't have given a toss about Val. He would only have entered the queerly shaped nook where Val lay – the result of eras of partitioning – in order to press a pillow over Val's horror mask and extinguish his flame-red nose for ever.

But he didn't have to, because the Martian was doing the job for him. Between trips to the offie, the Martian sidled about the St Charles. In an environment at once hurried and yet desultory, the staff barely noticed this nondescript figure; while if a clamp went missing here, and a scalpel there, then they barely noticed that either.

Over several days the Martian assembled all the equipment he wanted and stashed it in the cupboard in the corner of Val's nook. Each evening, when visiting hours were over, he went back to his house on Melrose Avenue, off Shoot Up Hill. If our chance wanderer – last seen lurking in the vicinity of Blore Court – had happened to creep through the overgrown front garden to the bay window, he would have seen a curious spectacle through its scummy panes: the Martian, standing stock-still in the middle of a completely empty room, waiting, hour upon hour, for the dawn.

On the morning of the day Pete Stenning killed Val Carmichael, he left his house as usual and travelled by minicab to Lidgate's, the organic butcher's on Holland Park Avenue. Here he collected a pig's liver that he had ordered by telephone.

The Martian doubted that the pathologist at the St Charles would wish to conduct a post-mortem: the uncertainty, in Val's case, would concern not the cause of death but how his life had been maintained for so long. Even if they did perform an autopsy, the pig's liver might still fool them.

There was also the undertakers to be considered. Embalming was not an issue – Val's cadaver was to be cremated forthwith – but the Martian knew some of them could be sharp-eyed; and some liked to handle corpses – that's why they took on the job. They left it to colleagues to honour the dead and comfort the living, while they poked about in the cremulator.

The Martian wasn't too bothered if his subterfuge was discovered. He was not an entity characterized by a sense of humour, let alone irony, but he did like to leave his mark. Much as Trouget blobbed three dots of paint in the bottom-right-hand corner of his canvases – thereby increasing their value ten-thousandfold – so the Martian considered his transplants a form of signature.

The Martian had a good feel about this morning, believing he had got his timing exactly right. He stopped at the convenience store for a bottle of Gogol that he concealed in the inside pocket of his suede jacket. Even this late in the procedure there was still the possibility of discovery and that would make things . . . awkward.

The pedestrians hurrying towards Ladbroke Grove tube station swarmed past the Martian not like flies – such an image suggests fat and hairy bluebottles – but midges fizzing over a puddle; while the vehicles coursing in the roadway had all the mass and heft of mosquitoes dallying above diaphanous netting. It was the same at the St Charles, where the medical and auxiliary staff swarmed through the corridors much as termites pullulate in a mound, while the patients lay in their beds: black and white grubs, nourished with pap.

The Martian moved through all this mini-beastliness decisively. If our chance wanderer had been back on hand, and noticed that this otherwise forgettable man, with his greenish hair – the result, no doubt, of a duff dye-job – seemed out of joint with his surroundings –

or, more specifically, out of *time* with them: jibing the underlying biological rhythms of human life – then that would have been a very fine piece of observation.

For, while one of the reasons the Martian had chosen the Plantation as his sphere of activity, and Val Carmichael as the subject of his attentions, was that the very stasis of the club – where it could take the best part of an afternoon for a member to make it from bar to toilet and back again – made it easier for him to calibrate to the behaviour of creatures who were, to him, as mayflies are to us, none the less, he had disciplined himself so well that he could not only communicate with them – a prerequisite, all would agree, of any successful animal husbandry – but also engage in intercourse with those creatures who were, to humans, as frenetic and transitory as we are to him.

The Martian could catch a fly in his nicotine-stained fingers – and talk to it.

Speeding up, slowing down, but mostly in sync – as a computer-generated effect is edited into an early silent film – the Martian went about his work. Once in Val's nook he became a blur: feeding Val sips of vodka through the straw; putting a frame beneath the bedclothes to give himself ease of access to the abdomen; removing the instruments and further equipment he required from the cupboard, then arranging these under the bed.

Timing was crucial: for the product to have the highest possible value, it had to be removed, entire, at the precise moment when the portal haemorrhage occurred. Too early and there would be too much blood in the liver; too late and there would be too little.

In the centuries since the Martian – or another of his kind – had nudged humans in the direction of 'discovering' the distillation of alcohol, there had been a few scores of them at work during any given epoch. All sorts of methods had been tried in order to perfect this *gavage*. The Martian had himself developed many different techniques, from performing 'split-liver' transplants of cirrhotic organs into the bodies of São Paulo street urchins, then tending them until harvest, to working with hebephrenic living 'donors'. He had force-fed his human geese with fine burgundies, arrack, poteen and cider; he had soused them with Marsala and drenched them with ale. But, after centuries of experimentation, he had decided that the best possible results were achieved when the *gavage* was undertaken at a natural pace, with voluntary subjects.

Pure grain alcohol imparted the most nodulous appearance to the necrotic tissue – a finish that was highly sought after by the Martian's gourmet clients.

Feeling the cold metal of the frame press his flesh, Val surfaced from the mire of his moribund brain. Seeing the concern on the Martian's face mask, he whined, 'Giss some acqua, Marshy', and when his carer obliged with the Gogol, Val sank back on the pillow, sighing, 'I'm croaking, Marshy, you cunt.'

The Martian nodded sympathetically to indicate that this was indeed true.

'Lissen.' Val's eyes, stripped of their shades, glittered unnaturally. 'I ain't got long, Marshy, but you'll grant an omi-paloni 'is final wish – won'cher?'

Again, the Martian nodded.

'Juss yer lapper, cunt.' Val groped for the Martian's hand. 'I ain't after a bloody jarry – only a fucking sherman.'

Even if the Martian hadn't understood Polari – which he did, perfectly – the dying man's feeble motions would have instructed him. As it was, Val's desires coincided perfectly with his own: with his hand on Val's penis, the Martian could both increase Val's sluggish heart rate, and sense the precise moment when the rotten wall of his portal vein ruptured.

Culinary savants differed on the question of how an animal's state of mind affected the quality of its liver, but most agreed that fear and disillusionment engendered a pleasing deliquescence to the fat-engorged tissue. With the more philosophically inclined beasts, it was even worth while giving them a snapshot – as much as their limited minds could take in – of the wider picture.

As he masturbated Val, the Martian spoke to him urgently. It would be onerous to translate from the Cockney, the back-slang and the Polari he employed, but the substance of what he had to relate was that Val's entire life had been leading up to this: at the very instant of his expiration, he, the Martian, would cut out Val's rotten liver.

So it was that Val Carmichael died, eyes wide with astonishment and horror, a final valedictory 'Cuuuunt' rattling between his bluing lips.

At once the Martian set to work properly, his hands a blur beneath the covers as he made the incision in the upper abdomen, then clamped and sutured with machine rapidity. A passing nurse – a wanderer in this city of death – chanced to poke her nose into the nook and, noting that Val's own nose was losing its angry hue, taxed the Martian: 'Is Mr Carmichael all right?'

And even though at that precise moment the Martian was speedily dividing all the ligamentous attachments – common bile duct, hepatic artery, portal vein – that held Val's liver snug in his abdominal cavity, he had also had the foresight to close the dead man's eyes and was able to say, with believable sincerity, 'He's just resting, sister, I think he had a difficult night.'

Convinced, the nurse moved off, leaving the Martian to complete in twelve minutes an operation that would have taken a skilled human surgeon – were he minded to transplant a pig's liver into a man – some five or six hours.

Pausing for a fragment of a second to admire the perfection of the *foie humain entier* that he had removed – its pleasing heft, its bloody-beige marbling, its glistening wartiness – the Martian wrapped it in the greaseproof paper Lidgate's had provided and popped it into his string shopping bag.

Instruments wiped and stashed, bed rearranged and cadaver rearranged in it, the Martian left the nook without a backward glance. No poultry keeper in the Dordogne – no matter how mimsy or sentimental – sticks around to mourn a goose; and I think we can all concur that, as geese go, Val Carmichael was one of the least endearing.

Dear, perceptive reader, you will have grasped by now that Peter Stenning, aka 'the Martian' (and aka, for that matter, 'Peter Stenning'), was an extraterrestrial – an 'alien' in common parlance. To see him wend his way through the mid-morning traffic on Ladbroke Grove – resisting a strong impulse to break into a run faster than the 100-metre World Record holder – would have been enough to confirm this for an acute observer; no sixty-something on earth has such a swift and supple gait.

But were I to tell you that, should he have wished to, the Martian could have taken to the air, flipping, rolling and weaving through the power lines, and between the chimney pots, at twice the speed of sound, I would, perhaps, stretch your credulity; or, rather, invite you to speculate on the nature of the Martian's real appearance, shorn of the fleshly overall of his assumed humanity.

Such speculations are useless. Insectoid, arthropod, protoplasmic blob, cyborg, robot built from purest iridium with laser-polished coltan fittings – these are the feeble projections of human imagineers on to the mighty screen that is the universe. It is sufficient to paraphrase Wittgenstein, and note only that if we were able to see the Martian as he really was, we wouldn't understand what it was we were witnessing.

So, on this basis, let us go with him to Totteridge, to the shuttered light-industrial premises between the Great North Road and the South Herts Golf Course that Stenning Offset used to occupy. Unobserved, save by us, the Martian undid the padlocks and went inside. As soon as the door was locked he resumed the pace of action last witnessed at the St Charles. Even so, it took him the best part of the day to fuel, programme and then load the craft that would carry Val Carmichael's liver on its 38-light-year voyage to the Martian's home planet.

Late that evening the Martian sat with Hilary and Her Ladyship in the snug back bar of the French in Soho. The Martian raised his glass and muttered 'Bon voyage'. The others had no idea what he was talking about and assumed that he was drunk. But the Martian had never been drunk in any of his two thousand, six hundred and forty-six solar years.

At that precise moment, in Totteridge, the roof of Stenning Offset exploded in a sheet of white flame and a smoothly tapered ellipsoid lifted off into the sodium-stained London night. It was invisible to either human eye or human instrumentation, and, although it left considerable devastation in its wake, no one was injured. Leant upon by the gas company, the insurers paid out without a murmur.

Val Carmichael's funeral was a desultory affair; only the older members of the Plantation Club even bothered to attend. To them Val was . . . well, something – but to the younger crowd he was merely an 'old cunt'. Those who live by the cunt, do indeed die by it.

As has been remarked, irony was not an attribute of the Martian; however, please feel free to consider how inappropriate it was for a man with a pig's liver transplanted into him to be burnt at Golders Green Crematorium. Moreover, why not indulge in a little *Schadenfreude* as you gaze upon the Dog, the Poof, the Cunt, Hilary and Her Ladyship, who, even in the brilliance of a summer's day, have the dazed-grey look of ghetto-dwellers about to be relieved of their remaining teeth by Nazis with pliers.

Mark only these two further things. If you feel aggrieved by the way this narrative has moved towards its – frankly sickening –

conclusion, proceeding not with straightforward honesty, but waddling through needless digressions and lunging into grotesque interpolations, then all I can say is that it has only been mimicking the Martian's own perception of humanity. For, where we are confronted with the nobility of feeling, high culture and deep spirituality, he sees nothing but the stereotypic behaviours of anthropoid geese.

Second, if you are inclined to feel bad when you contemplate the cosmic fatuity of a species that exists, in its given form, purely so that a few score individuals may be harvested for their cirrhotic livers, then don't: self-pity is such an ugly attribute of the human character, and one particularly pronounced in the alcoholic.

Instead, why not return with the other members to Blore Court and climb the two flights of stairs to the green baize door? Take off your coat, throw it over a stool, wink at the Prince Consort, then watch his glazed eyes begin to rove as the Poof pounds upon the piano keys, wrenching the Death March from its dusty bowels.

The gang are all here – all in their allotted places. The Martian would have had to decamp if things hadn't panned out in Totteridge, but now he'll be able to stay a while longer. See him sidle up to the bar – and note how attentive young Stevie is.

The Martian orders a round, specifying a triple for Hilary; and, in time-honoured fashion, Hilary pours a bit of his vodka into Stevie's glass of lager. All is as it should be as they raise a toast to the memory of Val Carmichael: the *gavage* is under way. It may take a while, it may perhaps seem cruel, but then there's no finer flavour in the universe than *foie humain*.

Leberknödel

Introitus

Joyce Beddoes – Jo, to her friends, Jo-Jo, sometimes, in frank intimacy, to her late husband, and also to her daughter, Isobel, when she was a child – wanted to get her head down between her knees.

'Are you all right, Mum?' Isobel – who insisted on the ugly sexlessness of 'Izzy' – asked her, maybe for the fiftieth time that morning. It was an inquiry, Joyce felt, that was aggressively pleading, devoid of any true concern.

'I–I just want . . .' She was going to say 'to bend down', but the fruitlessness of this desire – the seat was too cramped, she was too frail, and the sound of her own voice, more the hiss and cluck of a barnyard fowl than anything human – overwhelmed anything but the blunt articulation of need itself.

However, that didn't mean the sentence was incomplete, because Joyce did *just want* everything: the tray table, the fake tortoiseshell hairgrip in the stewardess's honey hair, the glossy magazine she could see through the gap between the seats in front. She *just wanted* that magazine – and what was pictured on it: the corner of a table set for a leisurely breakfast with elegant white crockery, a basket of croissants and a glass of orange juice. Joyce *just wanted* the shapely hand of the model in the photograph, a hand that held a teaspoon with studied poise.

Instead, Joyce had these things that no one wanted: nausea, sickly-sour and putrid; a painfully swollen belly and a hot wire in her urethra. Overwhelming all of them was a dreadful – near criminal – lassitude.

'Is it water, Mum, d'you want some water?' Isobel said; except to Joyce it sounded like 'warter', and what was that? A fifth element, a lumpy substrate on which they all thrived and died, like bacteria?

How she loathed Isobel's affected common accent – it made the young woman ugly or, rather, not young at all any more. She was, Joyce realized, increasingly resembling her father. Isobel had always been Derry's girl – and that was lovely. For Joyce, the great joy of motherhood had been to discover that the young man who had courted her with Stan Getz 78s and Turkish delight, and who had been as slick and assured as his Brylcreemed hair, was back again; but re-cast, played now by an adorable little girl.

But in the past couple of years Isobel had leapfrogged her father's mature good looks – his firm dimpled chin, his level brown gaze – and gone straight on to his middle age, when, *to be perfectly frank*, Derry had *run to fat*. Isobel, who was only thirty-three, had a dewlap beneath her own dimpled chin. Her brown hair – thick and straight to begin with, exactly like her father's – had been hacked about and dyed so much that it crackled like candyfloss on her round skull.

No, Joyce didn't want water – and besides, they had none. At Security their plastic bottles had been dumped in a bin – a sudden scare. And, although Joyce had asked Isobel to go and get some more, it was too late because the younger woman had already spent too long in the ladies.

They had only recently taken off and the plane was still climbing sharply: a tilted tube full of humdrum. At last, Joyce succeeded in wrestling her face to the window. The outside world would, she hoped, play the part of knees: she could press her burning cheeks against cool clouds, take deep breaths of fresh air and quell the nausea.

In the frame of the aircraft servomotors whined, the ailerons jerked, the wings' tips waggled, rivulets of moisture bleeding across them. Joyce noticed that each pimple of a rivet head was surrounded by a ring of infective rust.

The plane slammed into an air pocket. Joyce gasped, then

clamped her hand to her mouth, imprisoning the metallic bile that had sprung up her throat. Down below, way below, wheeled the English Midlands, their jigsaw of brownish towns and greenish fields bucked and then scattered. Joyce saw the slick beading of row upon row of new cars, fresh off a production line. Thousands of feet yawned between her wasting flesh and their toughened windscreens; she was – she realized, as once more the plane rocked and rolled – absolutely terrified.

Terrified of plummeting into a superstore's car park on the Coventry bypass. Terrified of her meagre hand baggage – a change of underwear, useless make-up, unspent money – being strewn over a rutted field. Terrified of being disembowelled by a pylon, or her limbs amputated by humming cables. Terrified, despite her, of all the forty-odd passengers on this flight from Birmingham to Zürich, having the least reason to fear death.

Even so, Joyce hunched up whimpering, while self-made homilies – *What will be, will be* – came to her parched lips. Joyce wanted her distant and yet jovial father – one side of his face bulgy with the gutta-percha used to replace the cheekbone that had been pulverized in France, the other smoothly benign. Joyce wanted to be on his knee, in a dappled woodland before the Second World War. But he was dead – her mother and Derry, too. And there could be no comfort in the arms of the dead: you couldn't feel them – and they felt nothing.

God, then – he would stop her from falling; God and the pure sounds of uncorrupted humanity.

Until the end of January, when she had felt too ill to continue, Joyce had been one of the Bournville Singers, who were rehearsing Mozart's Requiem in the canteen of the Institute. No one – including their insufferably vain director, Tom Scoresby – could have claimed that their performance was going to be either the most faithful or the most sonorous; yet, even with serving hatches for a backdrop, they had soared.

Requiem aeternam dona ets, Domine. Dumpy men in open-neck shirts – some former car workers, others retired middle-class professionals – their chests heaving; then Joyce and the other women panting up the scale: *et lux perpetua luceat ets . . .* She tried not to see Scoresby, his quaver of silver-blond hair bouncing as he whipped up his singers, but instead focused on those beautiful streamers of sound, chords looped over clouds so that the angels might haul her up. *Grant them eternal rest, O Lord, and may perpetual light shine on them.*

It was so stupid to have got on this flight; and *cretinous* not to have appreciated *everything* before she left – the row of storage jars on the kitchen shelf, rice, pearl barley, flour, sugar – but taken all that wondrously dispassionate order for granted.

If I ever get down from this sky I won't be making that mistake again, oh, no.

The plane surfaced in a sea of cloudy islands, then broke through into unearthly sunlight. Relief rippled audibly along the fuselage. The stewardess unbuckled her harness and stood, swaying, straightening her skirt.

'Water, Mum?' Isobel asked again, her plump features stuffed with the gutta-percha of concern.

The immediate anxiety fell away from Joyce, a dark plume dispelled, leaving the black truth behind: the nausea, the wire, the distension, the lassitude. *How mad, how mindlessly bloody insane to care if I die now, when in a matter of hours I definitely will.*

The rest of the flight was uneventful. There was no question of Joyce accepting the white roll filled with cheesy sludge – an alcoholic drink was unthinkable. The stewardess – *maybe she knows* – kept hauling herself along the plane to ask, 'Is it . . . your mother? Is she OK, yes?' Then she and Isobel – both of them, Joyce thought, a little bovine – would low: 'Would you like some water?'

Water! Joyce was pretty sure she'd wet herself on take-off. When they left the house, and she had locked the door for the last time and handed the keys to Isobel, Joyce was gripped by an unworthy rage. *What will she do with the good drapes and the seat covers? Her father's LPs and the Venetian glass?* She saw it all – despite her meticulous instructions – dumped in cardboard boxes outside the Sue Ryder shop in Shirley.

By the time Joyce got a grip on herself, they were in the cab heading for the airport – and it was too late to go back for the incontinence pads. And now, well, there must be a dark patch on the pale blue airline upholstery. *Shameful.*

The plane, moaning, hunkered down towards the ground. Wooded hills, bare fields, arterial roads flowing between the metal barns of light industry. The housing was as samey as that which they had left behind. There was no sign of the Matterhorn – or grassy Alps. No snow – but this was March – or cuckoo clocks, or chalets with wide wooden eaves, or Heidi running with the goats, or chocolate bars stacked like lumber. The only clichés were the airport, the runway, the plane braking to a halt, the co-pilot announcing: 'Welcome to Zürich, ladies and gentlemen, where the local time is 11.48. I hope you enjoyed your flight with us today, and on behalf of the crew I'd like to wish you a safe onward journey.'

Joyce, who had always been a tall woman – a *rangy* woman, Derry's expression, and she had liked it from him – couldn't extract herself from the window seat without Isobel pulling, and the stewardess, who had slid into the seat behind, pushing.

A moment before she got up, with a colossal effort, Joyce lifted her behind and slid the paper napkin beneath it. Fleetingly, she had a touching faith in the napkin's absorbency, but when she looked back there was an obvious pool of urine. The stewardess must have seen it, but she was tactful – a Swiss characteristic, Joyce supposed

– and offered to help Joyce on with her coat, indicating that she understood the need to hide the spreading stain on the back of Joyce's skirt.

Dr Phillimore – whom Joyce had first met when he arrived at Mid-East, a year before she retired – had known full well why she wanted a letter setting out the details of her cancer, its likely progression and definite prognosis. Although she had no great respect for him as a practitioner – Phillimore's manner was brusque and self-satisfied – at first Joyce was merely grateful that he didn't try to dissuade her; this implied that, despite the scant attention he had paid her when he could have been expected to keep her alive, now she had stoically chosen death he would aid her in the Ancient way.

So, no mention of the excellent palliative care team – which anyway would have been an arrant falsehood. Although Joyce hadn't had a direct hand in the hospital's administration for a decade now, she kept in touch with old colleagues at Mid-East and knew the threadbare condition of these things. Nor did Phillimore remind her of the many hospices with which the hospital had good working relations; nor yet still did he speak of the tremendous advances in pain management, which would allow Joyce the lucid repose of a Socrates up until she breathed her last.

It was only as Joyce shuffled off down the corridor – grateful for the handrail that she herself had arranged to have installed – that it occurred to her that Phillimore, far from being disengaged, might actively support her decision: not for philosophic reasons, but only because her removal would lighten his own caseload, enabling him – a plump arrow with white coat fletching – to stay within the concentric rings of his allocated budget and hit his targets.

Isobel insinuated under one arm, the stewardess tucked under the other, Joyce scraped her ankle boots over the concrete pan to the shuttle bus. Inside it black-clad businessmen and women urgently gripped their mobile phones. Ignoring their impatience and the damp chafing of her own underwear, Joyce paused, savouring the mineral tang of aviation fuel, the beat of heat and the echoey howl from taxiing aircraft. She looked back at the plane that had brought her, shackled now by gravity. On its tailfin the stocky white-out-of-red cross glowed: it was the opposite of an air ambulance, Joyce thought, bringing her here with great dispatch so that she might be lost, not saved.

Kyrie

Lord have mercy upon numbered bank accounts, neutrality and Nazi gold . . . Joyce shivered in the shiny arrivals hall, then shook as they shuffled along the shushed shopping concourse. She had no option but – *Christe eleison* – to allow her daughter to *get on with it*. Of course, they had taken only carry-on. Joyce may have been intending to stay for ever, but she could make do without a change of shroud; while Isobel would be flying home the following day.

Be that as it may, with her mother to tote, Isobel had to find a luggage cart and ask for directions – tasks she performed, in Joyce's eyes, poorly. Her daughter was at once loud and ineffectual; she moved with a mock-triumphant roll of her wide hips. Her outfit of high-heeled boots, tight jeans and cropped leather jacket seemed designed to emphasize how overweight she was. She had – Joyce thought, not for the first time – her father's bullishness but none of his charm.

Finally, they were in a cab, a Mercedes as snug and black as an *orthopaedic boot. You don't see those any more – all the victims of the polio epidemics after the war; grown up – dead, I suppose.* As the cab rolled away Joyce admonished herself. *Stop criticizing Isobel: this is harder for her than it is for you, because she's not like you. She'll have to go home alone – and there is no home for her, really. No boyfriend – or lover. What's she doing with her life? A photographic project of some kind – an installation, she calls it. Peculiar term, more military than artistic.*

Neubahn Birchstrasse. Glattalbahn. Flughofstrasse. The very words on the signs looked heavy, with their dumpy vowels and chunky consonants. The blocks of flats and factory buildings lining the roadway were as fat as the back of the cab driver's neck.

Isobel had told her mother that she was meticulously photographing the contents of some rooms in the Soho district of London, rooms that had been left sealed up decades before. She had grown animated as she described Mr Vogel's abandoned office, which was cluttered with Gestetner machines, rubber stamps, typewriters and all sorts of other office equipment from the 1950s – and even earlier – all of it still boxed up.

Joyce had nodded, making encouraging noises, while Isobel explained that hers was a visual inventory of objects that had, sort of, defied time. But really, her mother had thought, this was *a nonsense*, not proper work at all – and certainly not art – more a kind of *play* that the grown-up girl indulged herself in, and that various public bodies – colleges, councils, libraries – were prepared to indulge her in as well, by supporting it with grants.

Christ have mercy upon us! So dull this was: the plunge of the underpass beneath the haunch of the wooded hill.

When, up in the sky, Joyce had been *ridiculously scared* of dying – while not for a second considering the bursting of all those other bubble-worlds of thought, each so fragile and entire, each brilliantly reflecting the entirety of the others – the fear had blanked out the mundanity of her own well-administered death, which was all about her now, like cold dirty snow blanketing the verges.

Isobel got out her mobile phone and switched it on. Joyce blurted, 'Please, Isobel, we agreed –'

'I was only checking it worked, Mum,' she began calmly enough, then choked up the scale: 'I. Might. Need to make a call – later. Tomorrow. Y'know', before hitting the high note of tears. Isobel was suddenly a little girl once more, sitting on her bedroom floor, the minute displacement of a tableau of tiny dollies having provoked this huge grief. Then, it came – or, rather, Joyce moved ever so slightly towards it. Out from the shadow of her own death, Joyce crept into the wan sun of her love for the daughter she had borne and beared.

The two women cried in one another's arms, oblivious to the Mercedes's progress, which swept downhill between prosperous villas, then apartment blocks, then past the green splash of the university's grounds. A tram clang-ting-whooshed in the opposite direction, and to the right of the road the Limmat River shone, touched with the same golden lambency that played upon the domes, steeples and towers of Zürich's old town.

Joyce had read – because that is what she had been taught to do – a selection of the relevant literature. The liver cancer and the imminence of death itself – these would, she had been informed, take up all her energies. The workaday world would, almost comfortably, recede, milk deliveries and tax returns taking on the character of metaphysical abstractions, now that the most important unknowns were on the point of being known.

And yet . . . and yet, it hadn't been like that at all. True, she did find herself caught up – lost even – in the roomy soutane of death, its folds at once heavy and invisible, but there remained no escape from the trivial, the ugly, the banal.

Back in Birmingham they had argued about the hotel. Isobel favoured somewhere with all the four-star trimmings, while Joyce was set on thrift: not because she wished to deny herself – why bother? – but because she wanted, even at this late hour, to deliver a final homily to her only child on the virtues of parsimony.

'Why, Mum? Why do you want to spend the night in a shitty little guest house?' Isobel had been sitting in front of the PC, which was on the rolltop desk in the small room that used to be her father's study. 'This place', she tap-pinged the screen, 'is meant to be very nice –'

'Nice?'

'Well, stylish.'

Stylish. Joyce grimaced. Yes, she understood that this was hard on her daughter, but must she organize every single particular herself? This may have been a small administrative problem – renting the antechamber to death – but beyond it Joyce sensed Isobel's psychic hinterland as office suite after office suite, all staffed by time-serving incompetents, not one of whom would have had the *gumption* to order a toner cartridge for the photocopier, were it not for Joyce's assiduous management.

Phillimore's detailed assessment had to be obtained, and Joyce's birth certificate. There were the first phone calls to Switzerland, followed by the to and fro of emails arranging dates and details. Then the home visits had to be set up. Trained hospice nurses came, who acted as outreach workers. 'Suicide assistants', they called themselves, with what Joyce thought of as typically Swiss practicality. All of this she had had to do herself, the unspoken truth being that were Joyce to leave it for too long, Isobel would prove utterly incapable.

Joyce had been initially diagnosed in September of the previous year, but then, just before Christmas, she was given six months to live. Some present. Given them grudgingly, by Phillimore, in a way that, on reflection, she imagined that he considered flattering to her no-nonsense demeanour: 'Even with further chemo, Jo, 50 per cent of people with this kind of cancer will be dead in six months.' *Jo! Jo! The nerve of the man.* Some present. Some time. No hope.

Although it was now the beginning of March, Joyce didn't feel *too bad.* She might, under other, easier-to-delegate circumstances, have lingered into spring, to see the bulbs she had planted – a prayerful act, on her knees, hands pressed together in the wormy earth – come up in the garden. Lingered to see the cherry blossom spraunce up the suburb. Lingered to hear Scoresby's – and her own – Requiem performed at the Adrian Boult Hall. *Kyrie eleison.*

Might have, were it not that Joyce had seen enough people dying from terminal disease not to appreciate its awful, creeping normalcy: despite the black abyss being clearly in view, there was still this cup of tea close at hand, to drink or disdain; and so they nursed it – until it was too late.

Might have, were it not for her professional experience of doctors and their manner, which was nothing but the irrelevant furnishing of death, the shelves and bookcases installed in the earthen sides of the rabbit hole you tumbled down. As for treatments – what were they? A jar of marmalade you took up in falling – then dropped.

Might have, were it not that Isobel was incapable of filling in a form properly, and had to bring her grant applications – together with her laundry – home to Mummy in Brummie.

Standing on the cobbles of the Rennweg outside the Widder Hotel, Joyce felt the chill grit of her own soiled underwear and flipped into compassion for the *dumpy thing*, who was paying off the cab with burnt-sienna Swiss francs. Isobel, who tried to convince her mother that she lived an exciting bohemian life in London, but whose breathless accounts of hanging out at the notorious Plantation Club fell on sceptical ears: 'And Trouget, y'know, he was the presiding spirit for, like, years . . . until he died.'

The Christmas before last Isobel had brought home Hilary, the club's proprietor, who, although not nearly as inter-sex as his name, was *an obvious pansy*. He drank the best part of a bottle of brandy, while remaining perfectly polite. Isobel, *quite gone on him*, had done for the rest.

Hilary had then wet the bed in the spare room, and at 6 a.m. on Boxing Day morning Joyce came down to find Isobel in the utility room, sponging the mattress while the sheets moiled in the washing machine. 'Why?' is all her mother had said. 'Why can't you do this for yourself?'

These bitter ruminations occupied Joyce while her daughter completed the check-in formalities: dealing out her mother's credit card, copying out their passport numbers. The receptionist was no flinty-eyed Alpinist but a black-haired *chap* with sallow skin. He glanced once at Joyce, verifying that she existed, and she thought *he knows*: his sallow skin *spake unto* her jaundiced one.

The Widder was a terrace of old houses that had been knocked through by architects armed with steely beams and chequered marble tiling. The corridors morphed into walkways that traversed glassed-in cists; at the bottom of these were hunks of masonry, preserved under spotlights. *Stylish.* Isobel led her mother here and there, her heels clopping; she'd declined the services of a porter, then got a little lost finding the lift.

Joyce's *stylish* room was at once frigid and stuffy. There were four broad windows on the street side, and opposite them blond-wood cabinets with glass doors and mirrored shelves. In the seating zone, at one end of the long, squat room, shone the cold puddle of a mirror-topped coffee table. There was a mirror-topped desk cascading in the middle of the room; beyond it the white bed had a mirrored headboard. With impersonal funerary goods laid out for its occupant – chocolates, wine, fruit and flowers – Room 107 was an awful box in which to be penultimately alone.

Joyce watched her little old lady body totter into the bathroom. Then watched some more as she turned on the taps and slumped on the toilet; she watched herself take a quarter of an hour to struggle out of her reeking clothes, then roll her yellow body into the yellow bath.

Isobel kept calling: it made her anxious to be shut out. *Nervous of what? She can't be afraid that I'll die?* Joyce lay in her favourite nightie, cold in the bed, the phone's receiver beside her on the pillow: love reduced to a black plastic *dildo*. *Would it*, Joyce wondered, *shock my bohemian daughter to learn that I'd once used one?*

It seemed unnecessarily cruel to Joyce that these last few hours of her life should be spent not simply alone but divorced from anyone who had known her as truly vital, properly sensual; anyone who had touched and held her. *That's all I want*, Joyce gripped the black rod, *to be held one more time. I don't even care who it is. Just held.*

'Have you taken a sleeping pill, Mum?' The receiver resonated with tinny concern. 'Or morphine?'

For want of anything better, Joyce had taken both. Not that she really needed the painkiller, but in the last fortnight she had discovered that it dulled the anxiety of falling to sleep. Without the temazepam she couldn't sleep – and with it her narrowing vision was a catacomb hung with wind-dried cadavers, leading to a dark plain strewn with skulls.

'I'm all right, Isobel,' Joyce whispered. 'I just want to sleep now, please . . . Please let me alone.'

Why did she begrudge her only child any reassurance at this late hour? Why couldn't she be a good mother? True, it had been difficult to get between Derry and Isobel – who'd been every bit as close as loving father and only girl child should be – but it was Joyce who had sewn the name tapes, put the dinner money in the envelope and been there to comfort the cygnet in tutu and tights when she cried because she didn't get the part.

It was far too late for a re-evaluation of all this now. The gap between the narcotics was getting narrower and narrower . . . Joyce could no longer see the telephone; her visual field was a cranny, in which lay the Cartier watch Derry had given her for their twenty-fifth wedding anniversary, a digital clock, the plastic tub of pills with her *name tape sewn on to it*, the brown bottle labelled 'Oramorph 5 mg solution', the bedside lamp – a clear tube, its filament a glowing worm – the window, which was ajar.

From the street below came the click of well-shod feet over the cobbles and the chesty cough of Schweizerdeutsch. Joyce had supposed – what? That she might venture out? That she and Isobel would visit the Fraumünster, admire Chagall's stained-glass windows? Then, later – what? A heavy meal in an oak-panelled restaurant, a plank of beef with a knob of butter on top?

After the spat they'd had about the hotel – and Joyce's troubled concession – she'd read the guide. So she knew what to expect from Zürich: well made, orderly – pretty, almost, with its setting between wooded hills and either side of the Limmat, the swift little river that flowed into the long lake. The Zürichsee, with its pleasure boats, its bathing beaches, and its islets hollowed out by reclusive millionaires.

Zürich, Joyce gathered, was a country town masquerading as a global financial capital – or perhaps the other way round. At any rate, here the deep, cold current of money was obscured by surface ripples of tepid liberality, while the Zürichers hid their avarice beneath polite masks.

The benzodiazepine stroked Joyce's frontal lobes, the morphine caressed her cortex. In the cranny, the red numerals on the digital clock blinked from 14.18 to 15.18.

Zwingli, preaching at the Grossmünster, sways gently in a long black robe, his pale face uplifted to a vertical beam of still paler light.

Baptism is a covenant between God and Man, he says, making of faith a contract; it's a notion that appeals to the hard-nosed burghers who sit in the pews. The sacrament is symbolic, Zwingli says, a memorial rather than a re-creation. Again, this recommends itself to the Zürichers, geared into time's progress as they are, the ratcheting of moment to moment. As for music in church – isn't it the most obvious distraction, Zwingli asks. Why, you'd never countenance a lutenist in the counting house, or a drum being struck in time to the heavy beat of the coinage, now would you?

This, too, the City Fathers swallow – because he's a charismatic fellow, this priest, his holiness as unimpeachable as his own instrumental talents – for he can play like an angel upon the flute and harpsichord. At the same time as he preaches against liturgical music, Zwingli cannot prevent his angular frame from swaying in its natural spotlight.

Ba-ba-ba-ba-baaa. Babba-daaa . . . Zwingli swings. What were they called? The girls with long, ironed-down hair, the men in matching roll-neck pullovers. The Swingle Singers, that was it – but that was later, on Top of the Pops, *in the bright fuzzy fog of black and white television. I want earlier – the skiffle night at the Locarno Dance Hall. Derry said it wasn't real music, but, preachy as he was, he still liked to swing me around, crackling handfuls of crimplene. Later, cocoa at the Kardomah on New Street. Later still, smuggled past his landlady into his bedsit, the tremendous gift of his hands . . . Kyrie eleison . . . Christe eleison.*

14.21. Joyce slept. Half an hour later the pass key turned in the lock and Isobel tiptoed in. She leant forward at the head of the bed, holding her dyed-blonde hair to her neck, and listened to her mother's monochrome breathing. The porter stood in the doorway, massively indifferent in his striped hotel livery.

Isobel turned to him. 'She's asleep,' she said, and, taking the handset from the pillow, replaced it on the cradle. 'But I'll sit with her for a while.'

He left, and that's what she did. She sat, and, as the footfalls outside grew more and more scattered, she wept. The fog oozed up from the surface of the lake, infiltrating the narrow winds of the old town, pressing against the plate-glass windows of the underwear boutiques along the Rennweg, imposing its grey shroud of modesty on the brazen plastic models.

In the morning the fog was still there; daylight struggled to illumine the stony façades and blank windows. As she woke, Joyce recalled what the minicab driver who'd driven them to the airport had said.

The A45 was its usual coagulation, and he kept switching lanes, speeding up, then braking so hard that Joyce's bloated middle pressed uncomfortably against the door handle. 'Please,' she gasped. 'Please, really, there's no hurry – we're in plenty of time.'

'It's true,' he replied; the fight went out of him and he slumped over the steering wheel. 'You're a long time dead.'

Isobel winced, while Joyce thought: why is it that even those closest to me regard my dying as socially awkward?

Rising in slow stages, Joyce ran through the checklist that confirmed she was unfit for duty: the banging headache and the wire in her urethra, the painful numbness of fingers and toes, the cruel blockage in her oesophagus and the malevolent gravity of her internal organs.

She limped to the bathroom and pulled the cord. The woman in the mirror, with her sparse skullcap of grey-white hair, looked like Death's mother.

Not long after she had been diagnosed, while she was undergoing the useless chemo and radio, Joyce had begun marvelling at this aspect of her illness. All her life she had been engaged in a secret conversation with her body; whispered talk concerning the removal of her mucus, the blotting of her blood, and the evacuation of her bowels; consultations regarding the squeezing of her blackheads and the plucking of her hairs. In this, Joyce supposed, she was no different to anyone else. But now this chit-chat had been shouted down. Joyce's body had revolted. The respectable working-class liver cells had gone berserk, smashing the chemical refinery they laboured in, then charging down the bloody boulevards to carry their fervour to gall bladder, bowel and lungs. They would not stop until they had toppled the sovereignty of consciousness itself, and replaced it with their own screaming masses of cancerous tissue.

Peeing, then wiping herself, then fighting to brush her teeth, Joyce reeled once more under the revolutionary terror, and so remembered what day this was, and why she was in her familiar purple nightie, shaking in this strange yellow bathroom.

The imminence of her death – and the fact that she, herself, had booked the abattoir – pole-axed the *poor cow*. So she sat, stupidly sullen, while her milkmaid daughter helped dress her for the slaughter.

Isobel, who had barely slept, despite four massively overpriced gin and tonics in the hotel bar, was equally stunned. Ridiculously, they were late, and the continental breakfasts she had ordered for them lay untouched on white linen covered trays.

'Mum, I've asked them to get us a cab,' she said. 'It should be here in a few minutes. I'm sorry there's no time . . .' She gestured helplessly at the croissants, the furled Emmental and smoked ham, the freshly squeezed orange juice. Joyce ignored the breakfast gaffe (*Still, how many times have I told her that I mustn't eat before . . .*), 'Well, dear, you'll need to make up some time later if you want to pack and check out in time to avoid paying a supplement.'

Her parsimony, Joyce knew, was inhuman – and yet all too human.

Isobel had begun to sob uncontrollably. *But we have been over all this time and again!* Just as Joyce had forced her daughter through several tutorials in the study, so that she would be able to find all the papers required for probate, so Joyce had also rehearsed these last few hours and minutes, blocking out every move with precision and care, all but scripting lines for both of them.

Joyce understood intuitively what every executioner soon discovered: perfect choreography is essential if messiness and hysteria are to be avoided. So, although hustled towards extinction by her daughter's poor time-keeping, Joyce was determined to keep her cool.

For the facts were these: apart from Isobel's preschool years – the early 1970s, a good time to take a rest on the career ladder – Joyce had spent her entire working life as a hospital administrator; she had ended up running a large trust, responsible for many staff and patients. She had, she hoped, brought all this professionalism to bear on her own death.

Joyce struggled upright. She was wearing her comfortably lined ankle boots, a smart tweed suit, dark tights and a cream silk blouse. The emerald brooch Derry had given her on their twentieth wedding anniversary was pinned to her lapel. She hadn't troubled with an incontinence pad; *there's nothing left now*. Her mouth was fearfully dry; they had said no liquids or solids before arriving at 84 Gertrudstrasse, *but that can't possibly include Polos, can it?* Joyce fingered out one of the small white rings and slid it between her chapped lips; then, as they moved to the lift, she worked it with her tongue, savouring the dissolution of its minty wash.

Around her was the lift clunk and then the lobby chill. The Widder staff who opened the doors *knew*. *They know*. At each encounter there was a familiar *Grüezi* or a haughty *Guten Tag*. Then Isobel and the doorman were in hushed consultation regarding their destination.

'To live with dignity, to die with dignity.' That was their motto. What Joyce had appreciated most during her dealings with the executioners she had appointed was their commitment to best practice. All communications had been brief and to the point. She had made the 3,500 Euro deposit weeks before. The doctor's prescription for 25 grammes of natrium phenobarbital, together with his attendance and that of the suicide assistant, had been brusquely and competently organized.

Joyce chided herself, for had she not loved and been loved? Had she not run, swum and smelt? She might not have had all that she'd wanted – but there had been all that she'd needed. But then there was Isobel, unmade-up, her handbag a gaping straw basket in which the disorder of her life – multiple packets of chewing gum, cigarettes *and* nicotine lozenges, loose change, dumb trinkets – was on view for all to see.

As the Mercedes tumbril rolled over the cobbles of the Rennweg, then jolted into Sihlstrasse, Joyce marvelled at her own cold detachment: Isobel and all her disordered passions – her drinking and, no doubt, her drug-taking, her queer boyfriends and unpaid debts –

was an administrative problem that Joyce had been unable to shift to her OUT tray before she died. Isobel, who was crying again – although her mother, meanly, felt certain it was self-pity alone – remained PENDING. Joyce had so little faith in her that she had decided to do without a funeral: no matter how careful her instructions, Isobel would be bound to *muck it up*.

The fog lay low over the city, so that the tram cables underscored its obscure notation.

Joyce had read in the tourist guide that the Zürichers enjoyed the best quality of life in the world. They didn't look as if they were enjoying it much this morning, these black-clad revenants hurrying through the grey. Nevertheless, the cleanliness of the streets, the orderliness of the populace, the efficiency of the infrastructure – *you are never more than a hundred metres from the nearest bus, tram or train stop* – were there for all to see. It was utterly unlike the splurge of Birmingham, a city, Joyce thought, that no matter how much it *primped itself up*, always looked like it had got out of civilization's bed on the wrong side and was shambling across Middle England kicking housing estates and retail parks out of its roadway.

Put simply: Joyce hadn't wanted to live any more with this metastasized town, any more than she'd wanted to suffer the torment and indignity of her cancer. But if she could have continued with this dispassionate order? *Well, maybe . . .* However, such speculations were massively beside the point – *far too late*, because they had turned into Gertrudstrasse, a street of forgettable five-storey apartment blocks, and the cab was now halting in front of the dullest: a pedestrian exercise in the ruling of straight lines, which wouldn't have looked out of place in the Bull Ring.

'At every step of the procedure it is, how you say, practice – as well as our legal responsibility – to remind you of exactly what you are doing. Do you understand?'

'Yes.'

'This liquid is an anti-emetic, it is necessary for you to drink all of it, yes, and also to eat as many of the chocolates as you can; otherwise you may, how you say –'

'Vomit.'

'Exactly so, vomit the phenobarbital. Unfortunately with this particular drug you must take a lot, yes?'

Dr Hohl's accent was slight and his English of good cloth stretched over German syntax. He appeared unremarkable, the kind of vaguely rotund man – in his late fifties, his brownish-grey hair shaded in above his neat ears, his charcoal-grey suit jacket pushed apart by his paunch – that could be encountered in any side office, anywhere in the developed world. His medicalization was effected by gold-rimmed bifocals and a small gold caduceus lapel badge.

But this wasn't an office; it was a one-bedroom flat on the fourth floor of a Zürich apartment block; and, while everything had been done to make it seem, if not lived in, at any rate liveable, the air-freshened atmosphere remained determinedly commercial. It was, Joyce thought, the work place of an osteopath, a New Age healer or perhaps – although she had never seen such a thing – the better kind of prostitute.

The walls were papered pale yellow, the curtains were blue chiffon. Through an open door she could see a small bedroom. An Alpine landscape hung over the bed, which was a single with a thick mattress and a green coverlet.

The three of them were sitting at a round table, upon which stood a fresh candle, a garland of dried flowers at its base. The legal papers were spread out on the blue and white check tablecloth. Beside the official registration of her birth sat a camcorder, inside of which was a tiny Joyce trapped for all eternity, saying: 'I wish it to be known that my death has been entirely voluntary, and that I was subject to no pressure or duress by anyone.'

Treu und Glauben, that, she knew, was the Swiss's conception of themselves. Every contract was entered into with full faith and the required credit; to go over the small print was to impugn the other party's character. Anyway, she had read the papers already – there were copies posted on the organization's website – so she had signed them all – all except her will, which she had brought from England herself.

'So,' Dr Hohl said, fetching a silvery cardboard box from a wall-mounted cupboard, 'you will have a chocolate, yes?'

They were pimply truffles bedded in tissue paper. Joyce thought back to the Widder Hotel and the complimentary chocolates on the coffee table in her room. They had also been truffles – but white ones, caught in a cage of spun sugar. *Very stylish*. She and Derry had lived in Bournville for almost thirty years. Then, after his death three years ago, she was left alone in the idealized home. On days when the wind was in the east, the smell from the chocolate factory fell across the privet hedges and the lawns that had been mown into stripes. *Everything was sweet, sweet, incredibly sweet . . .*

The absolute horror of suicide gripped Joyce like a palsy: its mundanity and its profundity. The bulk of life, she now understood, was a succession of erasures, one action cancelling out the last. Not now. Everything that she was doing had a machined finality – *if only . . . if life could've been like this . . . such intensity*; and now to die with people *not much liked*, let alone loved.

She took one of the truffles and placed it in her mouth. It began to dissolve immediately. As if a spell had been broken, Dr Hohl went back to the cupboard, got out a plastic canister, opened it and began spooning the contents into a glass, while counting out in an undertone, '*Eins, zwei, drei, vier, fünf . . .*', all the way to '*fünfzehn*', when he was somehow back at the table, seated, and looking at Joyce with his gold-rimmed green eyes.

Dr Hohl put the glass full of poison down beside the papers and said, 'Now, the anti-emetic, yes?'

It tasted vile – at once ferrous and organic. Joyce almost brought up the stuff meant to stop her retching. This was why the chocolates were needed – to fill her mouth with sweetness, so that the bitterness wouldn't overwhelm her.

'Und now, another chocolate, yes?'

Joyce couldn't fault Dr Hohl's manner: he was devoid of any inappropriate levity, yet not solemn; deeply concerned and altogether *present*, while by no means intimate. He had managed to weld all three of them into a highly effective team within minutes of their entering the flat. The evidence of this was that Joyce wanted to please him, so took another truffle – although she didn't feel like it.

Only Isobel, Joyce felt, was letting the side down. Her daughter sat sideways on the straight-backed chair, her shoulders rounded in powder-blue cashmere (Joyce's own) and shaking. She had a wad of Kleenex pressed to her eye, while a second sent out soggy tendrils from where it was lodged in the sleeve of her cardigan. Isobel – who had hardly spoken to Dr Hohl – was being *barely polite*. Her hair, Joyce noted, was *a mess*: Medusa snakes of various blonde hues, and it was *far too long for a woman of her age*.

Joyce washed down the chocolate sludge with a second gulp of the bitter anti-emetic. 'Do please to remember', Dr Hohl said, 'that at any of these times, Mrs Beddoes, you are able to make the mind change, yes?'

He had said this at least three times before, and on each occasion Joyce had replied, 'I understand.' It was, she grasped, the very call and response of assisted suicide: Dr Hohl was the priest, announcing the credo, and she was the congregation of one that affirmed it.

Then, suddenly, the anti-emetic was all gone and there were only three truffles left in the box. Joyce couldn't recall all this eating and drinking, but the pads of her fingers were sticky, and her lips were tacky.

Dr Hohl poured water into the glass heaped with phenobarbital, then stirred it: ting-ting, ting-ting. It would've been better, Joyce thought, to've brought Miriam, or even Sandra – anyone, in fact, other than Isobel, *who simply can't cope.*

'Perhaps,' Dr Hohl ventured, 'you would be finding yourself more comfortable in the bedroom?'

'No, thank you,' Joyce said. 'I'd as soon stay here for the meanwhile.'

'In that case' – he held up the cloudy glass – 'I must tell you that if you drink this you will die.' He handed it to Joyce.

The glass was deadly cool to the touch; she hated her shaking jaundiced hand that held it. A memory came to Joyce, not of her beloved husband, her Derry, about to press his lips to hers, nor even of Isobel's slathered newborn features, but of a wasp batting against a windowpane.

It had been late the previous October, a mere six weeks after the diagnosis. The chemo had its own miserable side effects, yet they only partially masked her real symptoms; she knew it wasn't working. The stop-go of her bowels, the waves of fatigue and dread, the acid bile that rose up when she sang, *'Confutatis maledictis, Flammis acribus addictis, Voca me cum benedictis!'* And the insomnia. Sitting in the study, the curtains open, she had marvelled at the washed-out world without; it looked as if the greens and reds and blues would never return. Then, a tiny tapping at the pane. It was the wasp – tired, cold, its summer done – struggling for admission to the warmly coloured room.

'M-Mum.' Isobel had got her act together. 'Mum.' She slid a document out from the pile. 'You haven't signed this yet and we need someone else to witness it.'

It was the will; unless Joyce's signature was on it, her legal heir, Isobel, would be stalled and for the meantime *nothing could be done.*

Oh, oh – ooooh! This is why none of it has been as I expected. Where was the fast-approaching darkness? The series of mighty contractions she had imagined, clenching and then releasing, clenching and then releasing her from the world?

Joyce set down the glass and picked up the will. She folded the pages neatly in half, then began tearing them into small square pieces. 'I am not', she said, addressing Dr Hohl alone, 'going to go through with it.'

He was unruffled – so impressively so that Joyce nearly relented. 'I understand exactly, Mrs Beddoes,' he said. 'I have been thinking already this morning that it is too soon for you, yes?'

'Maybe, maybe too soon,' Joyce acknowledged, although she already knew that, having refused the poison once, she might never muster the courage to take it.

Dr Hohl got up and, wheezing a little, carried the phenobarbital over to the kitchen units in the corner. He put it on the draining board, took down a funnel and a plastic bottle marked GIFT from a cupboard, then poured the liquid into it. 'You appreciate', he called over his shoulder, 'that the payment you have made is non-refundable.' He came back and sat down. 'But it may be left as a deposit for if you will be making the mind change.'

'Yes,' Joyce said, choosing her words carefully, 'I do appreciate that, Dr Hohl, and I also appreciate the way everything has been organized by you this morning. Now, if you don't mind, would it be possible for you to call us a taxi?'

There was an old woman waiting for the lift. She had a matching hat and coat in synthetic brown material that looked *sweaty*, and as if the wearing of it would make you sweat. The three women stood in the breakfast-smelling lobby, listening as the building regurgitated the lift. The doors opened, and the old woman, peering intently at Joyce with glinting-coal eyes, said *'Bitte'* and ushered them in.

'Dankeschön,' Joyce replied, summoning up the remains of an evening class in German from two decades before.

On the way down the old woman scrutinized Joyce. Her gaze was disconcertingly vivacious: a much younger woman looked out at the world, through two eye holes that had been cut in the parchment of her face. *She knows . . . She's seen, what? Body bags slumped in this lift? She knows – and she approves. I've won a hand against Death.*

In the hallway, the old woman left ahead of them, pulling a wheeled shopping bag. Joyce watched her go and hated the kinship that she felt. *So what if I live a few weeks longer? I'll still be like her, trapped and used up.* Only moments before Joyce had been a heroine – *but now what am I?*

An ambulance and a police car were parked outside in the street. Their crews stood chatting and smoking. They were *surprisingly scruffy*: a paramedic's blouse unbuttoned to expose her bra strap; one of the policemen was unshaven. *They were waiting for me.* Joyce wondered if they were annoyed by this interruption in their schedule, or on permanent call, and therefore would remain in Gertrudstrasse until Dr Hohl – this time with more success – had methodically assisted another terminal case to drink up her phenobarbital.

A wave of exhilaration had pushed Joyce from the fourth-floor flat, sluiced her down and out of the building. In the street it broke: she was a sick woman, and, while not as old as the one with the shopping bag, old enough. She groped for Isobel's arm. Isobel, her daughter, who had yet to speak – to acknowledge this astonishing reprieve.

'What', Isobel said, 'are you going to do now, Mum?'

The tone was *not quite right*; the hand that closed over Joyce's felt at once diffident and *disapproving. She wanted me to go through with it – she's annoyed that I didn't go through with it!*

'What d'you mean?' Joyce said. 'Are you asking what am I going to do with the time left to me before I die, or whether I'm going back to the hotel? You don't, I may say, Isobel, seem that overjoyed to have me still with you.'

'No . . . Mum, that's not what I meant, it's –'

'Which? Which of those two options didn't you mean?'

'It's just . . . It's a shock – the plans you'd made, so carefully. I dunno – I mean –'

'You'd've rather I'd gone through with it, wouldn't you, my girl? That would've suited you fine, wouldn't it? Let me guess: you'd already decided what you were going to ask for the house, you'd already spoken to a broker about selling off your father's stock, you'd already thought about all the things you were going to do – is that it?'

'Mum, please . . .' She gestured to the emergency workers. They were staring at the two women – Joyce realized she had been near to shouting. She stared back at them, hard; and they kept on staring back. This must, Joyce thought, be the flip side of Helvetian rectitude, this unselfconscious *rudeness. Kyrie eleison.*

Sequentia

They didn't talk in the cab, which was an identical Mercedes, with another taciturn Swiss at the wheel. Isobel was crying again, and, even though Joyce had calmed down and was prepared to forgive her daughter (*It's shock – I'm shocked. She may be self-piteous – but then, she is pitiable*), she still left her to steep in her own brine. *It's all too irritating . . .* Despite which, there was an odd element of excitement: instead of being dead on that *ghastly coverlet*, Joyce had the whole day ahead of her; she felt as a schoolgirl does, when some confusion in the Olympian time-tabling of the adult world leaves her with a free double period.

At the Widder Hotel, the doorman, the concierge and the receptionist *Teste David cum Sibylla* looked at the two English women with ill-concealed surprise, as, arm in arm, they made their halting progess across the lobby to the lift.

'Mum,' Isobel said as she unlocked the door to Joyce's room, 'I – I mean, we. I mean, you have a return ticket, too. You remember – it was cheaper. The flight's booked for two o'clock, we've gotta pack up now . . .' She trailed off: her mother was giving her a censorious look.

'I don't know what your father would've said about your behaviour today.' As she spoke Joyce knew this was a low blow; Isobel, for all her self-centredness, had been unswerving in her love for *him*.

'M-Mum, that's not fair!'

Isobel had loved Derry more: *it was only to be expected*, but it *still hurt*. She had been so attentive during his last, *dreadful* illness; while since Christmas she'd spent *at best* three weekends in Bournville.

Joyce had had to ask friends to go with her to the hospital – a shaming thing.

'I don't know what's fair, Isobel,' Joyce hectored her under-performing subordinate. 'All I do know is that I'm tired' – through the open doorway she spied blobs of underwear on an armchair, beside it a plastic bag that she knew contained a sodden incontinence pad – 'and I'm going to lie down for a bit. If you want to take the flight, then it's your own affair. I haven't decided what I'm going to do yet, but, rest assured, whatever I do decide, I'll be fine without you.'

Joyce went into the room, shut the door firmly behind her and locked it. Then she fell against it and listened to her daughter snuffling like a *pathetic puppy* requesting admission. Eventually, Isobel went away.

The mirror behind the sink doubled the pill pots, the bottles, the tubes and the blister packs that Joyce had shakily laid out when she arrived the previous afternoon. It was the same device that cocktail bars used to convince drinkers of their alcoholic largesse.

Diuretics and antacids, sleeping pills and drugs to tamp down anxiety, painkillers and dietary supplements – *marmalade snatched while falling*. She had never properly questioned the justness of all these before: this was *what you did*, you took what you were told to take.

In the window of a pet shop at the shabby shopping parade in Selly Oak, she had seen them: *Scottie's Liver Treats*. Shrivelled, blood-dark excrescences packaged in cellophane. *That's what's going on inside me*. To begin with she had been accusatory of her own body as she watched it wasting in the pier glass she had inherited from her own rangy mother. *Is it you, or you, or you?* Breasts and bones and blood. But then Phillimore had confessed: he had no real idea where Joyce's cancer had originated.

'Although the most obvious, ah, tumour is in your liver, this is not where the cancer began – primary liver cancer is almost unknown in the developed world, Jo.' Phillimore seemed to be taking personal responsibility for this. 'Except among alcoholics and people with Hepatitis C.'

'So . . . where?' She was dreamy during these day-mares.

'Usually, when – as with you – we've done a biopsy, we can analyse the cancer cells and discover their origin, but in anything up to 15 per cent of cases this will remain occult.'

'Occult?' What was he talking about? A silver-bearded wizard? A voodoo priest?

Phillimore smiled at her consternation – how she loathed him. 'That's merely a medical term for something we don't know – yet.'

Yet, looking at all these useless salves and inadequate physics, then recalling the lead apron, the scattered footfalls, the spooky hum – it struck Joyce that 'occult' was precisely what Phillimore's treatment of her had been. *I . . . I . . .* It was difficult to grasp – peering through the eye holes of her old woman mask, at the woman in the mirror wearing the old woman mask – but in the suicide flat Joyce had somehow *begun talking again* with her body; they had recommended a conversation that was reassuringly pro-saic, full of itchy chatter and punctuated by companionable burps. This was a dialogue that excluded Joyce's questioning mind – for all her body demanded was a compliant listener, prepared to sit and nod, and occasionally mutter, 'Yes, yes, of course, dear' in response to its own moany self-absorption.

The capsules popped from their blisters straight into the toilet bowl; the pills plopped after them, followed by coils of ointment and splashes of linctus. Then she flushed five times, until the whole *business* was done.

There was one thing left: the Oramorph, a sticky solution in a squat bottle. *I'm in pain, now* – the pain of having to lug Isobel around with her, *she even has Derry's mouth. His mouth!* Decisiveness mutated into a deadly impulsiveness; she clenched and twisted the safety cap until it yielded, then took a swig.

What? To cease upon the Swiss lunch-time? She tittered, then wove through the Teutonic symphony of blond wood and clashing mirrored surfaces to where clean white linen offered quiet sanctuary. She fell across the bed and directly into her own fugue. *Mors slopebit et natora, Cum resurget creatura, Judicanti responsura . . .* Scoresby, naked, working himself up into a *right old tizzy*, bearing down on Joyce, quiff flicking like a baton; his blue-veined marble torso smashed against the bedside table and crumbled into dusty chunks. *He's only plaster!* Her horsey neigh took her back and back to the paddock of puberty, where she watched with a *queer hot thrill* older, richer girls posting *up and down.* Their jodhpurs stretched into hide, the girls transformed into centaurs with ponytails, their ponytails fanned out, iridescent, becoming peacock tails. The peacocks' beaks thickened into dolphins' snouts, the dolphins arched and dived into oceanic tea cups that shrank into dancing Disney crockery. Scoresby chased the string section up a spiral staircase, while ahead of them scampered the Singers. *Liber scriptus proferetur, In quo totum continetur, Unde mundus judicetur . . .* Even in drugged sleep, it seemed to Joyce that such a fantasia was pitifully wasted on a dying woman.

Her watch said it was five when she awoke; she didn't look at the 24-hour digital clock, and so assumed it must be the following morning, so deeply refreshed did she feel. She picked up the phone and dialled Isobel's room: no answer. She got up and opened the curtains: fog still nuzzled the panes. She dressed carefully, then further adjusted her clothing in the mirror, turning this way, then that, paying strict attention to the lie of her skirt – was it *becoming*? She had brought hardly any make-up, only lipstick, and blusher to give life to her moribund complexion; but it didn't really work, not on such jaundiced skin. Nevertheless, in the bathroom she applied these, marvelling at her own girlishness. *Death and Nature shall be astonished, When all creation rises again, To answer to the Judge.*

Going along the carpeted gantry to the lift, Joyce discovered Isobel slumped on a leather-padded bench. She was plainly drunk, her mascara smudged, her lipstick smeared, and her cheeks – without the assistance of blusher – as pink as any Heidi's. There was a stiff paper bag between her slack calves. *I see, a little retail therapy.*

'Mum, oh, Mum,' she gasped. 'I wanted them – I didn't know. I wanted them to go into your room – but you'd locked it inside.' Then, using Joyce's own thrift in recrimination: 'We missed the flight.'

Joyce came straight to the point: 'Well, you'll have to get another one, then – and pay for it yourself.' *A book, written in, will be brought forth, In which is contained everything that is, Out of which the world shall be judged.*

'Mum . . .' Those grovelling tones. 'What's happened to you?'

'Nothing much, but I've decided to stay here. And, Izzy, I may not have killed myself, but I'm still dying.'

Isobel was too saturated to absorb her mother's news, or note the rare diminutive; she slid down further on the bench, a cashmere heap.

'You're thirty-three years old,' Joyce couldn't forbear from reminding her. 'I can't go on carrying you for ever – and I don't want to.'

After that, for a while, she stood and listened to her daughter's sobbing, and the heavy whoosh of the approaching lift.

At reception Joyce handed her key to the concierge. He wore a cod-antiquated waistcoat with gold facings and striped sleeves. He had a 17.00 hours shadow and regarded her with the detachment of hotel staff the world over. 'Madam,' he began, 'we tried –' but was interrupted by a manager, a wispy man with a high-domed forehead, who appeared at his shoulder.

'Your daughter, Frau Beddoes, wanted us to enter your room – but I was not wanting to do this; it would have been second time in your stay.'

Joyce said, 'I didn't realize there was a quota.'

'Madam – please?'

'Nothing – really, nothing. I'm going for a walk now.'

'Do you know how long you will be making the stay with us? Your reservation is for one night, only.'

'I–I don't know . . . not indefinitely; why, do you need the room?'

The manager consulted the screen that peered up at him from beneath the brow of the desk. With one waxy finger he picked out a monotonous tune on the keyboard. 'I can let you have the room until *Sonntag* – Sunday – but then there is a higher rate for the Friday and Saturday nights.' He gave Joyce an avaricious smile, top lip tucked under lower for safekeeping.

'Very well,' she said. '*Sonntag* it is.' And went out into the street.

Where it was chilly, Joyce realized, with the approach of evening. Swiss sat suppering in the candlelit window of a restaurant opposite, the plump men correct in jackets and ties, their wives restrained by decent couture. From thirty feet away Joyce could still make out the food piled on their plates, and she felt the first quickening of an appetite long in abeyance. Pulling her coat tightly about her and buttoning it, she headed off uphill between the bright windows of the bijou luxury goods shops that took up the ground floors of the hunched houses.

Her saliva tasted sweet; the rumbling of her belly was unthreatening. Although she had forgotten an incontinence pad, Joyce felt no seepage or ominous swelling. The wire had been yanked out of her.

Leather goods as edible as milk chocolate; gold-nibbed fountain pens as suckable as teats; jewelled sweetmeats arranged on velvet-covered platters – Joyce gobbled it all up. She turned up a cobbled ramp, passed an inscribed Roman tablet set in a niche and reached a small hilltop park where linden trees with their first green tips stood in raised beds, and a water feature dribbled into a pool surrounded by empty benches. A low stone wall drew Joyce to it; from here she could look out over the old centre of Zürich. Close to, in the fading light, the twin domes of the Grossmünster, the tapered spire of the Fraumünster, all the other high-gabled buildings, with their steeply sloping roofs, weathercocks and gilded clock faces, jostled along the banks of the Limmat. The fog was lifting, scudding up as the darkness streamed down from the woods of the Zürichberg. In the suburban streets, the street lamps came on, braiding the trees. The Limmat unwound, a vinous ribbon between glassy embankments.

Joyce drank in Zürich's peace and orderliness. The city gave her a curious sensation of déjà vu, as if it were a picture that she had stared at, sightlessly, in childhood: a reproduction of *Hunters in the Snow* on a classroom wall. The breeze was fresh, with a note of last year's leaf fall. There was hardly any noise – no police sirens, no shouts, no traffic grumble, only the carillon of a distant tram.

Later, as she made her way back to the hotel, Joyce passed by the open door of a small Catholic chapel. A young priest, closing up for the night, was ushering out two late worshippers; his face was chubby, although his soutane hung loose on his rail-thin body. The sparse blond hairs on his bare head caught the light shining from behind the altarpiece, which was an *undistinguished* modern diptych: the Virgin Mary on one side, a frumpy mummy in a magenta housecoat; Jesus on the other, *not a baby any more*, and really *of an age when he should be expected to dress himself*.

The young priest said '*Guten Abend*' to Joyce, and she said '*Guten Abend*' back.

Hearing her accent, the couple, who had been hurrying off, stopped, and the man turned. He was middle aged and solidly built; when he came back into the light, Joyce saw that his otter head was sleek with dark-chocolate hair; he also had a rounded oblong moustache that was less groomed. It demanded, Joyce thought, to be waxed. He wore an Inverness-style coat, the cape fur trimmed. On most men this would have been *an affectation*, but, as he approached, Joyce saw that, somehow, he could carry it off.

'You are', the man said, 'English?'

'Yes.'

'If you were looking for a Catholic place of worship, I am sorry that this is only a shrine, joined now with the Benedictine monastery at Einsiedeln.'

'I'm not –'

The man rode over her denial; he was gently slapping the palm of his left hand with the gloves he held in his right, an insistent accompaniment to the information he had to convey. 'Father Grappelli und I' – he submerged his otter head; the priest smiled and half bowed, thumbs hooked in the cord at his waist – 'we are the committee people of the old parish here, we look after the restorations and these things.'

Joyce glanced at the man's female companion, expecting a complicit look, but the woman, whose features were pinched under tight curls, only stared back blankly.

Joyce tried again: 'I'm not a Catholic.'

'So, so' – the zealot wouldn't let her off the hook – 'but if you were wanting to be' – the moustache quivered – 'or are only needing the comfort of an English-language service during your stay, then Father Grappelli is one of the – *ein offiziants* at St Anton's in Minervastrasse. We' – he indicated the woman – 'are communicants there also.'

'P-Please.' Joyce held up a hand; she thought she was annoyed, but discovered that her voice bubbled with merriment. The priest and the cold woman chuckle-coughed Schweizerdeutsch over each other. Joyce assumed they were telling the natty man to *rein it in.*

'Please,' the man echoed Joyce, 'that is enough of it now, *Guten*

Abend, we are hoping to see you there.' He took the woman by the upper arm and escorted her away.

Joyce turned to the young priest, expecting him to say something – the scene seemed to demand it – but he only added his own *Guten Abend* and retreated inside the chapel.

Later still, Joyce sat on the sofa in her hotel room. She snapped off a spun-sugar span from the *stylish* confection that had sat on the coffee table since her arrival. Then, reaching inside the sickly cage, she took a white chocolate truffle.

Chocolate.

While the bonbon melted in her mouth, Joyce reflected on her odd journey; from one chocolate to another, from Bournville to here, to the Gertrudstrasse suicide flat, and now back here again. At every stop there had been a sweet treat.

After two more truffles Joyce dialled Isobel's room. There was no answer. She called reception: 'My daughter – Fräulein Beddoes – has she gone out?'

'She has checked out, madam, this evening at 17.00 hours, approximately.'

'Was it? Did she – did she leave a message?'

'Yes, madam, there is a letter here for you. Would you like me to send it up?'

Hoping this was generous, Joyce tipped the bellboy ten francs. She might need an ally. He smiled and bobbed his pillbox hat, but by no means obsequiously. Was it her imagination, or was there a certain brusqueness about everyone she had encountered since she had refused Dr Hohl's cup full of poison? An absence of the patronizing manner the living had towards those feckless enough to be dying; a manner that implied they were the parents of teenagers embarking on a permanent holiday, with very little luggage and inadequate preparation.

Joyce didn't open the envelope immediately. Instead, she lay on the bed, which had been remade and turned down while she was out. She picked up the aluminium stick and prodded the flat-screen TV into life. Trevor Howard materialized, saying: 'Go home, Martins, like a sensible chap. You don't know what you're mixing in, get the next plane.'

But Joseph Cotten demurred, 'As soon as I get to the bottom of this, I'll get the next plane.'

Trevor Howard gave a tough, realist's grimace – all the more commanding, given his homely features and bat ears. 'Death's at the bottom of everything, Martins,' he clipped. 'Leave death to the professionals.'

Joyce shifted on the fresh white pillows, curling up her legs, resting on one shoulder and an arm – it was a posture she hadn't assumed in months. She opened the small box of chocolates the maid had left on the other pillow.

The Snow Hill Gaumont, the cigarette smoke thicker in the gloom than the Vaseline smeared on the lens when Alida Valli was in shot. *Whatever happened to her?* Clattering down alleys between ruined houses, scrambling over mounds of rubble, splashing through the cavernous sewers – there went the past in its square-cut suit. Then they were on the Ferris wheel, and Orson Welles – such a spendthrift with his talent, in the way that Death was a waster of human lives – was saying: 'In Switzerland they had brotherly love, they had five hundred years of democracy and peace, and what did that produce? The cuckoo clock.'

In the still stiller middle of the night, when the television had dwindled to news and tombolas, Joyce finally read Isobel's letter. It was only the orphaned wail she'd expected; the 'you don't understands', 'it's so hard for mes' and 'if only Daddy were still alives'. Of course, the ostensible cause of all these *histrionics* was her own dying state – *Quid sum miser tunc dicturus?* – and yet Isobel had abandoned her. She didn't say where she had gone, whether Birmingham, London or that villa in Majorca belonging to a *useless*

99

rich friend – one of her *favourite bolt holes*. There was only *silly* omniscience; Isobel wrote that she would be 'watching out' for her mother, that, despite having checked out, she would be 'checking to see that you're all right'. Really, Joyce thought, if it weren't so pitiful it might be mystifying.

Over the next three days, Joyce called on the bellboy's services often. He brought her snacks and, while she lounged in a bathrobe with *Widder* across its left breast, took her clothes away to be laundered. His name, Karl, was also embroidered on his left breast. Joyce tried her seized-up German on Karl, but he blanked this: his English was fine.

There was no call from Isobel. It had been agreed that it would be best if she went back to Birmingham immediately after Joyce died. There was no requirement for her to participate in her mother's cremation, then the filing away of her dust – that could be *left to the professionals*. Isobel was needed for amateurish tasks: sorting stuff into boxes, humping some to charity shops, then asking Joyce's friends if they wanted to 'choose something' from the superior residuum, that in a few years' time their own friends would be asked to choose.

Late on the Friday evening Joyce called her home number and listened to the phone ringing in her own empty house. As it rang, she pictured the interior of the fridge, empty except for non-perishables: chutneys that wouldn't die and low-fat spreads awaiting Judgement Day.

The undertakers had been recommended by Dr Hohl's organization. Joyce called them on the Thursday morning – twenty-four hours after her reprieve – and their response had been as dispassionate as Hohl's: her deposit was non-refundable, as was the one for the columbarium niche at Fluntern Cemetery. Both orders could, however, be reactivated when necessary.

Joyce had let the phone ring in her own house for a long while, half convinced that Isobel was hiding from her mother, crouching in the walk-in cupboard in her parents' bedroom, her small shoulders shaking between polythene-sheathed dresses, her Start-rite feet planted between rows of shoes, all stretched by shoe trees. This was where Izzy had secreted herself when she was a little girl and evading elocution lessons or piano practice; but the phone only trilled on, duetting with the dunked-biscuit contralto of the Radio 4 continuity announcer, which had been left on to simulate the departed householder.

At long last Joyce had replaced the handset and gone back to the TV, which broadcast a succession of films – *Rebecca, National Velvet, It's a Wonderful Life* – that were a reassuring background to her resurrection. For, while to begin with Joyce was able to persuade herself that the numbness was due to her under-dose, by Thursday evening, when she felt hungrier than she had been in months, there was no denying that change was under way.

She didn't feel particularly well – how could that have been? But she wasn't not well: this dullness of body and mind was wholly unfamiliar, a state of suspension. There was no medication for her to take, yet she remained continent. On Sunday morning, when she put on her clean underwear and stood in her slip in front of the biggest of the many mirrors, Joyce was jolted from her inertia by the sight of her own flesh.

Which was no longer jaundiced. It sagged, certainly, but only in the way expected of an older woman who had once been *rangy, with beautiful high-rising breasts* – these last, Derry's words, not her own vanity. And while for two decades, the jibe between white lace and pleated skin had struck Joyce as the worst turn-off of all, she now found herself turning a little this way and a little that to admire the new-old birthday suit.

After four days of reclusion, the lobby was an alien planet. Floating from the lift to the reception desk, Joyce marvelled at the miraculous bubble-worlds of other people: an American mulling over a tourist map with his wife, a squat black maid struggling with an industrial vacuum cleaner.

With her cream blouse, neat brown tweed suit and her good coat from the new Selfridges in the Bull Ring – fake-fur trim, unlike the Inverness worn by the odd man she'd encountered outside the chapel – Joyce looked, she thought, *perfectly nice*. Around her neck was a heavy Victorian gold chain, given to her by Derry for their fortieth anniversary. *Perhaps a little premature, but . . .* he had said, presciently.

She placed her lilac carpet bag on top of the desk. Embroidered with gold fleur-de-lys, it was possibly *too young* for Joyce, but it was exactly the right size. Once the bill had chattered from the printer, it chewed Joyce up. Of course, there was Isobel's added on – including many and pricey spirits miniatures – but her own snacks, teas and laundry were also, in the normal course of life, *prohibitively expensive*. She did well to hide her consternation, giving away only her Visa card.

'You are wanting a taxi to the airport?' the receptionist asked, and, when Joyce denied this, she suggested instead: 'The Hauptbahnhof – the train station, maybe?'

'No.' Joyce shut the clasp of her bag with a definitive click. 'Thank you, I'll walk. It's' – she glanced at the revolving door which spun sunlight into the lobby – 'a lovely day.' She made to leave, then stopped. 'You wouldn't happen to know how to get to the Catholic church – St Andrew's I think it's called?'

'St Anton's,' the receptionist corrected her, 'on the Minervastrasse.'

At first hesitantly, then with increasing confidence, Joyce made her way down through the cobbled streets of the old town, then across the Münster Bridge. The fresh air was heady, and when, to the south-east, at the far end of the cobalt-blue lake, she saw the seven snowy peaks of the Churfistern, she gasped, then stood at the balustrade for several minutes, drunk with their *loveliness*.

It was only ten minutes' walk to the church; the tramp down Seefeldstrasse, between dull five-storey houses and apartment blocks, wearied her, but Joyce got there feeling *all right* – not nauseous. She hadn't thought ahead, and was oddly disappointed to realize she'd arrived at the end of a service. Father Grappelli was standing on the front steps, together with an older priest. Both wore snowy-white modern vestments, and long scarves embroidered with naive standard-bearing lambs. Joyce – despite not being a believer – thought the scarves demeaning of their office.

The priests were chatting with their parishioners: prosperous families of burghers – the adults had the *self-satisfied* expressions of the recently shriven. Joyce scanned the throng for the otter-headed man and his tight-faced friend, but was partially relieved not to see them. Then, affecting an interest in a plaque on the wall, she made her way along the side of the church. Here, she came upon the blockhouse of a 1960s vestry. The door was open, so she went in.

A teenage girl was bent over directly in front of Joyce, her long chestnut hair hanging down to the parquet floor, which was spread with newspaper. A woman of almost Joyce's age – but plump, ruddy-faced, and squeezed into *woeful* jeans – was aiming a spray can at the silky cascade.

'OK,' the old-hippieish woman cried, *'jetzt – aufstehen.'* The girl straightened up, and with her clawed hands vigorously backcombed her laquered hair until it rose up in a great ruff. *'Und . . . nächster!'* the woman cried, and the girl scampered away to be replaced by a second, who adopted the same posture and was duly sprayed.

'Well, so, you *have* converted, yes?' said a voice right behind Joyce. She jerked round. *Quantus tremor est futurus, Quando judex est venturus, Cuncta stricte discussurus. Breath on my neck, moustache prickle; night presses against a cold black pane, vast, impersonal, yet alive.*

'Uh – y-yes; sorry – I mean, no.'

The otter-headed man laughed. *I'm* sorry,' he corrected her. 'I gave you a jump. Marianne always says to me' – his nut-brown eyes slid away from hers, to where the tight-faced woman was examining a noticeboard – 'that I am too on your face.'

'I think,' Joyce said, 'the expression is "in your face".'

The moustache pouted. 'Exactly so, in your face.'

He was in a loden coat today, olive with horn toggles. *He really ought to have a Tyrolean hat as well* – its absence made his hydroplaned head seem that much sleeker.

'You must allow me to introduce myself,' he said. 'I am Ulrich – Ueli for shortness – Weiss, and this is my – how do you say it? – partner, Marianne Kreutzer.'

Hearing her name, the tight-faced woman came across and all three shook hands formally. Joyce put her in her mid fifties – older than Weiss – and with her gaunt, angular figure, she hardly seemed *mistress material.*

Joyce found herself co-opted by Weiss and the Kreutzer woman. They introduced her to some people: 'Frau Beddoes, she is visiting from England.' And showed her round the church. 'An undistinguished building,' Weiss said, 'you will agree.'

Joyce did. Anglican churches were *bad enough,* with their tepid air of state-assisted piety, but Catholic ones had always seemed *far worse*: musty battlefields, where lust and repression fought it out, in the process torturing wooden effigies, then nailing them to the walls.

The trio stopped in front of a headless figure that stood in a spot-lit embrasure. It wore a blood-spattered toga, and its head rested at its sandalled feet like a gory football. Joyce stared at the severed head; it stared back, the Aztec eyes maniacal.

'You would say,' Weiss lectured, 'St Antoninus, but here St Anton for shortness. He was the public executioner at the time of Emperor

Commodus, second century, and responsible for the execution of St Eusebius, among many other martyrs . . .'

Joyce registered that Weiss was trying to make all this interesting to her, but she was bored already. Sacred objects, she had always felt, needed to be so much more powerful and affecting than even the greatest artworks; if, that is, they were to perform the tasks assigned to them. Otherwise, what were they? *Useless tat*; and what did that make God? Only a fervent bargain-hunter in a long white dress.

Marianne – the Kreutzer woman – had strolled to the next embrasure along. Here she lit a candle and stuck it on a blackened spike spattered with waxy rime. Joyce searched the tight face – its grey eyes closed, its long top lip vertically creased – for evidence of prayer, or yearning, but saw neither.

Weiss droned on: '. . . then this fellow, this executioner, he is having a dream, you know, a vision thing, Christ comes in his face, yes? And he repents.' He brought his hand up abruptly, then dropped it. 'Then it is his turn for the chopping, a martyr also now.' Except that this sounded like 'Allzo nao'. Weiss smiled, and upper canines slid from beneath his walrus moustache.

'We Catholics have so many of the saints.' He took Joyce by the arm and led her on. 'Sometimes I think too many. No longer is there the selling of indulgences and all those corrupt practices; but the saints, I think this non-believers find hard to . . . accept: that a man, the Pope, can decide that the *naturgemäss* – the natural law – has been – how do you say it – suspended.'

Clearly, Weiss expected a response. Joyce said, 'I had no idea there were so many Catholics in Switzerland; in England we think of the Swiss as very Protestant –'

'No music, yes? No dancing. All in the black, yes?' He laughed. 'In exact fact there are more Catholics here in Zürich than the Zwinglians. Many Old Catholics allzo; y'know, who, ah, say mass in the Latin.'

They reached the end of the nave and went into the vestibule. Father Grappelli was seeing off the last of his communicants: an elderly couple, both with ski sticks, both swaddled in full-length quilted coats, who were haltingly making their way down the shallow stairs.

Seeing them, Joyce remembered that she was ill – *dying, in point of fact*. Felt, too, Derry's absence – as acutely as any human presence. Church bells were pealing across the valley of the Limmat, glockenspiel notes struck on bronze. Pigeons wheeled, Joyce's head spun. She staggered a little, and Weiss tightened his grip.

Marianne Kreutzer came up beside them, her face betraying little concern. 'But you are not well, so?' she said. 'I think this other time.'

'I'm all right, really.' Joyce detached herself from Weiss – his cologne was lemony, alcoholic, *Father's bay rum*.

'Perhaps you are hungry? It is lunch-time, we would' – he sought confirmation from his partner – 'be delighted if you would like to join us.'

'Off course,' Marianne said.

'Oh, I don't know.' Joyce gathered her carpet bag into her arms. 'I wouldn't want to impose.'

'It is not imposing.' Again, the wolfish smile. 'You are a guest in our country. Normal times we go to a bistro near to here – but of course you have visited the Kronenhalle?'

Joyce looked blank.

'No? But really this is too bad, this is the most famous eating place in Zürich; to be here and not to visit, it is almost a crime – you will please to be our guest.'

Father Grappelli was lingering, rolling and unrolling his scarf of lamb. He had a tentative expression on his boyish face, and Joyce guessed he was hoping the invitation would be extended to him. It wasn't. Weiss, coughing Schweizerdeutsch, took the priest's hand and shook it. Then he explained to Joyce, 'I will get the car', before skipping off down the steps while pulling on his suede gloves.

Joyce turned to Marianne: 'Please, it isn't necessary for all this . . .'

Her tight face clenched still more. 'Frau Beddoes,' she said, 'Ueli is not so ordinary Swiss person. He is *ausländerfreundlich* – you say, friendly to the aliens. That is his . . . thing, so, come, please.'

Not deigning to take his hand, Marianne Kreutzer nodded to the rejected priest, then indicated to Joyce the car that was already idling by the kerb, as compact as a travel iron. As he leant across to open the passenger door, Weiss's otter head dived out of it.

In the oaken burrow of the Kronenhalle, the Zürichers – sleek, black and dapper as moles – tunnelled their way through mounds of food. Many of them blinked from behind tinted Christian Lacroix glasses, as if even this subterranean ambience were too bright. The Zürich guilds' coats of arms were painted on to the creamy plaster of the walls, up above the wood panelling. Waitresses bustled among the crisply laid tables, while the hunched maître d' slowly propelled a trolley up and down the aisles, the silvery lid of which was rolled up, exposing a glistening joint of beef: the meaty pupil of a steely eye.

Stripped of his loden coat, Weiss was disconcertingly exposed in a black roll-neck pullover that was so sheer Joyce could see his nipples.

'So, here, you see' – the lecture was resumed – 'the most celebrated Zürich restaurant. Here in this place since the 1800s. Haunt of the writers – Dürrenmatt, Keller, Mann, Frisch. Music-makers also – Strauss, Stravinsky, Perlman . . .' He rattled out the names with scant feeling. 'I think maybe the artists' presence more obvious still – Miró, Braque, Chagall . . .' As he pronounced each name he pointed to their respective efforts: small canvases, their oils tastily effulgent beneath downlights. 'Und there, by your back, Frau Beddoes, Picasso.'

It was a blue boy on a lighter blue foreground, seated, with his naked arms encircling his bare legs. There was a pierrot's conical hat on his tousled head.

'Same family, see, the owners – two generations now – have been very clever.' Weiss leant forward, his black breasts resting on the white linen. 'Some are saying they took the paintings from the escaping Jews in the war . . . I think this is but only gossip. See, the, ah, presiding spirit of the place' – he gestured to a portrait of a formidably beaky matriarch that hung up high by the curved cornicing – 'Madame Zumstag, by Varlin.' He snatched at his own snub nose with all five of his plump digits. 'She does not, I think, look like an anti-Semite.'

Marianne sighed and rattled her menu card. She's bored, Joyce thought; *bored, disapproving and hungry. All three.*

A waitress halted at their table; in her trim uniform of black dress, white cap, black hose and white apron, she was perfectly timeless. A stilted bilingual interchange began, as Weiss – unnecessarily, as these were printed in English as well as German – explained the dishes to Joyce: '*Mistkratzerli . . . gebraten, mit gebraten . . . Mit Knoblauch und Rosmarin* – it's, you would say, a little bit of baby chicken, yes, with the garlic, yes, and rosemary.'

Joyce was fully intending to decline the food, or to have any drink besides sparkling mineral water. But Weiss prevailed upon her: 'Please, this is a Lattenberg Räuschling, an '05 from a local vineyard; we are right to have the pride, I think.' A moist and red lower lip pouted from the luxuriant moustache.

Because of its very rarity, the foody aroma of cigarette smoke in a confined space seemed a *special treat*. The hushed munching of the diners and the priestly garb of the efficient staff, all of it felt so . . . *enormously pleasing.* Then there were Joyce's insides, which were talking to her again, although not with the barely suppressed hysteria of incontinence, nor oedema's plummy nastiness. *I'm hungry,* her stomach blared. *A trumpet spreading a wondrous sound.*

The cerise wine was clearer than complete transparency. It smelt of fresh-cut hay. Joyce had to restrain herself from glugging. She had never been a drinker – or, rather, Derry had been a whisky drinker, and it always seemed *a waste* for Joyce to open a full bottle of wine, then leave it in the fridge, expiring beside the mayonnaise.

She ordered the baby chicken for a main course, and some of the *Leberknödel* soup to start. She hadn't consulted the English translation, so Joyce didn't know what *Leberknödel* was – or were – but soup was *always comforting*.

The Swiss ordered as well; then, after grudgingly asking whether Joyce minded, Marianne Kreutzer lit a long slim menthol cigarette. The minty acridity suited the woman, while the smoky threads pulled her face still tighter. Weiss began – gently enough – to probe Joyce concerning her widowed status, her former career and the rest of her life back in England. She was happy to impart; however, she remained vague when he asked her the reason for her being in Zürich, and the likely duration of her stay.

Their entrées arrived. Joyce's soup smelt so *heavenly* that she shifted uneasily on her seat: surely the hot wire would still be there, only buried deeper? But there was nothing; only the companionable rumble of her stomach, so she took a sip of the soup. It was meaty, herby . . . *tasty*. Fleshy dumplings floated in the life-giving broth, and Joyce spooned one up and bit into it, releasing tangible pulses of flavour.

'Mmm,' Joyce couldn't restrain herself from exclaiming, 'this is absolutely lovely!'

Weiss, who was digging at a tall seafood cocktail with a long-handled spoon, peered at her with his lustreless hazel eyes. 'I'm glad you are liking it; it is not a very typical Swiss dish – more the German, I think.' (Eye zink.)

'And what's in these dumplings?' Joyce asked, biting into a second.

'The dumplings? Ah, so, *die Bouillon mit Leberknödel*, yes, you would call them liver dumplings.'

Scottie's Liver Treats. Occult origin. Her body, sad and lonely, tossed without regard across the middle of the bed they had shared for ten thousand nights. Her own middle, a mass of alien tissue, *revolting*, poisoning her with its blind and senseless growth.

Joyce was laughing; a full-throated guffaw, the like of which she hadn't experienced in months. She laid down her spoon and picked up her napkin to cover her mouth.

'You – is everything all right for you, Frau Beddoes?'

Imagine that thick fur against your neck – or your thigh!

Marianne, having shuffled the lettuce leaves and slices of smoked meat on her plate, resumed smoking her lungs.

'I'm f-fine, really, thank you, Herr Weiss.'

She recovered herself – but only partially. Some blockage had been swept away by her hilarity, and now Joyce found herself telling the moustache – for the man was only a whitish growth hanging off the back of it – far too much: her illness, her loneliness, her pathetic and inadequate daughter, her miserable decline and Phillimore's indifference.

Then Joyce told Weiss how she had heard about Dr Hohl's organization because of a high-profile case in England: the woman with motor neurone disease haranguing TV news reporters and chat show audiences, then departing for Switzerland and the after-life, her wheelchair carried shoulder-high on to the airplane, the litter of a crippled warrior queen.

As she spoke, Joyce noticed that Weiss – whom she had mentally pegged as a *cold fish* – was becoming more and more agitated: his manicured fingers tugged at his napkin, he spun his wine glass by its stem. As she described her own decision to come to Zürich prematurely, Weiss stilled, grew intent; and Joyce played to this solo audience – for Marianne Kreutzer's attention was elsewhere, her cold eyes frosting the convivial quartet at the next table: elderly parents, thirtyish son and daughter-in-law; all hale, all hearty, all pink and flaking in a way suggestive of a recent skiing trip.

Joyce slowed down and, as any good storyteller should, took her listener by his figurative hand, led him on to the plane, sat him beside her while she lost control of her fear and her bladder, then led him off again, into the cab, on to the Widder Hotel, sat him at her bedside throughout the sedated night, then took him on again, to Gertrudstrasse.

When they were actually in the suicide flat, and Dr Hohl was mixing the phenobarbital with water, Weiss's white face swam up from behind his moustache, transfigured by a joyous agony. He was muttering, '*Schrecklich . . . schrecklich . . .*' and when Joyce told him how she had, at the very last moment, refused the poison, Weiss took his otter head in his hands, shook it, then exclaimed: 'Oh, but Frau Beddoes, this is so very wonderful!' Before urging his disengaged companion, 'Isn't it, Marianne, so very wonderful to be hearing?'

Setting her cigarette down on the edge of the ashtray, Marianne Kreutzer said, 'These are very bad people, Frau Beddoes; you have done something truly brave and important, we thank you for that.' Although her frigid tone suggested that she might just as well have administered the poison herself.

Weiss ran on: 'I am not very involved myself in this thing – but we have friends who are, *gegen Fanatiker* – who, you would say, make the campaigning against this dreadful thing that they do.'

Joyce stared at him – she felt foolish and vulnerable; of course, they were Catholics – she should've kept her mouth shut. *Mors slopebit et natora, Cum resurget creatura, Judicanti responsura. Death and Nature shall be astonished, When all creation rises again, To answer to the Judge.* She began back-pedalling. 'I'm afraid I'm going to disappoint you, Herr Weiss.' Her tone was correct, off-putting. 'My decision was impulsive – and nothing to do with Dr Hohl's ethics – I am still terminally ill, I may want to avail myself of their . . . of this service at a future date.'

Weiss was not to be deflected so easily. 'Please, Frau Beddoes, do not think we are *das fanatisch* – the fanatics – I understand, truly I do; my first wife died of cancer ten years ago. She was still a young woman –' He stopped short and asked Joyce: 'And you?'

Taken aback, Joyce found herself confirming, 'Cancer.' Then added, 'Of the liver.'

Marianne Kreutzer appeared to catch this very English irony; at any rate, her creased lips furrowed a little more – but Weiss missed it. Licensed by the revelation that they were both members of the *not very exclusive* cancer club, he began, energetically, to fill Joyce in on the local resistance to the goings on at Gertrudstrasse. Weiss confirmed her suspicions: there had been such grotesqueries as body bags propped up in the lift. Then there were the emergency vehicles in near-constant attendance, while the arrival – often by private ambulance – of the suicides seeking assistance created a despairing atmosphere.

'It is not helpful,' Weiss said, 'that there is a cemetery next to this building. The people who live there are not best-off type, but the city council – the canton, also – are thinking about taking the action. I think they will be made to move soon. (Moov zoon.)

'There is also Hohl. He is, you know, well – he is *ein Fanatiker*. He is offering now to the people with clinical depression his poison – nothing wrong in their body, only the head.' Weiss massaged his own smooth forehead, mussing his hair. 'This is making the difference – even non-Catholics understand this to be wrong.'

While these very weighty matters were being discussed, Joyce tidily dissected her chicken. The Swiss couple were equally methodical eaters, *although where she can be packing it away is a mystery*. When Joyce laid down her cutlery, Weiss responded as if this action were a diagnostic tool and bluntly asserted: 'You are in much pain, yes? On the drugs? So. I have talked too much; we can drive you to your hotel if you like this.'

The hunched maître d', whose short white jacket and cranky manner reminded Joyce of a lab technician at Mid-East, had abandoned his roast trolley for a copper pot, from which he was ladling large dollops of cream on to the strudels and tartes tatin of the diners. Observing this wanton consumption of criminally unsaturated fats, Joyce gingerly patted her belly beneath the table. There was no pain, or watery intimation of flux to come, only the tight sensation of healthy plenitude. The Leberknödel were in there, she thought, happily being digested.

'No, please,' she said. 'I am feeling quite all right. If it's not too much trouble I think I would like some dessert.'

After the cream pot had done two rounds and they had all been served with tiny cups of espresso, Weiss finally called for the bill. Joyce reached for her bag and began rummaging for her purse, but her host was having none of this. 'Please, please,' he said, warding off the threat of her contributing with open palms. 'You are our guest, we would be the most upset, wouldn't we, Marianne?'

Marianne Kreutzer didn't look as if she would be in the least upset; she had a compact out and was retouching her foundation. Even as a girl, Joyce had found such public attention by a woman to the appearance of her own flesh a *distinctly lewd* performance. Seeing this elegant – and slightly hostile – Swiss woman doing it, caused Joyce to speculate on the nature of her relationship with Weiss. The sex, she imagined, was necessary – but by no means the most important thing. Despite his assured manner, Weiss was a man-boy, gripped by his enthusiasms – and presumably by childish anxieties as well. Joyce found it easy to imagine his pink, freshly shaven cheek resting between her tired breasts.

Marianne Kreutzer dispelled her reverie by launching into this curious speech: 'Lenin,' she began, 'when he lived in Zürich, in the First War, he said of us Swiss that we could not be having the revolution, because when it came the time to attack the Hauptbahnhof – the train station – the crowd would be stopping to buy the ticket to go on – Ueli, *was ist der Name für Gleis?*'

'The platform.'

'That is it, the platform. But now, well, you are taking time to see Zürich and our beautiful buildings, our pretty lake, maybe also you are seeing our new kind guests. Black guests, brown guests. People are not so friendly with them; they are invited only by the Government in Berne, I think. There are some times not so long now, when the Swiss in the crowd are not buying the platform ticket!' She snapped her compact shut for emphasis.

Joyce didn't know how to respond; it wasn't at all clear whether Marianne Kreutzer's remarks had been an endorsement of this revanchism, or simply a description. Pointing out from her severe curls were ears as thin as a fish's fins; in place of lobes they had diamond studs.

'What is your hotel?' Weiss asked, twining his credit card with the strip of receipt.

'I was staying at the Widder, but, well, to be frank, I've decided to stay on for a while in Zürich, and . . .' Joyce bowed her head; she didn't want Marianne Kreutzer's accusing eyes on her: she didn't want to be kin of the uninvited guests. 'It's not that I can't afford it, it's just that it seems too expensive if I'm going to be here that much longer.'

Weiss looked at Joyce's bag. Its pattern of fleur-de-lys didn't, she thought, seem out of place in the Kronenhalle. *Perhaps I should stay here?* 'So,' he said, 'you are without a pension or hotel?'

'I'm afraid so.'

'We have a new kind of taking tax here, you know.' The waitress had brought Weiss's loden coat and was hovering by the table, but he showed no inclination to rise. 'If you are a tourist from European Union country, you may stay as long as you like, but only in a hotel. To rent – just a room only – you must register with the Fremdenpolizei, and then . . . well, so on and so on, they will check up on you; we know' – the moustache drooped shamefacedly –

'the reputation we have abroad. There will be many forms and stamps – too many, I think.'

Joyce rose to this: 'That doesn't concern me. I was a professional administrator myself for many years, I'm accustomed to that sort of thing; and if it's a matter of assets, well, I can produce evidence of sufficient.'

'Maybe so, maybe so.' Weiss wasn't taking Joyce's competence well. *He wants to hang on to me!* 'But foreigners can find it very hard to get the flats and rooms; they are always the last in the line, often times when they are the first – you understand?'

Joyce nodded.

'I have a friend – she is a member of our church. She has a very nice room. She would be happy, I think – I know – to have you as the *Pensionsgast* –'

'Really, Herr Weiss, you've been kind enough –'

'One call, one call . . .' He had his mobile phone out already, unfolded, the panel tucked up under his hair. He had taken the coat from the waitress, draped it over one arm, and now began tangoing it towards the door.

'Please.' Most unexpectedly, Marianne Kreutzer had placed her long elegant fingers on Joyce's sleeve. 'Let Ueli be the helper for you. I said one time, he is *ausländerfreundlich* – it is his *Natur*.'

The sky was still bright, although long shadows fingered the bolt of grey tarmac that was woven with tram lines. The compact Mercedes pulled up to the kerb and Joyce got out. *Antiquariat der Literatur* was stencilled on the window of a small bookshop, and a clothesline strung across this was pegged with different editions of a periodical called *Du*. Below them lay rows of German-language books with paper covers.

Coming up beside her, Weiss said: 'This is the university quarter, many culture people are living here. This lady, her husband is – was – a professor.'

Marianne Kreutzer extracted herself from the back of the car, but it was only to wish Joyce *auf Wiedersehen*. 'I am waiting,' she said to Weiss.

Opposite the bookshop stood a large, faintly ugly, Italianate building. It had a four-storey tower, and a three-storey wing with cast-iron balconies; two dismal dormer windows protruded from the tiled roof. 'Frau Stauben is on the top. Very good views, I think.' So saying, Joyce's protector led her across the road.

The views from Frau Stauben's apartment were an irrelevance – or so she seemed to believe. Her living-room windows were covered with both straw blinds and heavy, dark green velvet curtains that were half drawn. The furniture was dated, yet still of the wrong period: padded European Modernist slabs with tapered poles for legs and arms. The nylon covers of these chairs and sofas were time-faded beige and mauve, plush with moulted cat fur.

Frau Stauben – or Vreni, as she insisted on being called – was the ruddy-faced woman who had been doing the girls' hair at St Anton's. Upon Joyce and Weiss's arrival, she had first imposed a plate of pastries on her guests, then put them on one of the bigger slabs. While she hustled in and out of the adjoining kitchen preparing coffee, Frau Stauben chattered away in heavily accented English. 'It is *Gründonnerstag* soon now – that's what we say; in English, "Green Thursday", I think. The children will do their playing then – the day before *Karfreitag* . . . Good Friday.'

Weiss hadn't taken his loden coat off. He sat awkwardly on the edge of the sofa. There were patches of icing sugar on either knee of his immaculately creased black trousers. A large cat came padding into the room; it was – Joyce dredged up from some sink hole of memory – a Birman. A strip had been shaved out of its thick, smoky-blue coat, exposing disturbingly human skin and the fresh stitching of an incision. The cat advanced halfway across the furry carpet, then sat and stared at Joyce with malevolent yellow eyes.

Weiss accepted a cup of coffee and said, 'Frau Beddoes, please allow me to explain your situation to Frau Stauben in German.' Joyce fluttered her hand – a gesture she wasn't aware of having in her repertoire – and the two Swiss began spitting and lilting Schweizerdeutsch over one another.

Through the kitchen door Joyce could see wind chimes dangling above the sink; spider plants in string harnesses had parachuted into the corners of the living room; in the corridor there were framed homilies illustrated with tow-headed cherubs. It all reminded her of the drop-in centre at the hospital, where, together with a troop of other sufferers, Joyce had lain in vest and tracksuit bottoms on a tatami mat, as a tranquillized tape recording urged them all to *go into the garden*.

Joyce had wondered *why*? The garden at Mid-East was a *concrete waste land*, its only blooms *polythene*. But maybe the voice meant her own garden, which, although no *show-stopper*, had afforded her so much pleasurable absorption: the crumble of loam between fingertips, while she stared intently at the rippling ultramarine of an iris petal.

Or perhaps the voice had meant her to recall weekends in the garden with Derry. He hadn't been that attuned to the natural world – every seasonal change, right until the very end, remained a source of mild surprise – and yet he still dutifully assisted her, because her pleasure was his own. *In the last year or two, like a walrus in his old grey cords, pulling himself up from the weeding, elbows on to the seat first, then so slow and ungainly to stand. In bed at night the awful gurgling: everything draining away.*

And here was his widow, listening while one foreign stranger explained to another that, despite the fact that she, too, was dying, she also had to rent a room. *Hardly what you want in a prospective tenant.*

'She had – *was sagt man für Gebärmutter*?'

'A . . . well, *ich weiss nicht, eben* . . . She has had her womb – is it womb? – cut out of her.'

117

Joyce smiled. She hadn't realized how intently she had been staring at the cat; nor that the cat had continued to glare at her. 'Frau Stauben,' she asked, 'might I use your bathroom?'

Braced, Joyce voided herself. A smooth sensation: pleasing distension, holding on and then letting go. A rounded 'plop', a single cool splash on her left buttock. The shabbiness of the rest of the apartment was absent from this tiled confinement; the open window admitted fresh air and birdsong. *Maybe that's why I was relaxed enough?* Joyce mused, for if there wasn't diarrhoea, there was usually its hardened opponent.

But when she rose, wiped herself and looked back at the healthy brown bracket encapsulating the greenish water, she comprehended that the true explanation lay within: the vicious antagonisms – bowel screeching at stomach, gall bladder howling at liver – had been subsumed by a low hubbub, as of parish councillors mildly debating in a musty hall.

Joyce rearranged her clothes, flushed the toilet and checked her face in the mirror. Going back along the dim corridor, she noticed a ceramic name plate on a door; it was decorated with edelweiss and read *Gertrud's Zimmer*. The door was ajar and she could see candlelight blinking on a skirting board.

Joyce pushed the door open. It was a perfectly ordinary teenage girl's bedroom – or, rather, had once been. The pink flounce around the padded headboard of the bed was dusty and mildewed, the mattress was bare except for a quilted under-sheet. On the walls, the puncture marks of withdrawn drawing pins, and the tacky marks of ripped-off Sellotape showed where pop posters and hobby certificates had resided. The window was tight shut, the blind half drawn.

This was not a room that had been recently vacated; tiny temporal jibes – the cartoon decal stuck to the wardrobe door, a fluffy slipper sticking out from under the bed – informed Joyce that the girl who had once slept here was long since grown. Or dead, because the candlelight came from two rows of nightlights that had been arranged on a makeshift shrine.

Three planks, set like stairs on supports of increasing height, were cluttered with snapshots, drawings, glass figurines, china dogs and kittens. Among these were amateurish handicrafts, while in pride of place, in the middle of the highest plank, was a missal with a gold-tooled cover and a rosary looped around it, one bead a smooth football at the feet of a plastic ballerina. On the wall above the clutter hung an ornately framed photograph of the goddess of these small things: Gertrud herself, on skis, wearing a bright pink ski suit, and with a vanilla ice cream Alp over her shoulder. Her portrait was flanked by a crucifix: Jesus, hairless legs in white pants, and with a brasserie waiter's goatee, hung casually from the cross, having simply *dropped by*.

Joyce stood planted in the doorway; she hated that she'd intruded, yet found herself unable to retreat. The black silhouette of a bird flapped by the bottom half of the window: out there, in the daylight, were the living; while in this fusty room there were only brain-dead girls, their souls kept alive on faith-support equipment.

Frau Stauben bustled along the corridor. Joyce turned, flustered. 'Please, I'm sorry . . . I didn't mean to intrude – the candles –'

But her prospective landlady was unfussed. 'It is a silly thing,' she said. 'My daughter,' she continued, pointing at the girl in the ski suit, 'she dies many of these years ago, it was a cancer in the blood.'

'Leukaemia?'

'Yes . . . so. I am always meaning to do the tidy' – she made sweeping motions with her sturdy hands – 'but . . .' Frau Stauben left this, and the hands, dangling. Joyce looked into her periwinkle-blue eyes and saw nothing unusual, only the cliché of humanity. All at once she decided she would try to like Frau Stauben – *Vreni*; trust her, maybe.

'So,' the other woman resumed, taking Joyce by the arm and leading her not towards the living room but further into the bowels of the apartment, 'Herr Weiss, Ueli, he had to be gone – you were a long time.'

'Really?' Joyce felt not abandoned but relieved.

'Yes, that Marianne –' Frau Stauben pulled herself up. 'So, this is the room I am hiring.'

It was large, clean and, in contrast to the others, well aired. Twin beds were pushed together beside one wall, the fitted carpet was an institutional tan, the wallpaper a pattern of trellises and climbing roses.

'It is' – she made reckoning on her stubby fingers – 'two hundred and ten francs for the weeks, and I can be giving you *le petit déjeuner* – an evening meal also, if you're wanting?'

Treu und Glauben. 'That's fine, Frau Stauben,' Joyce said. 'I'll take it.'

Frau Stauben's grey hair lay in a mass of spirals on her rounded shoulders, the links of her spectacles chain were buried in the fuzz of her cardigan; the spectacles themselves rose and fell on her massive breast. She was still holding Joyce's arm. 'Please, you *will* call me Vreni – and . . .'

Joyce touched her own breast. 'Joyce.'

'Joyce. Exactly. Are you very sick-feeling, Joyce?' Frau Stauben's eyes were too blue – doll's eyes with bags under them.

'No, not very sick at all . . .' She hesitated, wondering whether to speak of her odd feelings since the abortive visit to Gertrudstrasse, but decided against it. 'I came to Zürich early, to – well, presumably Herr Weiss explained? My cancer is not very advanced, I don't think I'll be any kind of problem to you –'

'No, no, you are not understanding, Joyce!' Vreni Stauben became animated. 'I am not having any problems with this – I have seen the very sicks, the very sicks. I only wonder . . .' She twiddled an invisible dial, tuning in to her wonderment. 'But really, I am too rude!'

Vreni Stauben hurried about, breathing with the rumbling squeak of the obese. She fetched towels and sheets for Joyce, then made up the bed. She showed Joyce the kitchen cupboards with their plastic boxes of muesli, and the fridge with its quarter-litre tubs of yoghurt.

'If you are up first of time,' Vreni said, grinning conspiratorially, 'I will be frying the *Röschti* and the eggs.' Then she gave Joyce a set of keys and demonstrated the tricky manoeuvre required to turn the mortise lock. All the while, the smoky-blue cat with the shaved belly padded along behind them. 'She is the stupid animal,' Vreni contended indulgently – and Joyce, who didn't like cats, silently concurred.

When Joyce was alone in her new room, she sat down on the side of one of the beds, unzipped her ankle boots and eased them off. *You've been on us a lot today*, her sore feet complained. *We're not used to it.*

Well. Joyce bent forward to grasp first one ball, then the second. *I know that, but you may have to.* She lay back on the pillows, intending to rest for a moment, but unconsciousness mugged her with its soft cosh.

She dreamt of Isobel, a Tommy-girl in a khaki wool uniform, puttees wound round her milk-bottle calves, a salad bowl tin helmet on her crunchy dyed hair. Joyce's daughter was hunched up in a shell crater; illuminated by the bursting of *whizz-bangs*, one of her cheeks was shinily artificial. *Gutta-percha.* Ueli Weiss – in a full-length leather coat, Iron Cross at his high collar – stood smoking on the far side of a black pool, from the middle of which poked a skeleton's hand holding a pistol. Despite the shellfire it was eerily silent, except for Chopin's B Flat Sonata, played very softly by a virtuoso who was out of sight in *no man's land*. The melody insinuated itself within the after-tone of each note.

The Angel of Mons slithered down out of the hot orange sky. It was wearing Marianne Kreutzer's tight face mask, and its billowing white silk robe looked *deliciously cool*. Even though the Angel was fifteen feet high, once it had grasped Isobel under her arms, it was unable to lift her.

'I'll miss the flight, Mum,' Isobel said. 'Don't leave me here.' She pawed at her mother's blouse, her *stupid manicured nails* catching in the fabric.

Joyce cried, 'Get off me!' And woke to the terrifying banality of Vreni Stauben's cat, which was trampling her upper body. It was dark. After she had switched the light on and been to the toilet, she checked her watch: 3.44 a.m. She undressed, put the cat out the door and returned to the twin bed. She fell asleep immediately, and in the morning was hungry enough for both the *Röschti* and two fried eggs.

Offertorium

Every day, after breakfast, Joyce left the Universitätstrasse apartment and walked the Zürich streets. Vreni Stauben tried to persuade her to take cabs – or at least the tram or bus. But Joyce told her she preferred to walk.

In the mornings, when she set out on her expeditions, there were still misty rags hanging from the trees on the wooded slopes surrounding the city; then, as the morning wore on, the rags were torn away. There was a succession of high, bright, chilly days. With each venture she made, Joyce unwound the thread of orientation, down between the dully neoclassical museum and library buildings, then across the Limmat Bridge, before trailing it round the edge of the old town.

Vreni told Joyce about Weinberg's, and the cheaper department store, Globus, both of which were on Bahnhofstrasse. She took her time shopping, far more than she would have done at the Bull Ring in Birmingham. The shop assistants were no more *presentable* than those at home, *but, to be frank* – and since she was addressing herself alone, why shouldn't she be – they were far more attentive, and polite, and spoke *markedly better* English as well.

Joyce realized she was *building a wardrobe*, and it was from this alone she deduced that her sojourn in Zürich would be for *quite a while*: the hours sheathed in good-quality cotton underwear, the days helped into a comfortable, yet stylish, navy two-piece – this in a lightweight wool, since Vreni had told her to expect warmer weather in April.

At Apartment 7, Universitätstrasse 29, Joyce adapted herself to the rhythms of her landlady's life. It was much as she had always feared: the petty sumptuary rules, the cat-and-weather conversations, the talk of milk supply – and ailments. A pooling of sensibility with no sex barrier to prevent it: is that my support hose, or hers?

Joyce had always understood, rationally, that Derry would predecease her – the X chromosome, the single malts, the many cigarettes, the sedentary job – but worse than the fear of his absence was the idea of any other presence. In the darkest days of mourning him, when she didn't even dress herself, Joyce recoiled from the phone calls of even her closest and oldest friends, their very feminine concern. Her anxieties were half formed, and all the worse for it: the purgatorial doom of a shared scone in the café of a National Trust property, for ever and ever and ever. *Lord Jesus Christ King of glory, deliver the souls of all the faithful departed from the pains of hell . . .*

One morning, after Joyce had been a week or so at Frau Stauben's apartment, the two women lingered together over breakfast. Vreni was showing her photographs of the previous year's Easter play at St Anton's; this was, Joyce knew, her other way of memorializing Gertrud. Tossing aside the final photo – a particularly choleric cherub, tightly held by a long-suffering angel – Vreni said, 'Ueli – Herr Weiss – he called in the night before to ask me if you are being all good.'

Joyce didn't think this an inquiry after her moral welfare; she dug doughtily at the remains of her muesli. 'Oh, really,' she said, 'I'm perfectly all right – don't I seem all right?'

'It is – I – it is . . .' As Vreni was not someone to whom tact came naturally, she mangled on: 'I am not knowing what is the stage of your treatments, Joyce. I am so sorry, you forgive me for not inviting this talk, but I am confused, I do not know what to say to Ueli –'

'You don't have to say anything to Herr Weiss!' Joyce snapped, and was going to add that her health was *none of his business*, had not Frau Stauben tipped her glasses off the end of her long, veined nose and put the doll's eyes on Joyce. The morning sunlight was intense in the small kitchen, and a sort of nimbus edged her soft form. 'But I am thinking,' (Butt ai amm zinkin . . .) she mispronounced with great care, 'that you are not so ill at all. You have not the look' – she skidded into Schweizerdeutsch – '*Sie gsehnd nöd uus wie öpper wo Chräbs hätt*' – then back out – 'the look of a cancer person. I know this things, you see.'

The daughters of other women looked up at them from the table. Teenagers dressed as immaterial beings, their smiling faces blank and startled in the flash, waiting for experience to shade them in.

Without being aware of having taken her leave, or taken up her new coat, handbag and gloves, Joyce found herself outside in the street, the *fairly high* heels of her new shoes vigorously tapping on the paving. She followed the thread back towards the river; on the museum's portico a muscular goddess did dancercise with the globe. Joyce walked over the bridge, then climbed the stairs beside the gothic grotto to the Lindenhof, the small park she had ventured out to from the Widder Hotel on the first night of her resurrection.

Could it be true, what the fat lady said? Could Joyce be recovering from the cancer? Phillimore had said the origin of her cancer was 'occult'; might the dissolution of these tumours be equally mysterious?

In the dead of recent nights Joyce had awoken often, and looked across the empty twin bed to where the feline darkness rubbed against the jet windowpane. Was it outside, her cancer? Had it been *put out* there, to stare back in at her with eyes as round and black as an umlaut? Was it watching her body, huddled up in the duvet, for signs of defeat: the unruly cells, cowed, mending their own membranes, retreating into the milky opalescence of their cytoplasm? . . . *fac eas, Domine, de morte Iransire ad vitam . . . Allow them, O Lord, to cross from death into the life . . .*

Below her sun rays skipped, wavelet to wavelet. Pretty. Ordinary. Pretty. Beside her the Stadthäuser loomed. Sandy. Dull. Sandy. Joyce was beginning to read Zürich, a little; the individual buildings, the streets, the hills beyond – all were outlined. Some of these were filled in – with colour, texture and form – while others were simply labelled, e.g., 'Rathaus', and given a brief description. She went on, threading through side streets empty in the mid-morning. She had it in mind to pick up the bras she had ordered the day before yesterday – although she also knew that it was far too early.

In Bahnhofstrasse Joyce was arrested by a chocolatier's window. Here was the inverse of the edible leather goods in the old town; the slick brown *stuff*, melted and poured into the moulds of quotidian things – books and biros, coins and watches. It was tempting, this parallel world of sweet substance, and Joyce tried casting herself as a little old English governess, stuffing a Gladstone bag full of it, before boarding the train that would take her home across Europe.

The train home, *maybe I could take that?* The plane was out of the question: *if I feared death when I was on my way to commit suicide, then what would it be like now?* Every jolt or jostle threatening to pop this bubble of shiny, reflective awareness? Joyce walked across the road towards the station, eyes fixed, unseeing, on the stony breasts of the gods and goddesses guarding its clock. *What does Weiss want?*

A group of street drinkers were clustered convivially beside a plinth, upon which a bearded patriarch was ever-striding towards an industrious Zion. Joyce thought that, *this being Switzerland*, they were going about the business of intoxication in a sober fashion, the only thing to distinguish them from still soberer citizens a certain lack of registration that recalled the transfers Isobel used to rub on to cardboard panoramas with a pencil. They stood – two men, two women, one brown, three white – in kinship with the drift of last autumn's leaves. It was only when Joyce was within a few feet of them, and one of the women took a swig from her can of lager, then looked round, that she recognized her own daughter.

'Mum – Mummy!' Too loud, the closest living relative cried: an egregious acquaintance forcing intimacy in a crowd. The man with her was Asian – *a Tamil?* His face smooth – firm, yet fleshy – his lips symmetrical, his thick blue-black hair pressed down on his brow by a cream-wool hat.

Isobel set her can on the ground and rushed to embrace her unyielding mother. 'Oh, Mummy, I was so scared. Oh, Mummy, I thought you were –'

Dead. Joyce completed the sentence, internally, but it was Isobel she meant. She realized that Frau Stauben's Gertrud and her own Isobel had become mushed up in her mind, both household goddesses, the objects of useless and chintzy cults.

'Where've you been? I've been back to the hotel every day, I've waited there loads, they – they called the police in the end –'

'I'm not surprised, Isobel,' Joyce said firmly, disengaging herself from the beery embrace.

'Are you all right? Are you going somewhere – d'you want me to come with?' This, all in a rush. *Please take me with you, Mummy, please?* The teary little face imploring among the tricycles, *nurseries in those days, well, they were a bit like prisons.*

'I hardly think we want to discuss this in front of your . . .' Joyce eyed the Tamil man and the two others, who were *not so respectable after all*: the man had his front teeth missing, the woman an open sore by her ear. '. . . friends.'

Mother and daughter walked together into the front hall of the Hauptbahnhof: an enormous, barrel-vaulted space, with dingy light filtered down through many semicircular windows. The atmosphere was stale with diesel fumes and the odours of the departed masses. A bulgy, gilded dummy of a pierrot was dangling from the beams overhead; Joyce supposed this was meant to be *public art*. She stopped and said to Isobel: 'I'm not going anywhere, I told you that already. I'm staying here, in Zürich –'

127

'But, Mum –'

'I also told you, Isobel, that I'm fed up to the back-bloody-teeth with carrying you, girl.' From ancestral workshops came the bash and whine of her long-gone Black Country accent. 'If you're going to hang about on street-bloody-corners with this – this riff-raff, you can keep out of my road.'

'I'm worried about you, Mum.'

'Worry about yourself.'

'What about the house? What're you gonna do about that?'

Red and wet – was that how Isobel's cheeks were always going to be? Unreasonably – because she knew this was only the lost girl's compounded neurosis, *no home to go to at chucking-out time* – Joyce grew still angrier with her *grasping, ungrateful, sot* of a daughter.

'The house, the house – that's all you ever think about, Isobel. Worried you won't be getting your money any time soon, are you? Honestly, if your father could see you now!' *If he could, he'd give her a hug, stroke her stupid dyed hair. Comfort her.*

Isobel was now sobbing; Swiss travellers hurried past, eyes averted, heading for the ticket machines. Joyce got a pen and notebook out of her handbag, and, distraught as she was, Isobel still noticed this new acquisition. Joyce scrawled Vreni Stauben's address and phone number on a page, tore it out and handed it to her daughter.

'This is where I'm staying, if you feel you have to reach me. I don't want to know where you are, Isobel, not until you straighten yourself out.'

'But, Mum, I've got no . . . You see, my credit card –'

Joyce forestalled this *bloody beggary*, so at odds with the nation, its cavernous Alps stuffed with *hard cash*. She got out her wallet and slapped five rust-coloured notes into her daughter's hand; then she tried to walk away, briskly, without a backward glance, *deliver them from the lion's mouth*, but Isobel was still quicker.

The drunk woman grappled at Joyce's arm, and it took fifty or a hundred yards to shake her off. She fell back to the group by the statue, and the last her mother saw of her, when she did look, was Isobel being comforted by the Tamil man, who had put down his beer and clasped her in an embrace that – since he was a full head shorter – appeared *bloody ridiculous*.

Sanctus

Joyce used her own key to the apartment, and walked straight down the corridor and into the main room. Ueli Weiss and Marianne Kreutzer were on one of the sofa-slabs; Vreni Stauben sat quivering on a chair. The dusty curtains had been opened and the blinds rolled up; there was a figure at the window, and, when it pivoted to confront Joyce, it took a while for her to establish its sex.

Then he said, 'Mrs Beddoes – Joyce, if I may?' in flawless English, while advancing to take her hand. 'This is an intrusion – and an unexpected one for you – so, you must please forgive us?'

Is he wearing fancy dress? But no, it was a purple-trimmed soutane with wide, flaring skirts; a vivid purple sash cut across his tubular upper body; and a black biretta with a purple tuft was set on top of his head – the capital of this human column.

'I am Monsignor Reiter,' the priest announced – not without a trace of pride – 'but please, call me Jean.'

Joyce noticed the gold band on his wedding finger, and a white gold signet ring set with diamonds on his little one. He was young, this priest, and so white-skinned that he looked as if the pigment had been sucked out of him. He was also very tall, with a long El Greco face and black glossy hair so dense that even though he must have shaved that morning – evidenced by the fresh nick on his sharp Adam's apple – his hollow cheeks were already blue-shadowed by new stubble.

'How do you do,' Joyce conceded.

Vreni began flapping, asking Joyce if she wanted tea . . . coffee. Even Marianne, who was in an eau-de-Nil silk top *that must have cost a small fortune*, seemed a little awed by the prelate.

'Why,' Joyce asked him, 'are you here?'

'I am a papal chaplain,' Reiter explained, 'charged by the Curia with the task of assessing certain kinds of . . . well, perhaps the least prejudicial way of putting it would be to call them "unusual events".' He raised his eyebrows; it was a radical move that made of his face something comical and expressive; temporarily, he appeared dumbfounded by his own words, overawed by his own magnificence.

They were still standing. Joyce paced herself. She slowly unbuttoned her coat, retreated to the vestibule to hang it up – together with the woollen tam she had bought at Day's – then, returning to the living room, she sat down on the least comfortable of Vreni Stauben's chairs: an aluminium frame with a leather sling for a seat. She didn't feel particularly intimidated by the situation – priests, doctors, where was the difference? She had dealt with such professionals all her working life, and, as Derry had been a solicitor, she had also socialized with lawyers.

Joyce let her gaze track from one Swiss to the next. Vreni Stauben was cowed. 'Ueli – Herr Weiss,' she said, wheezing self-exculpation, 'he has been making calls all the days to say how is Frau Beddoes?'

'And you told him I was . . . fine?'

'You did not seem like the cancer patient to me, Joyce.' She allowed herself the upturned palms of a martyr.

Weiss held the tip of one finger up to his walrus moustache. 'When we first met, outside the chapel, I saw a very sick woman.' A second finger poked at the charged atmosphere. 'But when you came to St Anton's you were much better.' Weiss, Joyce thought, had the professional manner of someone who had no defined profession. 'I could tell, because I had already seen how sick you were . . . Und now, well, Frau Beddoes' – he withdrew the finger, laughed curtly – 'these big walks round the town, and – you must forgive her – but Frau Stauben, yes, she has been telling me with what – *der Appetit?*'

131

'With what relish,' said the Papal Chaplain, relishing the opportunity to correct his countryman's English.

'So, yes, exactly: with what relish you have been eating her *Röschti*. Und now, we see here a very sprightly, yes? Sprightly lady. Well, already when I was talking with Father Grappelli about you – and you saying what had happened with Hohl – I am thinking this is not usual, it is strange happening. So, well, we are being very careful – Grappelli, he is frightened, but I say we must –'

Leaning forward, Joyce cut Weiss off with a wave of her hand. 'Can I be right in what I'm hearing, Herr Weiss?' She was as matter-of-fact as if she had been querying bed allocation or late laundry delivery. 'Are you suggesting that what has happened to me is a' – she grimaced – 'miracle?'

Joyce wasn't at all surprised that Vreni Stauben crossed herself, but a little that Marianne Kreutzer did so as well.

'Aha!' Reiter interjected. 'This term – we don't use it so much nowadays; it is very value-laden, I think. The preferred expression – certainly during preliminary inquiries – is "perceived suspension of natural law".'

Joyce laughed at his bureacratic jargon of the supernatural; laughed with Falstaffian vigour. 'Gentlemen – ladies,' she said once her merriment had subsided, 'I can't deny that I'm feeling extremely well indeed – and I'm happy to discuss the possible reasons for this, but, before we go any further, two things: I think I heard the kettle boil, Vreni. I'm thirsty and I would like some tea.' Frau Stauben got up and, after soliciting the others' orders for hot drinks, clucked off to the kitchen. 'Second,' Joyce resumed, 'if I have been the . . . subject? Of a suspension in natural law, could you tell me, please, who has been doing the suspending?'

It seemed that Weiss hadn't expected her to raise this point so soon. The moustache winced, and he nervously shot the pink cuffs of his striped shirt. Marianne busied herself in her handbag – only the Monsignor had the sang-froid to reply: 'Well, now, Mrs

Beddoes, these are very early days, and the procedure by which such extraordinary events are authenticated is a lengthy one. I'm only on secondment here, preparing initial reports for the diocesan bishop –'

Joyce silenced him with another imperious wave. 'That's quite enough of that, thank you, Monsignor Reiter. Let me put it another way: if you want me to cooperate at all, you'll have to answer that question right away; otherwise I'll pack my bag and leave.'

Silence. *Holy, holy, holy, Lord God of Sabaoth, Heaven and earth are full of . . . dust and cat hair.* The eyes of the delegation all slid to the kitchen doorway where Vreni Stauben was standing, a spoon in one squashy hand, a tea strainer in the other. Her usually mild expression was tempered by an intensity Joyce hadn't seen before: a fierce parental pride, not in some mundane swimming, jumping or instrumental achievement – but in a transcendent one.

After Derry died their friends had drifted away. Joyce had expected this – been prepared for it, too. Derry had been far more gregarious than her; it was he who organized get-togethers. She prized this in him, just as he valued her asperity, her reserve. It was not that Joyce was incapable of friendship; loyalty, she felt, was akin to insurance payments – something you *kept up*. There were her two friends from girlhood: Ruth, now retired to the Yorkshire Wolds, and Iris, who had gone down to London, where she maintained a long-lasting lesbian union. Then, when Iris's companion had died, she uprooted again and returned to Birmingham. She had stayed with Joyce for a month the previous year, while she hunted for a suitable cottage in the Forest of Arden. An indefatigable presence, round-faced, petite, *vigorous*.

Then there were Miriam and Sandra, both former colleagues; although her friendship with the former, who had once been her secretary, was always *a little strained*. On several occasions Miriam had negotiated the tortuous arterial roads all the way from Snow Hill in order to take Joyce for her radiotherapy at Mid-East.

Sandra, who had been a long-serving and much revered consultant paediatrician, now reposed in the leafy splendour of Edgbaston. Every room of her Arts and Crafts villa was like a conservatory, while the entire house resounded with the song of grandchildren – or such was Joyce's impression on her infrequent visits. Sandra dispensed meals whenever required – came over, too – but she was hardly *proactive*. *I had to ask her to take me to the clinic – and that was hateful. Shameful.*

Self-pity was not in order, though: *I had a life*, and even, briefly, after Derry had died, *another lover*; a source – surely justifiable? – of considerable satisfaction. *Age would not wither me.* Despite all this, the way those couples had *dropped me* hurt. The self-satisfied solicitors and their WI wives, it was they who were withering as they dealt the pack of remaining individuals into bridge pairs.

Obscurely, Joyce blamed Derry for this, and related it to a failure in their intimacy: they had been *close*, *certainly*, yet the bulk of the unspoken communication between them had been that there was *nothing much worth saying*.

All this while the three seated Swiss looked at the one standing; all this while the Magi adored the Saviour's mother. It was preposterous, *most definitely*, the *dippy shrine* to the miraculous teenager; the beatification of Gertrud – first spotty, then holy. Oddly, Joyce now felt empowered by all those wordless decades she had spent with Derry. There was a shrewdness in them – a native cunning.

The Swiss had their coffee; Joyce took her tea. They talked, a devilish interplay between pragmatism and spirituality. It transpired that Ueli Weiss had a severely disabled son. 'A hard birth, there was not enough oxygen,' he explained, and Joyce thought *he's describing his marriage as well*. The baby had been – and this was stated like a menu choice – 'a vegetable': deaf, blind, dumb, paralysed. One day, Weiss, as had been his custom, took the persistently vegetative infant with him to visit Gertrud Stauben, who was in hospital, dying of leukaemia.

Joyce could envisage Vreni's daughter, her skin as translucent as dripping wax, stretching out her anaemic fingers to draw strength from the little boy's potato head . . . 'There are three classes of such happenings,' Monsignor Reiter said. '*Quoad substantiam* – this is the biblical act of the Saviour, and some of his saints.' The young prelate had sat and crossed his legs, the skirts of his soutane falling open to reveal tan cotton trousers. 'Then there is *quoad subiectum*, which, while not entailing the full resurrection of the dead, can nevertheless exhibit the full restitution – *restitutio in integrum* – of irreparably damaged organs; the growth, even, of new ones.'

So far as Joyce was concerned, it was this second kind of . . . not faith but collective suspension of disbelief that Reiter was investigating. The dying girl had laid on her hands more than fifteen years ago: 'My son, he was, as I say, a vegetable. Now, he is not the totally normal fellow – no one is saying this –'

'But he feeds himself, dressing too,' Marianne broke in. 'He can walk and is talking these few words, so.' She leant forward, her usually saturnine face animated. 'This was baby with no brain – *Siis Hirni isch Hackfleisch* –'

'The grinded meat,' Weiss put in.

'Now he is doing these things, but with what?' Her own struggle to be understood echoed this incomprehensible happening.

Joyce could picture the young man: wet-chinned, butting his big head at a door, his features grosser than his father's, and in place of Weiss's thick moustache the charcoal smudge of male puberty.

Reiter was pedantic: 'We don't expect the doctors to support what we're trying to prove for one second; nor do we look for doctors who are Catholics; the evidence is the evidence and we will abide by it. But even getting the doctors to give me interviews, the hospitals to release the records, and, naturally, arranging for Erich to have the necessary scans and examinations – this is taking the longest time, you see.

'Then there is the relationship between the diocese and Rome. We are,' he said with a smirk, 'like any other very large organization, so, there is much paperwork. Once already, the Bishop here in Zürich has referred this matter, but the report has come back: there must be more tests, further confirmation.'

It was easy to understand Vreni Stauben's motivation: better than memory – or formaldehyde – faith would be the ultimate preservative; an acknowledgement from the highest level of the beatification that every parent bestows on her child. As for Reiter, he was a functionary, and this was his equivalent of a doctor's cure; Joyce well understood how such statistics secured funding and advanced careers. But Ueli Weiss and Marianne Kreutzer? It was difficult to *peg them as zealots*. Was there a murkier guilt that needed assuaging, some sin of dereliction that must be shriven? Or was it only that this was a middle-aged man with a business card, who had never done much business worth speaking of? Vreni Stauben had mentioned a car dealership in Berne that Weiss had inherited; however, in her very glancing remarks there was the suggestion that this was a going concern, for which he had done very little of the running.

All this clicked through Joyce's mind with tight precision as she listened to Reiter. She was making the kind of assessments that had been integral to her work as a high-level administrator; an analysis of ways and means and motives that, since retirement, had seized up to become mere crankiness. Sitting on her Modernist throne, Joyce was empowered to make statements *ex cathedra*.

'So' – she put a stop to the Papal Chaplain – 'because I don't look as if I'm dying, you want – you want to believe – that I may've been subject to' – she savoured the phrase – 'a suspension of natural law.'

'*Quoad modum*,' Reiter said succinctly. 'This is the third class: a recovery from a fatal, progressive malady that is spontaneous, and that, even if it could be managed by medicine, would take a long time and a lot of resources. Yes, Joyce, we do believe this may have happened to you.'

Fac eas, Domine, de morte Iransire ad vitam . . . Allow them, O Lord, to cross from death into the life . . . Joyce laughed heartily again – and although the lay Catholics grimaced, she was pleased to see Reiter joining in her secular merriment. 'And how, may I ask, did Frau Stauben's daughter perform this, ah . . .' She fluttered her fingers in allusion to the politically incorrect miracle. *Mors slopebit et natora, Cum resurget creatura, Judicanti res-pon-sura* . . . The awesome phrases wormed their way into her inner ear.

'Here are two things for you,' Reiter said. 'First thing. You may not be familiar with what Catholics believe here; these intercessions can occur years later, called forth – provoked, if you prefer – by the prayers of the faithful. Second thing. On the evening that you met with Herr Weiss, Marianne Kreutzer and Father Grappelli . . . well, this little chapel by the Lindenhof, it is – it has become – entirely unofficially, of course – a lot like a shrine for Frau Stauben's daughter. Most days' – he looked to Weiss for confirmation and the otter head dipped – 'they go to pray there.'

Joyce had a vision of the power 'provoked' by their prayers: a neon thunderbolt that shot along the dull Zürich boulevards. It zapped into the flat at 84 Gertrudstrasse, where Joyce sat with Dr Hohl, and, by snapping open her jaw, helped to stay the assister-of-suicide's hand, before playing up and down her abdomen – crackling purple veins on the glassy skin of a van de Graaff generator – irradiating her diseased liver with the entirely free, and on demand, X-rays of faith.

They were all staring at her. Reiter had stopped speaking; Vreni Stauben was cradling the framed photograph of the dead girl, which she had retrieved from her own domestic shrine. Thinking back to her foolish confidences at the Kronenhalle, Joyce said, 'I'm not a fool, you know –' Weiss sucked air sharply, but there were limits to *Treu und Glauben* and she pressed on: 'This strikes me as a very smart . . . very political move on the part of the deity, given what Herr Weiss told me about Dr Hohl's organization, the city's government, the Catholic majority here in Zürich – and so forth.'

Reiter sat forward, gathering his skirts over his knees, an action at once sexless and coquettish. He pressed his slim white hands together and brought them up in front of his long expressive face. Joyce thought of Phillimore, who, with his flaxen fringe thatching farmer's features, was a *peasant* compared with this princeling of the Vatican.

'You are entirely astute, Joyce,' Reiter said. 'And, although there is nothing to prevent the Lord involving himself in the minutiae of local government, I concede that from outside the Church this would appear very . . . well, worldly.'

Joyce decided she was going to enjoy doing business with Monsignor Reiter – and business it was most definitely going to be. His English, of course, was *far too good* – especially for an Englishman. It made everything he said pitilessly clear: 'Should you decide to cooperate with our investigation, the medical examinations, any treatment you require, accommodation – also a per diem: all of these we would help you with.'

'I don't really object to Dr Hohl's activities at all,' Joyce shot back at him. 'Otherwise I wouldn't have gone to him. On the contrary, I think he and his organization are doing good work – giving people a real choice.'

Weiss's eyes were popping, and Vreni Stauben caught a sob in her fat cheeks, but Reiter was unperturbed. 'It isn't really a question of conviction, Mrs Beddoes,' he said judiciously. 'It's more a matter of finding common cause. Besides, the primary objective here is not to campaign against assisted suicide' – this phrase he couldn't forbear from grimacing over: bitter pips – 'but to investigate events of an overpoweringly spiritual nature: the evidence of God working through humanity.'

'I understand that,' Joyce remarked succinctly, although she didn't believe for a second that Ueli Weiss's prayers to Vreni Stauben's dead daughter had cured her of cancer. This odd feeling – not of health but of a kind of competent nullity – was simply a mundane plateau covered with a dusty rug, on all sides of which the abyss still fell away, deep and dark and deadly. Vreni Stauben's wombless Birman came padding into the room and over to where Joyce sat. It looked at her with its *stupid vain* eyes.

Ueli Weiss began talking with his tone of slightly egregious, boyish competence. The necessary tests, he said, could take weeks – perhaps months. Even if Joyce was in a position to demonstrate that she had considerable – and liquid – assets, obtaining a *Niederlassungsbewilligung*, or type C residence permit, from the federal government might still prove impossible, given her condition. But he, Weiss, in conjunction with the diocese, had access to the best immigration lawyers; and there seemed to them to be a prima facie case for Joyce claiming refugee status.

'Refugee status?' Joyce goggled at Weiss, who today was sporting a well-cut flannel suit in a highly neutral shade of blue. 'What exactly am I seeking refuge from, the NHS?' The Swiss looked blank, so she elaborated, 'The medical care in England, I mean.'

'No, no.' Weiss remained in earnest. 'We are thinking that you are asking for the *Asylberechtigung* from Hohl, his people – the pressure they made to kill yourself.'

I was subject to no pressure or duress by anyone . . . 'But they have safeguards for this, a tape recording, a contract –'

'So, so, we know this, *natürlich* . . .' He went on, reassuring Joyce that there would be no fuss – that wasn't the way things were done in Zürich. It would be a case of back-door representations, informal interviews, the subtle influencing of politicians and jurists. There was a case to be made – of that much they were certain; the shifting demographic of religious affiliation in the canton chimed with a gathering nationalism . . . *You are seeing our new kind guests. Black guests, brown guests.* How ironic, she thought, me and Isobel's Tamil friend. *Two of a kind.*

Joyce was surprised that Monsignor Reiter ceded all this suasion to the unpersuasive Weiss. Despite this, she had resolved to go along with them before he eventually finished speaking. She couldn't have said what her motivation was; certainly, it had nothing to do with their aims, while her own were inchoate. This wasn't, it occurred to Joyce, as they all stood and tramped down the dim corridor to dead Gertrud's *Zimmer*, to do with ends at all; but, rather, means: the filling out of forms would fill in otherwise featureless days. There would also be appointments to attend – this would be *comforting*, a small sort of *part-time job*. And then there was the prospect of her own flat. *I've got to get away from this bloody cat!*

Vreni Stauben, Ueli Weiss and even Marianne Kreutzer – they all knelt down, seemingly unselfconscious, in front of the shrine; bowing their heads before the schoolgirl's bibelots, hair ribbons and dag-tails of macramé. Reiter darted a sharp look at Joyce: a schoolmasterly prohibition on giggling or fidgeting. Then he began chanting, low and clear, in Latin, while the trio made the appropriate responses, '*Credo in Deum Patrem . . . Et in Jesum Christum . . . Credo in Spiritum Sanctum . . .*'

A flat of her own would involve Joyce in her newly adoptive city, allow her to become part of it – then she pulled herself up short. This was *ridiculous! I'm terminally ill! Quid sum miser tunc dicturus, Quem patronum togaturus, Cum vix justus sit securus? What then shall I say, wretch that I am? What advocate entreats to speak for me?* The righteous Swiss had Monsignor Reiter, his purple sash glowing in the gloomy bedroom, with its nightlights wavering in their faithful exhalations. Reiter had said the Church could not sanction Saint Gertrud's growing cult – yet here he was, tending its shoots.

If it hadn't been for the curiosity, awakened in Joyce by the cynical Marianne Kreutzer's incongruous piety, she might have headed back to her own house – but then it could never again be a home, not now; the final washing up had been done, and her underwear itemized for alms. Might have, even so – but then there was that dreadful fear of flying, and the insufferable burden that was Isobel. Might have – but then there was Switzerland itself, its reassuring orderliness, its stolid vitality.

Easter came and then went. Joyce attended the children's passion play that Vreni Stauben put on at St Anton's. It seemed no different to such productions in Middle England: the same halting declamations and belted-out song, the same painted faces and haphazard gowns. The narrative – which linked environmental concerns to the Resurrection – had innocent new flowers sprouting on *Gründonnerstag*, only for them to be scythed down on *Karfreitag*, as the Saviour was nailed up. Joyce found the play's spirituality as flabby as anything Anglicans might have originated.

She told herself she went out of simple loyalty; that the week she had stayed at Universitatstrasse had created a bond between her and Vreni Stauben, shared domesticity being more adhesive than any *mumbo-jumbo*, no matter how ancient or hallowed. The truth was that Joyce was lonely – achingly so.

The heft of the diocese had secured her a flat in a small block on Saatlenstrasse, in the suburb of Oerlikon, which lay beyond the wooded hump of the Zürichberg. With her refugee status under consideration and a temporary residence permit granted, Joyce was freed from the exposure of repeated interviews with Frau Mannlë, the Fremdenpolizei officer who held her dossier.

Her pension income continued to be deposited in her bank account; the running costs of the old family home were handled by direct debit. A small sum was also being discreetly paid into a Swiss bank account, so that for her Zürich rent and her nugatory expenses

Joyce could simply withdraw money from a cashpoint. Any questions of taxation might, an adviser at the lawyers' office told her, be postponed until her residency had been placed on a more permanent footing.

Joyce felt sorry for the solid, inter-war, Bournville semi, the tidy rooms growing mustier as spring quickened the world without: fluffing up the privet, greening the lawn, switching on the bulbs – white, then yellow, then red, violet and orange – in the brown beds. Yet this close dormancy seemed in equipoise with her new Oerlikon apartment.

She had welcomed the stripped-down state of the four small rooms. Light fittings, blinds, carpets, kitchen appliances – all had gone with the previous tenants; this was, Ueli Weiss had told her, the Swiss way. It meant that Joyce had to make several expeditions to the Sihl City shopping centre, where she had wandered the atriums and climbed the escalators, consulted catalogues and spoken with sales assistants. She didn't mind this, and such was the efficiency of the local service sector that the stuff was all delivered and installed within ten days.

By then, with characteristic competence, Joyce had completed her local orientation. She knew where to shop for groceries, where to buy the dockets that had to be attached to rubbish bags, and how to sort that rubbish so as to conform to the draconian recycling ordinances.

To begin with the neighbours in her three-storey block were, if not exactly friendly, pointedly welcoming. Herr Siemens, the stumpy, bearded man who lived in the flat on the other side of the landing, stopped to chat when they met on the stairs. Joyce guessed he was a computer programmer, and soon enough he confirmed this. He was middle aged, probably *obsessive*, yet altogether gentle and *decent*, she thought. In the evenings he played electronic music, and, although the beeps and oscillations were hardly raucous, Herr

Siemens came across punctiliously, every two or three days, to confirm that his neighbour still did not object.

It was the same with the Pfeiffers, who lived in the flat below. Their two children, Rolf and Astrid, were no noisier than any other under-fives Joyce had been exposed to – if anything, markedly less so – yet Frau Pfeiffer came up regularly to ask if they were disturbing Joyce. She was a jolly, sloppy, young woman, with uncorseted breasts hanging loose in her cardigan; but, however slatternly Frau Pfeiffer may have been, she was always perfectly correct: polite and distant. Her counterpart in Birmingham would, Joyce felt sure, have been tattooed, pierced and offhandedly abusive – for Oerlikon was a predominantly working-class area, convenient for the workers at the nearby industrial estate.

When Joyce had moved in, it was Frau Pfeiffer who told her about the local shops, and directed her to the Peter Tea Room, as a place where an Englishwoman might get a cup of her national beverage. The mannish hair-do that Joyce had had chemically induced was becoming unruly, and, once again, it was Frau Pfeiffer who recommended a salon. But that was as far as it went – no further intimacy was encouraged. She was not alone in this: Herr Siemens was the same, as was the landlord, Herr Frech, who collected the rent in person. All of them remained standing some way off, a people at once fleshily corporeal and nevertheless exiguous: *ein verschlossenes Volk* – a hidden-away people – as the Swiss said of themselves.

The language barrier didn't help, although Joyce felt little inclination to surmount it. Her old evening-class German carried her only so far into the impenetrable accent; it was almost impossible to feel out the syntax lying beneath the slushy Schweizerdeutsch. Besides, she feared that the lack of nuance she experienced conversing with these people in a collage of languages – a little English, *ein bisschen* German, sometimes a soupçon of French – would remain, even if their meaning became as pellucid as the windows of their spick and span homes.

Joyce went for strolls along the railway line where allotment sheds comfortingly clustered, then followed the path that ran beside the River Glatt. Apart from the shallower pitch of the roofs on the boxy dwellings, and the precision of the spray-painted graffiti on the concrete bridges, these could have been dull promenades through the under-imagined outskirts of any small English city.

Or else Joyce turned the other way out of her block and went to the Peter, to sit in its cosy uglification of melamine tables and gingham curtains, watching the slow explosions of cigarette smoke from the ruined mouths of other elderly patrons. After this, telling herself – but for why? – that she ought to work off the *Apfelstrudel* and the squirty cream, Joyce would plunge uphill on the switchback trails that led to the top of the Zürichberg. Spring sunshine groped the evergloomy limbs of spruce and pine. The blackened trunks of their predecessors, done for by decay, lay tossed into gulleys. The toadstools were white warts on their flayed trunks, the atmosphere was rich with the odour of rotting bark.

Over the course of a month Joyce's walks grew longer and longer. It was difficult for her to deny to herself that this erect figure in a neat tweed suit and good walking shoes, who crunched over pebbles and skipped across puddles, was a very *sprightly* lady for her age. On the day she was due to go into town for the results of the medical examinations to which she had submitted, Joyce walked all the way to the top of the hill – feeling not the slightest shortness of breath – then over its thinning brow.

The spires of the Grossmünster and the Fraumünster stood down in the valley, stonily *lonesome pines*. The cloud lay down on top of the Uetliberg – a mauve-grey muff. She walked on along the ridge to the gates of a cemetery. It was only after noticing the words *Friedhof Fluntern* cut into the blocks of the wall that Joyce realized the trim cinder path, disappearing down an avenue of silver birches, led to her own grave.

Judex ergo cum sedebit, Quidquid latet apparebit, Nil inultum remanebit. When therefore the Judge takes His seat, Whatever is hidden will reveal itself, Nothing will remain unavenged. Her mother had died before her father, clawed apart by the crab in those pinched years after the war. The tears were creamy on her father's synthetic face by the graveside. Joyce had been twelve, a bad age for a girl to lose her beloved mother – perhaps the worst. Later on she did not lack insight, understanding that this experience – being forced to mother her father and her younger brother – had helped to make of her a tyrant when it came to self-reliance and Best Emotional Practice.

Joyce had had high expectations of the interviews with the Papal Chaplain and Father Grappelli. She had hoped that even the lawyers engaged by the diocese to pursue her claim to *Asylberechtigung* – and the public relations consultant that they, in turn, had taken on to give currency to this politically sensitive case – would prove interesting interlocutors. The notion of a contemporary miracle was, she thought, so bizarre that anything connected with it would take on a diverting hue.

This was not so. Instead, shiny blue and black suits in the monotonous ambience of corporate offices. His subtle fencing upon their first meeting at Vreni Stauben's dusty apartment had, Joyce realized, been Monsignor Reiter's play for her – body and soul. Now he had her, she was subjected to a celibate's passionate indifference. In place of that delicious worldliness they had fleetingly enjoyed in each other, they sat either side of the Bishop's desk, surrounded by filing cabinets that could have belonged to any organization.

The long, thin prelate was coiled into a swivel-chair. His flared soutane and purple sash – which, in a domestic context, had struck Joyce as charged with exoticism – were here diminished: not-so-fancy dress. The biretta sat on the blotter, the toy of God's executive. And so the Papal Chaplain examined her, his questions derived from a pre-printed sheet.

There were interviews alone with Reiter, and also ones with the Monsignor and Father Grappelli, who, it transpired, was to amend the first diocesan report on Gertrud Stauben so as to incorporate the evidence of Joyce's recovery – and recover she definitely had. The results of the exhaustive testing undertaken at the university's Kinderspital on Steinwiesstrasse had been conclusive: the tumour in Joyce's liver had radically contracted. Comparing her blood test results with the records obtained from Phillimore at the Mid-East, the medics – although not oncologists – could definitively establish that once more the body's chemical refinery was working at full capacity: tidying away glycogen, synthesizing vital plasma proteins and emulsifying lipids to produce crucial, digestion-aiding bile.

When he saw these data, Reiter allowed himself a rare quip: 'The liver is the body's saviour, no? After all, it is the one organ that can fully regenerate itself – be born again. Your liver, Joyce, well, it has risen from the dead.'

But Joyce was not wandering in the dewy garden of Gethsemane, clad all in white samite; she was trapped beside a filing cabinet as massive and grey as any boulder, looking at a calendar of the Dolomites.

Father Grappelli was preoccupied by one thing alone; had Joyce touched – or been touched by – either himself or Ueli Weiss on the evening they had all met for the first time? Joyce thought it *rather crass* that an omnipotent super-being should work through such clumsy agents and crude methods; touch, prayer – what were these? Surely, mere metaphysical sleight-of-hand combined with wishful thinking – no great marvel when compared to the blinding complexity of the largest organ in the human body, with its million-plus lobules, through which the life-blood percolated, via the very *fenestrae*, into a thousand sinusoids.

The parish priest's English wasn't good enough for him to interrogate Joyce alone, so Reiter acted as interpreter. Again and again they anatomized the encounter outside the chapel beside the Lindenhof. Joyce remembered the open doors, the overgrown Christ child, Weiss's showy coat and edible hair – these were the things that had lodged in her memory. There had been verbal shuttlecocks flicked across the language barrier, but whether English stroke had followed through on to Swiss hand . . . well, the more they peered into the dim recency, the more opaque the run of play became: Joyce saw Weiss's suede gloves slapping on his open palm – had he also, perhaps, touched her arm?

Like a student confined to a library, Joyce found it impossible to concentrate, and it was visions of a sexual kind that came to her. She was surprised – although not immoderately. Whatever *people might assume*, she hadn't been wholly quiescent during her five years of widowhood; there had been one brief affair. Derry had been a carnal man, and even when ill-health had brought about the diminuendo of his own desire, he still desired hers. In life, the conversation of their bodies had been exclusive, yet open-ended: he did not seek to possess his wife from beyond the grave.

She hadn't been expecting it, but two years after Derry died she was ambushed by the leisurely urgency of reawakened lust. However, worse than an unfamiliar body, she thought, would be its revelation. Strange clothing discarded on a well-known chair, the alien tang and slack tone of a distorted musculature . . . Yet it wasn't these, but the very companionability of his caresses that had made her cease to want them. Why bother to get undressed when there was as much intimacy to be gained in front of the television? It was irrelevant whose the body had been – a widower's, of course, one of their old circle. She still saw him from time to time. There were no hard feelings; after all, there hadn't been any in the first place; and that, Joyce concluded, was the essence of desire – it was all hard feelings.

Now, here, with the two priests in the Bishop's office, the feelings were hard, hard as lust before the climacteric. Joyce sensed a hot flush rouging her face – *have they noticed?* Most disconcerting of all, it was Ueli Weiss who mounted this ambush; Weiss's body that she wanted to see, flayed of its bourgeois woollen skin; Weiss's unkempt moustache tickling . . . *my belly?* Healthy blush-blood jetted from Joyce's hepatic veins, through her inferior vena cava, into her heart, into her hot head, round and round. This – this had been one of the conversations the crab had scuttled her away from: the delirious gabble of arousal.

That afternoon Joyce left the diocesan office and, instead of taking the tram home, walked over the Zürichberg again. As she paid out her thread of orientation from the old town to Oerlikon, she thought on this: there had already been a small item in *Neue Züricher Zeitung* by a sympathetic journalist. Nothing showy – the Church was playing its hand close to its chest – still, enough to create some impetus. There was to be a meeting called by the Christian-Democratic Party in the canton. A follow-up editorial in the same newspaper had proposed another referendum on assisted suicide, singling out Dr Hohl's organization for especial censure – and, in particular, the move to offer clinical depressives their service.

And when Joyce reached the end of the reel, at Saatlenstrasse, there was the Minotaur: Isobel, bullish with booze, crashing up and down outside the apartment block.

Of course, it hadn't been the media references to 'the English woman who has cheated Doctor Death' that had sent Isobel bellowing and snorting towards Oerlikon, but Vreni Stauben, who, having had Joyce explain to her, perfectly matter-of-factly, that her daughter was an alcoholic, still insisted that it would not be *mütterlich* to so reject her only child.

Isobel kicked at the wheelie-bins in the front yard. She shouted,

'Mummy, what're you doin', Mum? Are you a fuckin' *ghost*, or what?'

At least the Tamil man – whose mouthful, Joyce had gathered, was Chandrashekra – wasn't with her this time. He had come on other occasions, and the way he loitered had seemed far more menacing than Isobel's acting up.

Since he wasn't in evidence – and her daughter was making still more noise than usual – Joyce let her come up to the flat for her handout. *The beast*, with greasy horns of hair on her spotty forehead, trampled from bedroom to living room. 'Very ni-ce, very ni-ce,' she snorted, laying hoofs on curtains and upholstery, her nasal vowels a bad impression of a Birmingham hausfrau.

Stupidly, Joyce offered her tea. Isobel laughed like a dirty drain: 'Tea? I don't want your fucking tea, Mummy.' She was staying with Chandra at some kind of refugee hostel; the wardens were 'cunts', but, so long as he smuggled her in late at night and she left early in the morning, she could get away with it.

'But what're you getting away with?' Joyce made herself some peppermint tea anyway, hating herself for her neurotic little sponge-dabs on the worktop; *old womanish*, fending off dirty disorder and dusty death with nothing but *habit*.

She sat on the sofa nursing the hot vessel. 'Why're you still here, Izzy? Look, if you go and get your things and meet me at the airport, I'll buy you a ticket home right away –'

'I'm not bloody going!' Isobel bellowed. 'I've told you that before, an' I'm specially not going now I know you really are the fucking saint you've always behaved like.'

'Sit down before you fall over, Isobel – and what do you mean by that?'

'I may not be able to read bloody German – but Chandra can; we saw the thing in the paper. Oh, Mum.' She fell to her knees and came snuffling across the carpet. 'What've you got yourself involved in – are you getting treatment from some quack?'

Sympathy, Joyce thought, didn't suit her daughter. To be on the receiving end of it was to feel *damp and mauled*. 'No,' she said firmly. 'I'm not getting treatment any more, Isobel, there isn't any. You know that – I'm terminally ill –'

'Terminally ill?' Isobel laughed bitterly. 'Have you looked in a mirror recently, Mummy, you look bloody better than I do!'

There was a deep pathos in this: the bland room, barely furnished – a show home for a second life; the bigger, younger woman, her face rubbed with alcohol and then scraped raw by distress, kneeling at the sharp knees of the older, trimmer woman, who would apply no salve.

However, this awareness came later, after Isobel had got her 200 francs, crashed off down the stairs, bashed through the front doors, then disappeared down the road in the direction of the tram stop, still bellowing. It came later, after Joyce had gone across the landing, then downstairs, to apologize haltingly to Herr Siemens and Frau Pfeiffer, both of whom had stared at her blankly, while denying that they had heard anything untoward.

This came later, when Joyce sat in the darkness, staring out at the spider webs that veiled the orange head of the street lamp below her window. *Quantus tremor est futurus, Quando judex est venturus, Cuncta stricte discussurus* . . . She couldn't pinpoint exactly when it had happened, but the abundantly rich and complex orchestration had drained away, while the polyphony had dwindled to a single, deep, dry voice that spoke to her alone, of a *dread*, when the *Judge* shall come, to *judge* all things *strictly*.

On Sunday mornings Joyce went into town by tram for the noon mass at St Anton's. She alighted at the Bahnhof Stadelhofen and walked the last kilometre, summoning herself for the ordeal. Many eyes surreptitiously tracked her each time she entered the church. She knew what they sought: the submissive self-quartering of a genuflection. It was not enough that she be seen to be saved by their god; it was necessary that, like a sulky child, Joyce say 'thank you'.

The service was always well attended, and Father Grappelli, together with his deacon, made up for what they may have lacked in soulfulness with well-choreographed aplomb, moving from altar to pulpit and back again: slow-revolving dancers in white surplices. The congregation were dutiful under dull stained-glass windows; they sang louder than English Anglicans, but no more tunefully. The children fidgeted, although not much. Modern Jesus leant against his big cross above the altar, a bad Giacometti with a face like a pious turd. Joyce followed the order of service, telling herself that mouthing the responses and hymns was improving her Schweizerdeutsch accent by the Suzuki Method.

When Ueli Weiss and Marianne Kreutzer were alone, they sat near the front on the right, but when Weiss's son was with them they took the last pew, and sat by the aisle so that Erich could come and go as he pleased. Joyce assumed the young man had cerebral palsy – he certainly moved in the crabbed, spasmodic fashion of some CP victims she had seen.

When Joyce first encountered Weiss with Erich, a fortnight before, he had been pushing him on a swing in the playground next to the church. It was an incongruous sight: the child big enough to be the father to the man. Weiss hadn't bothered with an introduction, speaking of the forthcoming festival of Sechseläuten, when the old winter – in the form of a straw dummy stuffed with fireworks – would be dismissed by flames.

As they had chatted stiffly, the young man's white face plunged between them, again and again, ferociously concentrated on his controlled abandonment. Erich was better looking than his father. He had a beautiful mouth, such as it was impossible to credit Weiss's moustache with concealing; and the chocolate eyes were deeper, more profound. Was it fanciful to see in them an anguished intelligence, which had been released by the dead girl's touch but remained trapped inside brain tissue petrified by anoxia?

While Father Grappelli intoned the eucharist, the manly boy ranged up and down the nave, in and out of the side chapels. When reverent men came up to assist with the communion, Erich exited into the churchyard; Joyce could hear him out there, groaning. Was it because of his status as a miraculous being that Erich was allowed such licence? Or was it only another aspect of the Swiss's peculiarly repressive liberalism, whereby the community permitted anything, if the individual could overcome his or her own massive internalized constraint?

Were it not for those accusatory looks, Joyce might have taken communion. The Lord's Prayer – this was the muzak of spirituality; and the sign of peace was a brusque handshake, a murmured '*Frieden ist mit dir*', then Grappelli and his deacon got the picnic ready on the already laid cloth. It was, she thought, no worse flummery than the Anglican rite, nevertheless she balked; bloodwine, fleshwafer, *Scottie's Liver Treats*.

This went on throughout Easter, all in a month of Sundays. There were no more convivial lunches at the Kronenhalle; after the service Joyce chatted with the priest for a short while, then made her way back to the tram stop. Not even Vreni Stauben seemed inclined to invite her to the Universitätstrasse apartment for coffee and cakes. As for Reiter – on whose companionship Joyce had pinned such high hopes – by the end of the month he was gone.

'It was only in the – *was ist beratend*?'

'Advisory.' Unusually, it was Marianne who made good Weiss's deficiency.

'Yes, so, it was only in the advisory capacity Monsignor Reiter was acting. The diocesan staff, they will now be making this second report. The Monsignor is a papal chaplain you know –'

'I know.'

'Good, so, he has returned to Rome.'

They were standing on the church steps, and Weiss spoke as if he regarded Reiter as a rival of some specialized kind, *Celibacy being – this was Derry's fruity, lawyerly disdain – only an extreme sexual perversion.*

It was a drear day, the cloud covering the top of the Uetliberg, the spires and cupolas of the old town brownish smudges on the near-distance. Marianne Kreutzer held Erich's hand cursorily, as if he were human rubbish and she were looking for a bin to drop him in. The young man moan-whistled; he was handsome, but the steady hand of consciousness was needed to draw finer features.

Weiss went over to talk to a man in a navy trench coat. 'That is one of Ueli's guild,' Marianne explained. 'They are preparing for the *Umzug* now.' When Joyce looked perplexed, she continued: 'It is part off the *Sechseläuten*, the men, you know, they are having the big gets-together, the big lunch, the big dinner. They tell these special jokes and things.' Marianne seemed *awfully bored*, and, observing the grey foreclosure of her handsome features, Joyce wondered, not for the first time, *why does she bother?*

'He will, I think' (Eyezink) 'ask you to go with him to the Opernhaus; there is a special concert.' This she said offhandedly, yet *this is what she wants. But why?* Stylized poses, Marianne and she as Sabine women, Ueli Weiss naked except for a crested helmet, his penis adamant below a moustache of pubic hair . . . *Ridiculous*. 'Und so, you will come to Baden with me, for the spa day? It is a good thing for us girls (Uzgurls) 'to be . . . *verhätscheln?*'

'Pampered.' Weiss had rejoined them. Was it Joyce's imagination, or were his chocolate eyes melting with a vision of this *verhätscheln?*

Marianne Kreutzer pulled up outside the Saatlenstrasse block the following morning in the compact Mercedes that looked like a travel iron. Joyce was surprised to see Marianne driving – she had thought her one of life's more accomplished passengers. When they were pressing north along the neat crease of a dual carriageway, Joyce continued her reappraisal. From the way she managed the car alone, Joyce judged Marianne Kreutzer to be no mere ageing geisha, schooled in Catholic ritual and cultural pursuits, but a competent woman of this particular world: the trim farms, neat business parks and geometric plantations of conifers through which the spring sunlight strobed.

Marianne piloted the car with tight precision – and at speed. Light music mingled with car air freshener. She spoke little, yet when she caught Joyce's eye in the rear-view mirror, she smiled; not her usual constipated smirk but a grin that displayed tightly packed and beautifully maintained teeth, the white pipes of a cherished organ.

'So, yes, we are going for one night – you have the night things? Good, so, we are staying at Hotel Blume in the Kurgebiet – the healthy district. It is having its own hot spas like all these hotels, also very high space inside . . .' She lifted a leather-gloved hand from the steering wheel.

'An atrium?'

'That is it, an atrium. There we will be pampering our tummies after the treatments.' Again the smile. 'That is my treat to you.'

'No, no, really Marianne, I couldn't possibly –'

'Please. You will be making me cross if you refuse. Also, when I was running my *Gesell* – my company, I have done public relations for the hotel, so I have discounts.'

'You were in public relations?' To her own ears Joyce's remark sounded tinnily silly: tenth-rate conference-morning-coffee-break chit-chat.

'Yes, I was businesswoman for many years, working all the times, but I enjoy it.' The grin. 'Und, so, I never marry at that time. It did not bother me. I have the company workers – the employees, yes?'

'Yes, employees.'

'They are being children for me; and I have my faith, *natürlich*.'

The way Marianne referred to this 'faith' was as a spiritual utility: supernatural gas, to mingle with her own sophisticated musk, a perfume that battled with the car air freshener for olfactory supremacy.

The Mercedes had been ironing along in the slow lane; now, seeing a gap in the faster traffic to the left, Marianne pressed her expensively shod foot down on the accelerator, and the car shot into it, stopping up the conversation.

As they left the main road and drove through the outskirts of Baden, Joyce sat, barely registering the picturesque jumble of buildings in the narrow upper valley of the Limmat, or the ruined Stein Castle high on its crag. She was fixated on *I never married at that time*. Was this merely the imprecision of Marianne's English, or had she meant to imply that she and Weiss were now married? Their being lovers had always seemed to Joyce to be incompatible with their status as pillars of ugly St Anton's; yet at that first meeting – and this inconsequence Joyce could vividly recall – Weiss had definitely introduced Marianne as his 'partner'.

As Marianne Kreutzer expertly manoeuvred the Mercedes into a parking place, Joyce slid about in these ambiguities of word and flesh.

Joyce had a *Holy, holy, wholly* bad feeling in the hotel room; everything that should have been soft and inviting coldly rejected her. There were too many pillows on the bed: bleached teeth gnawing the taupe silk of the headboard. The mattress, when she drew back the coverlet, shone like a white-tiled floor. The unsettling reversal continued in the bathroom, where, as she arranged her toiletries, the real tiles sickeningly yielded beneath her heels.

Joyce felt her forehead – a useless examination when practitioner and patient were *the same one*. *Is it my teeth?* She had looked after them – almost all were her own; nevertheless, there was the inevitable softening of the gums, the exposure of bony roots in the old mud of her mouth. *Not pretty.*

But no, a cursory probe with tongue and eye was enough to reassure *on that score.* Then she reeled back into the bedroom and bit down on the bed. Whatever had happened to her – whatever might happen – Joyce's teeth would, she knew, survive her flesh, dentine kernels popping against the perforated cylinder that revolved to grind her bones.

She and Isobel had scattered Derry's ashes into the Severn near Tewkesbury, where, for a couple of years, he had moored a stubby cabin cruiser – another thing father and daughter had shared, to Joyce's mild derision. His teeth had been intact. She saw them, perfectly clearly, as they fell gnashing into the grey puffs of his dust. Then they sank, and the dust had lain on the coffee-coloured bulge of the river's shallows, between yellow doilies of algae. Isobel had cried, but then *she always did.*

No, it wasn't her teeth; it was this room, with its heavy double shutters and oppressive atmosphere. They had checked in so early – and now they had the whole day ahead of them in this stuffed womb. A speedy reverse gestation: the rubbing away of hardened skin, the removal of adult hair, the tightening of slack flesh, until she and Marianne were thrust from the delivery room of the spa, twins identical in terry towelling, fresh and ready to have their little tummies *verhätscheln.*

It all reminded Joyce of the Widder, and those four strange days when she was – what? Reborn – resurrected? She didn't believe any of it, *not for a second*; all she knew was that she had come to hate hotels more than she feared the grave. She rose, checked herself in the mirror, picked up the key with its heavy-testicle fob from the liverish top of an armoire and left the room.

It was the revelation of Marianne Kreutzer's body that made Joyce anxious, more than the exposure of her own. She found it difficult

– no, *impossible* – to conceive of this elegant Swiss woman, childless
and of a brittle age, being comfortable in her own skin – even if it
was only under the eyes of an older, less beautiful woman.

This anxiety was misplaced; the spa at the Blume was a clinical
unit rather than a leisure centre. There was to be no girlish dis-
robing beside troughs of carefully graded rocks, or preliminary
chatting over peach tea and fashion magazines. Instead, they were
interviewed by a nurse-alike in a starched white tunic, who sat
behind a metal desk upon which lay blood-pressure equipment and
a stethoscope.

She was a tough-looking blonde with no English, so Marianne
translated, and Joyce declined *die Dickdarmberieselung*, *das
Enthaarungsmittel*, *die Druckstrahlmassage* and especially *die Abblät-
terung*. In German these treatments sounded scarily invasive: a
scouring out of her body, then the decortication of what little
remained. Joyce settled instead for the basic package: a dunk in the
hotel's own sulphur baths, followed by a brief laying on of trained
hands.

'She is asking to me,' Marianne relayed, 'if you are having the
heart conditions of any kinds?'

Joyce checked herself from saying 'only heartlessness'; it was a
problematic sentiment to translate; besides which, it had meaning
for herself alone.

She and Marianne separated. Joyce changed in a cubicle, and was
then led down sloping white-tiled tunnels into the hot bowels of
the hotel. Here she was submerged in the shit-tangy waters that
bubbled and farted in a giant stone basin. The orderlies, in their
plastic aprons, were unsmiling butchers and hustled her along:
another body part to be hosed down and then wrapped. The
masseuse – whose developed sense of her clients' modesty caused
her to work on one portion of their bodies at a time – gripped
Joyce's calves as if she were squeezing giant toothpaste tubes and
exclaimed, '*Ach! So dick! Sie Händ vil Musklä!*' Joyce, startled from

her drowse, reared up, and the woman scattered confused English: 'Madam, so sorry, I am only that you have very physical, *ja?*'

At last the peach tea, the recliner, the terry towelling. Lying in soft moist splendour, 'very physical' was, Joyce considered, a perfectly apt description of how she felt. The *Kursaal* was spartan – white walls hung with black and white photographs of highly toned naked bodies, strip lighting rebounding from the chequer board of white and black floor tiles – yet to Joyce it all seemed suffused with a roseate glow. *Pleni suni coeli et terra gloria tua. Heaven and earth are full of Thy glory.* Joyce hadn't thought she would ever again experience such a complete mingling of calm mind and easeful body.

When Marianne Kreutzer came in, her hair in a towel turban, a second wrapped beneath her arms, Joyce amazed herself. 'Oh, Marianne,' she gushed, 'this is heavenly! Thank you.' By way of acknowledgement, she unwound her hair, dropped her other towel and stood bare before Joyce's recliner.

What did I expect? The cruel scar left by the barbed bracelet of a Catholic sect? Or else fierce preservation – a body plumped, filled, implanted, and so engineered into artificial youth? Clothed, Marianne Kreutzer was *so poised*; yet, here it was; the sagging breasts and scrawny arms, the blue veins straggling through cheesy thighs and the pucker of cellulite on drooping buttocks.

'Come,' Marianne said, extending her left hand. *Had they always been there* – the diamond solitaire engagement ring, and the dull circlet of a platinum wedding ring? Or had Marianne slipped them on as she slipped her towel off? 'Come, please, Joyce, show yourself to me also, please.'

There was a full-length mirror by the door that was wide enough for the most brassy cream pot of a Zürichers, and Marianne led Joyce to this. Joyce didn't understand what this ritual was – yet grasped that full revelation was essential. Was it gratitude or pride that made it so easy to abandon a lifetime's reserve and divest herself? She could not have said.

They stood there looking at themselves, until Marianne Kreutzer said, 'Ach, Joyce, you are too beautiful. Really, too beautiful. This, I am thinking, is the miracle.'

Benedictus

As Marianne had predicted, Ueli Weiss telephoned the following week to ask Joyce if she would accompany him to the special *Sechseläuten* concert at the Opernhaus. Joyce was inclined to turn him down; he had, she felt, so neglected her. However, he smoothed his dereliction over with pat English phrases: 'I've been rushed off my feet,' he said, but it was 'time we caught up'.

Employing equally formulaic language – 'It would be a pleasure', 'At what time?', 'I'll look forward to it' – Joyce imposed a week-to-view grid on the shapelessness of her current life. *For if not there, on that green coverlet, beneath that Alpine landscape, then when? My father's death at Ypres had surely, given the odds, been inevitable. Yet he survived. And my own, also – now there's nothing ahead of me to look away from . . . I've been shifted into some other . . . Everything is possible – but nothing . . . heard.*

Joyce replaced the handset and twitched the curtain to stare across Saatlenstrasse. There was a noticeboard on the pavement opposite; the Zürich Nord branch of Die Heilsarmee had placed details of their services and their youth club behind glass, together with pious homilies printed on cards cut exactly so and edged with cotton wool to make little clouds of godliness. The biggest cloud – which Joyce, having time to kill, had already read several times – proclaimed, '*Hilf mir zu erkennen, oh Gott, dass die Dunkelheit in Wirklichkeit der Schatten deiner liebevoll augestreckten Hand ist.*'

She wondered if Sandra – who stood beside the noticeboard, and whose sea-green, incorruptible eyes were levelled at Joyce's window – knew enough German to understand this; to grasp how, according to the North Zürich branch of the Salvation Army, God played with insect humanity: they scuttled about in the spring sunlight, then He plunged them into abject terror by blocking out the sun with His august right hand.

Sandra still wore her ivory-white hair defiantly shoulder-length; while her black slacks and tan suede jacket suggested, to her former colleague and friend, that her retirement was being spent in coffee bars discussing airy abstractions. Sandra, whose lifetime of ministering to childflesh – in between *pushing out some of her own* – had bequeathed to her more practical support than she could *possibly make use of*. Sandra, who had none the less eschewed the assistance of her grown children – all competent medics themselves – and booked her own ticket, then driven herself to the airport and enjoyed the short flight despite the gravity of her mission. Sandra, who, with equal efficiency, had now taken a cab here, to Oerlikon.

To forestall the agitation of the buzzer, Joyce got her own jacket, snatched up her shopping bag and skipped down the rubber treads of the communal stairs. She tossed a pan-European 'Hi' to Astrid Pfeiffer, who was playing out on the landing with a lubriciously pink and naked doll. Joyce shopped daily – for freshness, and to give herself something to do; this encounter with Sandra would be like the others – with Miriam, with Iris, with Ruth – screened off by nylon mesh.

She isn't my friend. Sandra came across the patch of grass, smiling, her arms open for a hug. *She's only the ghost of an old acquaintance.* 'Joyce, what's the matter – Joyce!' she cried out, *far too loudly* for this quiet suburb, especially in the still mid-morning of a weekday.

'Joyce.' Sandra fell into step behind Joyce, as she hurried towards Beckmann's, the convenience store. 'I've come all this way to see you – to talk with you. Miriam told me –'

Joyce said nothing, silencing her with an angry glare. *Told you what? What? That she'd been given her marching orders, too?* Those other three had been bad daydreams, mercifully brief, easy to forget, for, although these women had sought her out here, where

161

Joyce lived, the reality was that *they're dead to me. We've said our goodbyes.* They might just as well have gone to Fluntern, strolled along the cinder path between the box hedges and paid their respects to the waiting niche. These corpses-in-waiting, stinking of the eau de toilette they applied for special journeys, were no more welcome than Isobel, stinking of booze. *They all want bloody handouts.*

Joyce's exorcisms of these domestic demons had been short and sharp: 'I have nothing to say to you'; 'I don't care what you've heard'; 'Leave me alone'. No pleases or entreaties; and, while a dispassionate observer – if one such can be imagined – might have expected her visitors to be more persistent, Joyce was so very vehement that, having once recoiled, none of them returned.

Sandra hung on a little longer. She shadowed Joyce to Beckmann's, then up and down the short aisles, examining swatches of kitchen cloths and jars of sauerkraut. Was Sandra, Joyce wondered, making the sort of three-way exchange comparisons – from Sterling to Euros to Swiss Francs – that were meat and bread to the bankers downtown? Or were these only *nervy displacements*?

Once Joyce had paid – exchanging pidgin weather chat with Frau Beckmann – Sandra came at her again, saying, 'Joyce, I'm your friend – Isobel called me as well. I – she – we're both so very worried about you.' Then she made the mistake of taking Joyce by the arm.

What did the passers-by see? And the lingerers across the road, outside the pensioners' drop-in centre? An old Englishwoman – crazy, with lank hair – shouting, while grabbing at that nice lady who lives on Saatlenstrasse, the one who moved in a few weeks ago and who, altogether understandably, *keeps herself to herself.*

The cotton wool cloud of Swiss opprobrium descended on Sandra as Joyce shrugged her off. 'I'm a doctor, Joyce,' she protested; 'I can help you.' But this was utterly counterproductive; a futile assertion that was her last. She dogged Joyce back to the apartment block, and as they reached the door to the flats Joyce at last spoke: 'There's a taxi rank at Schwamendingenplatz, five minutes' walk that way. But if I were you I'd go the other way, along Tramstrasse to the depot. You can get a tram direct to the airport from there; it's far cheaper – and quicker.'

Then, having fulfilled her duty of care, Joyce went inside and closed the door firmly in the former paediatrician's wrinkled and wounded face.

At Sechseläutenplatz there were fat green buds on the upscratching limbs of the lindens along the quayside. The sun was a dull silver disc, while haze lay on the lake. The crowd, being Swiss, struggled to achieve festive incoherence, one bright, primary-coloured jacket slicking against its neighbour. They watched, muttering their appreciation, as the Reitergruppe – the mounted guard of the twenty-six guilds – undertook its ceremonial canter around the bonfire of the *Böögg*.

Joyce had set out from Oerlikon at lunch-time, intending only to take her usual walk, up along the snaking paths of the Zürichberg to the Fluntern Cemetery. But, on reaching the far side of the woods, she could see ant-people milling across the Quaibrücke, and the flash of the *Umzug*'s penants, as the guildsmen, together with their floats, processed through the streets of the old town.

Gravity dragged her down the hill. With all this exercise Joyce's knees no longer creaked or groaned; she had bought some ski pants at Globus, and the foot straps transformed her legs into exo-tendons, giving extra snap to every stride, as Joyce marched down the Rämistrasse into town, barely breaking sweat.

She ate an apple fritter – hot and sugar-dusted – that she bought from a stall, then wandered among the guildsmen in their cod-medieval costumes. It was somehow predictable that Ueli Weiss would be in quartered hose, half of each leg yellow, half green. His yellow-green belly could be glimpsed between the sides of his leather jerkin, from the slashed sleeves of which escaped puffs of yellow cotton.

Weiss stood, together with a handful of others similarly attired, at the base of the bonfire. These paperbag manufacturers and loss adjusters were fooling nobody with their embroidered banners and velveteen cowpat hats; burst blood vessels, liver-spotted hands, bifocals pinching pitted noses – *in the fifteenth century this lot would be long gone*. All apart from Weiss, who, as ever, managed to carry it off. His aquatic head bobbed in the surly-burly of civic gaiety, his manicured hands gripped the varnished haft of a fake halberd, and the moustache bristled with martial pride.

Spotting Joyce in the crowd, he saluted her with his ceremonial weapon. They would, she thought, *have sex*; there would be no breathy tenderness, only *fat slug push* and *stubble rasp*, but *so what?* The axe head of the halberd chopped at spring air, Weiss grinned, and then his brown eyes rounded: he had spotted someone in the crowd behind Joyce. She turned, expecting to see Marianne Kreutzer leading the miraculous Erich; instead, there was Isobel, being dragged away by the police. Their white-gloved hands were under her armpits, yanking up her short leather jacket. The pale slab of her back was exposed, and the near-legible notelet of her underwear label.

Joyce was disconcerted – she hadn't thought that Weiss knew what Isobel looked like. But then he resumed his historical mummery – posing legs apart, the halberd sloped – and Joyce realized that he'd made no connection between her and the drunken beggar; it was only the disruption that had drawn his attention.

One of the policemen was now pushing Isobel down by her head into the back seat of a Volvo estate, his white glove grabbing her scrappy dyed hair. Joyce searched the crowd for the Tamil boyfriend, but he was nowhere to be seen. However, here and there, idling among the children rabbiting on toffee apples and their *gassing* parents, were the town drunks; it was they who were the festival's cosmopolitan element – some with brown or black faces reddened by wine – leavening the heavy Swiss-German homogeneity.

When Joyce looked back the police car had gone, and Marianne Kreutzer was standing in front of her, with Erich Weiss tethered by her arm. Marianne bestowed her cheek on Joyce – this had been the way of it since their spa break. To Joyce, giving her a peck felt less like further intimacy than being fended off by a shield of foundation.

'It is your date with Ueli this night,' Marianne said, while Erich spluttered, 'Sch-sch-schwess!' A leakage of breath and spit that was *surely* parodic of the tongue he couldn't twist his own around. He was so smart, Erich, and so handsome. At St Anton's, Joyce had been taken by this mad fancy: that Erich was no more handicapped than anyone else, that his tics, spasms, barks and yelps had been carefully rehearsed and his spasms blocked out. The English apparel – toff's canary-tan corduroys, the waxed jacket, the brogues – these, she felt sure, were Ueli's doing, although could anyone be stylish *and* subnormal?

'He will take you for supper at Casa Ferlin after the concert,' Marianne said. By this alone Joyce understood that she was not the first other woman to be so entertained, and nor would she be the last. 'Be making sure to have baby cow meat – the veal?'

'The veal,' Joyce concurred.

'It was the dinners for the *Umzug* last night – Ueli was with his *Schneider Zunft* until late times. He was ve-ery drunk.' She laughed.

'*Schneider*?'

'The men who do the' – she mimed sewing – 'making of clothes.'

'Tailors? I had no idea Ueli was a tailor, I understood he owned a Mercedes dealership.'

Erich cavorted over to his father, who was chatting with his fellow *Schneiders*; from a hundred feet away their hungover hilarity was still salient: shoulders shook, banners quivered. Erich fitted in, Joyce thought; his country squire's costume was more mummery.

St Vitus was Erich's patron – he zigged and zagged and boogied beside his dad, who, together with his friends, seemed oblivious.

Marianne laughed again, sourly. 'Aha, no, you see this is only the guild for the ceremony – they are not real tailors.'

Any more than this was the medieval era, with an abbess installed in the abbey church, although, as the big bells of the Fraumünster began to two-tone toll 'Bing-*bong*, bing-*bong*, bing-*bong*', a local government official in fancy dress stepped forward and fiddled with a lighter, until the brand he held licked into life. The tots in baseball caps cried out, as worshipful of fire as anyone, ever. The brand sent flames hopping and skipping up the flanks of the pyre. It was, Joyce judged, a cleverly constructed and very Swiss pyre: a giant inverted fir cone of precisely stacked logs. The *Böögg* himself, far from being a grotesque Guy, was an elegant wooden bodyform that would have sat well in the Kunsthaus. One of the vanquished Winter Spirit's arms was raised, and as the two women watched this was slit by fire and puffed yellow smoke.

'I hear nothing now from Father Grappelli,' Joyce said. 'Now Monsignor Reiter has returned to Rome, it's as if I . . . well, don't exist.' She fell silent, appalled by her own self-piteous tone. The *Böögg* was swaying in a fiery soutane, then the first of the fireworks packed into the effigy's shapely chest shot up through the linden boughs and arced over the river. 'I mean,' she resumed, 'what's happening with the political side of things – this business of a referendum? Father Grappelli seemed to think it would be easy to get the necessary signatures – fifty thousand, is it?'

Again the tightened face and the acerbic laugh; whatever creaminess Marianne Kreutzer had exuded in Baden had now gone off. 'You – you, well you are not understanding, Joyce. The referendums – no one is giving their votes. No one cares, you see. No one cares.'

More rockets launched from the burning manikin, as the crowd sighed with pleasure; a flight of pigeons lifted off from the *Badeanstalt* – the open-air swimming pool out in the river. The *Böögg* half crumpled, embers bleeding from his cracked ribs. It was a creepily human motion – as if the figure were a suicidal monk, who had doused himself in petrol, then sparked a match.

Marianne Kreutzer urbanely lit a mentholated cigarette. 'I was, you know, twenty-one when the Federal Constitution was changed to make the women do the voting – to give *me* the vote. By then . . . well, I was making my money already three years. There are some cantons – Appenzell Innerrhoden – where there was no women voting until 1990.' She took a pull on the cigarette and exhaled; her expression said it had lost its minty savour. She dropped it and ground it out with a patent leather toe; then she picked up the butt and clicked to a steel bin, where she discarded it. By the time she returned to Joyce's side, the *Böögg* was no longer humanoid – was no longer anything, and the *Sechseläuten* was only another bonfire.

'The churches, the state, the banks also – in Switzerland, Joyce, to have any of these – these *Grossfirmen* . . .' She cast about, almost wildly, having reached the limits of her English.

'Do you mean institutions?'

'Exactly so. To have any of these big institutions pay any attention to a woman – an older woman – well, this is, I think, also the miracle.'

In the interval Joyce followed Ueli Weiss to the circle bar, where, on a shelf supported by two gold-painted plaster cherubs, two gin and tonics were waiting for them. He used the paper napkin with his surname written on it to blow his nose and wipe his moustache, then he began an explanation. This was not the usual venue for this festival concert: it was normally held in the Grosser Saal of the Tonhalle; but then nor was it the custom to have a visiting orchestra playing – in this case, the San Francisco Symphony.

Joyce only half listened to his lecture on Zürich's musical politics; she sensed that Weiss was giving it not because he thought it of interest to either of them but simply to fill time: a verbal intermezzo.

Other couples, the vast majority in late middle or old age, stood having their drinks. The wealthy and cultured Zürichers were dressed in their habitual navy blues and shades of black – with, here and there, a youngster in her fifties who dared brown. Jewels sparkled at plump wrists and plumper throats; these women's bodies were *display cushions*, scattered in this gilded cabinet.

The programme, thus far, had not entranced Joyce. Her thoughts had not been about music – or music itself resounding in her mind, note-for-thought, tone-for-feeling, the organic development of mood – but preoccupied with how very un-musiced she felt. The musicians had clodhopped on to the steeply raked stage, frumpy cellists and tubby percussionists, their evening dress worn as lovelessly as traffic wardens' uniforms. Had they been this apathetic when they left the City of Industry, or had the pall fallen on them only as their flight descended into Zürich?

And there, in the shape of the local conductor, had been the cliché Joyce dreaded: he was a Francophone Swiss from the hinterland of Geneva, who was yet more Bavarian than a puppet in wooden lederhosen strutting from underneath a clockface. Tick-tock, tick-tock – he gestured from the waist, and hearkening to his Taylorization of sound, the assembled lines of players sawed and hammered and blew. The opening chords of the Overture Egmont, which should have been a Romantic storm surge, were instead a mechanical pumping out of sound.

As the San Franciscans laboured to the Swiss beat, Joyce despaired. There was no dizzying ascent into the orbit of the crystalline chandelier that dripped from the ceiling of the auditorium; instead, she was sent truffling between ankles, where she smelt the shit of toy poodles smeared on expensive shoes.

Back in Birmingham, back in time, on those rare occasions when she had thrust Derry before her to a concert – it wasn't that he was crass, or that he couldn't swing to a slower beat, only that he preferred his Laphroaig to hand, and to be able to turn up the volume when Dexter blew hot and mean – Joyce, not liking herself for it, would involuntarily cast her eyes to one side, again and again, gauging his response to what they heard and then, sickeningly, adjusting her own.

After the piano had been brought on for the soloist – with some huffing and puffing – the second piece in the first half of the concert began. The San Franciscans obediently transported him through the choppy waters of the Allegro, if not con brio, then at least with dispatch; then the young man – who, Joyce didn't need the programme to tell her, was French from the tip of his ascetic nose to the ends of his lily-white fingers – geared himself down for the Largo of Beethoven's Third Piano Concerto.

His forearms and thighs appeared to stretch out from his forward-canted trunk. Still, no fiery embers fell from this *Böögg*: he might have been *typing* so far as Joyce was concerned. To her left, Ueli Weiss's thumb supported his smooth-shaven chin, while his manicured index finger probed the soft barbs on his upper lip. Frozen and tantalized, she watched the white half-moon of his nail trace the wing of his nostril.

At the interval Joyce had been desperate to pee; she rose but Ueli remained solidly seated, until, the applause pounding her ears, she was compelled to clamber over his knees.

In the second half the San Franciscans abandoned their factory and went wandering in the Alpenglow of Strauss's tone poem. Joyce was too tired to accompany them, as they humped their harps and drums into deceptively pillowy couloirs and across polished blue glaciers. Besides, there was a fat lady, not singing but shouting *Domini, Domini*, as a *Brummie slapper* might bawl at an unwanted child, her every ragged warble bracketed by the still louder cries of the bass baritone, Derry, who stood outside the Top Rank Bingo Hall at Five Ways, intoning mournfully, *Dom-i-ni, Osanna in excelsis*. She ran away from him and found herself beneath the purple sky of Monsignor Reiter's soutane, with his pale face – *where it shouldn't be! –* the sun.

Either Ueli Weiss didn't deign to wake her, or he cared not that Joyce slept. She was roused by the deadening *réclamé* of the Zürichers, only to witness the spectacle of the mousy first violinist scuttling into a bouquet. As the clapping scattered, Ueli said invitingly, 'Und now, supper at Casa Ferlin.'

Joyce hadn't gone so far as to obtain a full fur, but the saleswoman at Weinberg's had persuaded her to buy a black leather coat with genuine mink at cuffs and collar. Her old-new coat was abandoned. Beneath the leather was a real dress, plum silk, cut on the bias; and beneath the dress there was an armature of more silk and wire, that, amazingly, provided her with a *not unbecoming* décolletage. The lank grey crop that the hairdresser in Oerlikon had treated with not much more than professional neglect – shampoo, set, trim, the hedging of old growth – was, at Marianne's instigation, borne across town to Schwartzkopf's on Urianastrasse, where it was artfully dyed, before having completely new topiary.

Joyce waited on the steps of the Opernhaus while the *Schneider* went to get his little clothes iron of a Mercedes. When he returned, and hustled round to open the door for her, Ueli Weiss gaped at Joyce – but was this because of the makeover, or the veil of night and the rouge of street lamps? He kept darting looks at her as he pressed the tarmac around the town to Stampfenbachstrasse. In the restaurant's vestibule Ueli uttered a small, animalistic grunt of appreciation when she disrobed; or perhaps, since there was a strong smell of pasta and *baby cow meat*, this was only coincidental.

Beside a slim golden pillar, with a tapestry-covered banquette scratching between her shoulder blades, Joyce scanned first the menu and then the room. The latter was nothing special, with its off-white walls, undistinguished oil paintings and fireplace stripped of paint in emulation of a rusticism that had never existed. Joyce might have wondered why Ueli Weiss's chosen women found such an ambience seductive, were it not that she already knew that seduction – in her case as much as in theirs – was not an issue.

The discussion of menu selections, and then, when the entrées arrived, of the music they had just heard, was as much a formality as these events themselves. The ear-worm of Scoresby's semi-professional Requiem bored into Joyce as she bent to scallops caught in a chicory basket. *Benedictus qui venit in nomine Dom-i-ni.* The quiff-flicking in the Arts Centre canteen – did it all lead, ineluctably, to this? And had the others – who, she was sure, whether young or old, had been lacking in self-esteem, seeking the stiffest, and shortest-lived, acceptance – been as numb as she? Drained of melody, what remained of anyone's life? A narrative trajectory as straight and dull, as discordant and crowded, as the M1. *Benedictus qui venit.*

Bread and wine were needed for a benediction. Joyce ordered tagliatelle, with an amatriciana sauce, and drank deep of the Gamaret, a *bloody* red that Weiss regally called for – first one bottle, then a second.

He talked, if at all, of his first wife and their damaged child. Her virtues, it seemed, were many – although they were lost in the retelling: a loyal wife, a doting mother, a superb homemaker – the very ideal of a hausfrau; lovely to gaze upon as well . . . The trauma of Erich's birth, the severity of his disability, these had been, well, there was no need for him to say this – the implication was as weightily present as he himself – but were it not for their faith . . .

Weiss had dealt with his own dish – some meatiness swimming in a *jus* – in double-quick time, and now his hands were free to flop in the orangey light flung down by the fake oil lamp on their table. They were hands, Joyce mused, that always seemed gloved – sheathed in their own tanned hide. She steeled herself, imagining what they would feel like flayed, then dug down between her buttocks and a mattress.

171

Joyce saw herself reflected in Ueli Weiss's brown eyes: the two tiny miracles of her birth and her resurrection. He said, 'She died of pancreatic cancer, you know.'

She hadn't. The waiter arrived, his hips epicene below his short white jacket, and asked if they would like cream with their coffee. Weiss declined, then said, 'Here in Switzerland we have the highest levels of pancreatic cancer – you are not knowing this, also?' His tone verged on the hectoring. 'It is the creams, the milk and the butter – the fats, you say, we are eating them all the times. We think, maybe, we are still up on the Alps, looking after the goats and the cows – like Heidi, you know?'

And this, she did know.

There could be no question of them going to the apartment that Ueli shared with Marianne in Seefeld – this was how Joyce thought of it, not, despite the evidence of the rings, as a marital home. She knew it was close to St Anton's, and, while they were at Baden together, Marianne had explained in some detail how she had renovated the top-floor flat where Ueli's parents had lived, bought a second flat in the adjoining building, then knocked through the walls to create a defiantly contemporary space.

Joyce placed Marianne in this chic penthouse as Ueli Weiss skimmed the rainy streets with the Mercedes. Marianne in black silk pyjamas on a black leather divan. Lobby music welled from concealed speakers while she turned the pages of a fashion magazine. Her abstraction – it was more integral to her than her faith.

As for Erich, it wasn't possible to place him in this rational environment; he must be in the basement, beside the roaring boiler, crouching in an outsized plastic sack, waiting to be put out with the rest of the rubbish.

Benedictus qui venit in nomine. Ueli had booked a room at the Widder, *Dom-i-ni, natürlich*. Either because they didn't care, or else because they were accustomed to his liaisons, the staff showed no particular interest in them; *and yet, and yet . . .* surely this was the point at which somebody should've balked and made a pointed remark?

Blood. Or even, ᗺᒪOOᗡ, estate cars idling in the Mid-East car park, URGENT BLOOD on their flanks, their snouts ɣbooɭd noses. Up in the treatment rooms, the operating theatres and the intensive-care wards there were plenty of bodies pulled back from the edge of the abyss; jolted with electricity and then pumped with factors 1 through 8. Were these rollings away of the stone any less mysterious than her own? She had witnessed them all her working life – and were the arisen any more grateful, any more content? Did they not subside, soon enough, into the dull mulch of ordinary existence, cursing their miraculously humdrum lives?

It was Karl – *her* bellboy – who showed them up and up, to a room in the converted attics of the old townhouse, although he made no indication of having recognized her, except for saying 'Good evening, madam' in English, as he ushered her in through the door.

Joyce had an impression of queered familiarity. Her previous room at the Widder, with its blond-wood mirrored cabinets, mirror-topped desk and coffee table, its riot of cut glass and urns of fresh-dying blooms, had been crushed to fit under the sloping roof. But she had no real time to take this in: Ueli switched off the lights and pushed her against the wall; one of his hands clutched her right breast, the other she felt coming up under the hem of her dress.

She did not mind the moustache that grew immediately on her top lip, nor the strange tongue that flexed in her mouth. A kiss – always a thrilling taste of the essence of another, from adolescence on: their sweetness, their sourness – the loneliness of the nervy cave, lined with tombstones, where the hermit I lived.

She did not mind the rush and fumble. She felt no sexual arousal, yet was excited by her own suppleness, as she backed and wove between the furniture, absorbing his onslaught until they toppled on to the bed.

When, in the mêlée of snort and paw, Joyce cried 'Stop it, Ueli!', he did at once. She rose and bade him unzip her dress, which she saw no cause to damage.

While in the dark and delusive room she searched for a hanger, he, rumpled by his urges, pulled the black wave of his jacket over his amphibious head, then kicked out with his trousers.

She did not mind the way he yanked her underwear, nor the push-down of limbs, then the drag-up of covers. They thrashed about, and Joyce wondered, where are the aches and pains, the cramping of ageing muscles, and the tightening of tendons that, over the decades, had hobbled their love-making? This wanton coupling belonged to a time when she and Derry were newly married and had overcome their shyness, when they fitted together: parts of a single organism engaged in complex self-pleasuring. She remembered the dry greasiness of the condom as she had rolled it on to him, and the live-wiriness of his penis. *Benedictus qui venit in nomine Domini!*

She did not mind when Ueli turned her over, nor when she felt him digging at and then into her. She did not mind the astringency of his cologne and the shellacking of his sweat, nor yet intermittent suffocation in the crisp Widder pillows; but she did mind, very much, when he stopped and, rearing up over her, began to describe upon her skin the botched geometry of his caresses.

She had gained her shaming night sight; flung from cabinet, to desk, to window, Joyce saw their mirror-images: the portly pink Swiss, his sleek hair mussed, babbling *love twaddle* to the cadaver coiled beneath him. She saw this, and she saw also that Marianne Kreutzer, who sat quietly on an upright chair by the door, had seen it, too. Then Joyce snapped: 'Don't fondle my bum, I'm seventy years old!'

After that he finished off brutally – three or four rams into her and all of Ueli went blubbery. He slid away, then collapsed beside her, panting. *Osanna in excelsis!*

Later, when Joyce was sure Marianne had gone, she got up and, feeling Weiss's semen trickling out of her, went carefully into the bathroom, where she encountered the pathos of the hand towels.

Agnus Dei

At dawn on 14 July, Joyce Beddoes awoke in the small bedroom of her flat at 34 Saatlenstrasse, in the Zürich suburb of Oerlikon. She did not lie there tangled in dream shreds, or stare woozily at the pictures on the white walls. For her there was no confusion between sleep and wakefulness, and nor were there any pictures in the bedroom. The only representations in the flat at all were two postcards: one propped on the thermostat unit in the kitchenette, the other leaning against a jar that Joyce had intended for rice but never filled. The first was a banal Alpine scene of picturesque peaks reflected in a limpid lake; the second a reproduction of a painting by Trouget, the great contemporary master of figuration, whose acquaintance Joyce's daughter had laid claim to, despite the very glancing, bar-room nature of their association.

Getting up, going to the toilet, then dressing – these Joyce did automatically. In the kitchenette she made coffee and prepared a bowl of muesli with soya milk. If she noticed the Trouget postcard at all it was not because of what it depicted – the artist's usual subject matter and conceit, a bourgeois in a suit, distressingly upended – but only to recall buying it; and the other card, from a visit to the Kunsthaus weeks before, *because that's what you did, didn't you?*

She sat by the window eating her muesli and drinking her coffee. She looked down into the dull street, along which came a figure with the draught-animal plod of a woman bearing heavy shopping. *But bought from where at this time on a Sunday?*

The day smeared ahead, hot, murky and ill-defined. *Dona eis requiem. Grant them rest.* There was no one for Joyce to meet, no place she had to go, or task she needed to complete. It was Sunday, *but what should I rest from?* She had stopped attending mass at St Anton's three months before – shortly after *Sechseläuten*. Since then Joyce had employed this, the most void of days, to fit in her household chores; but there were so few of these anyway that she soon found herself weeks in advance of her routine, with the Sundays to come purged of any structure at all. She discovered herself slavishly dusting individual Venetian blind slats, morning and evening.

This morning, once cup, bowl and spoon had been washed up, there was only Monday's rubbish to be put in its Züri sacks, ready for when the refuse truck came truffling along Saatlenstrasse the following morning. Joyce squatted down before the swing-bin in the kitchen and sorted through her meagre detritus, reducing it still further. Tin cans, clear, brown and plastic bottles she put to one side. These she would bag separately and take out with her on her walk, stopping at a recycling centre to post them into colour-coded dump bins.

All this order – what an oppression it had become. The necessary formalities; the correct paperwork; the importance of social responsibility rather than personal impulse. While during her first few weeks in Zürich, Joyce had been relieved – finally, she was among others who understood the virtues of careful administration as well as she – now this was no longer the case. Instead, the go-round of each identical week, with its shopping for solo meals, its washing of a handful of clothes, its payment of the odd bill, seemed like the reprise of a terminal exercise: the winding up, and winding up once more, of a pitifully small estate.

The mounting warmth, the silence in the flat – punctuated only by the Pfeiffer children's stifled play – the odour of the place that, no matter how much she sprayed and aired, still smelt so much of her, and her alone – it was more than enough to make Joyce swoon; and she would have done, were it not for the stupid, blind vigour of her body rising up from the kitchenette floor, forcing her into walking shoes, gathering the bag with the bottles and a second with her swimming costume and towel in it, then driving her out the door and shooing her down the stairs.

On her body went, frogmarching Joyce up the trails of the Zürichberg, while behind her the sleepy suburb slumbered. The previous Tuesday she had had a letter from Father Grappelli on headed diocesan paper. With tongue twice-tied – by formality, by estrangement – he had informed her that Monsignor Reiter would be returning from Rome in the next few days. The initial response of the Sacred Congregation for the Causes of Saints had been encouraging, and in view of this the Bishop would like to assemble a second report. Would it be possible for Frau Beddoes to –?

But no, she had thought, *why should I?* Not only assist in the beatification of the goofy Stauben girl – *a ridiculous notion* – but also be compelled to speak English again, with all the messy intimacy that this would entail. Confined, for day after day, to the certitudes of *Grüezi*, *Guten Abend*, *Bitte*, *Danke*, and the naming of small needs, Joyce had become *ein verschlossenes Volk* of one; she almost believed that this was the limit of any possible communication, while beyond lay only this hillside: the dense curtains of yellow and grey-green needles, the stink of their sap stronger than creosote; the under-growth parched and crackling, with midges swirling over the boggy hollows; and the grasshoppers pulsing like blood.

Her body wouldn't let Joyce stop for long at the gates of the Fluntern Cemetery, but shoved her on down the Zürichbergstrasse into town. It was still before nine, and under their wide eaves the deeply recessed windows of the houses were blank eyes on the world. What could they have seen anyway on this overcast morning? Only the flapping black silhouette, a ghost of the civic dead.

At the Bellevue Bridge, Joyce had to wait; the *Frauenbad* – the women's bathing area – wasn't open yet. A few other, younger women were lingering on the quayside by the Stadverwaltung, and when the custodian came to open the turnstile they roused themselves and headed for the changing cubicles at a neat clip. The enclosed pool, which was fed with water from the lake, was clearly visible from the surrounding buildings, yet a few of the women bathed here in the nude. Joyce had never considered doing such a thing, but this morning her *stupid blind body* made the decision for her, by folding its clothing neatly, placing this mound on top of its shoes in the locker, then chucking on top of this both towel and swimming costume.

Joyce's body threw her into the water – an aggressive dive; then its arms dragged her, while its feet kicked her, up and down the length of the pool. Up and down, up and down – two lengths, four, then fourteen. It was untiring, this body of hers, and the gaggle of girls who had entered the water with her gave up long before Joyce, disengaging themselves from its chilly embrace to pace the concrete surround. Their breasts and buttocks and thighs were, Joyce judged, babyishly soft, and wobbled as they rubbed themselves ruddy. When Joyce's body hauled her out – no need for the ladder – she couldn't fail to notice the contrast between her own trim, adult form and these graceless maidens.

Perhaps drawn by this elderly lady's vitality, they seemed to want to talk to her; one mountainous Valkyrie came over and offered her some mineral water. However, Joyce's body had other ideas: it hustled her away, towelled her down, dressed her and then escorted her off the premises.

Once she had regained the top of the hill, Joyce was fully intending to take the trail that led off behind the Zürichberg Hotel, through a series of grassy clearings, and so, eventually, home. A hot dry wind had begun to stir the trees, and she knew what this was – the *Föhn*. The oppressive feeling she had had all morning, that the very sky was smothering her, was this down-draught of hot air from the mountains.

Far from being enervated by the *Föhn*, her wild body hearkened to its soughing and pulled her the opposite way, on through the woods towards Rigiblick. Then, at the second waymarker, it forced her in the direction of Forch. From previous excursions Joyce knew that this was the beginning of a five-hour hike, and, with the temperature rising and no water with her, this would be at best uncomfortably debilitating; at worst it could prove *fatal*.

Agnus Dei, qui tollis peccata mundi, dona eis requiem. Agnus Dei, qui tollis peccata mundi, dona eis requiem sempiternam. Lamb of God, who takest away the sins of the world, grant them everlasting rest.

Joyce cavilled as sure feet took her along the trail. Combed by the *Föhn*, the myriad needles of spruce, fir and pine formed ominous figures in the undulating green carpet. She tried to ignore them and busy herself with memories of a convivial past, not lamb of God but leg of lamb, mint sauce, red wine. *A family Sunday lunch, Isobel – at her best age, ten or eleven, not rebellious yet. Derry vigorously carving the joint . . . the scent of rosemary*, as if a Provençal hillside had been raised up out of the Birmingham suburbs.

Her wayward body was having none of it; it got at Joyce's hurting head from behind, prodding her on through the forest: *Et-er-nal rest, et-er-nal rest*, the 4/4 beat of its footfalls a forced military march. On Joyce went, through the shuttered-up town of Forch, then back into the woods, and finally she arrived at the monument, the Forchdenkmal.

Joyce had visited this before and thought nothing of it, but on this fetid and dismal outing the iron blob on its wide plinth struck her as unspeakably disgusting, cream or excrement dolloped from the heavens. The legend *Die ewige Flamme* – 'The Eternal Flame' – had been inscribed in runic script on the stepped pyramid of the monument. There was also a desiccated wreath, and buried in its crispy core Joyce saw the white-out-of-red Swiss cross. But what war dead could this wreath possibly be honouring after five hundred years of democracy, peace and brotherly love?

Communio

Towards dusk Joyce returned to Saatlenstrasse. Her body showered itself, fed and watered itself, because that's what bodies did – but it wasn't remotely tired. The *Föhn*, a feverish zephyr, rubbed its sweaty flank against the apartment block, while inside the flats the static crackled.

When she moved in, Joyce bought a television and a radio at Sihl City. She'd never turned them on, preferring to listen to the orderly burr of the lives surrounding her. But this evening, with the temperature still rising, the Pfeiffer children were *running riot* up and down the communal stairs, and Joyce longed to shout them down. Eventually, young Frau Pfeiffer lost her temper and began screaming '*Bis ruhig! Bis ruhig!*' over and over again, until she sobbed up the scale, her hysteria in maddening counterpoint to the bleeps and peeps of Herr Siemens's electronic music.

As the dusk gathered, and a semblance of calm returned to the building, Joyce sorted through her papers and put them in order. It was necessary to write a long, lucid and fairly complex letter to the authorities, and another, shorter one to Isobel, who was being held on remand at Hindelbank, the women's prison outside Berne.

Joyce wished she had a computer – or at least a typewriter – with which to set down all these words: her fingers ached from the unfamiliar tension of holding a pen. Darkness seeped into the small living room as she scratched away at the thin sheets of paper; outside, a sparrow buffeted by the hot wind perched wonkily on the street lamp, then dropped to the ground.

If I stay here, then what? Joyce had experienced old age, and then her final illness, as the creeping normalcy of a bad habit. You took your pills and turned up for your treatments, because that's what people did. And, although you might have toyed with the idea of *ending it all when things got too bad*, what you discovered was the day didn't seem to come when it was *bad enough*; because, after all, they hadn't been *that good* the day before.

Joyce had never thought of herself as a rebel, but when she realized that soon she would have no fortitude left with which to resist death's conventions, well, this was a more nauseating abbreviation than chemo or radio, and so she did rebel – she made the call. Now Switzerland itself, with all its orderliness, had become the very creeping normalcy she had feared. With each sifting of the green, the brown and the plastic bottles, with each purchase of the state-approved plastic bags, she felt increasingly that it was this *rubbish* that was participating in a real life-cycle, whereas she was only a human residuum.

As she wrote the letter to her daughter, Joyce tried to imagine what a Swiss women's prison might be like – maximally orderly, she assumed. Isobel's letters – she had sent three – were hardly informative, consisting as they did almost entirely of protracted rants against her mother's heartlessness, her selfishness – and so *bloody, fucking on*.

Joyce finished writing, sealed the letters and addressed them. She arranged the envelopes together with the cardboard folders containing her papers on the serviceable table. All this was done as night completely fell, which was just as well, because Joyce didn't want to switch on the lights – she couldn't switch on the lights.

Requiem aeternam dona eis, Domine, et lux perpetua luceat eis . . . Grant the dead eternal rest, O Lord, and may perpetual light shine on them . . . The naked walls and barely used furniture suggested a show flat, not a place of genuine habitation. *Isobel could make an installation out of this*, like Mr Vogel's abandoned office. *My heart as contrite as the dust* that gathers on Vreni Stauben's ledges. *Dust,*

Joyce thought, *foolish of me to not understand that it has a kind of peace*.

Joyce's panther-body lunged at her: it had never been still. It mauled her into the toilet, where the flashing tail-lights of a jet coming into land at the airport sparkled in the water of the commode. Then the panther worried her back into the living room. These, Joyce realized, were the perpetual lights: the television, always on stand-by, the limelight switch of the electric jug.

The Zwingli Singers were back, jostling Joyce with their hideous 1970s frocks – *chiffon sacks, really*. It had been stupid of her to believe that anything not truly believed in could – Well, it was best left unsaid, *the sheer silliness of it*, a magic trick, a sleight-of-mind deployed against the gaunt inexorability of Death. *Babbababbada-ba-babba-daaa! What then shall I say, wretch that I am?* Isobel was thrashing about in her cell, the *graceless, clumsy, awkward, ungainly girl. She's a fat puppy, who gorged on Scottie's Liver Treats, just as I stuffed myself with hotel truffles and suicidal bonbons, then drank too deep of liqueur choccies*. The only palatable meal was a symbolic one: the *Leberknödel* of the Lord.

Joyce's body kept her up all night, a rambunctious teenager partying in the worn-out mind of an elderly woman. Towards dawn Trevor Howard came marching along Saatlenstrasse swinging his arms. A versatile leading man, he was playing Joyce's father, and Derry as well. He stood in the living room in his belted leather coat, waiting for morning to harden into day, while Joyce's body paced her up and down. Then, once office hours had arrived, he said to her: 'I tried to tell you, Beddoes, back at the Widder: leave death to the professionals.' There was no 'Joyce', no 'Jo', and certainly not the frank intimacy of 'Jo-Jo'; only the clipped 'Beddoes'.

Then, *A trumpet spreading a wondrous sound. He is offering now to the people with clinical depression his poison – nothing wrong in their body, only the head*. Joyce lifted the handset and dialled Dr Hohl's number. He answered on the second ring, and their conversation was brief and to the point. Yes, he was aware, of course, of the activities of the diocese, and *natürlich* he understood the possible repercussions; however, so far as he was concerned a contract was – and remained – a contract, *Treu und Glauben*.

Ite missa est. Go, it is the dismissal.

Prometheus

Prometheus stands, quivering, by the water cooler in the inert core of the open-plan offices of Titan, an advertising agency renowned throughout London – and beyond – for its genius at breathing fire into the most sodden products, and the dampest services; igniting them, then fanning them up, so that their notoriety leaps and spreads from demographic to demographic, until entire populations are consumed by a mania for their possession.

Prometheus, his prematurely iron-grey hair erect on his scalp – a magnetized ruff – rubs his cloven-toed trainers on the nodulous rubber floor covering, trying to earth himself; it's only seven thirty in the morning, yet he's already hopelessly jazzed up at the prospect of the day ahead.

Prometheus: his cotton clothes of Japanese cut are in shades of beige and mushroom, their kimono cuffs peel away from his kinked limbs like insulation from live wiring. His wrists are bony, with thick black plaited hairs.

Prometheus, he jigs, then bends to hit the spigot of the water cooler, releasing air bubbles that swell and burst. He swigs from the waxed-paper horn and smacks his lips, which then resume their normal expression: an endearing smirk. He's a handsome man – straightforwardly so; his Pantone 293 eyes keenly rectilinear, his smoothly shaven cheeks suggest the massaging of balms formulated by white-coated demi-virgins in the pseudo-laboratories of giant French cosmetics combines. A smattering of ancient acne pocks below each well-defined cheekbone are only grace notes, epidermal elaborations on the overall tautness of the composition.

'Tap,' Prometheus says. 'Tap, tap, tap!'

'What?' Epimetheus is befuddled – still drunk from the night before.

'Tap,' his partner carries on dripping. 'Tap, tap, tap . . .' Then he hits the spigot again.

Both creatives stare into the blue barrel of the water cooler, where another air bubble gurglingly gestates. It's big, this bubble, it swells and swells until it displaces all the water in the cooler, then rigid plastic ripples as it morphs into the ridged barrel itself.

'Whoa!' the admen cry, appalled and enthralled. They back off as the bubble goes on engorging itself, schlupping up ergonomic personnel pods of brightly coloured, injection-moulded plastic; brushed-steel laptop computers; novelty waste-paper baskets; scrawled-upon whiteboards; photocopier machines and swivel chairs with cheese-grater-padded backs. With each engulfment the bubble's transparency is momentarily occluded by the red-blue-green of these objects – but soon this clears and it resumes its awesome metastasis.

Prometheus and Epimetheus walk back towards the reception area of their agency – they're still excited by this phenomenon, and clutch each other's arms like little girls. A ridiculously basso voice-over begins incanting, 'Water, water everywhere but it all costs money', and, hearkening to this soliloquy, the bubble sends out quicksilver tongues to lap up stray biros and paperclips. 'Why pay more', the voice-over tells itself, 'for fancy labels and silly-shaped bottles, when tap water tastes just as good?'

Far from addressing the two Titans, the godlike voice pulls at that liquid part of them; besides, they've scrambled out of a Crittall window and are dangling off an old cast-iron fire escape: the bubble has sucked up the entire office.

'Five sixths of the earth's surface is covered by water, and the same fluid makes up 90 per cent of the human body.' Stated with such omniscience these schoolboy factoids take on the character of cosmic truths; the bubble, meanwhile, has engrossed London, then the south-east of England, then the whole British Isles, and is now vacillating over the Atlantic, Prometheus and Epimetheus soaring high above its leading curve: mythological man-birds with Muji wings.

'So why compromise on the stuff of life? Drink Zeus Mineral Water, it may be a little dearer, but it's definitely better than tap.'

'Tap, tap, tap!' With this Olympian endorsement the surface of the ocean condenses into a 3,000-mile-wide droplet that hammers the bubble back down: 'Tap!' It's country-sized. 'Tap!' It's regional. 'Tap!' It's a dome over the conurbation. 'Tap!' With the last hideously amplified blow of liquid on solid, it's driven back into the water cooler, and disappears in a milky cloud of its own tiny selves. All is as before: Prometheus whipping like an antenna, Epimetheus, bemused, saying, 'What the hell kind of fucking end-line is that?' Not that his mind is really on the pitch for Zeus Mineral Water at all – it's still on, or even *in*, the girl he picked up – or who picked *him* up – the night before.

It was in Soho House. She was blonde, bright-eyed, no more than twenty-five. Epimetheus was stunned when she agreed to go home with him, because he's no looker. Short, with bandy legs and an egg-shaped torso, no matter how much he spends on a haircut, Epimetheus always steps from the salon a 1980s footballer with a crap perm. Still, this was better than leaving his black waves to their own devices: flicking grease on to his griddle of a face, which was dominated by the fleshy T-shaped ridges of his nose and brows.

'Tap,' Prometheus keeps on, 'that's what punters ask for now: "I'll have a glass of tap", as if it were totally fucking exotic. It's getting like the States here – waiters've started pitching up with it before they're asked!'

A killer end-line should be like a garrotte applied to any

consumer's faculty for making a rational calculus of price and benefit – and these lethal ligatures were plaited in Titan's offices, in conversation pits of the kind favoured by imprisoning reality TV shows, in the pods where creatives were coddled by a warm albumen of piped-in pop culture. It was Prometheus who'd had the water cooler installed; his colleagues mostly eschewed it, preferring the hot froth dispensed from the coffee bar by the agency's own barrista, and then, by mid-afternoon, the cocktails that were shaken, without let or hindrance, by the agency's barman. For, as Menoetius, the chief exec – and Titan's founder, together with Prometheus and Epimetheus – was always at pains to point out: 'We're not in business to stifle appetites; we're all about satisfying them.'

'So what if punters ask for tap water?' Epimetheus snarls. 'It don't mean they wanna shell out for it.'

He feels like a Bloody Mary – right now. A Bloody Mary followed by a trip to the steam baths on Ironmonger Row, followed by a therapeutic wank in bed, then sleep for a week – or as long as it takes to shake this brain ache and liver jab. Prometheus is still bobbing and weaving; he yanks two waxed-paper horns from their holder, lifts them to his brow and paws at the rubbery turf with his cloven hoofs.

'Yes, indeedy – better than tap,' he snorts. 'And as for the graphic – on the labels, the PoS shit, the posters, whatever – that'll be a big fucking tap.'

This, Epimetheus grimly reflects, is the tap-tap-tap of water torture: wrenched from a bed in which he'd scarcely rested to slosh through dirty puddles and overflowing gutters, for what Prometheus hokily referred to as 'a blue-sky session'.

'C'mon, man. We've done the broadband stuff for him; we jiggled his insurance bollocks, too; if we luck out with this pitch we could make it on the roster, become his agency of fucking record. Think of the billings – then double 'em!'

This was Prometheus's voice, ever seductive, always with an

undercurrent of laughter, as it sounded issuing from Epimetheus's mobile phone an hour or so earlier; the mobile he'd found girded with the silky scrap of the girl's abandoned knickers – for Pandora herself was gone.

Now Prometheus chivvies him towards the plastic face of the Macintosh with flirty pinches and punches. 'He's lunching us at St John at twelve sharp, and I want something to show him.'

Seated at the machine, Epimetheus goes down into the pixel mine and commences searching, picking and grabbing, shakily assembling a series of images that can be used for a PowerPoint presentation.

'So,' Prometheus chortles as his partner grafts, 'who was she? Some tart, I s'pose.'

'Why d'you say that?' Epimetheus counters, but it's a flaccid denial; there's never any dissimulation between them, at least, not on his part. 'Oh, I dunno,' he groans on, 'she didn't swipe me card, but . . .' When he'd got up, he'd discovered that, while she'd left her underwear, she'd taken some of his outerwear. 'She took that Forzieri jacket I got in Milan.'

Prometheus whistles appreciatively. 'She's gotta nose, then, 'coz it don't look like jack, but it must've cost –'

'A couple of grand,' Epimetheus concedes. 'It's camel suede shearling – so she's either a tart or a thief.'

'C'mon,' Prometheus laughs again, 'same diff.'

He's still drinking water, but now it's San Pellegrino he's swigging from its dumpy green bottle. He's always drinking water. 'To keep me pure,' he tells anyone who asks why.

The madhouse of the bar, limbs contorted in seeming intimacy. Next, the big clatter-whoosh of the doors as they'd bolted into the gents and bolted themselves into a cubicle. Then the tiny rasp and teensy clatter as she had chopped and ground and swept the granules of cocaine.

The certainty that he was going to see her naked was unbearably sweet for Epimetheus, syrup poured into this golden cubicle. He wanted this to have happened already, so that he could be looking back on it. She was a natural blonde, her hair a perfect bell, the rest of her as smooth and rounded. Her skin had a furring of white-blonde down. Her features were worryingly pretty, and there was more than a hint of the catty in her slanting green eyes. And the nose? Too small, too snub. She wore a chocolate-brown dress of 1950s pattern – full skirt, tight bodice – and her breasts were pushed up high in its low-plunging neckline. When she bent down to feed, Epimetheus could see their pink snouts pressed into the fabric trough.

He finds a big steel tap on a photo library site; it looks capable of hosing away offal. 'Rustier,' Prometheus commands. 'Keep looking.'

He had haggled with the African minicab controller – but only for form's sake. The tarnished rain dashed Epimetheus's cheeks and the neon curdled on the slick pavement. Meanwhile, Pandora stood, her coat held up to protect her hair: a glamorous widow in an insurance advert. Epimetheus's cock, his balls – all the meat of him was engorged with the present; packed into skin and scrotum were cars and bars, commissionaires and au pairs, cycle rickshaws and ticket touts, 'roided clones and voided dossers.

In the vinyl glove of the minicab he put his hand up those full skirts and felt neat fleece through silkiness; then, dipping down, he walked his fingers into the clammy cleft, and Pandora eased herself on to these, at the same time as she pushed her tongue into Epimetheus's grotty mouth.

'That's the one!' cried Prometheus. 'That rusty fucking tap is gonna spurt out dosh – you'll see. Whack it down on a clear black field.

Do it dripping – then pouring, then fucking gushing. Always the same line. Big type: BETTER THAN TAP. Got it?'

Epimetheus gets it. He gets it bad.

There had been no preambles at his flat – a purpose-built New York loft next to Tate Modern. Pandora walked in, slung off her coat, shucked off her dress, stepped down from her shoes and fell out of her bra. Over her bare shoulder the floodlit dome of St Paul's boiled up: the mushroom cloud of the baroque. A split-tailed mermaid in her metallic tights, she flipped over the thirty-five feet of varnished floorboards to where Epimetheus's bed – a post-industrial slab of bolted-together railway sleepers – dangled by chains from the rafters and, without any ado, mounted it.

Then she had to mount Epimetheus, who, on joining her, discovered that he had no equilibrium at all. If he sat up, the bed's modest revolution threatened to topple him; even supine he couldn't keep his balance sufficiently to lay his hands on her. Pandora didn't appear to mind. She fetched the cocaine wrap from her bag and administered another line to them both. Then she coaxed his irrelevant nub with scarlet lips and delved with trowel of tongue, until it was significant enough – just – to penetrate her labia.

A Swiss Railways clock blooms on a silver stalk that bends over the rubbery allotment of the Titan offices. Its hands shiver to 10.57. The rest of the work spore have wafted in by now – account planners, researchers, secretaries and those eponymous heroes, the creatives. The creatives take to their pits and pods, and there they're brought printouts, or publications, or croissants – all by way of nourishment.

Prometheus says, 'I need a leak.'

'I'm not bloody surprised,' Epimetheus mutters.

Titan's toilets are well appointed: the floors covered with quarry tiling, the sinks hewn from granite blocks, the urinals old

Corporation of London horse troughs. The stalls, walled floor to ceiling, are equipped with the oak doors that once graced a Wren church in the City. Prometheus goes directly to the one at the far end, which is in the corner of the building and has its own window. Once locked inside, he takes out a key, unscrews the window locks, places them carefully on the sill and pulls up the bottom panel. He takes off his sack of a jacket and hangs it from the hook on the back of the door, then he drops his baggy trousers and his baggier silk boxers. He sits down on the commode and yanks up his jersey shirt, baring his narrow, almost hairless chest. He half turns to the window and bends forward, warping his long back.

Prometheus's ribcage expands under taut white skin; piss hisses in the bowl. His face is aimed at the stall's corner: he stares where tile, wood and masonry join.

Twenty-five thousand feet above Old Street a griffon vulture circles in the freezing air; twenty thousand feet below her a grey-brown lagging of cloud covers the city. The vulture's gyre takes her from Ilford in the east to Hayes in the west, from Potters Bar in the north to Carshalton in the south. Her bald white head, skull-like brow and double-curved beak are angled not down – for there is no carrion to be seen – but straight ahead. The bird is in a holding pattern; her buff wing coverts and darker flight feathers riffle in the slipstream; her short, stubby tail is tilted, rigid as a rudder.

Way down there Prometheus strains, shackled to his ceramic rock. Mysteriously, the vulture responds to this contortion from eight miles away. She tucks in her huge wings and slides sideways, plummeting to cloud level in less than a minute, then slicing through the vaporous wrinkles as surely as a surgeon's scalpel cuts through skin.

At once, the city is torn open for the vulture's gaze: a mass of viscid interiority, with its vital organs of governance and commerce, its sinews and arteries of communication, its intestinal retail concourses and media glands, and surrounding them all its myriad cells of human habitation.

Down and down the vulture swoops, then brakes, her wings wide and cupped. She sees the tumour of the Swiss Re tower, the tapeworm of the Thames, the fatty deposits of Broadgate and the Barbican, the sphincter of the Old Street roundabout. Buffeted, slipping to right and left, the vulture slides through phone and power lines, manoeuvres beautifully between a fire escape and a wall, then glides up to stoop on the sill of the window Prometheus opened five minutes before.

The creative stares at the vulture, and she examines him in return with eyes that have black pupils and yellow irises. Her countenance is utterly inhuman, yet possesses calm wisdom and complete understanding. The vulture's manifestation is terrifying: her wingspan is fully eight feet, and she stands as tall as a toddler. Her beak is perfectly designed to scythe, then rip; her ruff of white feathers cannot be anthropomorphized into Elizabethan courtly apparel and looks exactly like what it is: a sponge to sop up the blood of carrion.

She arches her muscular neck to gain entrance and comes into the toilet stall with dispatch, although careful not to create any noise or disturbance: a busy surgeon walking into a confined and cluttered operating theatre. Prometheus cants forward still more, so that every vertebra is clearly delineated. He bites the toilet roll. The griffon vulture spreads her wings with a scratchy rustle – the avian stench, musty, nitrous, is gassily pervasive – then abruptly lunges, plunging her beak under the lip of Prometheus's costal cartilage. With a sawing motion of her head, the vulture opens a ragged tear in him, revealing the glossy maroon mass of his liver. Then, without ado, she starts gnawing.

The adman makes no sound except a faint groan, easily interpretable, from without, as the labour of excretion.

★

He's visualizing a Sunday lunch in Middle England. Dad and two kids are at the table, while through the French windows we can see a trampoline standing on two tones of green lawn. Mummy gets up from the oven, her floral mitts gripping a sizzling pan. Dad and the kids are telegenically salivating, cutlery at the ready, when the French windows burst inwards. What's up there in the blue, blue sky? A swarm of bees? A cyclone? No it's a squadron of vultures in close formation.

One after another, they swoop into the kitchen and land on the table, their reptilian feet sullying the tablecloth. The happy family's grins somersault into girns – then they recover themselves; for these aren't real vultures, they're cartoon figures that link wings-for-arms and dance up and down, skilfully avoiding the dishes of roast potatoes and carrots, the beakers full of fruit juice and the sturdy earthenware plates.

The vulture chorus sings: 'Don't give Dad 'n' the kids fat 'n' bones, fat 'n' bones, fa-at 'n' bo-o-ones! Only give 'em a tummy fulla flesh, a tummy fulla flesh, a tu-mmy fulla fle-esh!'

One of the vultures breaks from the line-up and hops into the air to hover over the roasting pan. It grabs the meat with its talons – a scraggy half-burnt shank; the frame contracts to the vulture's pawky beak. 'Ooh!' it camps. 'What a dog's dinner!' The frame contracts still more, until only the bird's unblinking eye is visible, and the familiar basso voice-over urges: 'C'mon, Mum, don't serve your family carrion this Sunday, when prime beef from Olympus is only two ninety-nine per five hundred grammes!'

'You know my daughter, Athene?' Zeus says, employing a marrow-bone as a pointer. On the far side of the restaurant a bounteous young woman is in deep giggly conversation with another not the same. Allowing himself some moments within which to consider strategy, Prometheus watches the frond of marrow plipping dark spots across the white cloth.

'Uh, yeah,' he says eventually. 'We've met – did she tell you?'

'Some charity bullshit,' the tycoon says dismissively. 'I mean, I'm as philanthropic as the next man, but I don't want a badge for it, or a round of applause from wankers in penguin suits.' But all Prometheus hears is: *He doesn't know about you and her, and everyone says they're close – too close. Bit paedo in fact. Mummy's gone – she's his walker; either she thinks he won't approve, or she isn't sure . . . Besides, what about me? If he finds out I might lose the pitch . . .*

'Aren'tcha having the marrowbone?' Zeus resumes sucking on his own skeletal little columns, the architectural salvage from a temple of beef.

'No.' Prometheus gestures with his fork. 'I'm on the eel.'

'Probably wise,' Zeus says. 'This stuff's as dodgy as fucking fugu – swarming with prions. Metabolic time-bomb.'

Prometheus, despite having pitched to Zeus twice before, and running into him at half a dozen industry pissfests, still can't read the man. He's insecure, certainly, and who wouldn't be with those freckles and that ginger scrub, those tiny hands and that stocky peasant's build? Not that Zeus has come from nowhere; there are solid antecedents ranged behind him: moon-faced gentry execrably rendered in oils, staring down from the striped walls of airless parlours.

However, Zeus's Formula 1 racing team and his financial services company, his record label and his airline, his Premier Division football club and his cable TV network, his cranberry-flavoured vodka and his luxury leather goods range, his condoms and his cola – Zeus's products (or, rather, his *brands*, for every surface of his empire has a red z zigzagged across it) were a peasant's conception of what youthful Midases desire, plaster props from which the gold leaf was always flaking. Perhaps it was for this reason alone that he was so successful, that the all-consuming wannabes had taken him to their wallets.

'So,' Zeus says, taking a slug of his Haut-Médoc, 'whaddya got for me?'

It's one of the little great man's foibles that he takes such a close interest in the minutiae of his manifold enterprise. He has as many brand managers as Achilles has Myrmidons – and they're easily as ruthless – nevertheless, Zeus overrules them as a matter of course. He tinkers with the products, but in particular he mucks with marketing. Nothing seems to give him more pleasure than hiring and firing advertising agencies. He also loves to haggle with the media houses, calling the planners and buyers into his office to chew it out with them, muzzle to muzzle.

No bus T-side, billboard site, Adshel, display page in a provincial free-sheet or fifteen-second segment on an FM radio station escapes his attention. Zeus has been known to cost out a single instance of a pop-up ident on a webpage. He even gets between the media buyers and the salesmen. 'Take you to Chamonix, did they?' he barks at the pushy boys in their penny loafers, patterned braces and Hackett suits. 'I'll fly you to fucking Gstaad!'

And he does, just for the merry hell of it: winching them up over slushy corries to where his ski chalet squats, a megalomaniac's lair bought sight unseen, which looks like a mail order conservatory. There the boys frolic in hot tubs, the plugholes of which are choked with a thousand, thousand pubic hairs, shaved from the monses of models, actresses – whoever.

'I got this,' Prometheus says. 'I got this.' And he beckons to Epimetheus, who's nose down in a plate of chitterlings.

Epimetheus bestirs himself, pulls out a laptop and cracks open its brushed-steel slate. It's gloomy in the restaurant, despite white paint and yellow light, and, as the computer fires up, its sharp glare plays on the three faces gathered round: brain workers at a brazier.

Zeus goggles at the rusty spigot. 'Better than tap,' he snaps. 'What the fuck's that about?'

Prometheus laughs. 'Well, it is, isn't it? I mean, if it isn't as good as tap it's gotta be a total fucking rip-off, yeah?'

Zeus sticks a stubby finger in his own glass of mineral water and noisily stirs the ice cubes. Then he splashes water across the keyboard as he punches through the PowerPoint. 'Taps, taps, more fucking taps – what's it all about?'

'Bus bums,' Prometheus counters, 'two, maybe three hundred of 'em. The biggest programmable signboard in the 'dilly, all the arterial route Adshels – maybe some TV –'

'TV!' Zeus expostulates. 'For a bloody mineral water! Anyway, you don't buy my media, you're s'posed to be some hot-shot creatives. Better than tap – can't you do better than *that*? I mean, what does it mean?'

Prometheus isn't fazed – he never is, that's the essence of his charm – that and the gab. 'Exactly what it says. Look, Zeus, people are fed up with mineral water. You couldn't've chosen a worse time to launch one – it's a drag on the market. Eco-shit, recession chic – whatever. Besides, punters mostly know it's a con. Half the time when you order still, there's a bus boy down in the kitchens filling up the bottles from a fucking tap. That's why the waiters make such a palaver about cracking the screw top. This is a nod to that – a nod to the punters' sophistication. They'll like that; it's surreal, counter-intuitive –'

'Counter-intuitive!'

'And downbeat – it cuts through the crap, all that malarkey about purity. I mean, look at that.' He points at the tycoon's mineral water.

'This?'

'Yeah, that. Knowing this gaff it'll be kosher, but you've paid a quid-fifty for it, and they've bunged in a load of ice cubes. Did they make those outta the same mineral water, or what?'

'You' – Zeus picks up one of the ice cubes and pops it in his froggy mouth – 'have gotta point there.' Then he crunches ruminatively on the chilly bones of water.

*

Only a couple of birding office workers, whose chance itches throw their heads back on their collars, spot the griffon vulture as she dallies down over the Holborn Viaduct. It's not a day for tilting skywards in London – nothing encourages it. The cloud carpet's pile has thickened, and the Londoners are woodlice trundling beneath it. One of the irritated twitchers recognizes the vulture as a griffon; the other misidentifies it as a Ruppell's. Neither thinks much of it, after all; the city harbours so many aliens: refugees from the tyrannies of men and the market, *Gastarbeiters*, Russian oligarchs, black widows ridden in on a hand of bananas – why not this scavenger, too?

Who flies arrow-straight through the central arcade of Smithfield meat market, her scholarly gaze not deviating to the right – halved cattle, rigid as boards, anatomy like a drawing of same; nor to the left – scores of fowl, plump as eiderdowns slung over a washing line. She swoops up again, then drops down into the ancient court behind St John Street, where cigarette butts and dead leaves mulch the flags, and pigeon droppings ice every ledge. Hunched up, with folded wings, the vulture squeezes past the wheelie-bins and enters through a fire door that's been left propped open with a mop.

She works her way unerringly into the backstage of the restaurant, avoiding the staff by tucking herself into recesses or flattening herself behind equipment. She quests for the only foody aroma that interests her: the liverish thread. Prometheus is already waiting in the gents, snibbed into a cubicle, back bared. He hears the rustle and scratch of the bird's approach, admits this late luncher, then bites down on another toilet roll.

For luncheon the griffon vulture takes another fifth of Prometheus's liver. She clamps the hepatic artery and duct with one talon, the portal vein with the other. With almost half of the organ already missing she has to be scrupulously careful. The soles of her lunch's shoes beat a tattoo on the floor. When Prometheus returns to the table he's shaky and leached of colour.

'Are you OK?' Epimetheus whispers, but Zeus booms, 'You look like shit! What's wrong with you?' Other late lunchers peer up from their tripe and their oysters.

While his partner was away it's been a difficult five minutes for Epimetheus. At first, he tried to divert Zeus with talk of other accounts the agency handles: Devo, the giant Korean electronics corporation; Prosser and Beadle, tea merchants by Appointment; Lickstep Sportswear – but the tycoon wasn't impressed. Nor was he impressed by Epimetheus's talk of 'meaningful effectiveness data' and 'household penetration'. Epimetheus may art-direct, but his real passion is the quantitative and qualitative evaluation of advertising: looking back to the immediate past and judging how true has been the flight of cupidity's dart.

Zeus is so ineffably bored that he examines his nails. For the first time he takes in his companion's shady cheeks and the raw circles under Epimetheus's eyes. This, he troubles to conclude, is not merely the creative dishevellment of adland; this *scumbag* looks like he was up all night *snorting coke with some whore*. Epimetheus is on the verge of making a complete fool of himself, blethering on about 'interacting via text, phone or red button', when Prometheus is back, and gulping down water.

'It's nothing, really,' he gulps up. 'I'm fine.'

It's always like this in the first few minutes after the vulture has been feeding on him. There's a near-catastrophic collapse of Prometheus's system. His blood pressure plummets; the remaining portion of his liver, his gall bladder and his pancreas all swell with bile, threatening to rupture. Then comes a spasm, as of an anaconda choking down its own tail. Then the adman's internal organs right themselves and he begins to spiel, talking better than ever, quip after riff after sly dig, all accompanied by charming jerks of his handsome head.

Ah, Prometheus, he has the great salesman's knack of being able to convince whomever he transfixes in his charm-beam that he really *does* want to be their friend; and, moreover, that his amity is something keenly to be desired, a passport to carefree sunny uplands – a larger commercial featuring baking-hot pool surrounds, convertibles sweeping along a generic corniche, tipsy dawn serenades beneath the balconies of rapacious Rapunzels . . . and more – much more.

'OK,' Zeus silences Prometheus. 'You can do the fucking water, *and* you jokers can come on the roster.'

Both admen begin to thank him, but Zeus chops them down: 'Yeah, yeah, don't get overexcited, there's a poxy spend on this one, and you're gonna have to deal with my people, who'll cut the deal with the media house. There's no percentage in it for you shysters. And, while we're at it, I don't want one penny wasted – and I want results!'

Then he's up and toddling among the tables – there is no other word for the muleless rider – towards the glassed partition separating the restaurant from the bar-cum-bakery, where bankers with unsustainable levels of personal debt dab at olive oil with cubes of bread. Zeus pays the bill en route, standing by the maître d's plywood podium punching digits into the card-reader.

Next he's gone, and it isn't until then that Prometheus realizes the tycoon hasn't so much as nodded to his own daughter.

In recent weeks Prometheus has found himself contemplating this fine madness: that he was born out of Athene's head, in a wobbling caul, from which his features – like the bonnet of an implausibly high-performing mid-range saloon car – stretch towards the future. But this is absurd. He was fully formed when they met; thirty-five, well educated – no mere Hoxton haircut with a grab-bag of thefts masquerading as creativity. And yet . . . her energy, the kissing slap of her buttocks against his thighs, the report of her thought in his mind . . . She was yet quicker than him, she had twists of phrase that left him spinning, unable to retort – how could this be?

In private members' clubs and minimalist bars, in restaurants with anorexic decor, and at plumply uncomfortable country house hotels in the Cotswolds where horse brasses neigh from the walls, Prometheus applies the bellows to his soul-forge. There's no tight-mindedness in him at all, no ability to guard his ideas, he gives of all and to all freely.

'What we advertise', he says, 'is nothing much – things, and the things people do. But what we *do*, matey, that's the real McCoy, the full-fucking-monty. See, when a punter sees what we *do*, likes what we *do*, he begins to desire our ads more than the things – and the things people do – that they're selling. At that exact moment the whole fucking gig catches fire, because now the punter wants ads – covets them; wants to be in that mytho-bloody-logical realm where a guy can strap on a pair of homemade wings and fly, or a chick can comb snakes outta her hair – real ones! – with the right kind of conditioner.'

Prometheus's voice, that's his weapon. What he says? Well, on the page it looks like any other copy for the same old pitch: nothing for money. But his voice – it dips and soars and writhes its way into his listeners. His notes are deep or high, his tone rough or smooth, his accent posh with a street edge, or street with a layer of posh tar.

'One per cent of GDP! One poxy per cent! We can do way better than *that*; after all, we're growing all the time, mutating – business to business, virals, naming rights ferchrissakes. One day soon . . .' He pauses all eyes on him; his aptitude is such that once you're fixed on Prometheus you cannot look away. You covet him. '. . . one of us – and I'm not necessarily saying it's gonna be me – is gonna figure out a way of selling advertising directly to the consumer –' His ceaseless movement, his jiggling and darting, suggests not nervousness but unbridled potency. 'Social networking is only the beginning – some time soon, every man, woman and child is gonna become their own agency. Then it'll be 2 per cent, 5 per cent –

way more than defence spending; the billings, my friends, will be astro-fucking-nomical!'

The whiplash of his upper body reels them in, while Prometheus's piercing, square eyes give those that look upon him the paradoxical feeling that it's he who is searching for the best angle from which to view them.

But that was now – and this, also, is now. Athene's heart-shaped face is annotated by her black curls; her torso is armoured in gold lamé. Even from forty feet away, glimpsed among cotton trunks and woollen boughs, Prometheus experiences a voyeuristic thrill. Oh! To be her friend, to be privy to those girly secrets and party to that caressing mockery.

Athene stands and whips the cloth from her table so swiftly that plates, glasses and cutlery all remain in place. She slings the cloth around her shoulders and shimmies up the aisle. Other women arise in her train, whip off their tablecloths and don them. Their abandoned lunch companions drum on the tables and howl a Bacchanalian jingle: 'Oooh-ooh, you can't stop the children of the revolution!'

Athene slips the linen off her shoulder and arm – they're naked; her high-kicking legs are bare as well. All the sashaying women are naked beneath their robes, robes they hold up in front of themselves to make targets for the cannonade of food the sous-chefs are firing from tiny tungsten mortars. Tripe splodges, langoustines clatter, kedgeree disintegrates into rice shot and fishy shards.

The maître d' pushes forward a washing machine, and, as Athene sheds her soiled raiment, the other dancers strike arty poses to preserve her modesty. She stuffs the tablecloth into the machine, it hums, shudders and spits it out – all within seconds. It's cleaner than a void.

A plastic container fifteen feet square crashes through the ceiling and bursts open, scattering detergent capsules with muscular arms and legs. These bounce into the arms of the dirty tablecloth dancers, the couples go into twirls, magically cleaning the stained linen. The basso voice-over rumbles above the chorus: 'When you use Ceres, it's as if your washing machine spins faster than the earth itself! Gods and mortals all agree . . .' Athene's perfect red lips suck on your eyelids, her flawless white teeth nibble your earlobes; she cries out in ecstasy, 'Ceres biological washing capsules are truly revolutionary!'

Shaking the drooping Prometheus by his shoulder, Epimetheus says, 'You've gotta go and see the doctor, mate.'

'I'm going to have to put a shunt in,' Dr Ben Macintyre says; 'otherwise you'll drown in your own blood.'
    'A shunt?'
    'A transjugular, intrahepatic, portosystemic shunt . . .' What kind of a cunt, thinks Prometheus, could even begin to say that in these circs. '. . . is a tube. We've got to bypass your liver with a tube – there's a mass of scar tissue in there, and it's increasing the pressure here.' He has a scan clipped to a lightbox and lays his hands on these representations of the affected parts – it's as near as he ever gets to touching his patients. The tips of his thumb and forefinger are callused, dead skin of which Doc Ben – as he styles himself – is inordinately proud.
    Prometheus is leaning against a snowy rampart of pillows on top of an examination couch. His top half is naked, his flesh so meagre and jaundiced it looks like a yellow cloth slung over a birdcage.
    'I don't have the results of your bloods yet.' Doc Ben moves away from the lit-up interior of Prometheus and turns his back on the exterior man himself. He cannot forbear from caressing the machine-head of an original Fender Stratocaster that's propped on a stand. 'But my guess is that more than half of your liver is now severely damaged.'

Prometheus says nothing. What is there to say?

Doc Ben is a stocky man in his mid fifties; clever features are clustered on the front of his mostly bald head. He isn't a liver specialist but rather a medical generalist with a nice drip of honey for the moneyed. When he says, 'We've got to bypass your liver with a tube', what he really means is that a technician at the Portland Clinic, the London Clinic or University College Hospital will be subcontracted to do so. These artisans of the body are essential for the likes of Doc Ben, the interior decorators of health in their Harley Street showrooms.

'I told you months ago that if you didn't change your lifestyle you'd be in serious trouble.'

'I don't drink – at least not alcohol.'

Doc Ben can't hear this: it's nonsensical. There are only two possible reasons for a man of Prometheus's age having such extensive liver damage – and he doesn't have hepatitis C; besides, Doc Ben is picking out the riff of 'One Bourbon, One Scotch, One Beer' on the steel strings. He hasn't picked the guitar up, he's hunched over it in his magenta flannel blazer, a dreamy expression on his realist's face.

In his heart Doc Ben is an axeman – one of the greatest ever. He once treated Dave Knopfler, and the grateful Dire Straits guitarist gave him a silver disc awarded to the band for selling 150,000 copies of 'Money for Nothing' in Lithuania. They also used to jam together in Doc Ben's consulting room. Happy days.

Doc Ben wrenches himself away from the guitar stand. 'You're bringing up blood from your tummy' – this juvenile term is a very considered piece of medical jargon – 'you could have a portal haemorrhage. I'll book you in somewhere overnight; the TIPS is a relatively simple procedure, there's no surgery required. It goes in through the jugular vein – a roadie can do it under a local.'

'A roadie?' Prometheus groans.

'Sorry, I mean a radiologist.'

It's warm in Doc Ben's consulting room. There's a lot of tapestry on the walls: bold swathes of red, blue and jaundiced woolliness that he's brought back from his travels; trips he takes to record traditional gourd-strummers, with a view to writing a primitivist rock opera. There are these tapestries and an intricately patterned Afghan rug, two ottomans, five hassocks and four Moroccan floor cushions. Patients, Doc Ben finds, are softened up by all this padding.

Prometheus accedes readily enough to the room up the road in the London Clinic, and is driven the few yards there by some Portia or other; a blue-blood thickie in an Alice band who works for Doc Ben, providing a constant background hum of unrequited lust and workaday erections.

In Prometheus's wake Doc Ben sends a pinging of emails, detailing all the thinners, lacquers and zappers that his patient should've been taking: drugs, the prescriptions for which lie curling on the floor of Prometheus's riverfront penthouse on the south side of Chelsea Bridge.

The clinic smells inappropriately of buttered asparagus and *bœuf en croûte*. Nurses dressed like maids and maids dressed like nurses process in and out of Prometheus's room. They offer drugs, which he accepts, and buttered asparagus and *bœuf en croûte*, which he refuses. He languishes, watching through bleary eyescreens as animated flyposters paste themselves over every available surface – walls, floor, ceiling. They're copy-heavy adverts for a Kentucky bourbon, one he wrote himself. The dense lettering describes a slow day in the long life of a grizzled stillman stirring sour mash in a dry county.

Posters have just furled over the windows and door when Doc Ben arrives, tearing a ragged hole in the outsized label of the bourbon bottle. He's swapped his blazer for a leather motorcycle jacket that is padded in such a way as to give him an implausible musculature. 'Taking the pills?' he asks, although his mind is on other, more rhythmic things. Prometheus moans affirmatively. Doc Ben goes to the bedside cabinet, picks up Prometheus's mobile phone and footles with it, trying to see if it'll play chords.

'I'm off to the Roundhouse tonight,' Doc Ben remarks. 'Playing with Glenn Branca and his orchestra of a hundred guitars ... Y'know, Prometheus, I'm really excited about this gig, a hundred axes – it's a big rush, but I doubt I'll have more than a bottle of Becks all night. You should think about that.' Adroitly, he leaves.

Prometheus thinks about what Doc Ben has said for a few minutes. When a nursemaid comes in a little later, carrying a reader so she can swipe Prometheus's credit card, the patient has decamped.

It's a hobby for him, sort of, but Zeus works in money the way a gifted sculptor shapes clay, deftly changing it from amorphousness into this, or that. He squeezes, rolls, smooths and indents money – then he sends glazed examples of his modelling all over the world.

An offshore bank in which a blind trust has a controlling interest, lends to a cardboard-box manufacturer in Tampa, Florida, the non-executive directors of which are also managers of a chain of fast Indian food outlets in the north-east of England. Their buyout is financed by the same Cayman Islands bank that – off the balance sheet – sends seed capital to one of these men, to enable him to establish a series of off-the-shelf companies in Douglas, on the Isle of Man. One of these companies is a convenient entity through which to funnel the profits from AABA Escorts, an atomized brothel – the client book, office lease and website are its only assets – a net woven from electro-financial strands, within which to catch sexual cannibals so they can feed on each other.

One such is Pandora – 22, 5'5", 34DD, English. This stunning young lady is not only available for in and out calls, but will also, seemingly happily – in tabloid parlance – 'romp' with you and your partner, whether you be male, female or both.

Pandora, whose honeyed skin is intensified by the application of much Piz Buin – and sunlight; for every third week she jets away to a pimp's timeshare in Las Palmas. Pandora, whose every seam and join is caulked with commercially applied saliva. Pandora, whose body is a box for which her pretty head is the lid.

A prostitute never kisses a client – mouths are so much more intimate than genitals. And mouth-on-mouth, well, that will resuscitate those memories, open up Pandora's box; then, out will fly all the misfortunes of the world: the stepfather who put his penis in her when she was eleven; the glue bags she huffed in the park shelter; the orange-collared hypodermic needles her first pimp poked between her toes, so as not to damage 'the goods'. Inside, Pandora is as crushed and smeared and broken as roadkill, but for now the box still looks tip-top, eminently desirable, knick-knack-sado-whack.

Epimetheus was sitting in his simple past when Pandora rang. Sitting in his simple past, and sitting also in his loft, a dwelling that mimics a past assumed to be simple, when people – natives – bought and sold simply quantified goods that could be simply stored, instead of the maddening complexity of the present, when an adman sits in an apartment designed to look like a warehouse in another city.

Epimetheus was sitting and worrying a little about Prometheus, whom he hadn't heard from since he dropped him off at Doc Ben's in Harley Street. However, this anxiety was nothing much, a teaser for a campaign that never got going. Epimetheus had seen it tens of times before: his partner, bilious, black at the edges, sliding like a banana skin from the back seat of a cab into the converted townhouse, only to show up again the following morning, more than ready for that all-to-play-for pitch, as electrifying as ever, his spiel a never-ending webpage that scrolled up and up and up.

'It's me,' Pandora said, and her voice grabbed him by the scruff and dragged him to the full-length windows. Epimetheus pressed his eye against the wickerwork basketry of the city as a child stares into a hedge.

'You swiped my fucking leather jacket – have you any idea how much it's worth?'

'Like, duh, I wouldn't've if I didn't.'

But is it a pity she's a whore? He didn't think so. He had been sitting there, in his underwear, nursing a restorative beer and casting back a decade to the lager of male bonding. Menoetius, Prometheus and him, out on the town; pubs dissolving into clubs dissolving into after-hours bars; the flow of their ideas seeming as smoothly inevitable as the passage of a hoppy droplet through the condensation on a glass.

'Would you like me to come over?'

'How much is it gonna cost me this time?'

Casting back to his time at art college, Epimetheus remembered a collage he'd made, a griffon vulture soaring, its feathers so many carefully selected bits of black vinyl, buff sacking and white plastic; its beak and talons chrome trim scavenged from verges and gutters. His tutor asked, 'Is it a mind-child, m'dear?' And Epimetheus set him right: 'No, you see them in Cyprus.'

Flapping like airborne Turks over the carcasses of Greek houses, the walls of Nicosia bleached bone-white in the Mediterranean sun. In the hurly-burly of his parents' exile – in Newington Green, the Stroud Green Road, Green Lanes, all those London greenings – these abandoned properties remained, unusable annexes to their walk-up flats and tumbling-down terraced houses.

The three Greek Cypriot lads fought running battles with the Clapton Turks. Menoetius, Prometheus, Epimetheus – Titans, almost, especially when they were reinforced by hulking Atlas, who, unlike the others, dropped out of school. When Epimetheus had last run into him – a colossus in a crombie – Atlas was a bouncer at the Hippodrome. He said he still saw the Clapton Turks occasionally: 'Blue-metallic Mercs, profile tyres, personalized-bloody-number plates . . . iss smack, 'course, that cunt Osmun is up to his bloody elbows in the shit. Saw 'im giving it large in China White wiv a couple of tarts. I tellya, Epimetheus, we're well out of it, mate.'

Sadly, all Epimetheus thought was, what happened to that simple, uncomplicated male friendship – that bond? Thought this, and also – hearing the buzzer go, then seeing Pandora's old-girl face in the video intercom – envied Osmun his 2:1 ratio of prostitutes to consumer.

A certain savvy, skill sets and creative DNA are necessary to satisfy clients' service demands. The first pitch may've gone well, but the second still needs to be won on the bounce – in this case of Epimetheus's swinging bed. Last night it was toxic-induced impotence; tonight it's premature ejaculation.

Pandora copes – she can think on her feet, her back, her haunches. She eases herself off him as he slithers out of her, then slobbers down to do what is required. Later on, she teases out of Epimetheus exactly how his mother used to do him an egg, then coddles him one.

Recently, Pandora launched her own campaign: press ads with simple slogans, scanty body copy, end-lines that are an email address, no colour or graphics, and buried in an assortment of publications – *Private Eye*, the *London Magazine*, the *Daily Telegraph* – that her research department of other, smarter tart friends tell her are most likely to reach her target audience: *hommes d'un certain âge* ready to be led by the cock to be fleeced.

Pandora is violently tired – not even remotely curious. She knows what it will be like to be a mistress: humiliation on hire purchase, a drip-drip-drip of acid semen eating away at her soul instead of these corrosive gushes. 'Me, blonde poetess who needs to be kept in Krug. You, a cultured gentleman who knows the difference

between a sommelier and a sun visor. Temptress@demon.co.uk.'
She has a number of these prospects on the go, but is yet to close
a sale. So, if she gets sent this one, why not? He's both younger and
uglier than she'd hoped for, but he looks as if he may be able to
withstand all the misfortunes.

Four miles upriver, a grape stalk struggles to escape the lid of an
aluminium swing-bin; besides a couple of humans, this is the sole
organic thing to be found in this penthouse apartment. It's a fancy
absence – a thousand square feet of bleached beech floorboards,
the same again of walls so perfectly plastered they could be in an
art gallery – so long as its curator was defiant enough to exhibit
nothing. There are no pictures in Prometheus's home, no sculptures, mementoes or curios. His few personal effects are jammed
in walk-in closets; the fitted kitchen is sealed in white units.
A plain white futon lies in the middle of the floor; on it lies
Prometheus, and on him lies Athene.

'I was worried,' she says; 'you didn't answer your phone – and,
at the restaurant, you looked so ill.'

'It was nothing,' he husks into her neck, 'just indigestion.'

'You looked like you were dying.'

Her pulse is against his lips; he inhales the hydrogenated
wholeness of her. Belly to belly, breast to breast, they are grouted
by their spent passion; their hearts and lights and livers are the
shared organs of conjoined twins. Prometheus has never felt
better.

Athene rears up, is captured for a moment by those colour-chart
eyes, then falls to defining his face with her kisses. 'Huh, well' –
she's abashed – 'you're so beautiful – so healthy.'

It's true: Prometheus has a marvellous glow. And, while commit-
ted entirely to this moment – and to this goddess – he is also
looking forward to an attainable future, one in which video clips of
celebrities drinking Zeus mineral water infest social networking

sites; a virus leaping from PC to laptop across the only world that's worth being known.

Prometheus grabs the neck of a 1.5 litre plastic bottle, pulls its hard mouth to his soft lips, drinks awkwardly and points the bottle to the face of Athene, who arches her neck. Chilly spillage ungums the lovers, arousing them once more. Athene takes a mouthful of water and, moving down him, sleeves Prometheus's penis in this coolant.

Their motions those of sea creatures just evolved to move on land, the lovers resume the making of it; they creep over, then under, one another. Prometheus rears back, her trapezius muscles gripped like handlebars; this is not the explosion that tore Athene's clothing from her, hurling it across the beech flooring in the blast pattern of lust; this is ruminative lovemaking, as infinitely tender and considerately solipsistic as two geriatrics masturbating with each other's hands.

It is completely dark, yet seagulls are still mucking around the containers piled behind the chainlink, razor-wire and concrete fencing. Containers full of everything worth having – food, electrical goods, furniture, paper, metal, plastic, old photos, letters, locks of hair – that cannot be matched to anyone that wants it. The containers are waiting for dawn, when they will be grabbed, then winched on to barges, before being floated downriver from the Wandsworth Solid Waste Transfer Station to landfills on the Essex marshes.

The griffon vulture flies up to the massive beam of the winch, then accepts the gulls' mobbing as of right, smiling inscrutably out from the grey riot of their wings. Lazily, she takes once more to the sky; eighty feet up she yaws, then tacks across to the Hurlingham, then back to the Heliport, then from there to Chelsea Harbour, until her course takes her in past the Peace Pagoda to dock in one of the avenues of planes running along Battersea Park Parade.

The feral smell they sense as fear incarnate blows through dank boughs and raggy leaves, to reach blackbirds, pigeons – crows, even – and wake them from their citified sleep, safe under sodium lights. They limp into the air. As with the Wandsworth gulls, the griffon accepts their mobbing gracefully. Trailing the scrappy little airforce, she dallies over the floodlit tennis courts, then spirals up, the smaller birds falling away, fighter cover that has failed to bring the liver-freighter down.

Up, banking past the clapboard gasometer, soaring between the signature chimneys of the power station, then wheeling back round to approach Chelsea Bridge Wharf, not, as its developers might have wished, to take 'Another Look' – their own end-line for this terminally uninteresting development – but in order to land on the topmost of the curved balconies, which, in as much as they resemble jetties at all, are ones only suitable for the loading and unloading of brioche.

So considerate, the vulture, so intuitive; she enters with the aplomb of a third lover, en route to join the two entwined on the futon. Hearing the rustle and scratch as she beaks, then necks open the sliding glass door, Prometheus stirs but does not turn over – he knows who it is. Athene's hip is smooth and rounded in his palm, her wheaten belly rising against his finger tips. In pleasured drowse, she senses the cold air and murmurs a sing-song, 'Y'all right, love?' Only to be reassured by his face pressing further into the arch of her neck.

The vulture insinuates her head under the duvet, and Prometheus bites his lips hard enough to draw blood as she makes her expert incision, reopening a wound only superficially healed. As the bird feeds, her feathers – black, buff and white alike – are suffused with the pinkish wash of the external floodlights; a colour scheme that will, its developers hope, make of the wharf a pleasing property sweetmeat. Highly edible.

With pulp-tipped claws the grape stalk pulls itself out of the bin, while inside Prometheus's fridge an old Roquefort rind shudders into life; then a celery stalk rocks, rolls and tips upright. For a split-second the earth stops spinning and its magnetic field is neutralized: the fridge door unsuckers itself. Rind of Roquefort, stalk of celery, four squares of Swiss milk chocolate – all sprout cartoon limbs as they jump down to the white beech floor; in the fridge light they jeté to join the pirouetting grape stalk.

Throughout the wharf women light scented candles as they make ready to recline in tubs frothing with stress-busting bubbles, and men surf channels to rediscover the Discovery Channel. They are oblivious, seized only by relaxation, gripped by little more than reverie. So it is that the contents of their fridges and freezers are able to rustle, crack and rumble into life.

Lifts rush down into precisely ruled courtyards where bought rocks cluster in frigid beds and water features; the animated food-stuffs waltz out of their metal doors. The double-sized figures of wholesome chaps and winsome chapesses tear themselves from the billboards, where for four seasons they've languished tapping little ends with huge teaspoons. These demigods and demigoddesses feel not the cruel west wind that parts their mighty terry-towelling robes; they round up the food, cajoling frozen chickens, lassoing pots of clotted cream, trawling bags of Ethiopian sugar-snap beans and arresting jars of pesto. The subdued food is shovelled into an immense cone that one young Hercules has fashioned from a sheet of corrugated iron torn from a nearby scaffold.

The billboard deities choreograph a *tableau gigantesque* around this horn of left-over plenty – and this, truly, is worth Another Look. Then, with no sense of movement, no crude disjunction, we're back in the penthouse, back in the kitchen, back in the fridge – where a single slim tin of energy drink, lit by its own inner taurine and decorated with the silhouette of a naked youth that's blazoned 'Ganymede Up All Nite', half bows, crunching itself a waist.

And still the vulture feeds, its frightful ruff saturated with Prometheus's blood.

Doc Ben doesn't, as a rule, do house calls. 'Whadda vey fink eye am,' he says dropping into Mockney for the benefit of his Portia, 'a fucking tart?' A strange denial, because that's precisely what he is: after all, he puts himself about by the hour and deals drugs on the side – although, admittedly, not very nice ones. Doing out-calls is not the distinction between medical whoring and doctoring.

Nevertheless, Doc Ben feels differently about Prometheus: *the guy is three chords short of a punk song*, too crazy even to be considered as a proper patient. He revolves through the Harley Street consulting room every fortnight, his liver rotten to the core, *then off he pops, it's almost as if*. . . But Doc Ben is way too preoccupied to make the diagnosis any open-minded practitioner would be compelled to: that Prometheus's liver is being eaten away at, then spontaneously regenerated. Way too preoccupied by finding a parking place for his Porsche – and not just any berth. The underground car park at the wharf is *way wrong*; no security, poorly illuminated, and the mad axeman – who's actually an amateurishly poor plucker – has two Gibson Les Pauls in the boot worth *a cool fifteen grand*.

When he eventually finds a safe on-road space, then ascends the lift, Doc Ben discovers Athene waiting for him at the front door to the penthouse. A stench of organ failure hangs in the costly void. Below the plate glass prow of the block, the woolly-brown river knits and pearls itself. Lying face down on the futon, the impassioned lover of the night before resembles a used condom stuffed with offal. There's a large bloodstain by his latex belly.

Doc Ben thinks, there's always more sex the morning after than there was the night before; he has a nose for these scents, and Athene hasn't showered, only pulled on underwear, skirt and blouse, rolled-up stockings. He clocks the hot veins on the insides of her wrists as she presses her razor-thin mobile phone to her cheek. Idly wondering *how the fuck does he get it up*, Doc Ben kneels to give the adman a rare probe.

'He discharged himself from the London Clinic yesterday, did he tell you?'

Athene, who has introduced herself only as 'a friend', blanches.

'He was meant to have a liver shunt put in today, but it's too late for that now. There's massive distension here – his tummy is full of blood.'

Doc Ben is a good enough doctor, just, to notice this; although not good enough to spot the long, curved feather that's wedged between patient and mattress. 'I'm gonna call for an ambulance – he needs to be in an intensive-care unit as soon as possible. Do you know who his next of kin are, Ms . . .'

'Athene,' she concedes, then asks, 'Is he going to die?'

'Die? I dunno about that.' He could be speculating on poor ticket sales for a Deep Purple reunion gig, so mundane is his tone. 'I can tell you this: if he can be stabilized – and that's a fairly big if – he'll need a liver transplant, deffo. His liver's . . .' He pauses, regarding her well-used voluptuousness at the same time as he, belatedly, registers her name; then allows himself a definitive 'fucked'.

The griffon vulture watches from the summit of the north-west chimney of Battersea Power Station as Prometheus is stretchered from Chelsea Bridge Wharf to the waiting ambulance. She's driven away the peregrine falcons – London's sole pair – whose nesting site is this modernist ruin: a redbrick cliff-face, saturated with sulphuric acid and carbon, the best monument possible to human-kind's transmogrification of the earth.

From her lofty vantage, the vulture stares down on traffic, river, park greenery and the mop-top of Athene, who skips to the far side of the road, intent on hailing a cab to get her away from this awful wharf.

★

A fortnight later Epimetheus met up with Neil Bolton for a drink at the Sealink Club. Epimetheus didn't bother much with the Sealink any more; the ad industry's social interaction, such as it was, had headed east, to where the new generation of mono-nominal agencies – Mother, Naked, Poke, Dare and Titan itself – had gone to ground amidst the artists' studios and Bangladeshi sweat shops of Whitechapel and Shoreditch.

As for Bolton, he'd never been an habitué of the Sealink, which, despite having suffered new owners and revamped decor at least twice in the past decade, still had a car-ferry ambience, what with its safety lights caught in wire basketry, three-legged triangular chairs and raised door sills. The gents' urinal was a waterfall in a zinc trench, the stalls a storm in a space shuttle. This, the quintessence of chic circa 1980, was all far too modish for Bolton, who longed to strip the skirts from the yattering women who frequented the club, if only to put them on the table legs.

Bolton, who in recent years had become the narrator of a fiendishly successful TV sketch show – think *both* spin-off dolls *and* hagiographies of its originators in the qualities; think of catchphrases as widespread and involuntary as sneezes – now gave himself airs that would've been insufferable coming from Kean. When Epimetheus came in, Bolton was standing centre bar, his big fleshy face hanging in the air like a bruise, poorly bandaged with several loops of a long woollen scarf. He was holding forth to the barman, and his basso voice, like Pavlov's tinkling bell, recalled insistently to the minds of all who were hearing it the mineral water, meat, detergent and, latterly, energy drink it had been used to advertise, as it rumbled through the bar, inexorable as waves crashing on a shingle beach.

Spotting Epimetheus, Bolton boomed, 'My dear boy, how's Prometheus?'

'He's fine, really Neil.' Epimetheus ordered a gin and tonic.

'That's not what I hear,' Bolton told everyone. 'I've heard he's in and out of hospital every few days – some sort of liver thing.'

Liver thing. Bolton managed to deliver the words with coloratura at once bloody and bilious. Liver things – Bolton knew all about these: his last decade or so had been a cellular go-round, from bar, to recording studio, to rehab, and back again.

'Shush, Neil.' Epimetheus went so far as to take the old thespian by his boneless arm and give it a squeeze. 'Please, I don't want any more talk.'

This was a futile admonition, given that Bolton was *nothing but* talk; besides, the cutting-edge creatives may no longer have supped at the Sealink, but their older, blunter colleagues were all there: client directors, chief strategy officers and group accountants from Abbott Mead Vickers, Bartle Bogle Hegarty, and Saatchi and Saatchi, who, while they may have lost the ability to create particular standout, still retained good noses for the bouquet of distress and the stench of failure.

'He's absolutely fine,' Epimetheus continued, signalling to the barman to get them both another drink. 'As it happens, we've gotta big pitch tomorrow, Hermes.'

'Scarves?' Bolton said, tugging on his own.

'No, the other lot – mobile phones.'

This wasn't a work drink. At this point in his liverish life cycle Bolton was useless to Titan; he was so bloated with fine wines and TV residuals that he'd completely forgotten the voice-over he'd done for Zeus mineral water only ten days previously, and instead blethered on about his finest theatrical performances. His Falstaff (Southampton Gala), his Henry Higgins (Stamford Arts Centre) and, of course, his triumphant Hamm at the Peacock.

Epimetheus, whose knowledge of Beckett's plays was sketchy, kept hearing *Endgame* as 'end-line', which dragged him back to advertising, and his own naive faith in luxury goods, graven images and idols with everything of clay. Which dragged him back to . . . Pandora, who had brought oodles of vice and insanity into his life.

The previous evening he had arrived back from Old Street to find her fucking a stranger in his own bed. Epimetheus drubbed the man from the place; his last sight of him was a bare bottom impressed with the tread of his boot. He threw the man's clothing out the window, then had to endure Pandora's full-fledged psychotic breakdown: handwashing without soap or water; a 'Pakki' called Andy beating her, who likewise wasn't there; then the spewing of five dirty tongues with her delicious little one. And then – shameful this – he ravished her, after which they did drugs together.

In the ten days since she had moved into his loft, Pandora had begun to abstract Epimetheus's goods. They were bizarre thefts – a single cuff link one day, a solo stereo speaker the next. The smooth materiality of his existence was being peppered with holes – yet still he cleaved to her; they would, he avowedly hoped, be together in old age, snuggling down into the soft ruin of their bodies.

Hence this get-together with Bolton, for advice on where Epimetheus could send his love so that she could 'get better'. Who better than Bolton, who'd done 'em all? Primary treatments, secondary ones; halfway houses, three-quarter ones; then first-through-third-stage sojourns. Bolton, slobbing out in front of wonky tellies watching fake dramas, while the real tragedy of his life was right to hand – at his feet, where poorly laid carpet tiles curled up from the carpet tiles that had been poorly laid by the last batch of recovering alcoholics.

Ach! Bolton! So washed away by the longshore drift of his alcoholism that he could no longer tell which group he was not a part of. Were these stacking chairs circled for talking or drinking therapy? How should he pitch this old tale of derring-tipsy-do, as pathos, bathos or self-flagellating realism? In his old haunt, the Plantation Club, Bolton was nothing but a joke – and a bad one.

To abandon his drinking comrades once was a betrayal; to do it again and again was their equivalent of a war crime. Hilary, the Plantation's commanding officer, had stripped Bolton of his old moniker and given him a new one; he was no longer 'the Extra' but only 'the Prop'; because, despite having been barred, he still insisted on coming back and propping himself against it. The bar, that is.

Epimetheus was drunker than Bolton, and the actor did indeed have to prop the adman up, as, wavering in and out of blackout, they proceeded to Blore Court by way of Piccadilly Circus.

Sony PlayStations and Nicorette patches; Halifax mortgages and Nokia mobile phones; Coca-Cola and depilatory cream; the giant girlies of a mythic present – apple-cheeked Hesperides, star-fucking Pleiades, Hyades suffering with water retention – rode juggernauts and scaled the sides of buildings in their armour of lights. Cars transformed into robots and duelled down Lower Regent Street, while Eros fired arrows that were tipped with soft-centred milk chocolates.

Epimetheus reeled through the throng, each face a semi-transparent pop-up ident swelling in his monitors: clay faces, not yet set, gashes for mouths, indentations for eyes, slick with the water they swigged from plastic bottles, each labelled with a rusty tap-tap-tap graphic. Overhead, the electronic signboards bellied out, their surface tension a deliquescent blare. Clay and water, flesh and.

Blood and bile flowed through the veins of the liverish city; coiled conduits that merged, then branched out into the biliary tree of Soho. In Blore Court the two drunks tumbled through the visceral peritoneum, before being sucked into the porta hepatis. They staggered on the stairs, slammed against the door of Mr Vogel's long-dormant import business, recovered themselves, fell up the next flight, collapsed through the filthy plywood door – its baize long since gone – and, partially recovering themselves, entered the bar-room with all the nonchalance of five-year-olds stealing biscuits.

Hilary was on his stool by the cash register, an illegal cigarette between washing-up-glove fingers, a vodka and tonic in front of him. Behind the bar, Stevie was slotting a new bottle of Bacardi into an optic, while on the other side the Cunt and the Poof raised their animalistic faces from small pools of alcohol.

The smoking ban had been in force for only a few months, yet witnessing someone smoking in a bar was like seeing an old film. Epimetheus's lazy eyes rolled down the blue-grey grooves of smoke to where these merged with the inflamed veins networking Hilary's swollen nose. He looked away, and discovered the Martian deep in conversation with Isobel Beddoes, who, since she had been released from jail in Switzerland, had assumed the position formerly occupied by Her Ladyship. Margery De Freitas, dead drunk for years; now simply dead.

Isobel – known in the Plantation as 'Come-to-Beddoes' – was tolerated by Hilary because she had an inheritance to squander. Her miserable devotion to him was another bad joke. Sometimes he made her fuck Jones, the resident cocaine dealer, in return for a gramme for them to split – he and Jones, that is.

There were two or three other members in the club – a Scots sculptor who specialized in Holocaust memorials, a fashion writer for a mid-market tabloid, Cal Devenish, the ailing television personality and one-time literary enfant terrible – but even to Epimetheus's untutored eye they were an irrelevance. He saw only the old ads for cable-knit cardigans tacked to the bamboo-patterned wallpaper; the gibbous letters of an ancient flyer that bellowed BLACK SABBATH AT THE MARQUEE CLUB; and a tin hoarding showing two cloth-capped kids, their nostrils flared to suck in a meaty ribbon, which had had its slogan customized to read 'Ah! Cunto'.

''Allo,' Hilary said after an age, 'it's the fucking Prop – and oo's this ugly cunt 'e's got viv 'im, eh?'

Billy tittered and took a slug of his vodka-spiked lager. Bolton swept off his mohair fedora and addressed the company magniloquently. 'Ladies, gentlemen, my residuals are far from negligible, courtesy of this fine and principled advertising executive. I'm in a position to offer you and your leader' – he half bowed to Hilary – 'many libations.'

Paper cuts an already raw mucous membrane. Insufflation: the shrapnel blast of cocaine granules. Jostled by flying blood boulders, the tiny colourless creatures embark on the next leg of their fantastic voyage.

Abruptly, in the still, sweaty eye of his drunken storm – and after a score of nights the same – Epimetheus remembered that last night was especially not right. In the small hours, while Pandora whimpered beside him, crazy little grunts falling from her parted lips, he was gripped by an ague so intense that the chains of his dangling bed clinked. He knew it then – he knows it now still more – his body had new visitors, and, unlike so many of the others, these would stay.

The eggy reek of a forehead drenched with feverish sweat, the watery flux of the bowels; if only, Epimetheus thought, this was some earlier era when such supernatural rumblings could be propitiated, when there was a gross, yet effective, match between anatomy and belief. Instead, he would have to make an appointment to see Doc Ben – this, too, impinged, a rock in the maelstrom of alcohol – so that those callused fingers could prod the buttons, make the calls, arrange the further appointments at which Epimetheus's organs would be peered into by X- and gamma-rays.

'Oi! You! Ugly cunt – bonehead.' It was Hilary.

'Me?' Epimetheus beheld the ancestral nose.

'Yeah, you. What're you 'aving?'

He was having a nervous breakdown – drowning in the splenetic fluids of the Plantation, a hepatocyte in a lobule in a lobe in a liverish city. London, a metropolis that had itself been breaking down cultural toxins and processing rich nutrients for two millennia, yet could only do so by manufacturing hectolitres of bile.

Never before had Epimetheus been so transported by all the rough and scumble of lived life: the blurring of feeling and texture that lay below the slickery of his visuals – an icy surface that human desire skated over, describing figure eights, pound and dollar signs.

'I said, what're you FUCKING 'AVING!'

A frozen moment, indeed. Nowadays, Hilary was prone to lashing out, and Stevie was a girl who walked into doors. The Cunt said, 'Shall I give 'im the old 'eave-'o 'ilary?' But the Martian, who was fetching his and Come-to-Beddoes's drinks, took the matter in hand, picking Epimetheus up and lifting him on top of the bar.

For the art director was nothing but a perspex torso, such as are used in pharmaceutical advertisements. His transparent outer layer would allow a camera lens to discover green gall bladder, pink pancreas, blue guts, brown stomach and red liver; all the better to convince the superstitious peasantry – for whom medicine remains a cadet branch of magic – that they should leave their innards to the professionals.

The Martian slipped on a crisp white coat and brandished a pointer; Stevie hurried around arranging the chairs and bar stools for the presentation. The neon tube on the ceiling spluttered, then flared solar, annealing every scumbled thing until it was white-tile-hard and bright. The audience put on the same expressions of serious concern. The Martian picked up a jug of water from the bar and poured some into Epimetheus's reopened fontanelle; it trickled down, a silver stream that the Martian followed with his pointer, while saying, 'Pegasys is an injectable form of pegylated interferon alpha . . .' The water coursing through his veins and converging on his liver felt icily dangerous – not that Epimetheus, object lesson that he had become, could do a damn thing about it.

'Success,' the Martian snapped, 'you can depend on all the way. Patients in clinical studies, overall, had a better than 50 per cent chance of achieving sustained viral response. Pegasys helps the body's immune system fight the hepatitis C virus; Pegasys is the most prescribed medication of its kind.' The small audience was rapt, their eyes following the Martian's pointer as it tapped first one lurid organ, then the next. Epimetheus's liver was brimming with bubbling water – his own clever visualization, intended to express the mortal combat of the winged horse and the viral Furies.

Understanding very well that timing was everything, Bolton, thorough professional that he was, constricted his range and enormously increased the speed of his delivery. The result was – to paraphrase Coleridge – that listening to him was like reading the index of the *A–Z*, while someone kept flicking a lighter that obstinately refused to ignite.

'SeriousadverseeventsinhepatitisCtrialsincludedneuropsychiatric disordersseriousandseverebacteriologicalinfectionsbonemarrow toxicitycardiovasculardisordershypersensitivityendocrinedisorders autoimmunedisorderspulmonarydisorderscolitispancreatitisand ophthalmologicaldisorders.'

As this babbling of side effects went on, nobody noticed the flight feathers curled round the edge of the plywood door, fresh as paint. The griffon vulture sidled in along the wall, her buff wing coverts rasping against the bamboo-patterned flock. She hopped up on to the piano keyboard, her talons striking the opening chords of Chopin's *Marche Funèbre* – music oddly appropriate for an anti-retroviral advert.

The griffon hopped up again and, biding her time, pecked the Prince Consort's sightless eyes. She didn't have long to wait: the Martian was reaching the end of his thirty-five seconds of enlightening, his pointer, tipped with a ball of green lightning, poised over Epimetheus's carbonated liver. The vulture flapped down and came barrelling through the audience of drinkers. Hilary swung his hornbill towards her beak. 'Blimey!' he exclaimed. 'Who's this birdy cunt?'

It was too late for Epimetheus, for, with the crazyological cutting of a TV advert, the vulture grabbed his liver in her talons, then, taking off across the bar-room, smashed through the sash window, swooped along Blore Court, banked into Berwick Street and began to climb over Raymond's Revue Bar, up into the contusion of the London night.

It was to be a civilized drink to discuss the future of their relationship – if it had one. The venue: the champagne bar at the Savoy; here, among solid leather footstools, there would be no footsie. Then, at the final hour, Athene is overpowered by the wanting of him, so calls and suggests that Prometheus come instead to her father's huge penthouse apartment, high above the river at Vauxhall.

He takes the call while watching a financial services advert on cab TV; he's on his way from the City, where he's been making a pitch for another such. Making it alone, because Epimetheus has been getting flakier and flakier in the past fortnight: dead scalp on the padded shoulders of a clerk in the offices of a building society. Perhaps.

'Oh. OK,' Prometheus says, 'but what about your old man?'

'He's in Zürich seeing his bankers. I've sent the staff away for the night and the doorman's stoned on qat.'

She's thought of everything – except how she'll feel when, for the first time since his *boudin noir* body was fed into the ambulance, she sees Prometheus. He's so tanned, so planed, so pivoting on the moment, that all the lines she rehearsed, sitting at her dressing table clipping on Bulgari and spraying Clive Christian No. 1, evaporate. She was going to say, 'It's drugs, isn't it?' Because nothing else could begin to explain his total collapse, followed a few hours later by a blithely apologetic call assuring her he was 'on the mend'. At the time, Athene hated him as much as the cliché; but, instead of remonstrating with him, she says, 'I want to tell Zeus about us.' A thought not arrived at until precisely now, for she's in thrall to her father and knows no other life than the lifestyle that goes with compliance to his whims. Athene is used to wealth – swims in it like an element, and has no understanding of its true clagginess.

Prometheus says, 'I'm shocked; I'd assumed I was only a bit of rough for you.' He moves towards her, his trainers soundless on the dark marble with its liverish veins and swirls.

Zeus's penthouse is enormous; its twenty-foot-high windows imprison within their dark aquaria the big oily fish – Rothkos, Trougets and Freuds – that are mandatory catches for the ultra-rich. The fossilized trunk of an ancient hardwood rears up out of an equally ancient Japanese basin, its sinuous boughs embracing the plush atmosphere. Zeus's interior decorater convinced him this feature would 'bring the outside in, to integrate the domestic with the natural'; but what it actually does is to demonstrate that most of us are doomed.

Prometheus takes Athene in his arms, his hands in her warm hand-holds, and presses his cheek to hers. 'I want to be with you, too,' he says, although his mind is racing ahead. Where will we live? He sees an ugly Victorian house in Wandsworth, the sheet of grey paving in front of it punctuated by the commas of dog turds, a recycling bin hooked over the railings, evidence of a repetitive task that is all the more Sisyphean for its pretension to virtue. He sees Athene, grown plump and ordinary and matronly, no longer a fabulous deity, only another upper-middle-class woman, a function of her taste and her credit rating: a target group of one.

'I want to be with you, too,' he reiterates, 'and we've gotta talk, but –' He twitches, and his skin tightens, sensing the vulturine approach, and he wonders if this, also, could be accommodated in Wandsworth. 'First I've gotta use your loo, I'm busting.'

Athene wriggles out from him, frowning. He waggles the half-empty bottle of Zeus mineral water, and she points the way down a malachite passage to the third door on the gauche.

In the oasis, a clear pool beckons to Prometheus from between ferny fronds. He looks for Polynesian beauties offering him half coconut shells brimming with milk – then remembers this was a chocolate advert in his childhood. There's no window in the bathroom, only the ceaseless moan of aircon. Prometheus frantically dithers, caught between the demands of bladder and vulture. He succumbs, unzips, relieves himself, then, using his inner Ariadne, he makes his way through a maze of smaller passageways to the service entrance, where he finds the griffon vulture already waiting for him, a superior look first in one yellow eye, then the other.

Farce ensues as Prometheus tries to smuggle the giant bird back to the toilet so that she can feed on him in peace. He has to hurry – he's been gone a while and Athene is bound to be suspicious. The vulture isn't helping, uttering peremptory feeding cries – pig grunts, goose hisses – as she butts at his thigh.

They gain the toilet and are about to go in, when there's Athene, her amethyst eyes flashing, the words 'It's drugs, isn't it?' expiring on her ruby lips.

Prometheus stretches out the wings of his jacket, attempting to hide the scavenger; the griffon defeats his efforts by stretching out her own wings. Prometheus hustles right and hustles left, as if this two-step can obscure the vast span of feathers, the bony brow, the delving beak. 'So,' Athene says redundantly, 'it's not drugs.'

'No,' Prometheus begins. The urge is upon him to explain the griffon vulture away – to riff, to spiel, to sell himself – but for once he's tongue-tied and can only mutter, 'It's not drugs.'

'I should've guessed!' she spits. 'Your stupid Greek name.'

'I am Greek' – he paused – 'ish.'

And there it was: he had subsided into a simpler past, and so discovered a different, more honest, eloquence. 'She comes,' he explained, 'most days, and feeds. Obviously, I feel . . . like shit the next day, but then my liver – it grows back.'

'Regenerates.'

'Yeah, that. And when it does I feel better than ever, every time. Stronger, cleverer, too – more able to win pitches – bigger pitches with bigger spends. The first time she came I won the Zephyrcard account from your –' He faltered.

'My father.' Athene, despite his revelations, and the vulture's presence – its antediluvian vibe, its reek of nitrogen and rotting flesh – was disengaged, bored.

The vulture was becoming more agitated, spluttering and chuckling, working her head up the back of Prometheus's clothes, desperate to feed. 'I *have* to . . .' He gestured hopelessly.

'What're you saying – that the two of you require privacy?'

'N-No, not exactly privacy, but somewhere out of the way.'

'I should've bloody realized,' Athene mused; 'the stains on your futon, and I thought it was my period – then that creepy doctor came.'

'Yeah, yeah, he is a creep, isn't he. No, we – she – doesn't need privacy, just somewhere I can sorta bend over and be, um, *braced*. I normally do it on the bog.'

'No.' Athene was emphatic. 'This I've got to see.'

She led Prometheus back to the main room of the penthouse and pointed to the tree trunk. 'How about there? You can brace yourself against that.'

'It's hardly private, Athene. This is a glass box – anyone could see.'

'Bullshit!' Her colour was up: two burning spots in the centre of each olive cheek. 'No one can see in here – unless they're sitting on top of Tate Britain with a fucking telescope. Now, get on with it – that bloody bird's starting to nauseate me.'

Which was fair enough, because there was something not right with the vulture; her talons scrabbled on the marble floor, her wings hung limp, and her deep chest spasmed. Prometheus stepped towards her, then, arrested by Athene's furious scowl, retreated to the columnar tree trunk. He took off his sorrel jacket, then began to pull his mushroom shirt over his head. The bird *was* sick – that much was obvious. He was gripped by dread: if she couldn't feed, then what of him? He knew that what they had was a compact: her liverish treat gave him his gift of the gab, and so won Titan their new business; deprived of it, he'd be only another pedlar, crying his wares without the city walls.

Prometheus turned his back on the bird, and, bending over, shackled himself to the petrified wood with his own arms. He willed the vulture to be peckish.

Athene cried, 'Oh my God!' Prometheus whipped upright as the vulture arched her long neck and began to wretch. Together they watched, appalled, as a lump travelled up the bird's gullet; she coughed, then evacuated rubbery red chunks across the liverish marble floor. Blood and bile splattered the legs of Athene's sky-blue satin lounging pyjamas – she leapt for the shelter of the dead tree. But Prometheus went forward.

And knelt. How could this be? He sensed recognition in the regurgitated carrion: it knows me, he thought, and – more to the point – I know it. He picked up a chunk between thumb and forefinger, then held it to his nostrils; the vulture made a lunge for it with her imperious beak. Prometheus beat her off. 'You fucking murderer!' he shouted. 'I know whose this is – I know.'

Athene was no longer repulsed – it was all too strange for that. In lieu of repulsion she felt that overwhelming need for comfort that she remembered from mummyless childhood; so, like any other hurting little girl, keeping the tree between them, she backed away from bird and man and blood, and ran to her bedroom. Atop the dais of her bed, curled up on a tasselled cushion, lay a cute Scottish terrier, a tartan ribbon tied round its furry white neck. 'An-gus!' Athene sang. 'An-gus, come to Mama!'

The puppy raised himself up on his paws, his tufty eyebrows twitching; with his bearded muzzle and squared-off head, he had the angrily seraphic expression of Nietzsche after the philosopher's syphilitic breakdown. 'Come to Mama,' Athene called again; however, the Scottie had other, more significant impressions: a line of fresh meat aroma had been cast into the bedroom, and the hook had caught in his nose. He sprang from the bed, went wide to avoid Mama's open arms, and was gone.

'Epimetheus, oh Epimetheus – you poor guy!' Back by the framed hyper-realist paintings of night-time London, Prometheus sobbed over the chunk of liver. 'I should've paid attention – I should've listened to you.'

An absurd spectacle, no? A man, stripped to the waist, and addressing a bit of meat as if it were his boyhood friend. Not so, for Prometheus, so long a stranger to the backward look, now saw the whole terrain revealed. He saw the futile obsession that Epimetheus had for Pandora – a mad love that would lose him most of his liver, and perhaps also his life – and he surveyed the delusive hope that blanketed all human affairs, blanketed them like a toxic miasma, a smog over a city. Tightly woven, thickly piled hope, beneath which trundled millions of lice, buying and fucking, eating and sleeping, loving and working; hope, which hid them from the godlike perspective of their own, evolved consciousness.

Yes, Prometheus recognized that this was Epimetheus's liver, and realized also what it contained: it was he who was the technician able to analyse the biopsy the bird had performed. Every human misfortune was in Pandora's box, but the worst of all was delusive hope – and it was this that Prometheus had been feeding on. The delusive hope that this purchase, that sex act, those shoes, this person, another meal . . . would make it *all right*; and so, fashioned from mortal clay and shaped with costly bottled mineral water, they would go on and on until the big firing.

The Scottie raced across the marble floor yapping madly; the vulture, hissing, stretched out her fearsome wings and back-flapped from the mess of adman. The Scottie leapt to snap the meaty titbit from Prometheus's fingers –

'Tap!' The steel frame of Zeus's penthouse shuddered, then shrank. And why, thought Prometheus, haven't I noticed before now that here in Zeus's own home, there's no branded thing? 'Tap!' The half-naked man bending over to pet the cute puppy – at least, that's what any lazy viewer would think, seeing this single image graven for all eternity. 'Tap!' It would've been so reassuring to have been able to think of it all as a myth, a fable or a dream, but, as Neil Bolton's portentous voice-over came rolling upriver – 'Give your dog Scottie's Liver Treats and show him you love him as much as he loves you' – Prometheus was gnawed at by the most excruciating end-line conceivable.

It was all an advert.

Birdy Num Num

What's my name? My name is legion, for I – we – are many. Many and colourless. I'm in him – and her, and them; I'm in some of those over there, the ones shopping for travel adaptors in Dixons. The pair of semi-whores – squeaking on high stools in leather skirts, eating caviar with their sour daddy at the granite lip of the seafood bar – I'm far deeper in them than he'll ever be. As for that one, I'm most definitely in him, I'm *loaded* into him, the windy horse of a cleaner who, emaciated in his worn blue-denim fatigues, is invisible to these fervent believers in universal healthcare: the African, pulling his cartload of bleach and plastic bags from one village-sized toilet to the next.

I am not death, for death has no persona; death is only an absence – not even a mask. True, for some I am death's helpmeet, but I'm not a psychopath, only a cytopath. I, too, am alive. I, too, have feelings – ethics as well. If I am known at all, it's by my effects rather than my causes; in this I am antithetical to humans' gods. Be that as it may, I am powerful, I am ancient, I am constantly changing, and I – we – are, if not omniscient, privy to a lot.

Y'know, some bio-theologians think I'm the First Cause, a primitive form of all the life on this dirt ball – that every animal evolved from an organism like me; others take the contrary view, that I – we – are fallen angels, cast out from the heaven of advancement, deselected and so become parasitic and unsexed.

I say, surely it's a question of scale? Looked down on from a mile up in the sky – the holding pattern of a god – this air terminal is a body, the living tissue of which is bored into by bacterium planes, subterranean trains and hissing buses. Humans swarm through its concourses, virions with credit cards.

Soon, I – some of us – will be thrust into that steep vantage, the sky, then propelled over land and sea to another city; Helsinki, as it happens. Before I go, let me – us – tell you how this has come to pass; let me tell you about this generic Tuesday afternoon – because, let's face it, it's *always* Tuesday afternoon. Allow me to assemble a cast of characters, as well or as woodenly drawn as any in a whodunnit. They were all my accomplices; your task is to identify the victim.

November 1998, a Tuesday – the day teetering on noon's fulcrum. Georgie Maxwell was walking along the first stretch of Kensington Road; she passed the gates at the end of Kensington Palace Gardens and then the driveway of the Royal Garden Hotel. In the fluffy onset of a fine drizzle, the hotel doormen moved smartly to marshal brass luggage carts and beckon taxis beneath the jutting portico with its inset lights haloed in the damp gloom. Over the shoulder of the hotel – a 1960s thing, granite-faced and angular – stretched the late autumn brownery of Kensington Gardens, and beyond them, Hyde Park, its black tree spars rigged with dead and dying leaves. In the middle east a dark mauve sky, its fundament coiled with ashen clouds, squatted over Bayswater.

Walking is perhaps an overstatement. Georgie's progress was halting, despite her being encumbered with no more than a tabloid newspaper, a pint carton of semiskimmed milk and a packet of milk chocolate HobNobs, all in a plastic bag. She clunked from stiff leg to stiff leg, swinging them from her hips as if they were stilts. The hem of her skirt rose first above one thickly bandaged shin, then the other. The skirt, eh? Well, it had a Minoan motif worked into it – geometric designs embroidered with gold thread; once pale green, it was now stained and blotchy. People walking in the other direction, from Kensington Gore, didn't take in the skirt, or the rusty raincoat, or the espadrilles unravelling from both swollen feet. They merely checked her against their internal list of street people – alcoholics, junkies, schizos and dossers – made a positive identification, then dismissed her from view.

Up close, and personally, Georgie smelt of sepsis. There were open sores under the chicken skin of her crêpe bandages; craters, really, in which bacteria, numerous as Third World miners, hacked at the exposed tissue-face. Thankfully, the day was fresh, and neither the hurrying working girls nor the strolling young ladies out shopping could smell this. However, besides looking crazy Georgie talked to herself: a twittering commentary in real time – 'She's crossing the road, pelican crossing, not a game bird, crossing the road' – that kept her company as she did, indeed, cross the road at Palace Gate, stump back along the far side, then traverse the junction of Gloucester Road and turn left into De Vere Gardens.

Why did this street – no different to scores of others in the area – feel quite so bare, so baldly threatening? On either side magnolia-painted six-storey Victorian terraces loomed in the thickening drizzle; the pavements were anthracite glossy, void of any rubbish, or even the occasional bracelet – or tiara – of costly dog shit. The kerb sides were cluttered with tens of thousands of pounds' worth of cars – cetacean Porsches and squashed Maseratis with Dubai plates – and, as she peg-legged by these, Georgie kept up her rap, a well-spoken psychosis, 'Maybe he'll be there – maybe he'll come soon. Maybe-baby, if I don't TREAD ON THE CRACKS!' She shied away from the spear tips of the railings, then, halfway along the street, lurched towards them and, pushing open a gate, awkwardly descended an iron staircase into a savage little area full of bullying bins.

I – we went along for the ride – although we were also waiting inside.

*

237

Inside Billy Chobham, who, in turn, was inside the bath; which was inside the bathroom; which, in turn, was inside Tony Riley's basement flat. The cell-like bathroom had no windows, and only a single lightbulb that dangled, unshaded, from a furred flex. The harsh light beat the limpid surface of the bath water, below which Billy's pubic hair bloomed, silky as pond algae. The bath water had long since cooled – Billy was colder. He'd been in there for over an hour, his fair skin going blue, the ends of his fingers puckering up into corrugated pads. However, Billy was experiencing no discomfort, because, unlike the chaotic Georgie, he had had a get-up hit. Billy always had a get-up; this was part of his professionalism. 'I'm a junky,' he'd tell anyone unable to escape. 'I don't make any bloody bones about it. I don't try an' stop, an' I ain't sayin' it's not my fault neevah – I wanna be a junky. I like being a junky – I'm good at it.'

It's debatable whether it's possible to be good at being bad, and it's a discussion I – we – would be happy to join in. This being noted, let's not trouble with the theory for now, and instead present the actuality. Billy had jeans that stood up straighter without him in them, and a red mohair pullover given to him by a girl in East Sheen. If he was shod it was in prison-issue trainers. He had no fixed abode, but throughout London – and still further afield, in Reading, Maidstone and Bristol – there were small caches of his belongings: a T-shirt here, a paperback there, an exercise book full of mad ballpoint drawings of invented weaponry way over there. Billy never asked the occupants of the flats and houses where he crashed if he could leave these things; he just shoved them down the back of shelves or into cupboards, so that he could return days or months later and clamour to be readmitted, on the basis that 'I've gotta get me fings.'

There were warrants out for Billy from Redbridge to Roehampton for crimes beneath petty: kiting ten-quid cheques, exchanging shoplifted underwear at Marks and Spencer, forging methadone prescriptions. There was nothing aggressive in Billy's felonies; he took no part in the great metropolis's seven and a half million fuck-offs, the abrasive grinding of psychic shingle on its terminal beach. Be that as it may, wherever Billy went, doors came off their hinges, baths overflowed and fat-filled frying pans burst into flame. His life was a free-pratfall, as, flailing, head over tail, he plunged through year after year, his fists and feet – entirely accidentally, you understand – striking mates, siblings, the odd – *very* odd – girlfriend, but mostly his old mum, who, while fighting depression, did the payroll for a chemical plant in St Neots and remained good – or bad – for a loan.

Billy, the career junky, always had his get-up: the brown-to-beige powder in the pellet of plastic, which – after being tapped into a spoon, mixed with water and citric acid, heated, then drawn off through the cellulose strands of a bit of a cigarette filter – was thrust inside his veins, making it possible for the muzzy show to go on. Locked in bathrooms with taffeta mats, crouching in back of couches, planted in the bushy corners of conservatories – Billy stayed in these spaces for as long as it took, watching for the bloom in the hypodermic syringe, his gift of a houseplant.

Georgie, who had forgotten her key, tapped on the glass panel of the kitchen door. Her face was a sharp, feline triangle, tabby with dirt and misapplied make-up; her taps were as diffident as the blows of velvet paws. No one heard her. In the cold bath, Billy gouched out, sunk in the hot Mojave desert of his habitual reverie, a corny old Blake Edwards vehicle for the comedian Peter Sellers called *The Party*.

Billy had first seen the film on television when he was four or five years old; but even then – it was originally released in 1968 – its depiction of flowery fun was painfully dated: the beautiful people of Hollywood cavorting the night away. Besides, it was a crap film with a dumb script – no plot to speak of, only a series of farcical sight gags for Sellers, browned up to play Hrundi V. Bakshi, a

useless Indian who haplessly destroys the house where the eponymous party is being held, a party he has been invited to in error,
and that is being thrown by the producer of a movie he's already
sabotaged with his stupid mistakes and brainless antics.

It was on the location for that movie-within-a-movie that Billy
habitually began his drug-dreaming. So I – we – were inside Billy,
who was inside the bath inside Tony Riley's flat. In there with
us was a ravine, somewhere out beyond Barstow, chosen for its
superficial similarity to the Hindu Kush; and in the ravine were
Hispanic extras playing Pathan tribesmen, together with more
Hispanic extras playing sepoys. A detachment of Hispanics marched
along the bottom of the ravine, accompanied by an Hispanic pipe
band miming their instruments. The Hispanics playing the tribesmen – and a few light-skinned, Caucasian-featured blacks – reared
up from the rocks above and made ready to fire. Frantic to frustrate
the ambush, the half-Jewish Sellers – who, presumably, had been
sent ahead as a scout – reared up as well, blasting a bugle. The
Hispanic Pathans turned their rifles on him and he was struck by
their volley. The bugle notes flattened into farts, Sellers collapsed,
then reared up again, crazily tootling.

This was where Billy, as Peter Sellers, as Hrundi V. Bakshi, made
his entrance: a junky in a bath in a fantasy of a film. He had seen
The Party next in his teens, again on television; this time he was
banged up in a secure hostel on the Goldhawk Road. This second
viewing confirmed for Billy that this was 'his' film: an acid-pastel
ball, in which he could perceive his dull childhood transmuted to
the plinkety-plunk beat of a Henry Mancini soundtrack. Eventually
Billy had acquired his own videotape of *The Party*. It was wrapped
in a pair of bloodstained combat trousers and pushed behind the
hot-water tank in a bungalow near Pinner.

Billy's white body, fishily flattened by refraction, undulated in
the cold water as he mimicked the flips and flops of the comedian;
who died in 1980 of a heart attack – his third – brought on by the

amyl nitrate he huffed on the sets of movies such as *The Party*. Billy's wide mouth – which could be described as generous only if what you wanted was more plaque – stretched into a rictus. Outside, Georgie's taps increased in volume as the drizzle percolating De Vere Gardens bubbled into rain.

Along a gloomy corridor that ran the length of the basement flat, between Dexion shelving units stacked with papers and paperbacks waiting to be burnt, then between a thicket of cardboard tubes that sheathed old point-of-sale materials and posters, then in through an open door, the minute sound waves pulsed, to where Tony Riley, the Pluto of this underworld, sat on a sofa in his boxer shorts, his unshaven muzzle clamped by the transparent obscenity of an oxygen mask, while the cylinder lay on the cushion beside him, steely and fire-engine-red.

I – we – were in Tony, too, not that this mattered; the catch, then gush, as his own febrile inhalation triggered the valve and yanked a gush of oxygen into his defeated lungs, drowned out everything: hearing, thought, intention, feeling. Tony was hanging on to life by his teeth, which were sunk in the plastic mouthpiece. Shitty disease, emphysema; shitty paradoxical condition. Tony sat in a stale closet, into which every small sip of air had to be dragged down a long corridor wadded with cellulose, while beneath his rack of ribcage his lungs were already abnormally distended.

Tony Riley's legs were kite struts in the flattened cloth of his boxers; his sweaty T-shirt hung on him like a scrap of polythene on a barbed-wire fence; his dirty-brown hair was painted down on to his canvas scalp; his grey eyes streamed behind once fashionable Cutler and Gross glasses. Up above him, on the purple and taupe striped wallpaper, hung a Mark Boxer cartoon of Tony in his heyday. It was a prophetic casting of inky sticks: the Roman profile and laurel wreath of hair simplified to a few thin and thick lines. Two decades on, the caricature was as good a likeness as any photograph – perhaps better. No photo could have captured the way Tony's breathless need for heroin simplified the awesome clutter of the large, low, subterranean living room – its middle-aged armchairs and smoked-glass coffee tables, its Portobello Road floor cushions and swampy Turkish kelims, its portable commode and novelty coat tree – into two white dimensions of nothing.

Beside Tony's meagre thigh there lay a scrap of tin foil, on which trailed burnt heroin. Chasing the dragon? For Tony it was more akin to staggering after a snail: he huffed, he puffed, he struggled to exhale, so that he could carve a tiny pocket in the necrotic tissue of his lungs to fill with the narcotic fumes.

Tony spat out the mouthpiece, snatched up the foil and, from the coffee table in front of his sofa, a gold Dupont lighter; then he grabbed a rolled-up tube of tin foil, poked it between his lips and hunched to his labour.

'In the primitive environment,' Lévi-Strauss wrote, 'the relevant is the sensational.' But really, in Tony Riley's basement flat, it was too primitive even for *that*; here, sensations were muffled and numbed by mould and opiates; the rain falling on the roof five storeys above penetrated the slates, then joists, plaster, paint, carpet, floor boards and more joists, until it pattered on to the jungly floor between the chief's bare feet. The parrot of addiction flapped across the dank clearing to perch on the edge of a serving hatch. Oh, that noble psittacine! Longer lived than humans, perfectly intelligent, and well able to imitate the squawks of their most awful mental pathologies.

Outside, Georgie's tapping had finally risen to a determined rapping. It was only 12.20; nevertheless, the most dissolute of establishments still have their routines. There were chores to do, calculations to be made, the supplier to be contacted; then, soon enough, the customers would begin arriving. She rapped, the glass bruising her clenched knuckles. She had once had a body that, like any affluent woman's, was a gestalt of smell, texture and colour – but now that had all flown apart: she was as dun as a cowpat, you wouldn't want to touch her, her smell was in your face.

'Whereis'e? Stupid Billy. Fucking Billy. Open up. Gotta do Tony's meds. Call Andy. Gotta do Tony's fucking meds. Call Andy. Gotta do Tony's meds –' This aloud, the narrative of her staggering thought replacing the saga of her limping walk along Kensington Road.

Skin pancaked between bone and glass; the raps marched through the kitchen, along the sepia corridor, and into the room where Tony was trying to recapture the thrill of the chase. He left off, let fall his impedimenta, stood and lurched to the doorway. 'Billy!' he shouted in a crepitating whisper. 'It's her – get the fucking door!' Then he crumpled up as thoroughly as any scrap of tin foil.

'Brill-ll-llerowng! Brill-ll-llerowng! Brill-ll-llerowng!' Billy had discovered that if he plugged his ears in a certain way and pressed his mouth against the side of the bath, his submarine ejaculations sounded – to him – like sitar chords. Billy, as Peter Sellers, as Hrundi V. Bakshi, sat cross-legged on the floor of his Los Angeles bungalow, wearing a long-sleeved, collarless linen shirt. The big bole of the instrument was cradled in his lap, his browned-up face concentrated in mystic reverie. 'Brill-ll-llerowng!' When the letter-box flap lifted, a letter fell on to the mat, and the flap clacked shut. Clacked shut. Clacked shut again. It wasn't meant to do that – this was the invitation to the paradisical party, and he, Billy-as-Hrundi, was simply meant to pick it up, open and read it; but the *fucking flap* wouldn't stop clacking!

Billy lunged up in the bath, in time to hear '—king door!' in the calm after the splash. Then he was all action: out on the wet lino, twisting a thin towel round his nethers, then into the corridor. He knelt over Tony. 'All right, mate? Y'all right, mate?' A ghastly simulation of Cockney mummy concern.

'Juss, juss, juss –' Tony shudderingly inhaled, then sputtered, 'Get the fucking door.'

Calcium hydroxide, calcium chloride, calcium hypochlorite. In a word: bleach. We don't altogether fear it – there are too many of us, and we're too small. Far too small. I'm small even for my kind – maybe fifty nanometres across, which is fifty billionths of a metre. That's smaller than the wavelength of visible light, so why should I fear bleach? For I can have no colour. Anyway, Georgie doesn't apply bleach to the insides of syringes or spoons, nor does she dunk razors or toothbrushes in it. All her bleaching activities are confined to the laminated surfaces of Tony Riley's kitchen. In the days when the disorder in her life was a tea mug unwashed up for the odd hour, or a book left face down on the arm of a chair, Georgie used to say, 'It doesn't matter how messy things get so long as you have clean kitchen surfaces.'

Of course, that was when things weren't really messy at all. That was during the eight clean years, when Georgie attended her self-help groups, built a career as a television producer, had a couple of happy-then-unhappy relationships, visited her parents, paid her taxes. That was before the craters full of sepsis and the shrinking of her head; that was when she had her own studio flat in Chiswick, not two black plastic bags in the dark corner of Tony Riley's damp bedroom.

Now the clean kitchen surfaces were the only ordered thing in the mess that was notionally her life. After cooing, billing and heaving Tony back to his oxygen cylinder, Georgie adjusted her dressings – fallen down around her ankles, obscene crêpe parodies of old women's stockings – before setting to with bucket, hot water, brush and bleach. She didn't stop until the Formica was lustrous and the aluminium draining board gleamed.

Shitty disease, emphysema. Admirably shitty: chronic, progressive, degenerative – a bit like civilization. And here we have the gerontocracy of late capitalism that Sam Beckett – himself a sufferer – would undoubtedly have recognized. With their faces – one browned by neglect, the other blued by anoxia – Georgie and Tony were typecast as Nell and Nagg. He nagged her, wheezing demands, while she nellied about the flat, fetching his anti-cholinergics and bronchodilators, administering his steroids and checking the levels on his oxygen cylinder. Setting to one side the ghastliness of a carer almost as sick as her patient, there was a ritualized and stagy desperation to their relationship; because, of course, there is *no more painkiller, the little round box is empty*, and everything is *winding down*.

Yes, a stagy desperation heightened only by their cloying affection and their treacly endearments: Chuckle-Bunny, Sweetums, Little Dove, Ups-a-Boy and Noodly-Toots for each other; and for the drugs: smidgen, pigeon, widgeon and snuff-snuff. To behold them, passionately engaged in the chores of moribundity, was to intrude upon the intimacy of a couple so old, so long together, so time-eroded into a single psychic mass, that they seemed ancient enough to have had children that must've grown up, gone away, formed partnerships of their own, had their own children, grown older, then themselves died. Of old age.

Tony was fifty-three, Georgie forty-one. They had known each other for six months.

From time to time, Georgie would break out of her stagy desperation and peremptorily order Billy to fetch this or do that. This may have been a ship of fools, but it was a tight one. There was no room on deck for shirkers. Billy had shed his moist breech-clout in favour of a neatly pressed tan linen suit, white shirt and red tie – perfect protective colouring for a hapless Indian actor attending a Hollywood party. The 'plink-plink-brill-ll-llerowng!' of his sitar had snagged the twang of an electric guitar; now a snare drum brushed up the tempo, as Billy, in a dinky three-wheeler car, pulled out of the driveway and buzzed off down the boulevard lined with palms. It was an iconic image of Los Angeles, undercut, if only he knew it . . . Ach! Fuck it! If only he knew *anything*; and if only he didn't behave as if his entire life were a pre-credit sequence.

Because here it was: *Ars Gratia Arts* captioned a lion roused from torpor and petulantly roar-yawning. But a better motto for Billy would've been *Pro Aris et Focis*; for, as he piloted the joke car of his narcotized psyche down the corridor of Tony Riley's flat – a boulevard lined with the drooping fronds of old advertising flyers and press releases, the domesticated foliage of Tony's once wildly successful career in public relations – Billy was reverencing his deity and preserving this hearth.

The order of the credits for the production was this: Tony, the hotshot producer whose mortgage arrears couldn't now catch up on him before the repossession of Death. He had the De Vere Gardens flat and a few more quid in the bank to chuck on the pyre. Every day he re-erected the set upon which the film of the party was shot – but he couldn't do it without Georgie. Georgie was the director: she assembled cast and crew, rehearsed their lines, consulted with script editors and cameramen – without her there would've been no action. Since her legs had started to rot – abscesses from shooting up, did you really want to know? – she could no longer act as a runner for a different production, the big one, overseen by Bertram and Andy's crew.

Then there was Billy, who lived from hand to hand – because his mouth rarely entered into it. He gofered for Tony and Georgie in return for wheedling rights on the drugs that flowed through the gross anatomy of the flat. Billy, most weeks, couldn't even get it together to go to pick up his emergency payment from the social in Euston. So, no leech, but by default an exemplary sole trader, engaged in the arbitrage of small quantities of merchandise, while offering piffling services. He probably should have received an Enterprise Allowance – or a British Screen grant.

*

At the venue for the party, the capacious and ugly modern home of capacious and ugly Hollywood film producer Fred Clutterbuck, Billy manoeuvred Hrundi V. Bakshi's three-wheeler between two ordinary-sized cars, and then had to climb out the top because he couldn't open the door. In this, Peter Sellers was only aping many episodes in Billy's own life: the insinuation of his simian body into spaces it wasn't intended for – tiny toilet windows, constricted shafts, tight transoms; and places where it wasn't wanted – nice teenage girls' bedrooms, the locked premises of chemists'.

The Clutterbucks' front door was answered by a uniformed black maid. Beyond her stretched a long hallway, with a walkway running over an artificial stream that flowed alongside a bamboo screen. When Billy was a kid, it was the insane largesse of this interior rill that made of the Clutterbucks' home – or, rather, Blake Edwards's production designer's conception of the Clutterbucks' home – a domestic pleasure dome. (Fernando Carrere, died 1998.)

It might be surmised that with age and experience any child would be disabused of this impression by other, more stylish domains, so that, upon reviewing *The Party*, he would wince at the tackiness of it all: the painted plywood cladding on the walls, the funnel-like light fitments, the circular fireplace – all of which were to be travestied, and travestied again during the next two decades, until such 'features' ended up skulking in chain hotels by motorway intersections, on the outskirts of a thousand cities that no one chooses to visit. Not to mention the stream itself, which was no Alph but a mean little trough, its bottom and sides painted with durable, aquamarine paint.

Might be surmised – but not by Billy; Billy was never disabused. True, on TVs in the association areas of remand centres, then latterly, on those clamped in the top corners of cells, he had glimpsed these other, more stylish domains. There had also been times, on the out, when, like an anthropoid tapeworm, Billy had lodged himself in the entrails of others' evenings – usually because he'd sold them a blob of hash or a sprinkling of powder – and so ended up in their fitted flats or architect-designed houses.

While his unwitting hosts grew maudlin and clumsy in the kitchen, Billy roamed the other chambers, examining such innovations as rag-rolling and glass bricks with an aficionado's eye. When he left he'd take with him a silver-framed photograph or leather-bound book in lieu of a going-home present. He'd seldom been invited in the first place – and he was never asked back.

So, Billy – he wasn't disabused; for him, Chez Clutterbuck remained the acme of warm and sophisticated hospitality, to which he was invited back again and again, despite the fact that each and every time he arrived with mud coating one of his white moccasins. Oops! What should he do? Billy, as Peter, as Hrundi, had trodden in the oily gunk in the parking area, and then tracked black footprints along the pristine walkway, a dull single-player version of that quintessential sixties party game Twister.

Billy and Hrundi – they're both peasants, basically. A stream of water in a house must be for washing arse or hands, so the dabbling of the muddy shoe in the stream was only – like all slapstick – logical. Basic physics. It floated away, a jolly little boat, leaving Billy to encounter that stock character, the drunken waiter, while hopping on one bare, browned-up foot.

The waiter was young, with sandy hair, and in full fig: tailcoat, high white collar. He dutifully presented his tray of cocktails. Then Billy – as Peter, as Hrundi – got to deliver one of his favourite lines in *The Party*. Recall, he was a career junky, a professional. Heroin, morphine sulphate, pethidine, methadone – all opiates, synthetic and organic, these were his stock in trade; but alcohol, apart from when he needed it to sedate himself because he couldn't get any junk and his chicken bones were splintering in his turkey skin, well, 'Thank you, but I never touch it.' And so, unsullied, Hrundi hopped off to retrieve his moccasin that, like Moses's basket, had grounded in some rushes. Behind him the waiter, who was every straight-living hypocrite Billy had ever known, took a glass from his own tray and knocked it back.

All this – the fragments of remembered dialogue, the off-cuts of scenery, the comedian's fatuous mugging – was projected on to Tony Riley's blank basement, while the other two parties to the ill-lit production got set up for the day's shoot.

Once wiped down and medicated, ornamental Tony was replaced on his sofa with a cup of tea; and Georgie, having done the surfaces, retired to the bathroom, where, under the bare bulb, she put a bird leg up on the bath and unwound four feet of crêpe bandage to expose the open-cast bacteria mine. In the enamel ravine below lay strewn the rubble of Billy, his horny nail clippings and fuse-wire pubic hairs, the frazil of his dead skin left high and drying on crystalline ridges of old suds.

Georgie winced as she dusted the gaping hole in her shin with fungicidal powder. It was perhaps a little bizarre that, given the exactitude with which she measured, then administered, palliatives to Tony, she so woefully mistreated herself; but then, by sticking to her story that these septic potholes were 'just something I picked up', she could maintain the delusion that she was 'run down' and 'a bit stressed out', so necessitating certain other medications, which the authorities, in their infinite stupidity, saw fit to deny her.

The truth was that Georgie was dying as well – and she knew it. She'd been clean for long enough, before relapsing back into the pits, to no longer be able to cloak her mind – once swift, airborne, feathery and beautiful – in the crude oil of evasiveness. She had resolved to die with Tony, to go with him into the ultimate airless-ness of the emphysemic's tomb, as a handmaiden for the afterlife.

Be that as it may, in the time left to her there was work to be done; so, once the pits had been powdered and crêped, Georgie retreated to the inner sanctum she shared with Tony, the master bedroom, in order to make The Call.

Georgie had met Tony when she was a runner for Bertram and Andy's crew. Bertram, at one time a paper-bag manufacturer in Leicester, had been lured down to London ten years before. No one's saying Bertram's paper bags were any good: he didn't maintain the machinery, skimped on glue and abused his Bangladeshi – and largely female – workforce. His bags often split. I know, because I was also in Leicester, in some of Bertram's workers; remember, I am legion – and non-unionized. Bertram also knocked his own wife around.

Bertram liked whoring – and he liked whores still more. He panted down the M1 to London on the expensive scent. While in town, he treated his 'ladies' like . . . ladies, just as back home he treated his women like whores. He particularly cherished nice girls from good families who had fallen on to his bed of pain. He bought the fucked-up Tiffanies and Camillas he hired – at first by the hour, then by the night – as if they were nobility, dressing them up so he could take them to Fortnum's for tea, or to Asprey's for ugly silver fittings.

Bertram was a medieval miller of a man, complete with jowls and an extra brace of chins. His great girth suggested the washing down of capons with many firkins of ale. His thick thighs cried out for hosiery, his paunch bellowed for a codpiece. On his first chin was stuck a goatee the approximate size and shape of a Scottie dog. The beard looked as if it had flung itself at Bertram's face to get at the liverish treat of his tongue.

Bertram didn't do drugs – but his 'ladies' were clopping about in the muck. He soon realized he could secure himself cheaper favours if he took up dealing. During a brief sojourn in Pentonville – the result of a contretemps involving an electric kettle lead, his pivotal arm and a girl who wasn't a 'lady' – Bertram met

Andy (real name, Anesh), who dissimulated about everything, including his skin colour. At night, even in the nick, he rubbed whitening powder into his tan cheeks – an inverted Hrundi V. Bakshi, playing Peter Sellers. Andy was small Asian fry, but he had big Jamaican and Turkish connections. When they got out, the paper-bag manufacturer and the fraud went into partnership.

The viral quality of vice, well, we have to stop and admire it – for an instant. Bertram and Andy's business plan was simplicity itself. This was the early 1990s and crack cocaine, a recent arrival, was stupendously dear. Most of Bertram's whores used crack with their clients, as it made everything go – if it went at all – quicker; and the clients, many of whom had been as ignorant of hard drugs as Bertram, ended up using smack, too. Through nose-shots and cold-vagina-calls Bertram cemented his client list with blood and mucus.

They never wrote anything down, and the crew was built up on a cellular basis: Bertram made the wholesale buys; Andy portioned out; the Tiffanies and Camillas brought them runners, addicts who were unemployable, yet still presentable. Best practice was straightforward: they wanted only white clients in good standing – no blacks, no Social Security jockeys. Their delivery area was exclusively the West End, Kensington and Chelsea, Hammersmith and Fulham. None of their crew would cross the river – although, like motorized rats, they'd make a skulking meet in Oakley Street. Late each morning, Bertram and Andy rendezvoused with their four top runners at an hotel by the Hammersmith flyover, in a room held vacant for them by a compliant and heavily addicted manager. Those four, in turn, subdivided their allocation among other runners, and so on, for as many links as were necessary – drugs rattling in one direction, cash in the other, the entire saleschain cranked by desperate need.

If the runners used up too much of their stock, they were compelled to sell more; if they grew flaky they were brushed off like the dead skin they were fast becoming. At least, that's how it was all supposed to work; in practice Bertram and Andy weren't good managers, and they lacked a Human Resources department. They had their weaknesses – Georgie being one of them. Once the holes in her shins had become too large, and her tinkling accent a church bell that tolled the knell of her; well, by rights she should've been given her limping orders, but Bertram had some strange affection for her. Was it sexual, or still more venal? Best not to start out in that direction – let alone go there.

Aquila non capit muscas – 'The eagle does not hunt for flies.' Georgie was pensioned off to this queer care home in De Vere Gardens, and instead of running drugs she sat still and waited for them. The gloomy basement, squishy with dust, barbed with Tony's PR tat, was a carnivorous plant into which the flies spiralled, only to trigger the sensitive hairs that ensured their gooey absorption. Eagle-eyed Andy – neither he nor Bertram were fools enough to touch their stock – had only to wait until the trap-flat was full.

Piles of discarded clothing, together with the previously alluded to black plastic bags, smoothed the corners of the master bedroom. The brocaded drapes muffled the hammering of the rain in the basement area. A bedside lamp illumined the altar of pillows and cushions that had to be constructed just so, then mortared with smaller pillows and cushions, each time that Tony tried to sacrifice himself to sleep. It was Georgie who built the altar, and who had to arrange the stiff loops of Tony's oxygen line so they wouldn't kink and block during his provisional oblivion.

This was a boudoir – we always felt – that, with its huge old water bed, exerted a lunar pull on body fluids, encouraging their wanton exchange. We swing from ape to ape by pricking stick, but sex – especially low down and dirty sex, sex with lesions – will do.

Georgie picked up the receiver of the antiquated Bakelite phone on the bedside table and made The Call. Georgie never had a get-up; she was lucky if there were a few sugary sips of methadone linctus to stave off withdrawal. The dialling alone was torment to her hurting fingers, with each circuit feeling as if her entire body were being pulled apart on a torturous wheel. Georgie made The Call, and listened with the acuity of great suffering as the impulses nattered away under the London streets.

To a recently completed block of studio flats in Brook Green, where Andy was lying with a nearly sixteen-year-old girl called Pandora, whom he'd liberated from a pimp called Bev, so that she could be pressed, by his hand, into the bondage of his thighs. Pandora, who, at this early stage in her misfortunate life, despite the miseries that boxed her in, was still given to the giggles and hair-flicks of girls her age, girls who'd never seen the (men's) things that she had.

The mattress sat on a carpet that stank of rubbery underlay. Pandora sprawled across Andy's thighs and smelt the ghee that Meena, his wife, used liberally in her cooking. The ghee and the traces of urine in his sparse pubic hair. It was taking Andy a long time to get aroused; Pandora's mouth was available to him whenever he wanted it, so such congress had the ordinary sensuality of squeezing a blackhead. He groped for the chirruping mobile phone without troubling to shuck Pandora off.

'Any poss' of getting over here firstish?' Georgie said without foreplay. 'We're gagging for some albums – soul and reggae.' This was the kids' club encryption they used: heroin was 'soul', crack cocaine 'reggae'. Only if the interceptor of their calls had been a complete ingenue could crew and clients have escaped decoding; of course, such naivety was a given.

'Is anyone else there?' Andy asked.

'Er, no, not yet – but they probably will be soon. Please, Andy, I –'

'Not now. I haven't got any albums. I'm busy – it'll have to be . . .' He searched his sparse mental terrain – rancorous swamps, low hills of contempt, the isolated crag of violence – for the name of the runner currently serving Tony's patch. 'Quentin. Yeah, give Quentin a call in a couple of hours.'

Georgie knew it would take at least two hours for Bertram to see the Jamaicans and the Turks, then another for Andy to do the portioning, packaging and distributing. It wouldn't be until late afternoon that Quentin came padding down the stairs of the mansion block, the complexion of his motorcycle leathers clearer than the hide they hid. It'll be too late by then! Georgie's body yowled, I'll be mush!

'P-Please,' she sobbed into the phone. 'Andy, I know you've got one or two, you've always –'

'Can't talk now.' He cut her right off. It was true, Andy held a small stash, enough to keep Pandora . . . busy, but this was the way it was: the eagle does not hunt flies. The flies would be buzzed into Tony Riley's trap-flat, and by mid-afternoon Andy would relent and make the drop himself.

Andy liked to keep Georgie and Tony on a tight leash, feel them tugging as they walked to heel. It was all in the desperate doggy tug of their need and their obedience that Andy's mastery inhered. Back in Southall he was a nothing, the bad third son who'd been to jail for thieving; but in the Royal Borough it was white women like Georgie who bowed down before him.

Billy, still slow in the syrupy glow of his get-up fix, enjoyed this time: the elongated hours before the dealer came. It was when the party got under way. The hack combo in the matching blue nylon jackets picked up the beat and strolled with it; the drunk waiter circulated with his drinks tray; the cowboy actor with steer-horn shoulders mock butt-fucked his starlet date, as he pretended to teach her pool; Clutterbuck and his cummerbunded cronies drank cocktails and smoked cigars – 'I still have a few left over from the pre-Castro days.' Hrundi V. Bakshi leant on pillars or hid behind bamboo, and shyly observed the gay scene.

As the guests trickled in, alliances were made and concordats formed. These weren't minor Hollywood players pretending to be slightly less minor Hollywood players, but the flies who congregated at Tony's flat and waited for the eagle.

'Oh, my goodness, it is you! Wyoming Bill Kelso!' Billy said to Bev, Pandora's old pimp – a big Yardie bulked out still more by a puffa jacket. 'I am the biggest fan of your movies –'

'What the fuck,' Bev said, pushing past Billy, who had answered the door. Billy fell back, muttering, 'Howdie pardner.'

Bev could pick up where he lived, in Harlesden, but the gear Bertram and Andy's crew served was reliably better; besides, his girls worked in Earl's Court. Bev had intellectual pretensions. He was reading *Heart of Darkness*, and, plonking himself down in an armchair opposite Tony, engaged the suffocating ex-PR man in a conversation about the impact of colonialism.

Between chuffs on his oxygen Tony was eager to participate; he was wobbly-bubbly, oscillating in his start-the-day steroid high. That he'd never read Conrad's novella himself didn't matter in the least.

Billy, wearing a trim maid's uniform, checked the video intercom, then buzzed in Jeremy, who came ambling through the upstairs lobby and down the stairs. Jeremy, in Oxfords, jeans, and with a silk handkerchief snotting from the top pocket of his tweed jacket. He appeared every inch the scion of a minor squirearchical house – which is what he was. However, his account at Berry Brothers and Rudd had been stopped and his Purdey pawned; Jeremy's career in stocks was irretrievably broken, yet still he brayed, such was his sense of entitlement – to drugs.

Next to the party was Yami, a Sudanese princess as tall, elegant and unexpected in these dismal surroundings as a heron alighting in a municipal boating pond. She stalked along the corridor of the flat, so leggy her legs seemed to bend the wrong way. Everyone assumed that Yami whored, yet her almond eyes, salted with contempt, held no promise of anything.

Billy followed at her high heels, chuckling, and when Yami rounded on him, Hrundi V. Bakshi said, 'I missed the middle part, but I can tell from the way you are enjoying yourselves it must have been a very humorous anecdote.' Yami looked at him with regal hatred.

Then Gary arrived, a bullocky little geezer, with his hair damped down in a senatorial fringe, and a thick gold chain encircling his thick neck. Gary, who was in jail garb – immaculate trainers, pressed tracksuit and freshly laundered T-shirt – touched fists with Billy as he came in. 'Safe,' they said – although it was anything but.

And so the party filled up. David arrived, a failing screenwriter of spurious intensity, his face dominated by a gnomon nose, its shadow always indicating that this was *the wrong time*. With him was Tanya, his stylist girlfriend, a *jolie laide* who had to drop cocaine solution into her blue eyes in order to dilate her pinprick pupils, so her colleagues couldn't tell she was doing smack. As if.

Finally, there was an estate agent with boyish bad looks, who tore at the sore in the corner of his mouth with a ragged thumbnail. While he was cluttering up the living room of Tony Riley's flat, his own prospective buyers were getting soaked in Acton.

They parked their arses and groaned the same old addict myths: how far they'd shlepped, how hard they'd fought, how the fucking Greeks kept pushing wooden horses within their justifiably guarded walls. They slumped on chairs, floor cushions and couches, a layer of cigarette smoke slow-swirling above their vaporous heads, waiting for Circe and lotus leaves at forty quid a bunch.

Tony Riley still had a smidgin of heroin left, and each time he spat out his mouthpiece to take up his foil buckler and suck pipe, the double-bores of their withdrawing eyes followed his every move. Tony compounded their anguish by sharing with Bev; they were, after all, far up the River Congo together, with the pimp bamboozled by Conrad's semantics: 'Yeah, I mean, like, when 'e calls 'em "niggers", 'e don' mean it like "niggaz" do 'e? I mean, 'e weren't a bruvva, woz 'e?'

Tony, taking a chuff, aspirated 'ho', by which he meant 'no'.

On the lesser of the two sofas – an intimate two-seater, deep and softly upholstered – the screenwriter and the stylist were struggling not to touch. From moment to moment they became more mutually repulsed: he could not stand to look upon her needy face, while she was appalled by his pores – so very big, they threatened to engulf her.

Gary slumped on a floor cushion by the radiator, his fists held in front of him. The knuckles were scrawled upon in blue ink: God, Elvis, Chelsea – the council flat trinity. Scrawled upon with pins, in prison, which for men of Gary's ilk was only the continuation, by other means, of double maths on a wet Tuesday afternoon.

Tired of propping herself on a skimpy windowsill, Yami commanded, 'Shift yersel'', and Gary hunkered over, so that she could curl herself round his back, assuming a child's nap posture. He may've found himself cupped by Yami's thighs and belly, her breasts snuggling against his back, but Gary experienced no arousal. Like all the other waiters, his libido was further underground than the tube line from Knightsbridge to Hyde Park Corner: they could sense sex rumbling through the earthy element above them, but down here it was frigid and still.

Georgie kept nellying in and out of the room to check that her meal ticket was all right: Tony was as thin and translucent as a potato crisp, and might crunch into powder at any time. Every three minutes she nellied down the corridor to the bedroom and called Andy again. 'This number is currently unavailable, please try again later.' Georgie sat, the phone cradled in her rotten lap, picturing with ghastly clarity the dealer journeying across the city in his metallic-green Ford Mondeo, a car so anonymous that to look upon it was to see nothing. Her feverish imagination summoned up cops and crooks and tidal waves on Scrubs Lane; anything, in fact, that might get between her vein and the needle.

Thunder bumped over the rooftops as Billy went from one huddled waiter to the next, asking if they wanted a cup of tea. It was all he could bring to the party. In the kitchen he clicked on the electric jug and lost himself in his reverie. Through the serving hatch he could see the pompous Clutterbuck and his stuffed-dress-shirt pals, while he, Hrundi V. Bakshi, tiptoed along the margins, concealing himself behind shrubberies, pressing himself against fake veneer walls, lurking artlessly below the watery amoebae that were evidence of Alice Clutterbuck's awful taste in abstract painting. If he approached the guests with 'Oh, hello, hello, good evening – what a beautiful evening it is, to be sure', they turned their backs on his naked gaucherie.

The jug clicked off. Billy slung bags in cups and rained hot death down on them. The rejected Hrundi had found a parrot in a cage. The parrot gave him a hungry look, and the borstal boy playing the manic-depressive comedian playing the washed-up Indian actor cocked his head charmingly, then said, 'Hello.'

'Num-num,' the parrot clucked. 'Birdy num-num.'

'Num-num?' Billy queried aloud, and from the living room came 'What the fuck're you on about?' It was Jeremy, whose well-tailored accent was finally fraying, along with the cuffs of his Turnbull and Asser shirt.

'Birdy num-num,' the parrot reiterated and rattled its claws in the bars. Looking down, Billy spotted a dish on the floor. He picked it up so that we all could see: it was full of bird food and printed on the side was BIRDY NUM NUM. 'Oh, my goodness,' Billy chortled, 'birdy wants num-nums does he? I'll give him num-nums – I'll give you your num-nums.' He began spooning sugar into the mugs lined up along the gleaming counter – squat, fine bone, chipped. 'Here, birdy, here!' The parrot pecked at the grain strewn on the bottom of its cage, while Billy poured milk into the mismatched tea set. 'Num-nums, num-nums, birdy num-nums,' he continued muttering, as he fetched down from a cupboard the packet of milk chocolate HobNobs.

Hrundi V. Bakshi was hugely enjoying feeding the parrot; in the ecstasy of interspecific contact he forgot the stuffy Clutterbucks and their snobby guests. His browned-up face glowed with boyish enthusiasm as he sowed the bottom of the cage; but then, 'Num-num is all gone!' The num-num was indeed all gone. He had nothing more to offer, so had to put down the bowl and walk away, dabbing his damp palms on his linen jacket, glancing round to check he hadn't attracted attention.

Billy lined the teas up in the serving hatch and knocked on the wooden frame. He popped his satchel lips and made a 'pock-pock' sound, as a techie does when checking to see that a microphone is working. The waiters strewn across Tony Riley's living room ignored him; they were listening to something else: the music of their agonized nerves, tortured by craving the way a heavy-metal guitarist tortures the strings of his instrument; they heard their nerves screech – a chord that seemed to have been sustained for ten thousand years.

Hrundi V. Bakshi had found a control panel sunk in a wall. The array of buttons and dials was connected to he knew not what, but he pressed one anyway, then, hearing a speaker crackle, spoke into a grille: 'Birdy num-num "pock-pock". Howdie, pardner.' This latter an allusion to his cringeworthy encounter with Bev, the Yardie pimp playing the B-actor playing Wyoming Bill Kelso, the cowboy actor.

Warming to his medium, Hrundi blew on the mic again, 'pock-pock', then announced: 'Waiting for more num-nums. Num-nums is all gone!'

'Bi-lly,' chided Georgie, who knew all about his counter-life.

259

'No, seriously,' Billy said, 'I'm not fucking handing these round, they can come and get 'em if they want 'em.'

Birdy num-num. Birdy num-num all gone – this was the key scene in *The Party* so far as Billy was concerned. The parrot had had his fill, yet still craved more. Much more. Billy came round from the kitchen and, one by one, checking who wanted sugar, handed out the teas. For specially favoured guests he also offered a milk chocolate HobNob.

Like an army chaplain giving extreme unction on a battlefield, Billy bent down low to present them with their sweetened solution, and while subservient he offered this pathetic intercession: when Andy came, he, Billy, would speak to the dealer on their behalf. Andy always disappeared into the master bedroom with Georgie, who'd taken their orders in advance. Then there would be a further long wait, as she negotiated her and Tony's cut for concentrating the market, trapping the flies.

Billy, in return for a pinch of smack here, a crumb of crack there, offered to ensure that their orders would be filled priority, or else suggested other tiny services that he could perform: the feeding of meters, the obtaining of works, pipes and foil; perhaps even the making of calls to employers/wives/husbands/children to explain – in sincere, doctorly tones – the entirely legitimate reasons for so-and-so's non-arrival. This marginal service sector paid only because of Billy's preternatural ability to gauge the extent of his clients' desperation, and so adjust his pricing accordingly.

They clutched his sleeve and murmured pitiably, 'I was meant to be in Baker Street at half eleven' or 'My kid's out in the car, go check she's OK, willya?' or 'I gotta have a hit before I leave!' And Billy would nod gravely, accepting downpayment for these indulgences; the pope of dope with his dirty chuckle of absolution: 'Er-h'herr.'

'Waiting for more num-num, num-num is all gone,' Hrundi said to Billy; then Billy said it aloud. The coincidence between the hunger of the parrot in the cage at the party and the cold turkeys in the cage of addiction never ceased to amuse him – like a custard pie thrown in the face of the world.

And still Tony nagged for breath on the sofa, and still Georgie nellied in and out of the living room. 'Ha-ha-ha –' he gasped.

'What's that, Ups-a-Boy?'

'Ha-ha-ha –'

'What're you saying, Noodly-Toots?'

'Have you, have you –?'

'Have I what, Noodly?'

'Have you, have you "euch" called him?'

'Oh, you know I have, Ups-a-Boy, just this second.' So it was that they conformed to all the ordinary amnesia of the long-term married.

Every three minutes she would make the same forlorn calculation: their desperation factored against Andy's irritation; but, whatever the result, she'd still bruise her fingers dialling.

Billy retreated once more to the kitchen. He opened a cupboard door and the band were all in there smoking a joint. 'Shut the door, man.' The sax player comically honked. Next, Billy found the control panel again, and dickered with its switches. At the party in *The Party*, the statue of the little boy peeing in the ersatz rill increased its flow all over Wyoming Bill Kelso; the fire burning on the circular hearth flared up; the bar where Clutterbuck and his cronies were standing retracted into the wall, scattering glasses with tinkly abandon.

Billy watched these dumb happenings delightedly, superimposing them on Tony Riley's living room, so that it was Gary and Yami who were slammed against the mouldy wallpaper; Tony's Dupont that threw flame at Bev's face; and Jeremy's mug from which the tea jetted.

What of us? Does it ever tire us – me – our swarming behind the sightless eyes of the junkies and the tarts? Do I remain as amused

261

as Billy by the slapstick of addiction, the inability of these Buster Keatons to do even one thing properly at once? Well, yes and no. True, I never grow bored with my own imposture; each time I break into a cell, rip off a strand of DNA, patch it into my own RNA and so reproduce myself, I experience anew the thrill of creation.

Jean Cocteau – a junky, true enough, although before our time – said that all artists are, by nature, hermaphrodites, as the act of creation is one of self-insemination, followed by parthenogenesis. I – we – would concur with this, except that we are *far more* inventive: we mutate so quickly within the galleries of our patrons, simultaneously gifting them originals and multiples.

Then there's time, the most significant dimension of creation. Size may matter, but time diminishes all things, bringing them down to *our* level. We – I – bide our time; we savour our own side effects, the minor symptoms of accidie and loss of appetite, the insomnia and the biliousness. We aren't one of those Grand Guignol maladies, half in love with its own horror show. We do not seek to liquidize tissue in seconds, then send blood spouting from every orifice; nor do we see any beauty in the gestural embellishments of the cancers – although, all in good time, we may bring on those cellular clowns. Consider the slapstick of cancer, its crazy capers, the way it messes up the metabolism, chucking buckets full of tumours about the body.

No, they call what we do disease, but we know it's art; and the art of life is a process. This is what we do: we hang in there. We loiter – we don't hurry, we take years – decades, perhaps. For us, human death is a failure; unless, that is, enough of us have blasted off to colonize new worlds.

They are mobilizing against us. Pegylated interferon alpha, Ribavirin – crass names, brutal mercenaries. *They* don't even know how these drugs work, but let me tell you – it's not pretty. Figuratively speaking, they cut off our balls and stitch up our cunts . . .

Still, let's not dwell on the future; for now, it's still that Tuesday afternoon, in November 1998, and at Tony Riley's there're *loads* of us. Loads in Billy, Georgie and Tony himself. Loads in Bev and Jeremy, loads in Gary and Yami, loads in the screenwriter and his stylist girlfriend. And not forgetting the estate agent – there're loads of us squatting in him, as well. An abundance of mes, two million in every millilitre of their blood – a whole earth's population in one individual.

We bide our time. 'It is good', as Peter Sellers, as Hrundi V. Bakshi, said to Claudine Longet as Michele Monet, 'to be having a good time.'

'What the fuck're you on about?' said Tanya, the stylist.

'I am saying to you' – Billy waggled his head from side to side, his black locks swinging – 'that it is good to be having a good time.'

After the encounter with the parrot, and the revelation of its empty dish, this was Billy's second favourite moment in *The Party*. The girl, in her filmy, lemon-yellow mini-dress with the spangly bodice, was obviously meant for him – why else the soft focus, her slim yet shapely form, her air of sexualized neurosis, the ski jumps of her hair? Moreover, she was being harassed by her date, who was none other than Herb Ellis (as himself), the boorish director who threw Hrundi off the set out beyond Barstow, with the ringing cliché, 'You'll never make another movie in this town again!'

How many times had Billy heard *that* before. Still, here he was, looking deep into Tanya's eyes – which were brimming with sickness – and they'd clicked, hadn't they? 'Lissen,' Billy went on (as himself), 'I've gotta bit of gear if you want, not much . . .' He glanced at David, but the screenwriter, unable to cope with his enfeebled conscience – it was his kid who was outside in the car – had dropped a Rohypnol.

'I dunno . . .' Tanya muttered. She was chubby-cheeked with gingerish hair – not at all like Michele Monet.

'C'mon,' Billy said, insistent, 'meet me in the karzy in five.' He wandered off, avoiding the sandy-haired waiter, who, having downed most of the drinks on his tray, was now completely pissed.

But at first the bathroom was locked, and when the synthetic cockatoo who'd been using it emerged – a woman who, earlier in the evening, Billy's antics had gifted with a roast chicken for a hairpiece – there was a second waiting her turn. Ever gallant, Billy let her go in front of him.

Hrundi V. Bakshi climbed up a spiral staircase to the second storey of the Clutterbucks' extensive and ugly dwelling, crept into a bedroom that was an atonal symphony of nylon and velour, then finally found his way into the en suite bathroom. By now he was risibly pigeon-toed, his knees half crossed to sustain his full bladder. He'd been refusing alcoholic drinks throughout the party – but he'd drunk a lot of water. Then there was the strawberry soup he'd sipped sitting on a daft low stool, while to either side of him the sophisticated Hollywood types exchanged banter.

The Clutterbucks' bathroom was intimidating to a fake Indian. There was shag-pile carpeting, tiled steps up to a shower and pot plants everywhere; still, at least there was the comic relief, the slackening of Sellers's funny face.

Tanya came in. She was wearing a ribbed sweater, one of David's; the sleeves covered her hands except for her gnawed-upon fingers. She sat on the edge of the bath and peered down at Billy's silt. Billy busied himself at the sink, setting out works, spoon, wraps of smack and citric acid on the shelf.

'I won't fuck you, y'know,' Tanya said dully. Through his filmy lens Billy saw Michele Monet singing of love, while accompanying herself on an acoustic guitar.

'It is good to be having a good time,' Billy said in his stupid golly-gosh Indian accent, heating the spoon with a Bic lighter. Tanya sighed – she was used to idiots and snapped, 'Gimme that.'

But Billy thought this precipitate; he whipped his belt from the loops of his jeans, half garrotted his arm and dowsed for a vein. When, eventually, he handed the syringe to Tanya, the barrel was full of blood. Or should we say boold? The sucked-up back-flow of his circulatory system. Billy's viral load wasn't particularly high, and it was only a one-mil' syringe, yet there we were, a Varanasi's worth of virions, our isocahedral capsids jostling together in the tube like so many footballs floating down the Ganges.

Not that Tanya didn't have plenty of us, too. When she kicked off her flip-flop – in the fashion industry they dubbed this 'heroin chic', but, trust me, it was only junky *déshabillé* – pulled her foot up in front of her on the bath and, taking the syringe, bent to tend it between her toes, she paused to remark, 'I can't have a hit in my arm – they check there.' Then asked Billy, 'Are you negative?' To which the only realistic reply would've been, are you fucking joking? This guy is nothing but negation piled upon negation! But once he'd gruntaffirmed 'Finkso', she let herself have us.

How was it for me? Think of that numinous – but, for all that, real – moment in any party, when it all begins to slide into mayhem. The guests are tipsy; the band are getting looser, louder and funkier; darkness has come to press against the picture windows, and shadows swell in the swimming pool; sensual possibilities tickle everyone's extremities; and the drunken waiter falls backwards into the kitchen, where he knocks off the chef's toupee.

That's when the influx comes: younger, crazier, happier gate-crashers, prancing and dancing, and twisting their minds off, a gay cavalcade with a baby elephant they've liberated from the zoo and daubed with corny hippy slogans: 'The World is Flat!', 'Love is a Sugar Cube!' and 'Go Naked!'

That's what it was like for us as we gatecrashed Tanya.

No, they didn't fuck, but they were slung together by the plush impact of the heroin, ribbed pullover against mohair woolly. Tanya thought of little else, and Billy, as Sellers, as Hrundi V. Bakshi,

265

flushed the toilet once, twice, a third time; then, fool that he was, lifted the lid of the cistern and fiddled with the ballcock. One of Alice Clutterbuck's vile daubs fell off the wall into the cistern; Hrundi pulled it out and jerked the end of the toilet roll for some paper to wipe it. The roll began to spin, disgorging loop after skein of toilet paper on to the fluffy floor of the bathroom. Alarmed, Hrundi stooped to gather up an armful and, in so doing, predictably, dropped the cistern lid. Down below a lump of plaster fell on to the snare drum. The band played on. Hrundi rubbed the blotchy purple painting with the toilet paper; it smeared, but he put it back on the wall anyway, then stuffed the bundle of toilet paper into the toilet, shut the lid and flushed it. The toilet began to overflow; the bidet turned into a fountain. Billy watched – numb, enthralled – as a new interior rill formed a course across the Clutterbucks' bathroom.

Five minutes previously, in the catacomb of the master bedroom, cadaverous Georgie was strung up upon the wire for eternity when she heard 'I'm coming myself.' Andy had cut through the static, then broken the connection.

Andy slid through the chicane on Kensington Church Street and stopped at the lights opposite the Polaris bulk of Barker's. When the feeder light changed, he turned into Kensington Road. This junction had no resonance for him: he thought not of Biba hippies and Kensington Market honking of patchouli; nor, as the Mondeo headed east, did he ruminate on William and Mary's big move. The previous August, Andy hadn't so much as registered the cut-flower embankments that, overnight, had piled up along the railings of Kensington Palace – the most expensive compost heap in history.

For Andy, those strange August days had been business as usual; the same *plus c'est la même chose* of pick-ups and divvying-ups, of driving and serving, of screwing ruined under-age girls in empty flats, then heading back to Southall to play the overbearing and abusive paterfamilias – a role that Andy performed magnificently.

There was no prescience for this man, either; he could not sense the future, the coming Muji-Bouji's-woojie of dizzy dancing on ceaseless credit. No, Andy saw what was there in front of him: sheikhs, transplanted desert blooms, their pot bellies tenting their robes, their masked womenfolk ambling along behind. He saw men in shirtsleeves boring themselves to death in the overheated conference rooms of the Royal Garden Hotel. He saw cabs and buses and a faux-vintage Harrods delivery van. He didn't feel, as anyone else might, the vapid cosmopolitanism of this quarter of London, where the corner shops sold Swiss watches and the postmen knew no one's name.

Back in Tony Riley's flat, the chord that seemed as if it might sustain for ten thousand years was chopped off. Georgie jerked into action: all must be as the grim little god wanted it. Bev must cut short his seminar and, together with Yami, go into the small back bedroom, where more relics of Tony's gift for public relations were stacked and piled. The two black people came to rest on a large leather pouffe, sitting at the feet of a life-sized cardboard cut-out of Tony dressed as Wyatt Earp, his six-shooters blazing from the hip, a speech bubble poking from the side of his Stetson. 2-D Tony was saying, 'Meet me at the OK Corral on Old Brompton Road for fun that should be outlawed!' Bev and Yami didn't have speech bubbles.

Georgie fluttered among the remaining whites. 'C'mon, get up.' She ordered the sedated screenwriter: 'Giss yer money. Tell me what you want – Andy's coming.' The junkies dug out their linty notes – Gary even had the shame of change. The binary listing, brown/white, began. Tony left off his oxygen to do the count.

All at once, the party was in full swing. Jeremy stood and, locating a mirror, held it up so that he could comb his hair. It was as if he were *courting* drugs. Gary got up, rolled his shoulders and then, leaning against the wall with his arms held out, stretched first one leg then the other, just another bloke in a tracksuit limbering up.

David tottered off up the corridor. He tapped on the bathroom door. 'I know you're in there, Tanya.' Knew, and didn't really mind; theirs, like all drug economies, was a hard scrabble for subsistence: you did what you had to. 'Lissen,' he continued, 'Andy's coming – I've put in our order, but I'm gonna get Poppy from the car, so you better come out.'

Why would anyone bring their small child into this miserable place at the precise moment when the drug dealing – and taking – was about to begin in earnest? Answer: risks incalculable for those to whom responsibility is a given. The child had been in the parked car for over an hour, the rain was slackening off, traffic wardens and dog-walkers would be out on the street. There were these factors, and also the screenwriter's naive faith in the capacity of a little girl to summon up compassion – credit might be forthcoming.

But not with this little a girl, and not from Andy, who was riding the clutch at the pelican crossing beside the De Vere Hotel. Riding the clutch and holding Pandora's crotch, as any other sales rep might fondle the Mondeo's controls, its gearstick or steering wheel. He knew she was eight days shy of her sixteenth birthday – and felt both more and less secure because of it. Bertram had warned Andy off Pandora sternly; but his business partner pointed out that the girl's mouth was multipurpose. With the wipers slicing semicircles of London out of the drabness, Pandora sat behind the windscreen, a chipmunk with cheeks stuffed full of Class As.

We were in Pandora all right – in her for the duration. When those hateful anti-retrovirals became widely available, she wouldn't have the modicum of self-discipline needed to administer them. Yes, we'll be in and out of her for decades – and, given what she gets up to, and who gets up her, we have reason to be grateful to this air terminal of a girl, through which our kind transfer with conspicuous ease.

We were in Pandora – but we weren't in Andy. I know, I

promised you a victim at the outset; but, sad to report, it isn't Andy. No matter how deserving the dealer may've been of a debilitating and progressive disease, he was in no danger of contracting this one. As has been remarked, he didn't take drugs – except for a joint when a girl was sucking him limp; and for the purposes of fellation, he wore not one but three condoms. Andy didn't subscribe to the African idiocy that a sweet wasn't worth having with a wrapper on it; because it wasn't a sweet for Andy at all, it was a grim staple, sexual sorghum that he had to shovel down because famine might come at any time.

He parked the Mondeo at the far end of De Vere Gardens. Parked it scrupulously, sending Pandora to fetch a ticket from the machine, while he scoped out the other parked cars, then looked up and down the street for possible tails. Sometimes Andy carried a scanner that flipped automatically through the police frequencies, but mostly he didn't bother: he knew that when the bust came – and come it would, eventually – he would've been set up by a fuck-wit junky.

No screenwriter, no matter how inventive, could have got down on the page the scenario that unfolded as Andy and Pandora, together with David and his daughter, were buzzed in. As the plausible quartet took the short lift ride down, the junkies crowded into the corridor. Tanya emerged from the bathroom, with Billy snuffling in her train. Georgie came limping at a run along the corridor and herded them all back towards the living room. 'Get in there! Keep outta Andy's way!' Answered the door, then hustled the dealer and his jailbait away. David's daughter said something fivish, like, 'How long're we gonna stay here, Daddy?' And Billy, as Sellers, as Hrundi V. Bakshi, took a direct hit in the forehead with the sucker dart fired by the Clutterbucks' kid, who was romping in his plaid pyjamas in his toy-stuffed room. 'Howdie, pardner,' Billy mugged, reprising his embarrassing encounter with

Wyoming Bill Kelso, and the little girl – traumatized by an hour alone in a parked car in a London residential street on a rainy Tuesday afternoon in November – started to cry.

Slapstick is, in essence, the ritualized worship of causation, something humans place more faith in than they do their gods. *Post hoc ergo propter hoc* – 'after this, therefore because of this'. Anyone watching a comedian attempting to do two things at once – or even one – will be familiar with this instinctive belief: *of course* you would try to stop the toilet overflowing by shutting the lid; *of course* you would stuff all that toilet paper down the pan; *of course* you would – given your state of shock – allow yourself to be fed with liquor, despite having been refusing drinks all evening; and *naturally* your obeisance before the great god Necessity would be rewarded with the vestal virgin Michele Monet; she in nothing but a towel, you in an orange jumpsuit because you've had your trousers pulled off you by Fred Clutterbuck and Herb Ellis. *Of course.*

These effects follow their causes far more surely than night follows day; and so it went: Hrundi decried the desecration of the sacred Ganesh, and the hip protesting young folk decided to wash the slogans off the baby elephant in the pool. Then the drunken Hrundi climbed out of an upper window and rolled down a projecting roof into the deep end, and people dived in to save him. Then the crapulent waiter messed with the controls and the dance floor slid back, dumping more jolly guests into the water – water that was frothing with the washing-up liquid used on the baby elephant. A great glinting-white mass, such as children of all ages delight in, began steadily, like some beautiful and alien organism, to creep up on the band, who kept right on laying down the groove, despite the suds that spattered across the snare drum, each multicoloured bubble – caught by the adequate cinematography of Lucien Ballard (died 1988) – a world. Possibly.

★

Post hoc ergo propter hoc – but Billy's gofering was a triumph of the will. Andy sat at a kneehole desk, banknotes piling up in front of him as he took pellets from the stoppers Pandora had removed from her gob. Georgie fluffed, then stammered, 'I h-hope y'd-don't mind, Andy, it's just that B-Billy was crashing here last night, and he's a help – what with Tony being so ill . . . He keeps them in line, and better they pitch up here – doncha think?' However, this was a conversation that, having only one participant, was going nowhere.

Billy gave Andy the orders in monosyllables – 'Two brown, one white' – while Andy uttered profundities such as 'Here'. Billy darted back into the living room, distributed the goods, watched them being unwrapped, took his cut, returned to the bedroom and did the same again.

David and his dysfunctional family left at once; as did Yami, Gary and the estate agent. They tucked their stoppers into their gobs and put on workaday faces. They took the lift back up to the lobby of the mansion block, walked past the console table neatly stacked with junk mail, then stepped out the weighty oak door, with its brass fittings, and took the tiled steps down to the geometric street.

Yami turned right, towards the Brompton Road, moving with the pantherish totter of a tall woman on too-high heels. Gary splashed over to a van that was amorphous with dents and bashes. David, his daughter, and his abetter in her criminal neglect, climbed down into an MG Midget that wasn't theirs.

None of them said any goodbyes – what would've been the point of *that*? Nor, of course, were we required to say our farewells; we went with them all – including the kid. Went with them as they horizontally transmitted us across town.

Now the drugs were on the premises, the party in the basement was in full swing. Bev returned from the back bedroom to resume his seminar on the literature of colonialism. He and Tony sat either side of a coffee table strewn with the apparatus of derangement, and, while Tony battled to insinuate a poot of crack smoke into his lungs, Bev gently coaxed him, 'C'mon, bruv, thass it, I'll 'old the lighter.'

Jeremy hunched in the furthest corner of the room, his cheap gold hair wreathed in dear fumes. In between hits he interjected: 'But don't you see – I mean, Kurtz is – I went to Africa – once.' Disjointed remarks, made with tremendous sincerity and not intended to be ingratiating, because he had no need to be – the brown and the white had done it for him.

Crazy intimacy frothed up from the sunken pool of the living room, then shivered along the corridor to the master bedroom, where Billy – as Hrundi – had found a new Michele. What happy mayhem as the Hollywood party descended into anarchy. Billy was still in the swimming pool with the gay young folk, overseeing the bath time, while Pandora sat atop the baby elephant; coincidentally, she was wearing the same clothes – blue jeans and a grey T-shirt – that Michele Monet had been lent after her own dress was soaked.

Yes, Pandora sat on the baby elephant in the room – her own babyishness. It was irresistible. Billy saw them leaving together – leaving the wild party saturated with crack foam, where a Russian balalaika band that had just happened by was whipping the revellers into a frenzy of dreadful dancing. It was dawn, and the LAPD were standing by their squad cars. They had no warrants out on innocent Hrundi, so he and Michele would get into the funny three-wheeler – Michele with her mini-dress back on again – then they'd bumble down the palm-lined boulevards of Kensington and Knightsbridge, searching for a cute bungalow smothered in bougainvillea, where Billy could declare his hapless love.

On a Tuesday afternoon in November?

Andy goaded his mule – 'Going' – and handed her the remaining rocks of crack and pellets of heroin, all wrapped up once more. She

272

popped the stoppers in her cheeks. They exited the bedroom, Andy moving with the slow lollop of a creature that knows how to conserve its evil energy. He paused, seeing Bev by the coffee table, and snapped at Georgie, 'No blacks. I told you no blacks. I won't come by here if there're blacks.' Then he headed for the front door, Pandora walking to heel.

Before he reached it the buzzer went. The foamy, cracky vibe shuddered, then popped. Georgie squeezed past Andy to get to the intercom. 'Who izzit?' she demanded. 'Jones' crackled back at her.

Jones. She could see him on the poxy screen in his trademark, wide-lapelled velvet jacket, the sleeves rolled up to his elbows. Jones, partially sighted behind shades-for-all-seasons. Jones, looming on a grey day with his white black man shtick. Jones, who, like a sponging relative, invariably turned up exactly when Sunday lunch was being served. Jones, who sold powders in the West End drinking clubs. Jones, who held court at Picasso's on the King's Road with a big bunch of keys squatting on his crotch. Jones . . . but don't fret, we'll soon've seen the last of him: split ends on sharp shoulders.

'Let him in,' Andy commanded; then they all waited until there came a knock on the front door of the flat. Georgie heaved it open, sucking Jones and another man into the cramped vestibule. They all stood silently for several seconds – Pandora, Georgie, Andy, Billy, Jones and the new man – recompressing in the airlock of their drug paranoia. Presently, Andy – who knew Jones – said, 'You should've called.' Then he and his mule disappeared off up the carpeted mesa.

It took a while for the party to get back under way. Georgie remonstrated with Jones: no call – and who's this, then? This was, Jones explained, Cal Devenish, the bad-boy writer, whom he'd picked up at the Plantation Club in Soho. The celebrated Plantation – where there was a wake going on for the world-famous painter

Trouget. Jones related these things breathlessly, as if they were momentous: names, reputations, achievements – they meant nothing to him, although he knew they had currency.

Not much with Georgie; she wasn't impressed by Jones dropping Trouget's name, despite death being a career move she herself was about to make. As for Devenish, she'd heard his name in her arts programme producing days; seen him at parties as well. She knew nothing of his work, but held fast to the received opinion that it was glib, and that he was an egomaniacal pasticheur. However, his bona fides as an addict weren't in doubt; he hovered there in the vestibule, his stringy form dangling from his swollen head, its taut, rubbery surface dimpled with acne scars, puckered up with fresh scabs. At night, in front of the mirror, Devenish picked away at what other people thought he was – distressing his public image, while destroying the private individual.

'I, yeah – sorry,' he said to Georgie, for he'd immediately grasped that she was the chatelaine. 'I was looking for a bit of . . . gear? And Jones –'

'Come in, come in.' Georgie was all scary smiles, Billy bowed and scraped, because Andy had left a little smidgen-wigeon-pigeon behind on tick, and that meant there was a mark-up to be had. The beat combo struck up again as they trooped past the Dexion shelving; the Amazonian girl with the Mary Quant crop gyrated by the poolside, the foamy beast reanimated.

Billy hustled around, making the introductions, finding Jones and Devenish seats, explaining to Bev that this was a *real* writer, who had written *real* books. Billy kept taking sidelong looks at Cal: assessing his financial potential, certainly, but also taken by the other man's air of hopeless bewilderment.

Cal Devenish was quite drunk, a little coked up and oozing shame. Nowadays, he left a silvery trail of shame wherever he went; and, still more snail-like, he carried his bed of shame with him. He had reached a stage where seconds of euphoria cost him weeks of abject self-loathing. He was on his way to Finland, to promote one of his books that was being published there, and had only dropped into the Plantation to have a single drink and to commiserate with Hilary Edmonds on his great financial loss.

There was Jones with his white lines – and now Cal was sticky with Scotch, bristling with feathery cocaine and being ridden out of town on a rail. He took a seat next to Tony Riley, a bit disgusted by the dying man in the oxygen mask – but then that was only natural. He got out cashpoint-ironed twenties and bought into a rock of crack that Bev was crumbling into the foiled mouth of an Evian bottle pipe. All the while Billy watched.

This Devenish, could he be another Hrundi V. Bakshi? Whited up, and playing his superficial role, while inside of himself he dropped Michele Monet off at her sherbet-yellow Art Deco apartment block? Was Cal, like Billy, suggesting that Michele hang on to the cowboy hat that Wyoming Bill Kelso had given him; suggesting this, so that very soon he could call her up and, on the pretext of getting it back, ask for a date?

Oh, no, Cal Devenish wasn't at *The Party* at all. With his first hit on the crack pipe all the fuzzy foam had condensed into icebergs clashing on the frozen Baltic. What would Helsinki be like, Cal wondered. He suspected exactly the same as London, except for better modern architecture, together with publishers, journalists and publicists who appeared troll-like.

Georgie came into the room and passed the writer a pellet of heroin. Billy scampered to fetch the mirror and, placing it on the coffee table in front of Cal, said, 'Any chance of a little bump, mate?' Then added, 'D'you want me to get you some works?'

Cal looked up and then around at the drugged bedlam: Tony, huffing and puffing and blowing his body down; Bev, talking *arse* about Conrad *of all things*; Jeremy, squatting in the corner, his eyes saucers that needed washing up. He thought of the late Trouget's paintings – what might they be worth now? Those solid bourgeois and yelping dogs, upended and gibbeted by his barbed brush, their faces either obscured or rendered far too vividly.

'No,' Cal told Billy. 'No, thanks, I'm gonna snort some, but you can take enough for a hit if you want.'

Billy could take some, because Cal knew there would never be enough to sate himself. He was going to be hungry *for ever*. Cal tapped some of the beige powder on to the smeary mirror, *had elves been skating on it?* Billy, by way of being a good egg, rolled up his one remaining fiver and passed it to the writer. The parrot of addiction – unlike the owl of Minerva – will fly at any time of the day or night; so it flapped across the clearing from the serving hatch to land on Cal Devenish's shoulder.

If Cal had troubled to unroll the banknote, he would have seen the fresh bloodstain that wavered along its edge: an EEG that plotted a fine madness. Whose blood was it? Does this matter? I – we – told you at the outset, this was never a mystery, or a crime procedural – this was never to do with who done it, only who got it. Or us.

Cal bent to rub noses with his doppelgänger at the same time as he shoved the rolled-up note into his already raw nostril. 'Slap', the sharp paper edge, struck the mirror at one end, while 'stick', the other end, burrowed into his mucus membrane. Snuffling, feeling the numbing burn, Cal dabbed at the blood that dripped from his nose, then asked Billy, 'You couldn't get me a tissue, could you?'

As if he could blow *us – me –* out!

Where is the redemption in all this? Where is the reformed character on day-release from prison, teaching kids with learning difficulties and through them rediscovering his shared humanity? We don't know. I'll tell you one thing, though, our flight's been called – and we simply *love* flying. C'mon, Cal, up you get. That's OK, you look perfectly presentable – apart from your messed-up face. Still, not much chance of any official interest in a flight to *Helsinki*.

If he were to get a pull? We're not bothered – we like prison as much as flying. Possibly more. C'mon, Cal, Gate 57, one foot in front of the other, there's a good chap. Past the windy horse of a cleaner in the shafts of his disinfecting cart; past Dixons and Wetherspoon's; past W. H. Smith's and the Duty Free hangar.

No, Cal, that's not the way to approach a travelator – anyone who's anyone *walks* along it, doesn't just stand there. Ho-hum, we're going to be with you for a long time – years in all likelihood – so I suppose we better get used to your petty vagaries, your inability to do one thing properly at once.

At least we're well cushioned in here, buffered by blood and bile in our basket of lobules, ducts and veins. *Foie humain, Leberknödel Suppe,* Scottie's Liver Treats – we love 'em all. But most of all we relish birdy num-num. Birdy num-num. Num-num. Num.